I0652622

THE EX FACTOR

PRAISE FOR THE ART OF TAKING SECOND CHANCES

"Full of drama, angst, and multifaceted characters, *The Art of taking Second Chances* by Varsha Chitnis cogently explores first love, heartbreak, and forgiveness against the backdrop of familial obligation with adroit prose."

— INDIEREADER BOOK REVIEW

"Amazing debut novel by a conscientious and smart writer."

— DR. AMANDA LEWIS-NANG'EA

"Highly recommend this delightful romance. The characters are well drawn, with strong interactions."

— DR. SKYLAR BRE'Z

PRAISE FOR THE RULES OF PLAYING WITH FIRE

"Varsha Chitnis doesn't just tell you a story, she takes you on an immersive journey through the lives of her characters. *The Rules of Playing with Fire* is visceral, honest and powerful on every page....Grab your emotional support ice cream and cancel your other plans, Sona and Mihir need your full focus."

— ANNA P., AUTHOR OF LOVE IN WILDES SERIES

"Clever, compelling, and impossible to put down, *The Rules of Playing with Fire* brings the heat—and the heart."

— ALLIE OLEANDER, AUTHOR OF WILLING PREY

THE EX FACTOR

THE DALLAS CONNECTION SERIES
BOOK THREE

VARSHA CHITNIS

© 2025 Varsha Chitnis
The Ex Factor
First Edition, June 2025

July Showers Press
California
varshachitnis.com

All Rights Reserved.

The Ex Factor is under copyright protection. No part of this publication may be reproduced, distributed, or transmitted in any form or by any means, including photocopying, recording, or other electronic or mechanical methods, without the prior written permission of the publisher, except as permitted by U.S. copyright law. For permission requests, contact Varsha Chitnis at author.varshachitnis@gmail.com

NO AI TRAINING: Without in any way limiting the author's exclusive rights under copyright, any use of this publication to "train" generative artificial intelligence (AI) technologies to generate text is expressly prohibited. The author reserves all rights to license uses of this work for generative AI training and development of machine learning language models.

This is a work of fiction. Names, characters, places, events, locales, and incidents are products of the author's imagination or used in a fictitious manner. Any resemblance to actual persons, living or dead, or actual events is purely coincidental. No AI was used in the writing, editing, and cover image of this book.

Editor: Sherri Shackelford
Cover Artist: Zuchal Rosyidin

For Vaibhav,
my very own Sujit,
kind, brilliant, generous.
Now, if only you were a billionaire 😏

And
For all my people with a glasses kink,
Sujit has been created especially for you.

A NOTE ON CONTENT

Dear Reader,

Thank you for choosing *The Ex Factor*. The story of Aarti and Sujit begins with the HEA of Tara and Sameer. This is a standalone romance and you don't need to read my debut, *The Art of Taking Second Chances*, before you read this book. However, you will get a better, fuller perspective of their situations if you choose to read both books.

This is a relatively low-angst story compared to my first two books, but I do want my readers to be aware of a few things.

The premise of this book is the heartache that both lead characters have suffered in their past relationships. As such, discussions of pain and betrayal forms the backdrop of their love story. That said, this book deviates from the norm of demonizing exes. There is an attempt to take a more mature and healthy approach to romantic love and social relationships, especially in the context of the history of these particular characters.

A tertiary character in this book is from Kosovo, and there is a mention—albeit no on-page description—of the Kosovo conflict, where she lost her two young sons. Another tertiary character comes from a toxic home and there is a mention to emotionally unavailable parents. Neither of these are spoilers for the story.

As always, I have tried my best to be sensitive to my characters, and by extension, to you, my reader. I hope you love this book as much as you have loved the first two, or perhaps, more.

With much love,
Varsha

SUJIT

*I*t was the second time the word Dallas had crossed my desk that morning.

I stared at the screen before me, trying to read the code again. I knew it like the back of my hand, but it looked Greek to me. Scratch that. I had taken courses in modern Greek in college, so that language actually made sense to me. What script *was* Greek to me?

Telugu, my mother tongue. That script was definitely alien to me. I wondered why my parents hadn't insisted that I learn to read Telugu. Although I understood the language and could speak it, my English and French were more powerful than my mother tongue.

I was aware this was a distraction tactic, trying to avoid going back to that wedding invitation tossed into my desk drawer. Not with hatred or resentment, just put out of sight so I could hurt less. Or so I had convinced myself. It hadn't worked. I was still obsessing over the glossy ivory cardstock embossed with the tasteful, delicate paisley while pondering existential conundrums like why my Greek was better than my Telugu reading skills. With one eye on the clock in the top right corner of my laptop screen, I was also trying to see how long I would last before giving in and reaching for the invitation once more.

Devi saved me from that embarrassment when she placed a single knock on the glass door and walked in without waiting for my response.

"Did you take a look at the document?" she asked in her usual calm demeanor.

"What document?" I peered at her over the metal rim of my glasses, a frown of confusion creasing my brow even though I knew exactly what document she was referring to.

The document that had the word Dallas scrawled all over it.

As my executive assistant, Devi was used to my absent-mindedness. She leaned across the desk, pulled a thick set of papers stapled together from under my laptop, and placed it on the keyboard. I preferred to read everything digitally, but Devi was old school. She preferred paper. She insisted that this was the most effective and efficient way of getting things done right. If it was tangible and in your hand, you couldn't avoid it or put it out of sight.

She waited patiently while I picked up the document and went through it page by page again for her benefit. It wasn't the first time I was reading it, but having it in print did have a poignant impact. Devi was right about that. I glanced at her before tossing the stack across the desk. She knew the exact reason for my reaction, and I heard her pull in a soft breath.

"It's finally happened," I said, mildly annoyed. Although, at this point, I couldn't pinpoint the exact source of my annoyance.

"Yes, as Walt told us months ago," she reminded, shuffling her planner from her left hand to her right.

While everyone else had moved on to iPads and tablets, Devi

trusted her paper pad, her paper planner, and the power of her colorful pens.

"Walt's a good man," I observed absently.

"Yes," she said.

"But this is unacceptable."

"Again, as Walt warned us when he sold this property."

"To some swanky realtors based in Texas, I see," I said with a gentle frown.

She knew I had omitted the name of the city for a reason. They all knew. For months, I had drowned in shame and embarrassment before they teamed up to convince me that I'd come out swimming at the other end, happy and intact. I had yet to reach that promised land.

"To call them realtors is like calling Lata Mangeshkar a singer. She was an institution, as are they. I think empire might be a more appropriate term."

Devi was teasing, but her tone might as well suggest she was rendering a vital consultation on a global crisis.

I frowned at her. "Oh good, royalty! They can be *so* accommodating."

I picked up the papers again and reread the terms while she stood with the stoic face I hated, the pen steady in her hand. That was the face she made when I went on a rant, and she waited for me to be all vented out.

Devi was smart, capable, efficient, and my sister-in-law's best friend from college, so she could take liberties with me that others wouldn't dream of. Not that I was particularly hard-ass, but I could be difficult. Mainly, though, the deference and respect I garnered were on account of my success and the wealth I had amassed in the short time since I'd founded my first start-up.

"So, what now?" I asked.

"We need to renegotiate the lease and sign a new contract."

"For a higher rent?"

"You can bet on it. I've already sent El a heads-up."

Eleanor headed our accounts department. For all intents and purposes, she *was* the accounts department.

I pushed the papers away with a frown. "How's Kitty?"

Devi greeted that with a disapproving sigh. "You know she hates it when you call her that."

"She's seven, and she loves it. *You* hate it," I said while she kept her dazzling glare trained on me.

"*Katyayani* is better. It turned out to be a sinus infection," she said.

"Good. And her useless father?"

"He'd come over on the weekend for his bi-weekly visit."

"Did he behave?"

"He has no choice if he wants to keep seeing his daughter."

"And you?"

"What about me?" Devi asked.

"How are you?"

She gave a slight nod. "I'm financially secure and have a beautiful daughter. If he wants to spend his life with that woman, that's his choice. I'm happy without him."

"Good," I said and picked up the papers again. "That's good."

"They need your approval to move ahead with the renegotiations," she reminded me as I read the document again.

"Is there a way out of this outrageous rent hike?"

Devi's lips curled up as if this was the question she was waiting for. She took a step toward me and tapped her pen on her colorful planner. This year's planner was floral. Peonies. "There is. Meet with them and present our case."

I frowned like she knew I would, but before I could get a word in, she contended, "It will give our case credence, you know, coming directly from the boss, someone as influential as you."

My frown deepened. I didn't have time for unnecessary meetings, especially when they involved drawing on my limited resources to ingratiate myself for the sake of my business. Not that I wasn't good at it. I just hated doing it. I had done a lot of it during the early years when I was looking for angel investors and VCs. But I didn't think I would need to do it at this stage in my career.

"That's our final resort, Sujit," Devi declared, and I glanced at her as she gave me a pointed look.

She only called me by my name when she stepped into the role of an adviser, and she was a darn good one.

I let out a deep sigh and returned the papers back to the desk. "Alright, set up a meeting with this new real estate whatever. Let me talk to them. But if I'm getting involved, I don't want their minions. I want to talk to the boss."

Devi grinned. "You're in luck. She arrived this morning. I've emailed her assistant for a meeting."

"You knew I'd say that?"

"I knew I could talk you into it. You're so easy," she teased sans a smile. "I've only known you since you came to work in shorts and a T-shirt like a college kid."

"I *was* a college kid!" I cried with a defensive frown.

This time, she graced me with her warm smile before leaving my office.

I was a college kid when I started tinkering with the idea of starting a software company. I use the word "kid" loosely because I was in the final year of my master's degree when the idea materialized. Three years later, the company took off successfully, but jeans and "tees" remained my ensemble of choice, as it is for most engineers. When we feel desperate enough to don a three-piece suit, we shift gears and go to business school.

I chuckled again, aware of the fact that every thought finding passage through my mind right now was only to distract me from thinking about the heartache rolled up in the word Dallas. My mind raced back to the card locked up in my desk drawer.

Stepping over to the glass wall of my 22nd-floor midtown suite, I gazed down at the Manhattan streets, always busy, always alive. My office was silent as a smile, but I could hear the city's buzz in my head. The constant chatter of people on the streets, the shouts of panhandlers, resident New Yorkers cursing bloody tourists for messing up the flow on the sidewalks. I could hear the drills and the thrills that made this city my home. The fall had set in hard, and it would be only a minute before it dragged in the cold, harsh winter.

I sighed, setting my gaze at the horizon.

I'd started the company in a shed in Brooklyn, but moved into this uppity building at the insistence of my angel investor. Over the years, I had leased a total of four floors in the building, Walter's reasonable rents being one of the incentives. Walt had held on to this property because it was his father's choicest possession, but as his age advanced, the kind man saw no other option but to sell it off to someone who had a more proficient management team. He was getting ready to retire to Florida and had sold the building to a real estate company whose headquarters were in Dallas.

I hadn't shown Devi the bitter bile-like taste that erupted in my mouth when I first read that, but I knew she knew. I was grateful she was kind enough to underplay it.

Back in my chair, I finally succumbed to the temptation and pulled open my desk drawer to retrieve the wedding invitation. I allowed my fingers to glide over the embossed gold paisleys and the gold leaf motif adorning the border of the card.

Mrs. Rekha Kadam and Mrs. and Mr. Pavan Rehani
request the honor of your presence
at the wedding of their children
Tara
And
Sameer

I dropped the card back in the open drawer with haste and banged it shut.

About six months ago, my then-girlfriend Tara went to Dallas for a consulting job and reconnected with her ex, Sameer. Tara was the art consultant I'd hired to help decorate my expansive upstate vacation home. I found myself taken with her since our first formal meeting. She was smart, beautiful, humble, gracious, and kind. Everything good rolled into one, and I thought I was in love. Until she returned halfway into her assignment to tell me, she still had feelings for Sameer and wanted to see if things could work out between them. This was after I'd introduced her to my family at a surprise birthday party I'd planned for her. She'd been the first woman to meet my family, and by that evening, we were broken up.

So, yes, whenever I heard the word *Dallas*, my recoil was involuntary.

It wasn't that I hated Tara. On the contrary, some part of my heart still belonged to her. It would have been so much easier to deal with the heartbreak if Tara was a horrible, conniving liar. But she wasn't. The only hitch in our relationship had been that she didn't love me enough. At least not more than she loved her ex. To her credit, she'd been honest about her feelings, forthcoming about her dilemma and guilt.

At our final meeting, I'd magnanimously declared, despite the gaping hole in my heart, that I was reverting our status back to friendship. The jubilant card in my desk drawer was a testament to this changed status quo.

My eyes darted to the papers on my desk, and I released a sigh as the office phone lit up.

"The Congressman is returning your call," Devi said from her desk outside my office. "And Mr. Roth from Direct Solutions is here for the next meeting."

I put the papers in a drawer and waited for Devi to connect me to the Congressman.

SUJIT

*T*hat evening, I was on my way to the Baccarat with the re-leasing information resting on the seat beside me. My driver battled against the busy evening traffic, his impatience rising high with every passing minute. His hand was steady on the horn, but he resisted honking because I disapproved of the impolite act.

"Let it go, Imran, take a breath," I consoled as I caught him looking at me in the rearview mirror.

"I am breathing. I am calm," he said with a grin.

"Of course you are."

"You'll be late."

"I'll apologize. No use stressing about things we have no control over."

Imran didn't curse on principle, but that didn't prevent him from honking. He jammed down the noisemaker on the steering, unleashing his anger in his preferred way.

When I looked at him from above the rim of my glasses, he argued, "Did you see that? That foolish delivery guy on the scooter!"

"Breathe, Imran."

"Breathing...breathing...breathing." He was a spirited guy driven by youthful impulses.

Imran was not just a trusted employee who wouldn't peek at my business papers if I left them in the car or sell that information to my competitors. He was a close confidant, and our relationship was more familial than formal.

I'd never been sold on the idea of the successful lone wolf. Even when I had taken the riskiest of decisions, I had at least one person who believed in the risk. Someone who believed in me. I was surrounded by a tight group of trusted friends and allies. It was an ecosystem that was often informed by mutual benefit, but sometimes by pure, unadulterated human connection.

I smiled at Imran's back as my gaze darted to the papers beside me. The owner of SB Real Estate, Ms. Bhatia, had graciously granted me a meeting the next day, but she wanted to meet over a quick drink before we discussed the lease. My guess was she wanted to size me up to determine her negotiating options. It was a great tactic and a good opportunity for me to figure out how much pushback I could safely get away with. The new lease document in my hand quoted three times the rent I'd been paying for the past several years. That was a lot of money, even for a successful company like mine.

I'd thought of doing a quick Google search about SB Real Estate and its owner, but I didn't want online information to color my judgment or my impression of her. My instinct was usually pretty vocal and always yammering on, unlike me.

Unfortunately, it had been deceptively silent about Tara. And there I was again, all set to go down that rabbit hole. Luckily, my mother called.

"Kanna!" she cried in her sweet voice like she always did. My mother was quadrilingual, and the Kanna was on account of her proficiency in Tamil.

"Hello, Amma," I said with a smile, momentarily drowning out Imran's impatience.

"How are you? Did you like the rava laddoo I sent with Padma?"

"Yes, Amma, I loved it."

"I wanted to send the punugulu, but Padma said they won't travel well."

"She's right, Amma. They would have gotten all soggy and soft."

"But you have that fryer gadget, no? You could reheat it to crisp it up," she argued, and I laughed at her reference to the air fryer that she'd insisted on buying for my kitchen.

"Yes, Amma, but what's the fun in eating reheated punugulu?" The lentil fritters, like all fritters, were best when eaten hot right out of the fryer.

"I could never out-argue you," she said with a huff.

"I'll plan to come over soon. Then you can feed me all the punugulu you want. Also, bobbatlu. It's been a while since I had that."

The thought of the sweet stuffed flatbread flooded me with memories of a very happy childhood. As the younger of two kids, I was definitely spoiled.

"Anything you want, Kanna. Just let me know when you plan to come."

"I will, but can you stop bothering Padma with errands like this? The poor girl spends more time bringing me food from you than she does in her studio." I was exaggerating, of course, and Amma dismissed it promptly.

"It's not a bother to bring food to a brother! She knows it," Amma said in her usual chiding manner whenever I tried to create distance between families and relatives.

Padmaja was my cousin. A budding sculptor, she was Amma's sister's daughter, but there was no concept of cousins in our family. It was all sisters and brothers and uncles and aunts. Padma frequently traveled to the posh suburban hamlet where her parents and mine resided. And Amma never failed to send back some delicacy or the other with her for me. Then I had to arrange for Imran to get it from her so she wouldn't have to travel all the way from Brooklyn to Manhattan to deliver me homemade food. Of course, Padma didn't mind. She kind of expected Amma to do that. If she didn't, she would assume that either Amma was sick, or that I was. And even though she was a few years younger than me, she was the older child, and like everyone else in my extended family, she fussed over me.

"That reminds me," Amma's voice in my ear brought me back just as Imran banged his hand on the steering wheel in frustration and boredom. Our eyes met in the rearview mirror, and he grinned sheepishly.

"Yes, I remember," I said to Amma. "I remember about Padma's exhibition. You've only reminded me nine hundred times," I teased.

"Indeed, Kanna, because I know how diligent you are about these things. If it wasn't for Devi, you'd never remember any of the important social events," she chided.

"That's not her job, Amma. She's my professional assistant, not a personal one. I know she's like family, but don't bother her with this stuff."

"She doesn't mind. Plus, it was Cathy's idea. She suggested I use Devi's proximity to you to our advantage. Or something like that."

I smiled. That definitely sounded like my sister-in-law. She and Devi had been tight since undergrad. After Devi joined the workforce, Cathy went to business school, where she met my brother. Since Tara, everyone in my family had been treating me with kid gloves, especially the women. That included Devi, who traversed that boundary between personal and professional with impeccable ease.

"Here's Nannagaaru now," Amma said, handing the phone off to Dad.

"Hey, Dad," I said, often forgetting that Amma preferred us to call him Nanna. But Dad was our first friend, mine, and my brother, Srijan's.

"How are you? I know you're probably busy, but I just wanted to say hi," he said, always consciously aware of our time and commitments.

"Doing well, Dad. How's your new book coming along?" I asked.

"Slowly," he said with a chuckle that was the best sound in the world.

"Wish I could help, but you know my understanding of math is elementary compared to yours."

"That's not important. What's important is what you do with the knowledge you have, and I'd say you're doing pretty well," he said with another soft chuckle.

That made me smile from the bottom of my heart. Despite the freedom my parents had given us, it was no secret that both Srijan and I lived for their praise. Their accolades meant more to us than any of the numerous awards I'd received over the years.

"Thanks, Nanna," I said, granting him the respect he deserved.

"Ah, your mother wants to speak to you again," he said and disappeared from the line before I could say bye.

"About Padma's exhibition," Amma said, back on the line. "Buy something of hers to support her. And get me something for my gudi." That would be the room that housed her altar. Her sanctum sanctorum.

"Yes, Amma, I will."

There was a brief silence before she spoke again. "I also spoke to her about redoing the vacation home," she said.

"Amma, I've said it several times. Just because Tara is out of my life, it doesn't mean I'm getting rid of the pieces she chose for us. She did a very good job. Those paintings are unique and perfect for that space."

"I know, Kanna, but they'll remind you of her every time, no? It's better to get rid of those memories to move on."

Tempted as I was to tell her that Tara had sent me the wedding invitation, I knew the kind of trouble it would open up. In addition to admonishments for Tara's actions, it was bound to unleash another tsunami of sympathy and pity for me. I would receive more phone calls from the entire extended family than I'd be able to handle, probably more food and desserts than I could eat in a month. It was best to keep my mouth shut.

It had been an impossible task to explain to my family that I didn't carry any ill will toward Tara and that she was a good person who had been honest with me. Yes, she had broken my heart and shattered my ego, as my family surmised. But that was on account of my own foolishness in flaunting her before them without warning her. Now, all they saw was poor, injured Sujit, and wanted to eliminate everything Tara-related from my life.

When Amma and Cathy learned that I was still in touch with Tara's friend, Sona, who was also a friend now, they lectured me on how I needed to distance myself from her, so I didn't think of Tara. They stretched their imagination to assume that I saw Sona as a substitute for Tara. Watching too much television and reading too many pop psychology books had ruined their perspective on how friendships grow and thrive.

I still had my friendship with Sona. I also had my friendship with Tara's mother, who texted me about the progress she was making in learning English. She hoped to someday be able to converse effectively with me in the language. I saw no reason to let my relationship with Tara undermine my friendships with either of those women, and I didn't. Of course, I didn't tell that to Amma or Cathy, although I suspected Devi was aware of it, but that no one else knew about it reassured me of her discretion.

"Kanna?" I heard Amma again.

"I've moved on, Amma," I lied. "And I won't get rid of those paintings. It would disrespect the artists if I let my relationship with Tara determine their worth to me."

Amma sighed. "You and your Nanna are two peas in a pod. This is exactly the kind of philosophical stuff he would say."

"Well, he's a philosopher," I said amicably. "Math is a philosophy like he says, and he's kind of a badass at it."

"Tsk, don't use such words," she reprimanded. "Your father is a monk, if anything."

"That he is," I said and hoped our conversation would end now. Amma took the hint and said, "Alright, I'll let you go. Don't forget Padma's exhibition."

"I won't because you'll remind me again several more times, and I know you've had Devi add it to my calendar."

She laughed in her sweet voice before hanging up.

Imran had resigned to the traffic that had turned into a parking lot and turned on his favorite retro radio channel. Sweet Hindi melodies resounded in the quiet car. While I got busy replying to emails on my phone, Imran managed to breach the thicket of the evening rush, and we reached the hotel.

I walked in toward the bar where Ms. Bhatia would meet me, as her assistant had informed Devi.

Sitting at the bar was a tall woman, her back straight, and long legs crossed gracefully under the counter. Glossy black hair, straight as her posture, ran down to her waist. I saw her thumbing her phone while a glass of red wine sat before her, possibly untouched. The slender fingers on her lean hand looked uncharacteristically powerful from this distance.

Quick scenarios ran through my head, much like a simulation. I played around with multiple variables—my first approach, her first impression of me, my perception of her—all of which would chart the course of our subsequent interactions and determine my negotiation tactic.

It all faded away like a cloud of smoke in the wind when I approached her and said, "Ms. Bhatia, Sujit Rao."

She turned to me with a smile, which quickly disappeared as she left her seat and stood tall to face me.

Before me, in the flesh, stood Sameer's ex-fiancée.

AARTI

I only had a quick second to decide how to approach the situation.

Professionally, my brain insisted.

"Mr. Rao." I extended my hand. "Nice to meet you."

I wondered if he had recognized me. We had met in person only once, and for a few minutes. But the look in his eyes and his stunned body language seemed to answer that for me. Mercifully, he'd chosen the same approach as me. Ignore the acquaintance. Avoid the humiliation.

"Ms. Bhatia, thank you for meeting me at such short notice."

"Please," I said, inviting him to take a seat. With his tall legs, he perched on the barstool effortlessly. "We can sit in the lounge if you prefer. But I was hoping for a quick meeting."

"This is fine," he said with a smile that put slight dimples in his cheeks.

"What will you have?"

"Whatever you are having," he said.

Ingratiating himself to me, I thought, because I had a glass of red wine before me and he definitely didn't look like a wine person. But I played along.

"One more, please," I told the bartender.

I didn't usually drink red wine unless I was in a meeting where I had to pretend to drink. This was one such occasion. We sat in silence until the bartender placed a glass before him, its crystal dispersing a gorgeous tint of red on the counter. I watched as his strong hand advanced toward the glass and lifted it.

"I hope your flight was good," he said after a sip.

"It was uneventful. Thank you."

"I don't suppose this is your first visit to New York?"

"No, my close friend moved here a few years ago, and I've visited her a couple of times."

"It's great that you'll have a friend in the city while you're here," he said.

"Actually, she doesn't live in the city anymore." I don't know if it was the kindness in his voice or a desperate need to fill the silence, but I shared with him more than I normally would. "They have a penthouse here, but they live upstate most of the time."

He gave a small nod, and soon enough, the dreaded silence engulfed us.

I threw a quick glance at him. His eyes met mine, and a strange mix of feelings coursed through me. Dread, that he had figured out who I was. Shame, that he knew what I had been through publicly. Fear, that he might use it to leverage his negotiation. Anger, that the stain on my personal life threatened to invade my professional identity. And...a smidgen of sympathy, that perhaps he'd had his heart stomped on mercilessly too.

What would it be? Embarrass me, humiliate me, intimidate me? Under normal circumstances, it wasn't easy to get under my skin, but he was Tara's ex, and that was enough to ruin both my poise and my grit. I waited, peering into his face, waiting for him to capitalize on any of these several openings available to him.

To my surprise, he didn't. He cleared his throat and opted instead for the universal subject of small talk. "So, how are you holding up to the weather here?"

A palpable wave of relief washed over me. My body relaxed. My grip on the stem of the glass loosened. I hadn't realized I had been strangling it between my fingers.

"It's so cold here already!" I said, with a slight, grateful laughter.

"Yes. How's the weather in Dallas?"

"It's nice. It's getting colder, so some of us are freaking out. Bring out the puffy jackets!"

He chuckled, but it was a gentle sound. Suave, sophisticated, classy.

"I hope you brought all your puffy jackets with you because if you think it's cold now, just wait until it snows."

As I looked at him, my eyes met his warm gaze, and a strange feeling ran down my spine. I looked away to my wine glass promptly. "Definitely not looking forward to that. I would've postponed the visit if it wasn't important."

"Important like?" he inquired.

Peering into his eyes, I wondered if he knew why I was in New York, miles away from Dallas, at this particular time.

He shot me a restrained smile, but I couldn't return one.

"Important, like figuring out the condition of the properties we just bought."

His eyes softened, as if he knew this was a ruse, and I'd rather not acknowledge it. "Sounds daunting, especially in this weather," he said.

"Yes, thankfully, I don't have to physically survey everything, just oversee the overseers."

He chuckled an uncomfortable sound. This time, when our eyes met, his back stiffened as he returned his glass to the counter. He was doing his best to maintain this charade of formality between us, but the discomfort was starting to wear me down.

"I'm wondering how long it will be before we acknowledge the elephant in the room," I said, finally making peace with our ill-fated meeting.

He slumped slightly. With his posture, I would've imagined it was impossible his body knew what real slumping meant. "I was hoping it wouldn't come up," he confessed and followed it up with a gentle sigh. "It would've been so much simpler if we'd never met."

We had met in Dallas at the opening night of Tara's exhibition. "If this whole fiasco hadn't occurred, do you think you would've remembered me?" I asked.

He laughed as he removed his glasses and placed them on the counter. "Yes," he said. "Unfortunately, I'm terribly good with faces. Not so much with names, though."

"Aarti," I offered.

He laughed again and ran his fingers along the stem of his glass. "Yes, unfortunately, yours is a name I do remember."

"That's an awful lot of unfortunates for you," I observed.

"I apologize! I didn't mean it that way," he said. Sitting upright, he put his glasses back on. "I meant in the context of this conversation. It would've been easier if we hadn't met."

"Don't worry, no offense taken," I offered truthfully, placing both hands around my glass that stood turning warm on the counter.

"None was intended," he said in a very sincere voice. "So, how about you?" he asked after a long pause. "Would you have remembered me?"

I didn't lie often, but sometimes, I employed white lies, as was the nature of my business. But I felt that I couldn't lie to this sincere-sounding man sitting beside me. "Probably not," I said, "but then again....I do remember you, don't I?"

"Professional hazard?" he asked.

"Something like that." This was a lie. A white one, but a lie, nonetheless.

"So...how do we proceed from here?" he inquired.

"Well, we can shove all emotions under the rug and continue with this business very professionally." I brought my wine goblet to my lips.

"Or?"

I smiled as I returned my glass to its spot on the counter and pursed my lips. I was highly impressed he knew there was an *or* coming.

"*Or* we match our stories and drink away those memories."

"I'm game," he said, his body perking up. "Unless you have another meeting."

"No, that's an excuse I use to get out of bothersome ones. It's safe to say you haven't annoyed me enough yet to employ that excuse."

This time, he laughed heartily, giving me a full display of two very deep, very attractive dimples.

I invited him to the lounge and asked him to order a bottle of whisky. There was only one way to melt the awkwardness of our meeting, and that solution lay at the bottom of a bottle of whisky. He ordered a well-aged highland scotch. I'd always been a wine drinker, never a whisky or bourbon connoisseur like the rest of my family. But that evening, I knew my salvation lay not in a slender bottle of wine but in the thick, formidable glass of scotch.

"To us, the jilted lovers," he said, clinking his glass to mine.

"To fresh starts," I responded defiantly.

"To fresh starts!" He sipped with a satisfied look on his face.

I let him ruminate in the pleasure of the first sip before I asked, "Did you hear about the wedding?"

He looked up as if the news had shocked him. Then, relaxed

his back against the couch and said, "Yes, Tara sent me an invitation."

My stunned brows launched upward. "She invited you to their wedding? That's cold."

He promptly shook his head and said, "It isn't. It's not malicious like it appears. The last time we talked, when she came clean to me, I told her we would continue being friends. We ended our relationship on a positive note. The invitation is just her sweet way of keeping our friendship alive. It's her way of showing she still cares for me and that she values me in her life."

"So, you had a chance at closure, then. You are lucky," I said with mild bitterness, suddenly envious of their relationship. When he didn't respond, I added, "You certainly seem to have a high regard for her."

"I do. It wasn't a slight decision that I had intended to spend my life with her. She is a good person. It's a pity she didn't love me enough."

I knew what he meant. Love, desire, passion, or whatever else we call it, was strange. There was always scope for us to love more than one person, but the falling in love part was so messy it felt like there could never be another.

"If you're truly the person who's sitting here right now, she didn't deserve you."

He peered at me over the rim of his glasses, and my heart took a sudden, completely unexpected dip. I suspected he saw it too, because he pushed his glasses up the bridge of his nose and looked away.

"Unless you're not, and she did herself a big favor." I was nothing if not brutally honest.

He surprised me by taking no offense at my words. "Only she can answer that for you."

I studied him for a quick moment and shook my head. "She didn't deserve you," I declared, this time with conviction.

"Alright, let's share notes. I'll be a gentleman and begin first."

"How's that gentlemanly?" I frowned. "Shouldn't it be ladies first or some such nonsense?"

He shook his head. "Not when it involves embarrassing oneself. Then chivalry is making yourself out to be the biggest chump, so the lady feels less like one."

I returned a slight grin. "Your argument is convincing. Go on."

It was difficult to keep my mind off those brilliant eyes and that beautiful mouth while he shared the tale of how they met and how easy their relationship had seemed to him. He was a stunning man, and I understood what Tara saw in him, although in the end, she'd stomped on his heart like Sameer had on mine.

"So there we were, driving upstate, where my family and close friends awaited our arrival for her surprise party, and all the while, she was wondering how to tell me she was breaking up with me."

A sudden pang of pity pierced my heart as he finished talking and took an elegant pull of the smooth whisky.

"So, she tells you this after the whole surprise birthday event? After she's met your parents?" I asked.

Of course, I had heard every word he'd uttered despite my simultaneous internal monologue. I was an excellent multitasker. An overachiever, my friends and competitors called me.

"Yes, but in her defense—"

"Why?"

"Why what?"

"Why are you defending her?"

"Because it's the right thing to do. She didn't know what I had planned. That one is on me. I'm responsible for making a fool of myself."

"So when was she planning to tell you?" I inquired with curiosity.

"That afternoon at lunch, which *I* turned into her birthday party."

"Well, you were definitely more generous than I was. Wanna hear my story?"

"Wait," he said and picked up the bottle, "we need a refill." He poured two fingers into each glass, then dropped an ice cube in them.

"Go on," he said, handing me my glass.

"Sameer left for India the night we got engaged. He'd been gone for a week, and I was dying to see him, so I went to his place and found them sharing an intimate dinner. Turned out it was Tara's birthday. Sameer was sans his engagement band, and the looks on their faces told me everything I didn't want to know. But I used the choicest words in my repertoire to convey my displeasure."

"That must have been hard. I'm sorry," he said with a look that echoed his words.

I had seen that look before in many eyes, on many faces, after Sameer ended our relationship. The only difference was Sujit knew exactly what I'd been through. His pity wasn't hollow. It was empathy. It was the connection between two kindred souls.

Still, I hated that look. I frowned in response. "Do you want me to defend him too?"

He shrugged. "Only if you feel you must."

This man was an enigma. Powerful men weren't supposed to be like this. They were supposed to be macho, steeped in their misplaced alpha mentality, walking on earth like they did the rest of us a favor by merely existing. I had seen too many of them around me since I was a young girl.

The influential billionaire sitting beside me was an anomaly. It made me want to get to know him better. Was this all a front, and was I really missing something? As much as I wanted to hate Tara, I knew her well. Well enough to be convinced that she wouldn't have been with him if he wasn't the person he was projecting to be.

"What are you thinking?" he interrupted my musing.

"I forgot what we're talking about," I confessed.

"You were about to tell me the whole story," the astute man answered and slipped me a light smirk.

I sighed. "In Sameer's defense, I had proposed marriage to him in front of two hundred odd people at my parents' anniversary as a surprise, a day before he was supposed to break up with me. There, I said it."

"I'm sorry, Ms. Bhatia. I really am. Love is never easy, but nothing prepares you for this." He relaxed on the soft couch and savored his drink with his eyes closed.

"Love is irrational," I replied. "The concept of love is stupid. I don't think it really exists, and if it does, it's fleeting. All we ever catch is a brush, a light touch, a whiff...if we are lucky."

He opened his eyes to look at me, and it was the first time I noticed his beautiful lashes. And his deep brown eyes, full of wisdom and kindness. Darn, that man was gorgeous!

"You sound like a cynic," he observed and drew another sip of his drink.

"I'm practical," I countered with some indignation.

"And me?" he asked softly.

I wouldn't have blurted out the truth, but there was enough alcohol in me to lower my inhibitions. "You're a romantic. You believe in fairy tales. You believe in happily ever after."

"And you don't?"

"I believe in surviving right now. I believe in facing the truth with grit and vengeance, not patience or humility."

His face changed a smidgen like I had pinched a raw nerve, but he'd trained himself not to show it. Only I was really good at reading micro-expressions. He planted his gaze on mine with an amused look as if he'd also figured out that last part.

My heart skipped a beat, and my stomach took a tumble. That look of his, that peering from behind his glasses, with a slight smile on his lips, made me throb in all the wrong places. I found myself damp between my thighs. And yes, I was going to blame the alcohol for this misplaced, ill-timed, and completely inappropriate arousal.

His smile widened, and he gulped down the last of his drink. "I think we should call it a night."

"That's probably a good idea," I agreed, eager to get away from him before I said or did something I'd regret.

He signaled our server. When I saw him reaching for the wallet in his jacket, I said, "I'll take care of it, don't worry."

"Maybe next time."

"Do we hope to get wasted again?" I asked with a drunken grin.

"We could if you need a friendly ear," he said and dropped the card in the plush leather folder the server had presented.

I grinned again. I usually didn't grin. It was a part of being a socialite, you don't grin, not even when you're happy. You need to be picture-perfect every waking moment. But sitting here with Sujit felt different. It felt like I could breathe normally, like I didn't need to pretend. He saw me, the real me. I could tell he could read my thoughts, so I allowed myself the grins I'd withheld in the past.

"My car service is available if you need a ride back," I offered.

"Thank you, my driver is in the parking," he said. "But I'll walk you to your room first."

I straightened my back. I hadn't realized when I'd let my posture slump. It was uncanny the way I was at ease in the presence of this stranger. But I'd never enjoyed the prospect of a man holding the car door open for me, pulling a chair out, or escorting me to my room.

"That's alright," I blurted rather curtly, "I don't believe in old-school chivalry."

My tone would have bruised the fragile ego of a lesser man, but Sujit merely stated, "This isn't chivalry, and you'll soon find out."

I watched him place a generous cash tip on the table as I gently rose to my feet. But the room spun so swiftly that I sat back down.

"Exactly," he said, without any semblance of triumph at being right.

I couldn't help but allow myself another grin. "Alright, you may walk me to my room."

With a warm smile, he held out his arm, which I grabbed rather gratefully.

Yeah, I was definitely not a whisky person.

AARTI

*W*e took the elevator and gingerly walked to my room on the eleventh floor. Retrieving my keycard, I held it to the touchpad. The red light didn't chirp. When it remained stolid after a second attempt, I huffed.

"The key isn't working," I cried in exasperated embarrassment.

"I think that's your Visa," he said, glancing over my shoulder at the deep blue card in my hand.

"Oops," I deadpanned and retrieved the room key from my clutch. The light turned green, and the door clicked open.

"I'm *not* drunk," I argued.

"Yeah, neither am I," he said with dazed eyes that held mine for a few seconds before we both burst out laughing.

He was the first to regain his composure. "Well, it was a pleasure to meet you, Ms. Bhatia. I look forward to our meeting tomorrow."

Disengaging my eyes from his, I pretended to smooth my skirt. "It was nice to meet you," I said, stealing a glance at his magnificent face. "Good night."

As I turned to the door, my foot caught on the jamb, and I stumbled sideways. Sujit thwarted my fall.

"Steady," he whispered near my ear, as his arm closed around my waist. His voice permeated to the deepest parts of me, leaving me with a heady rush.

The exquisite liquor on his breath caused a ripple to snake across my skin. I became aware of his scent. The cologne smelled fresh and clean. My brain quickly calculated that he'd come to the meeting from work because this was a day scent, not an evening one. I wanted to lean in and soak up his smell. His touch. I wanted to luxuriate in the feeling of his arm around me that felt wonderful and comforting.

But I was unaccustomed to comforting. I quickly pulled myself upright, and he removed his grip on my waist.

"Thank you," I said with haste. "This was embarrassing."

"Not in the least," he reassured. "Chances are, I won't even remember it tomorrow morning."

"Didn't you just say you weren't drunk?"

"Uh-huh, and so did you, remember?"

We both stared at each other only a moment before bursting into giggles yet again. When our silliness ended, I found myself holding the door ajar, my eyes fixed on his magnetic face.

"Hey, I hope this won't affect our meeting tomorrow," he asked, leaning in.

I shook my head with a smile. "No, not from my end. I'm a professional. How about you?"

"I'm as dispassionate as they come," he said, and I was convinced he believed it too. But I was smarter than to buy it.

"No, you're not," I argued softly. "You're kind, and you're in pain."

He held his pause for a long second. "Perhaps. But that won't affect my business dealings with you."

I nodded. "Thank you for today, thank you for this," I said. I didn't know what exactly I was thanking him for, but his presence had felt reassuring all evening, so familiar for the stranger that he was. Kindred spirits, for sure.

"For the giggles?" he asked, and a glance into his eyes made my heart rumble.

"And more," I said, clutching the door tighter to keep myself steady on my feet. "Thank you for being kind. You're a genuine man, Mr. Rao. I hope this episode with Tara doesn't change who you are. Your kind of people are a rarity."

Those words, I'd definitely attribute to my buzzed state. I was a guarded person. I rarely let people see my real thoughts, let alone spell out my feelings so clearly. Why was it that this man was evoking feelings in me that I thought were dead?

Like the hurt that I had buried deep inside me. I didn't want to exhume that grief. I wanted to thrive in my anger. But it was too late. At that moment, the pain became unbearable. I felt my face turning warm, and before I realized it, tears were stinging in my eyes.

"Why does it still hurt?" I asked with childlike naiveté and allowed the tears to run freely down my face.

"Hey, hey...let's get you inside," he said and offered me his arm again.

As he led me in, I heard the door lock shut behind us with a soft click, and I broke into audible sobs.

For all these months, I had held on to my resentment for Sameer. Not only had he broken my heart, he'd humiliated me in front of all my friends and the society I knew in Dallas. But now that I had spelled it out on Sujit's insistence, I realized the humiliation was my own doing. I had put my own foot on the axe, as a version of the Hindi proverb goes. It was so much easier to deal with grief when I could place the blame on someone else's shoulder. But there was a stark difference between grief and anger. At that moment, I wasn't sure which one was behind my tears.

"Sometimes, hurting is good," I heard Sujit's soft voice and turned my body toward him. "We need to let it all out so we can heal effectively."

I put my face in my hands and kept sobbing silently. His gentle hand landed on my shoulder and stayed there. The reassurance of his light touch broke me further. And now, one more emotion had thrown its hat into this shit show. *Embarrassment.* My mother was the only person who had ever seen my tears. Sameer and Tara had been witness to a few, but no one else had been privy to them.

"Fuck!" I said finally, wiping my eyes and face. "I hate this."

I stepped over to the fridge, retrieved two bottles of water and threw one to Sujit. He caught it with the dexterity of a ball player, another thing I hadn't expected of him.

Walking toward him, I slid down against a wall to the plush carpeted floor. Sujit followed suit. I heard the crack of his bottle cap as I gulped from mine.

"Will you be alright?" I heard his soft voice.

"Yes," I blurted. "I might be in pain, but I'm not fragile." I had no idea why I was lashing out at him, but he remained composed and collected.

"It's healthy to cry. It's not a weakness," he said as if I had granted him access to the innermost recesses of my psyche.

But instead of pulling my guard up, I retorted, "Did *you*? Did you cry after Tara?"

"I did," he said in an unflinching confession. "For a bit."

His composure somehow added to my ire. "And you're healed now," I fumed again.

"Not really. I still think about her. Sometimes, I miss her. And it hurts."

"So letting yourself hurt didn't help then, did it?" I challenged with renewed defiance.

He chuckled. "It's a process. We both will get there, I'm sure of it."

I let out a snort. "You met me two hours ago, but you assume you know me?"

"No," he said with a soft laugh. "You are a very difficult person to read. But per your own assessment, I am a romantic. I have hope in hope."

I looked into his buzzed eyes and said, "That's the biggest load of nonsense I've ever heard."

"Yeah, it is. I have no idea what all those words mean right now," he said and burst into a peal of laughter.

Even though I had no intention of joining in, that infectious sound from his mouth made my lips turn upward. First, a smile, then a giggle, followed by full-fledged laughter. When I couldn't stay upright against the wall, I allowed my shaking body to recline sideways against him. My belly had begun to ache from the laughter.

"Yes, we both are absolutely not drunk," he said, and we laughed more uproariously.

"Shit!" he cried, looking at his watch. "I should leave. Imran needs to get home."

"Who's Imran?" I asked, suddenly envious of this person whom Sujit would care for so much.

"He's my driver," he said. "He'll have to be up early to get me to work on time. I didn't realize it was this late."

"Alright," I said and stood up with him. "I accept complete responsibility for keeping you, and I'll be happy to explain it to Imran if need be."

He nodded as he readjusted his jacket and tie. "I'll be sure to let him know."

We walked to the door, and I held it open for him.

"Thank you again for today," I said, and he turned to look intently into my face.

"You'll be okay, right?"

I nodded. "I've been taking care of myself since I was eight. I'm sure I'll be fine."

"Aarti," he said, then immediately corrected himself, "Ms. Bhatia, I'm here if you need a friend. You don't have to process all this alone. Neither of us do."

This time, when he looked at me, my heart beat so audibly, I was sure he'd heard it. I took a step back, putting distance between us.

"Thank you," I said, calling it a night.

"Good night, Ms. Bhatia." He returned a clipped nod and a short smile that barely dented his cheeks. I watched him walk down the corridor, wondering what he was thinking.

I, for one, was wondering what perverse idea of fun the universe had in mind when it dropped Sujit beside me that evening. There were awkward encounters, and then there was whatever the hell we'd just had. In a world defined by six degrees of Kevin Bacon, this was a one-hundred-eighty degree of *what the fuck do you call this connection?*

As I changed and turned in for the night, I resisted the urge to curl up into a ball and let myself weep.

AARTI

I couldn't pinpoint the exact moment when my relationship with Sameer had taken shape.

My dad and Sameer's uncle were old friends, and when Sameer migrated to the U.S. about thirteen years ago, we started out as friends. As we grew into mature adulthood, everyone around me suddenly began suggesting, in obvious and implicit ways, that we would make a beautiful couple. I'd harbored a mild crush on Sameer, but he had never shown any interest in me, or any other woman, for as long as I had known him.

It wasn't difficult to be smitten with him. With chiseled features, a sculpted body, and perfect etiquette, he was the definition of charming. When he spoke to you, the world ceased to exist. He had that knack of making people feel special and appreciated. I had seen him flirt quite effectively on occasion. But he had his mind set on getting his degree and learning the business from his uncle. He had no space for anything or anyone outside it.

Then, one day, he let his mask slip for a minute, and I found myself falling for him. Our group of friends had returned home from college and sat around with bottles of beer, sharing tales of our wild experiences. Sameer, the life of any party, was unusually quiet until one friend joked that he seemed hung up on someone. I'd watched his face change instantly, but he'd recovered fast and spun rakish tales from his college days in India. It had sounded fictitious because it was completely antithetical to his personality since the time I had known him.

"What changed, dude?" the friend had asked.

He'd shrugged and replied, "Shit got real, and I had to sober up."

It was at that moment, when I'd spotted a look of sincerity and uncharacteristic humility on his face that I had possibly begun falling for him. He was no longer the casual friend I'd had a mild crush on. I had found myself wanting more of him. For years, my subtle hints had gotten no reaction from him until our parents stepped in.

"We are not going to force you into a marriage," my wise mother had said, "but he seems like a person who'd make a great life partner for you."

I had grabbed the opportunity with both hands, but Sameer took months to ask me out on a formal date. It was as if his heart had never been in it from the start.

The next summer, Tara had come to Dallas as a consultant at the art museum and my world turned upside down. The first time I'd seen her and the way Sameer had looked at her, I had suspected there was more to their friendship than he was letting on. But he had remained adamant in insisting that she was his cousin's best friend, and that was the extent of their relationship. I'd been a fool in love with him, and bought every lie he pushed my way.

Then, I found the opportunity I had been waiting for. It was my parents' wedding anniversary, and I had arranged for a grand party to celebrate them. A few nights before the event, Sameer's father had come over with a suggestion that I should surprise Sameer with a proposal at the party. I'd assumed we would get engaged sooner or later. Our parents had wanted an extravagant celebration and were hounding us to come up with a date, but Sameer had been dragging his feet for months.

So, when his father granted me this golden chance, I had no reason to hesitate. A little voice, though, had warned me. I had called Sameer's father twice that week to ask if Sameer would find this transgressive of his trust in me. He had reassured me that Sameer was in love and would be thrilled. I tamped down the doubt raising its venomous head and revamped the event to accommodate my proposal to Sameer. My family was thrilled. My father had decided to offer Sameer a partnership in our company. With his investment firm and our real estate company, they began dreaming of establishing a formidable financial dynasty of sorts.

That evening, I'd been dressed in a specially commissioned designer gown from India, with exclusive jewelry that had existed only on fashion show ramps. A special kind of Kundan setting that had yet to make its way into mass production. I had ordered and reordered sherwani sets for Sameer until I'd found the one I liked, one that matched my gown. I had wanted everything to be perfect.

It had been the most beautiful night. Almost every influential member of the South Asian community was present at the party. Every important member of the city was there, including the mayor. I was swimming in love and adoration from my family and friends. It had promised to be one of the happiest nights of my life.

As the choreographed dance sequence with my family came to an end, I stood on the stage with Sameer. The crowd drowned us in claps and cheers. The flashes from cameras blinded me, but I found comfort in the presence of the man standing beside me.

Dad quietened the cheers with a mic in his hands, then announced to the world his plans to make Sameer a partner in his company. With bated breath, I watched all this unfold, as I had meticulously planned. I waited for Dad's cue.

The moment Dad announced, "All I want in return is that you keep our Aarti very happy," the spotlight had shifted from him to Sameer and me. Promptly dropping down to my knee, I'd said with a barely steady breath, "My dearest Sameer, will you marry me?"

Petals of roses rained down on us. Candid photos populated every camera present there. My grin spread from ear to ear as I gripped Sameer's ice-cold hand and stepped down from the stage with him like a royal couple. We were engaged to be married amid a heavily public display of love and wealth.

My happiness lasted a week. Turned out he'd been planning to break up with me the next day. He had realized he would always be in love with Tara, but he didn't want to ruin the evening for me. If he had, it would have left me broken-hearted and humiliated at the party.

He never got a chance to tell me any of this, because the night of our engagement, he left for India. It was much later that I learned the whole story. Sameer had been away to take care of a clandestine family affair. He hadn't trusted me with any of this. He had kept his family's secrets guarded and out of my reach.

A fool in love that I'd been, I had missed him while he was gone and decided to drop by unannounced the day after his return. I'd still not figured out if it was a good decision or a bad one. Would it have caused me less heartache if I'd allowed Sameer to come clean like he had planned?

That evening, when I arrived at his condo, I found him sharing a candlelight dinner with Tara. I was so furious I blasted them with the choicest vocabulary I could muster in my rage. In a moment so vulnerable that I'd repent it for days to come, I had allowed them both to witness my tears. In all the long years he'd known me, Sameer had never seen me cry. None of my friends had. But that evening, I let my weakness show. I let myself grieve.

My anger had kept climbing as Tara and Sameer explained the intensity of their affection for each other. I had wanted to hate Tara, to be angry at Sameer, but all I had found myself doing was getting angrier at myself. Angry that I had been played for a fool, angry that I hadn't seen it coming. Angry that both Sameer and his father had made me a pawn in their acrimonious relationship. I was angry that Tara wasn't the unkind, unrepentant, evil bitch I could hate with impunity. But all this anger was my burden to carry, my cross to bear. When I'd left his home that evening, I'd determined to never let my weaknesses sneak out again.

The breakup wasn't an ordinary one. That fucked up party had been one of the biggest events that season. People had left with memorabilia and favors commemorating the evening. The names Sameer and Aarti were etched on people's minds, flowing effortlessly off their tongues. How did one deal with a breakup of that magnitude?

The gossip and the rumors erupted immediately and mushroomed fast. Even though it was Sameer who had an affair, people alleged that he had broken it off because I was in love with my younger brother's best friend. Aakash's best friend had always been like a brother to me, but it didn't matter to the gossip machine. There was also the rumor that Sameer had moved on because he'd realized I was an evil, manipulative shrew. He'd be better off without me, the machine proclaimed. The more sympathetic ones claimed we'd caught the evil eye because we were perfect together. Too perfect for it to be realized.

I'd always hated that word, *perfect*. That's how everyone described me, everyone who hadn't known me before I *became* perfect. It was only Mary Beth, my closest friend since grade school, who saw the perfect me when I was gloriously imperfect. The rest of the world saw my tall body, my curves, slim waist, full lips, big eyes, and slender fingers and called me perfect. I hated it because once I was labeled as perfect, I found myself striving harder to be so. I was a successful businesswoman, yet I couldn't let the woman part of me come out and play.

The men, my father, and brother, could harness the so-called masculine values of assertiveness and aggression with little backlash. I had to keep myself aloof enough to be taken seriously, yet I couldn't display my anger or displeasure without being called hormonal or hysterical. That was the reason Sujit surprised me. He was not only kind to me when I was in tears but didn't let my vulnerable condition undermine my capability as a professional. He was the kind of friend I really needed right now. Maybe we could be...friends.

My thoughts drifted to Sujit. It was a cruel thing to happen to a beautiful human being who believed in the goodness of people. I was stronger and more practical. I knew better than to believe in such myths as people's goodness. And yet, our situations were quite similar.

Sujit had also had a tough breakup, albeit much less public than mine. But confronting a faceless crowd and drowning out the phantom of public opinion was easier than facing loved ones who are aware of your broken heart, day after day. I knew this firsthand. I wondered how Sujit handled being left sad and distraught before his family. He must have felt rather comfortable and confident in the relationship to involve his parents at a surprise party for Tara. As comfortable and confident as I had felt in my relationship, I thought, and broke into a hysterical laughter.

SUJIT

A slew of discordant thoughts swirled around in my head as I walked toward my car. The morning had already attempted to upset my equilibrium, and now I was walking away from Sameer's ex-fiancée. It felt like my world had tilted on its axis.

I'm in the wrong place. That was the first thought I had when I saw Aarti that evening. Since Tara's departure from my life, I'd had that feeling an overwhelming number of times. The time I was invited to the New York Philharmonic, and when my friends dragged me to a live performance by Tara's favorite Bollywood singer. The time I got the Innovator of the Year Award and ended up hostage in a conversation with an influential but incredibly boring guest. If Tara were with me, she would've efficiently deflected him or found an excuse to pull me away.

Tara had been at my office the day I'd received the letter, an honor bestowed upon me by a committee of my peers and industry experts. She had gifted me a tie that week, a tie my family forbade me to wear to the event. I think it eventually found its way to a thrift store somewhere, thanks to Cathy.

I had felt out-of-place multiple times over the last months. Yet, as I walked away from the evening with Aarti, I didn't wrangle with the feeling anymore. It felt as if I was exactly where I was supposed to be.

Talking to Aarti had been refreshing. Purifying, even. The rot eating at us to our core had been exposed and purged. Sharing our stories, honest and heartfelt, seemed to have eased the pain. I didn't need to hide my hurt and humiliation from her, and I was glad that she didn't either. The giggles, the tears, the laughter, the warmth, it all came gushing—unfeigned and unfettered.

An acute feeling tugged at my heart. Was Aarti alright? Had it been cruel to leave her alone when she was fighting off loneliness and hurt? Would it be a good idea to go back and comfort her?

No. My mind declared, resolute in its decision. I didn't know her well enough to go knocking on her door at this hour of the night.

As I stepped into the biting cold, Imran came around to hold the door open for me.

"Are you okay, Boss?" he asked as he drove me back home.

"Yes."

My mind remained preoccupied with Aarti's thoughts. There was something compelling, something *very* powerful about her that seemed to have sparked a longing in me. I couldn't say for sure what it was. All I knew was I wanted to see her again.

"Same time tomorrow?" I heard Imran again.

I looked at him. "What?"

He appeared perplexed. "Same time tomorrow morning?"

"Yes," I said and saw the lease documents on the seat.

"What's wrong, Boss?" Imran asked, noting the change in my demeanor.

"Everything is alright. No reason to worry."

After he dropped me off, I texted him to come half an hour sooner than our usual time.

THE NEXT MORNING, I was en route to Aarti's hotel with a tasteful bouquet in tow, reflecting upon our connection. What was the nature of my concern for her? She was a business associate I barely knew, who was also my ex's partner's ex. My ex, who was also her ex's former lover, and now our exes had ended up together again. Whichever way I looked at it, that was a lot of *ex* factor for comfort.

"It'll be okay, Boss," Imran said in a soft voice, and I caught him studying me with concern in the mirror. "Whatever it is, it's going to be fine. I know you'll make it right."

I gave a nod, grateful for his unshakable camaraderie. Years ago, Imran, then hardly twenty-one, worked as an errand boy at my office. His younger sister was sick back home. She had a congenital heart condition, and he needed money. But money wasn't the issue. He needed to get her to the U.S. to help her avoid getting pushed into a premature marriage before she completed her education.

I helped him bring her over and paid for the treatment, which wasn't much of an expense. Since that day, he'd trusted me with blind devotion. I kept advising him to be smart and not to trust someone so completely.

He always responded, "I don't trust anyone else. Only you."

His optimism about my current situation was colored by this faith in me.

Taking the elevator, I alighted on the eleventh floor, slightly surprised that I remembered it from last night. Walking up to her suite, I pressed the bell. A few quiet moments elapsed. The floor was silent. Had she checked out? I rang the bell again. This time, the door opened, and I stood face-to-face with Aarti, holding a rather expensive bouquet of flowers in my hand. Instantly, I felt like a fool.

She saw the flowers and looked at me. "Suj—Mr. Rao!"

"Ms. Bhatia..." It was too late to hide or ditch the bouquet, but I pulled it out of her face.

"I'm about to leave for a meeting." Her hurried words matched the impatience in her body language.

"This won't take long. I wanted to make sure you were alright after last night."

Her stern lip turned into a slight smile. "Are those flowers for me?" she asked with a glint of mischief.

My eyes drifted to the flowers in my hand and I held them out. "Yes."

She nodded. "Come in."

I stepped inside, and she closed the door.

"Thank you. I am okay. I'm much better, actually. The tears might have helped but I'm not ready to lose this battle of the egos with you, so I'm going to firmly deny that they did."

I laughed. "Well, good," I said. "But just so you know, I'm not fond of losing either."

"Is that right?" She cocked her hip and raised a brow.

"Yes, I've been preparing my armor for our meeting this evening."

"Well, I hope you shine it nice and bright. Get all kinks out of those pins and hinges."

I gazed at her as her eyes shone with amusement. I could gaze into those eyes for a long time...

I cleared my throat. "See you at the restaurant this evening?"

Her smile disappeared at my words, the softness and mischief replaced by an impassive, formal look.

"Actually, if you don't mind, I'd like to meet in your office," she said. "Not that I'm not grateful for your concern and for... these flowers." She raised the bouquet for effect. "But I think it would be best if we conducted this business in a formal capacity."

"Of course," I said and took a step back from her. "I just wanted to ensure you were alright. See you at my office at six?"

"That works."

"I'll have my assistant send you the address."

She nodded. "I must apologize for yesterday," she added. "I'm not a woman governed by her emotions, and certainly not before someone who's a business contact."

We were not just business contacts, but I didn't contradict her. I was convinced she was reiterating it for her benefit, not mine.

"No harm done. Business or otherwise, you have lost no respect in my eyes, Ms. Bhatia."

"Yes, but I wanted to clear the air from my end. It was an aberration and completely out of character for me."

When I returned a silent nod, she pulled in a deep breath. "You know, we'd be having a completely different conversation right now had we not been who we are."

"Exes' ex-exes' exes?" I said, and she looked at me with amusement.

"How much time did you spend coming up with that?"

"Well, there was traffic," I joked. "If we weren't who we are, we wouldn't be having this conversation in this room at all," I observed and was glad that we were.

She smiled, then pulled her hand over her forehead and ran her fingers down her dark, glossy hair. "Those two have quite literally messed us up, haven't they?" she cried.

"Not if we don't let them. We do have our own lives and identities. Our future lies ahead of us, not behind."

She blinked at my words. "Sorry, but I really need to leave. I do have a meeting. It wasn't just an excuse." She slipped me a tiny smile.

"I wouldn't know," I teased in return and was treated to a wide smile and a shake of her head.

As I walked back to my car, a blanket of calm surrounded my heart. I felt something I hadn't in a while now. I was happy. I had no reason to be, but I was.

"See, I told you that you'd fix everything," Imran said, spying the relief on my face in the rearview mirror.

"Maybe I didn't fix it this time. Someone else did," I said and looked out my window.

"Ms. Devi called to ask how long you'll be."

"Why didn't she call me?"

"You left your phone in the car." He pointed to the seat beside me with his eyes.

"Oh!"

"I said you weren't ready yet. Didn't want to tell her where we were."

"Thank you."

"That doesn't mean you're getting off easy," he teased with a twinkle in his eye.

Devi ran the place with an iron fist, but she got the work done. If it were up to me, I would've happily spent hours tinkering with codes and experimenting with new ideas without taking care of the *business* part of my business. She was the one who made sure I didn't relapse into my nerd mode.

Devi came barging in right behind me as I entered the office. "Where were you?"

"Woke up late."

"Were you out late last night? Do I need to reschedule your meetings?"

"No." I removed my coat and hung it on the stand in a corner.

"Don't get too comfortable. Your first meeting is in fifteen minutes. I hope you are prepared. Do you need Vaishali to sit in with you?"

"She owns the codes, so yes, I want her here. Make sure she brings the notes from last week."

Devi nodded and began to walk away. "How was you meeting last night?" she turned at the door and asked.

"It was alright," I said with my eyes deliberately planted on my computer.

"You think she'll be open to negotiating on the rent?"

"It's a difficult call. We'll see what happens. She's coming here at six."

"She's coming *here*?"

I nodded, still pretending to be deeply engrossed in my screen.

Devi closed the door and stepped back in. "I thought you were meeting her at Marco's, that you were going to use food as one of your bargaining positions."

"Change of plans," I said solemnly. "She's coming here. And email her office the address."

"But I'll be gone. I have Katya's violin recital today, I told you."

"I won't need you."

"Are you sure?"

"Yes. Email them the address."

She hesitated at the door but left without another word.

AT FIVE MINUTES TO SIX, Aarti's tall figure appeared outside my door. I promptly got up and invited her in.

She wore a knee-length skirt like last night, a deep blue against yesterday's black, with a light blue silk shirt and a stylish McQueen blazer. Obviously, I would've never known this if not for my brand-savvy sister-in-law and her frequent insistence that I go shopping with them. One of her many attempts to get me out of the house after my breakup.

"This is a very nice office!" Aarti said as she entered and scanned the tastefully decorated space.

"Thank you, long years of sweat and hard work to come up with just the right furniture, the right art."

"Or money, a lot of it," she countered matter-of-factly. "And a fantastic interior decorator."

I killed a chuckle as she looked over my shoulder to gaze at the city lights behind me, glimmering against the darkening sky. I realized why she had asked to meet in my office instead of the restaurant. She wanted a peek at the space, and now that she had, she knew exactly what it was worth.

Impressed and intrigued, I invited her to take a seat on the plush leather couch away from my desk. I lowered myself to a chair across from her.

"I hope you're not thinking of evicting us so you can rent out this place for a higher price, now that you know how spacious these offices are."

She shrugged elegantly, placing her bag beside her. "That's one option," she said, crossing her legs. She appeared more somber this evening.

"Let's talk about the numbers you've sent us," I said promptly.

This was a business meeting and the sooner we established this connection, the sooner we'd get over the weird one that linked us currently.

"We are not charging any more than the going rate in the area," she replied coolly and unhurriedly. It was a perfect power move to my impatience.

"But it's three times the amount we're paying," I countered, now matching her tone. "Three times what we've paid for the last several years."

"Walter was soft. He lowballed the rent for all his properties, initially out of inexperience but then out of the goodness of his heart. And look where that's gotten him. He let his emotions run his business into the ground. He's had to sell three of his toniest buildings."

"To you?"

She shrugged noncommittally.

"We can't afford that amount, Ms. Bhatia. We need to somehow survive in this economy."

"You lease four floors in this building, and I've heard you've been scouting another location for a satellite office. I'd say you are more than surviving the economy."

That knocked me off my game. She was good. I had made some very discreet inquiries about another space, and if she knew that, she was terribly well-connected. But instead of being annoyed at her for doing her research or embarrassed that she had better connections than me, I found myself genuinely impressed. She was certainly running this meeting, and she knew it.

"I can't agree to the amount you're paying, Mr. Rao." It didn't escape my attention that the way she addressed me—her tone—was more formal than was warranted by the situation. I wondered if it was just in keeping with the professional context of the meeting, or an attempt to create distance between us.

"You need to come up with a better number. I don't do these kinds of meetings. Our office takes care of that. I am extending a friendly hand here. This is a lot of prime real estate, and Walter told us you are a good person. We'd hate to lose you."

"Walter is also a good person." I leaned back in my seat and interlaced my fingers. "That's why he's losing in this cruel world."

Her face hardened. "Me, on the other hand...cutthroat, maneater, all the B, C, and F words. I've heard them all."

She looked fiercely into my eyes.

"I wouldn't say that," I said with a crooked smile.

"What *would* you say?"

"Astute, smart, assertive. A woman who knows her business interests," I offered, leaning back in my chair.

She was visibly taken aback. Her mouth gaped a little, and her body leaned back.

"I wasn't expecting that," she said softly.

"I wasn't either. Coffee?"

She shook her head. "No, thank you."

I steepled my fingers. "What's the F word?" I asked with authentic curiosity.

It surprised her, and she reacted with a short laugh. "You know the one. Feminazi. Used for every woman who knows how to effectively speak her mind."

"Ah, that one," I said.

"And since you didn't ask about the other alphabets, I suppose you know which ones I'm talking about."

Sadly, I did know those. I nodded.

"How do we break this impasse?" I asked, returning to the issue at hand.

"Come up with a reasonable number."

"I'll check with my accounts department and see what we can afford. I hope you will honor our offer."

"If it's reasonable. Please ask around, Mr. Rao, we're really not fleecing you. That's not what we do. We need to survive too."

"I was told you are real estate royalty. I think you're also more than surviving."

That earned me a smile. "Reasonable number," she said, "and we'll talk again."

Remember I said I wasn't much of a hard-ass? Well, she was! And she had me completely floored. The woman who had wept in my arms last night wasn't the one sitting across from me right now. Or perhaps she was but had learned to masquerade her deepest emotions too well.

"I'll see you to your car," I offered as she rose.

"Thank you, but I'll be fine," she said, and I walked with her to the elevators as a professional courtesy.

Back in my office, I watched the short video of Kitty's violin recital that Devi had texted me. She was good and played better than a seven-year-old should be expected to play. Then I answered emails that needed my urgent response. Half an hour later, when I packed up and went down, I saw Aarti sitting in the lobby with an impatient look on her face, typing furiously on her phone.

"Ms. Bhatia, you're still here?"

She looked up. "My stupid driver had a fender bender. The service is sending another car."

"You know there are cabs and rideshare services in the city, right?"

She looked at me like it was an alien concept or a highly dubious one. I laughed.

"Let me drop you," I offered.

"No, that's alright."

"It's not a big deal. It's not a long drive to your hotel, and it's on the way to my place. Please, I insist."

She sighed and stood.

"Let me call the service and tell them I don't need the car here."

I nodded and waited while she placed the call. She indicated we walk while she talked. Imran pulled the car around, and I opened the door for her before she reached for it.

"Allow me, Ms. Bhatia."

"Sujit," she whispered near my cheek, and the hair on my neck stood to attention. "I sobbed in your arms last night. You've seen me whimper like a child. I think it's safe to drop the honorifics."

"I thought you said you wanted to keep this formal and business-like," I teased.

She responded with a frustrated grunt before slipping inside the car. I don't think I did a great job of reigning in my amusement as I came around through the other door because I saw

Imran watching me in his trusty mirror with a twinkle in his eye. But I made sure to keep my eyes off him as we rode in silence.

Beside me, I felt the soft touch of Aarti's perfume. A gentle, pleasant smell. Unique but not overpowering. And yet, strangely powerful. Or maybe that's how I felt about her. When I threw a glance in her direction, I found her looking at me with a tender gaze.

"Thank you for the ride," she said in a voice meant for private conversation.

"Sure," I replied. "It's no bother."

The uncertainty of our dynamic was starting to trouble me. One moment, we were joking and teasing, and the next, the gravity of our situation, our curious connection, came bearing down on us. I could see it in her behavior as well. She wanted to put last night behind us, reverting to her professional detachment, yet I saw her soft eyes when she smiled and teased.

"Would you like to join me for dinner?" something prompted me to ask, but I instantly regretted it. When she threw a quick glance at me, I added, "Unless you already have other plans, of course."

"No," she replied with a decided haste in her voice. "I have nothing else tonight. Dinner sounds good."

"I know a nice bistro. Let's see if they will accommodate us."

"I've looked you up, Sujit. Something tells me they will," she teased.

And there it was again, the lighthearted exchange. I decided I liked this better. I enjoyed her teasing. I liked her quippy mouth.

"Marco's, Imran."

There was a twinkle in his eye, but with a perfectly courteous voice, he said, "Yes, Boss."

SUJIT

𝒶 regular at Marco's, I had my own table, a quiet spot in a corner.

"What will you have?" I asked Aarti when Fernando came for our drink order.

"A glass of the sparkling white, please."

I ordered whisky and waited until Fernando left.

"The name sounds familiar. Is this where we were supposed to meet today?"

"Yes," I replied. "I thought the good food might make you more amenable to kindness."

"Then you underestimated me," she said with a straight face.

"That was a joke. I really like this place."

She sipped her water. "There's something I must tell you. I didn't know what to make of your visit to my room this morning."

"How do you mean?"

She didn't respond to my question. "Can I be honest with you?" she asked instead.

"I hope you do."

"Why is this so complicated?" I caught the exasperation in her tone. She waited a full two breaths before continuing, "On the one hand, we have this formal business relationship, and I need to honor that. On the other, I feel like you know exactly what I'm going through right now, and that kind of weakens my position."

"Hmm, if I understand what you're going through, it's because I'm in the same situation. Doesn't that also weaken my position? And come to think of it, don't they cancel each other out?"

Fernando returned with our drinks, and we silently raised our glasses and took our first sips.

"This is crisp and really refreshing," Aarti said, pleased.

"I'm glad. This place has never disappointed me."

She began to peruse the scant menu placed before us.

"What did you mean when you said you couldn't figure out why I visited you this morning?" I asked.

"I'm putting aside our business relation for the rest of the evening," she said, returning the menu back to the table.

"I thought we did that already when you asked me to drop the honorifics," I argued.

Her lips lifted at the corners. "Okay, this is what confused me. I was conflicted about whether it was genuine concern for me or..."

"Or?" I said curious about the dilemma on her mind.

"I couldn't figure out if you really cared about how I was after last night, or was it merely..."

I smiled. "Merely a way to appease you so you'd reconsider the rent hike?"

She lowered her eyes to the table. "Something like that."

"And have you arrived at a conclusion?" I asked.

"I'm going with genuine concern," she answered, then put the wine glass to her lips. The shape of her mouth around the clear glass created flutters in my stomach. I promptly redirected my gaze to her eyes. "If you were someone who believed in playing games, Tara would have flung you away as far as she could throw you."

I picked up my glass. The color on her bronze face resembled the liquid gold I was holding up. "None of what happened yesterday or this evening, neither our business association nor our past, precludes us from having a friendship, does it?"

She looked up at me as if my words had shocked her.

"But I wouldn't impose either way," I added quickly.

"No," she replied with equal haste. "That's...exactly what I was going to suggest. If you were amenable, that is."

"Amenable?" I said with a gentle frown. "Didn't we decide to suspend our business relations for the night? That's a rather formal word, I believe, business-like even."

She smiled. "Okay, smarty-pants. Is that better?"

"Much." I smiled back.

Fernando came back with our food and laid it out before us with graceful finesse. Marinated chicken breast on a bed of mushroom risotto for her, and a steak with seasonal vegetables for me.

"Thank you, Fernando," I said and signaled him to bring more wine for Aarti.

"I don't think we need to read too much into it," I said as I sliced into my steak. "Seeking camaraderie at this time, especially with someone who knows exactly what you're going through, is natural, normal. It could be healthy. Who knows, it might even help us move on from the heartache."

A faint curve danced on her lips while she sliced a small piece off her chicken breast. Her eyes stayed on me as she placed the knife back, returning the fork to her right hand.

"Like I said, you're a romantic. You believe in hope and rosy endings."

"And you believe in surviving the now. Our friendship helps with both situations, as I see it," I contended.

"One of these days, Sujit, I *will* have the last word. I promise."

I laughed. "Okay, I will shut up."

"Don't," she said softly. "I like hearing you talk."

"Yeah?" I pulled myself upright comically. "Is it the sound of my voice, or is it my words that you enjoy?"

Fernando came back with her wine and brought another whisky for me even though I hadn't asked for one. He knew me well, and I offered him a grateful smile.

"It's everything," Aarti confessed when we were alone again. "It's your gentle spirit, your kindness, your intellect. It's your subtle wit. It's everything," she repeated.

I decided to underplay the weight of her compliments. We both were vulnerable at this moment and it wouldn't be smart to read anything into what she was saying.

"Well, now I know the reason for your success," I said instead.

"Oh?"

"You know how to read people."

She relaxed back in her chair and picked up the wine glass. "It's an acquired skill. Cultivated out of necessity."

"And you do it very well."

"Couldn't read Sameer or Tara, so it's been pretty useless in my personal life if you ask me. Although," she said, taking a sip of the wine. "I did ask Sameer about Tara the very first night I met her. I knew something was off. So maybe I just trusted the wrong person."

"Let's talk about something else," I suggested. "How's the city treating you?"

"It's still bloody cold!"

"Winter is just a long, circuitous route to Spring," I said and watched as she resisted rolling her eyes.

"Where are you getting all these? *The Hopeless Romantic's Handy Guide to Platitudes*?"

I feigned shock. "How did you know? Do you also own a copy?"

We both split into what I'm certain was impolitely loud laughter.

"Tell me about this place you're scouting," she said as she picked up the orzo on her fork. "What exactly are you looking for? Maybe I can help."

I hesitated. It was too soon in our relationship, business or personal, to confide in her about my new project. But if anyone could help, it would be her. She had that clout and the brilliance. Was I getting enamored by her?

Reading my hesitation, she smiled. "It's not for a satellite office. It's something you can't share yet." A statement, not a question.

"It's for a new project I've been thinking about," I found myself blurting. She had the knack of rendering me defenseless against her brilliance. "There are maybe five people who know about it."

She picked up her wine. "I can keep a secret if you feel inclined to share."

Inclined, I was.

"My younger cousin is a sculptor, and during a conversation with her some months ago, I thought of creating an online marketplace for freelance artists."

"That's why you're looking for places in Brooklyn. I thought it was only because it's cheaper than leasing another place in Manhattan."

Her changed posture suggested that she had put her business-woman hat back on. She sat upright, and her legs were crossed under the table. With the wine glass in one hand, she pulled her free arm across her chest,

"Price is one factor," I replied.

"What's the other?"

"I'm thinking of a workspace, a studio of sorts that artists can use when they need to."

"That's a great idea, Sujit. Like a rent-an-office space."

"Yes, but less pricey, and will offer more flexibility for short-term rentals and be close enough for effective and practical use."

"I think you might be on to something interesting here. Tell me how I can help."

"I need a space for backend work and a large space for multiple studio offices."

"I think we might have just bought something that I can offer you for a reasonable rent. Let me talk to Dad."

My hand stilled at the mention of her father. Would he agree to lease it to me if he knew who I was?

Again, Aarti read my face with the perceptiveness that I had come to expect of her by now and said, "Of course, I wouldn't mention who you are."

Her words intrigued me, maybe stung me slightly.

"Would that be a problem? Knowing who I am? Or was, rather. It's all in the past now, isn't it?"

"I wish we could shove it aside that effortlessly." She sighed. "Dad took my breakup the hardest. The night of the party, he had stood before the city that respects him and declared he was making Sameer a partner in his business. A couple of weeks later, Sameer had made him look like a fool. But it was my broken heart that made him the most furious."

Her eyes glazed for a moment like she was revisiting that day in the past. When she finally steadied them on me, I said, "For me, it was my sister-in-law Cathy who took it the hardest. She wanted to call Tara and blast her for her behavior, but of course, that would've hurt me, so she didn't. She wanted to, though."

"My dad called Sameer's father and went off on him. He threatened to ruin Sameer, and I think he did cause some damage to his reputation and business. Mom is magnanimous. Dad isn't.

He still keeps oscillating between injury and anger. So, yeah, he hates Sameer, and he probably hates Tara and everything associated with them. He's like a wounded lion right now, especially with the extravagant wedding Sameer has planned. I'd definitely not mention you to him."

"I wouldn't want to put you in an awkward situation, Aarti. We both have been through enough. I don't want more trouble."

"Please!" she said with a whiff of dismissal for her father's anger. "If I couldn't keep emotions out of business, I wouldn't be here. Dad's not that person, either. But Sameer hurt his daughter, and somehow, that took precedence over everything he's held about running a business. It's silly if you ask me."

"Can I count on you, then? I'll stop my inquiries immediately, especially because I don't want the idea leaked before I have a chance to implement it in its entirety."

She returned her wine glass to the table and nodded. "I'll take care of it, Sujit. If we don't have something to offer, I will find you the right place. You can rest assured. It's off your plate. You don't need to worry about it anymore."

"Are you helping as a friend or as a business associate?" I don't know if I should have asked that question, but her tone and words compelled me to.

She gave me her most elegant smile. "A friend. We suspended our business relations for the evening, remember?"

And suddenly, I was glad I asked because the warmth that coursed through my body at her words felt different than the whisky running through my system that night.

"I owe you a dinner," she said when I dropped her off at the hotel. "Thank you for a wonderful evening. I'm glad we did this."

"Me too," I said, holding out my hand. "Goodnight."

I saw Imran grinning wide when I returned to the car, and we started toward my penthouse.

"Go on, say what's on your mind."

"Is she the one who fixed what you couldn't?" Imran asked.

I smiled.

"I'm happy to see you happy, Boss."

"It's not happiness, it's relief."

"Whatever you say, Boss," he said and grinned wider.

"Drive, Imran."

"It's been a long time," he murmured, then sighed.

He wouldn't be this pleased if he knew who she was. No one in my family would be pleased.

I had no doubt in my mind that our connection needed to remain a secret.

AARTI

I slept well that night. Definitely better than the previous one. I kept thinking of our chance meeting and the impromptu sharing of our common grievances. Befriending Sujit, confiding in him, had comforted me. Learning that he had been hurting just as bad had somehow reassured me that I wasn't guileless and weak. Knowing that a man as smart as Sujit had also been fooled by love's lure made me feel less like a loser. It convinced me that there was perhaps hope for us both. A hope for a fresh start.

My condo in the city was the beginning of this new start for me.

Since our business in and around New York was expanding fast, I had convinced Dad to let me buy a place to use as a base of operations. I was already envisioning an office in the region. It would take some effort to convince him—taxes and all—but I had got my assistant gathering numbers.

That week, I checked on the status of the renovations at the condo. It had been stripped, re-floored, polished, and painted. The interior designer was working round the clock to make it good enough for me to move in soon. Staying at a luxury hotel had its perks, but home had always held a special charm for me.

I still owed Sujit a dinner. During another meeting at his office that week, I told him about the additional floor that had just become available in his building. Although I spotted his eyes light up at the offer, he gave me a diplomatic answer that he'd think about it. What I didn't tell him was that I had cut a deal with the small business on the floor just above his, giving them two floors in another building a few blocks away offering a lucrative price for the first year.

Sujit was a good person and deserved some kindness after what he'd been through with the whole Tara affair. At least, that's how I justified this business decision to myself. My heart, though, was smarter than to be plied by such flimsy excuses. It was also smart enough to know the futility of the path it wanted to go down.

For one, Sujit was a different person when we met alone than when I was at his office. Perhaps, like me, he also wanted to keep the lid on our connection to Tara and Sameer. The thought caused an involuntary twinge in my chest that our association will always be shrouded in shame and guilt. And for no fault of ours.

But to wallow in self-pity or seek out sympathy wasn't my modus operandi. I was known to forge ahead through thick and thin. And that's what I did.

That week, I called to invite him to dinner.

"How delicate is your palate?" he inquired when I asked him to recommend a restaurant.

"I've been known to survive all kinds of foods."

"I know a terrific Korean place. The food is a bit spicy, but if you can get past that, you'll never find anything better in life."

"I'm in. Send me the name, and I'll have my office make a reservation."

"Let me take care of that. They usually don't take reservations, but I have a connection."

"Is there any restaurant in New York where you don't have a connection?" I asked, part curious, part amused.

"What can I say? A man needs to eat."

I laughed. "That he does, and at very exclusive places, I see."

"This isn't an exclusive place. It's just incredibly good and almost always crowded. That's the reason I'll use my contact. Otherwise, we'd have to wait an hour for a table at the minimum."

Sunday evening, he picked me up at the hotel.

"No Imran today?" I leaned in and whispered when I saw a new person driving us.

"He has the weekends off. I use a car service on the weekends and holidays."

"I'm in dire need of good food today," I said. "I had a hectic day."

"No rest for the wicked, eh?"

"I was at the condo making sure things are ready so I can move in."

"Move in?" The lilt in his voice matched the jump of his eyebrows.

When I told him what had kept me busy all week, he confessed, "I had a very different image of you when I saw you at the bar that evening."

"Different how?"

"You don't mind the hard work. For the owner of a company so big, you don't mind getting your hands dirty."

"Well, technically, Dad owns the company. I'm just an employee, and I need to earn my wages."

His smile reached his eyes, his admiration deep in his dimples.

"What's that smile for?" I asked.

He shook his head. "So, how's the place?" he queried instead.

"Do you even need to ask?"

He let out a low chuckle.

"If you want to be my neighbor, there is another unit available," I blurted, then instantly regretted it. What was it about this man that made me drop my guard without thinking?

He flashed me the smile that was a salve to my soul. "I wouldn't mind if you lived here," he said softly. "But you are a visitor. You'll eventually return, and then I'll be twice as lonely."

"True." I nodded. It wasn't the time to mention the possibility of a new office and perhaps my move to the region. Not yet. Not before I'd talked with Dad, anyway.

That was another thing I was keeping from my father. After Sameer, I wanted to move out of Dallas. It was getting claustrophobic. Not that I'd be hung up on him for life, but the waters had been muddied. Moving in the same circles in the same city ensured some amount of awkwardness, no matter how repentant and gracious Sameer and Tara were.

When the car dropped us at the very crowded restaurant, a man in a lightly stained apron promptly directed us to a quiet table in a secluded corner and disappeared just as mysteriously.

"Let me guess, you know the chef," I said.

He tried to evade the question by looking down at the menu in his hand.

"Sujit?" I said in my sweetest voice, and it got me the desired result.

He looked into my eyes, and my heart stumbled over itself before he answered, "I've been coming here since I was in college. He wasn't this big, celebrated chef at that time. We both were just...ordinary people," he said with a shrug.

I smiled. "Those are the best kind of connections, but I doubt that you were ever *just ordinary*, Mr. Sujit Rao. Don't forget, I've studied you and your résumé."

"Oh?" he cried with raised brows. "Have you now?"

"Indeed," I said, trying to choke the smile that was threatening to bloom on my face.

"And what have you learned?"

He placed the menu back on the table and crossed his arms. I caught his biceps bulge through the powder blue cashmere sweater he had chosen that evening. My mind rushed to the night he'd put his arm around me to thwart my fall. The gentle scent of his fresh cologne combined with the luxurious smell of the whisky on his breath had a visceral effect on my body. I'd found myself wet and turned on like I had never felt before.

My breath turned heavy at the thought, and I quickly redirected my eyes and my mind to the menu before me.

"What would you recommend?" I asked, pretending to sincerely peruse the menu. There was only one authentic Korean restaurant in Plano and like this place, it was always crowded with impossibly long wait times.

"I love their grilled pork ribs and the gamjatang."

"What's that?"

"Pork bone soup."

"Sounds good. Could we get some bibimbap?"

"You're paying. We can get whatever you want." He cocked a smile.

"Are you always this sassy? There's a term in Hindi, haazir jawab."

"Don't know much Hindi. Barely know my mother tongue."

"What's your mother tongue?

"Telugu. I do speak it. But badly. Keep forgetting words. The closest I can get is Tenglish," he said with a shrug.

I creased my brows in thought. "If your more dominant

language is English, shouldn't it be Elugu instead of Tenglish? How do portmanteaus usually work?"

"Hell if I knew!" he said, then looked at me with what I knew to be the start of one of the most precious things.

The laughter that emerged from his mouth was the most beautiful sound in the world. It was promptly swallowed up by the crowd around us, but that made it even more special. His laugh was just for me. Only I was privy to its melody, and the world had better feel envious of it.

Infectious as it was, I couldn't last more than a few seconds before bursting into a squeal myself. It was ridiculous. The joke wasn't even that funny, and yet here we were, laughing like we had just outdone the best comedians of the world. My eyes rimmed with the kind of happiness I hadn't felt in a long time. The kind of tears that I really wanted instead of the ones I had ended up with after Sameer.

We only stopped because a server walked to our table with a bottle of fresh, crisp white wine and stem glasses.

"I hope this is okay," Sujit said as she showed us the bottle. "I took the liberty."

"It's perfect," I approved with a nod.

While the server poured us the wine with impeccable etiquette, I looked around and spotted soju and beer on every other table. A rush of warmth filled my core as I realized Sujit must have made this special request when he called for the table.

A vague memory rustled past me with a silent whisper. *It's the little things.*

As the sweet bubbles of the wine danced on my tongue, I watched him push his sexy glasses up the bridge of his nose and gaze at me. "So what's that term you were talking about? Haaz something?"

Extricating myself from the power of those brilliant eyes, I answered, "Haazir jawab. It means quick-witted, someone who has an instant comeback for everything."

"So you are fluent in Hindi, then?"

"I understand it completely." I smiled. "My dad's family speaks Punjabi. Mom speaks Hindi, and that term has been seared into my brain because, growing up, it used to be my mother's favorite criticism of me. That I was haazir jawab. Always ready with an answer. And I used to say, guess where I got it from."

"Mom?"

I nodded. "She's as smart as they come but didn't get a chance to fly with the full extent of her wingspan."

Shit! Had I just shared my family's private matters with him? I had always regretted that Ma didn't get to be who she could've been, but I had never voiced it so fiercely, so fearlessly before. Not even to Ma.

When I got my eyes to focus on Sujit again, I caught him studying me with intent. He picked up the wine and said, "Judging from your success, your wit certainly seems to have served you well."

I relaxed in my chair. I was getting more comfortable in his presence, and it unnerved me. I had always been guarded since I started working, and suddenly, I was smiling, laughing uninhibitedly, and sharing my family's secrets with a person I'd known for a couple of weeks.

When the food arrived, I graciously declared that it had stood up to all the hype that Sujit had built up.

"I didn't think we would end up finishing so much of it," he said as he refilled our glasses.

"Why, just because I'm a slender woman, you thought I was a salad-munching girl? That's such a tired cliché."

He looked at me from over the rim of his glasses—my stomach did a silly flip—as he returned the bottle to the table.

"Aarti, not everything I say comes with the premise that I'm talking to a woman. I was merely making an observation."

I nodded, suddenly embarrassed of my defensiveness. "Sorry," I said. "It comes with the territory. I've been operating in a man's world for too long."

"I know," he said, and it conveyed everything he'd not said.

I blinked rapidly. "Are you thinking of filing a patent for Elugu?" I asked for lack of another distraction.

"I don't know, but it gives me an idea for a language-based software that can help students in countries without proper schooling systems. You are brilliant! Thank you."

Apologizing for the interruption, he pulled out his phone and typed something fast and quick.

"You're not joking!" I cried, partly amused.

"I never joke about software."

I stared at him with a serious face.

He smiled. "That was a joke."

I shook my head and basked in his presence.

AARTI

*a*ll through dinner and on our ride back, I kept thinking of polite ways to invite him back to my room. Given the tenuous nature of our association, there was scant chance we would share a carefree evening like this anytime soon. Sure, we'd meet to discuss places for his new venture, but what was the probability that it would turn into a relaxed and fun dinner date?

I had thrown caution to the wind all evening, so why stop now?

When he came around to open the door for me, I brashly offered, "Come up with me."

His hand stilled as I stepped out of the car.

"Come up for a nightcap," I said with a smile.

He conferred with the driver, and I saw him drive off.

"How will you go back?" I asked.

"Cab. I might be late, and I don't want him waiting into the night."

"Into the night?" I teased with an expression of faux horror. "Whatever gave you that idea?"

"Not that way, Aarti," he protested, my name creating a

perfect sound in his mouth. Of course, my stomach did its thing, dropping and tumbling like it had no other business.

How about trying to digest the food I'd just had, stomach? Why don't you focus on that instead of making me hyperaware of Sujit's presence beside me?

"What way then?" I teased with a straight face. "I don't know what a man would be doing in a strange woman's hotel room into the night."

"Alright, smarty-pants," he said and bumped his shoulder with mine. "And you aren't a stranger. Not anymore."

And there it was again. That strong tumble in my stomach and the steep dip in my heart like it had taken a plunge straight down a tall cliff.

"Why is it that you always have to have the last word?" I complained.

"Hey, I told you, I don't like to lose."

Except you lost Tara to Sameer, my errant mind prompted me, but I kept my mouth shut.

Up in my suite, I invited him to take a seat while I excused myself and returned with a bottle of his favorite single malt. I'd ordered the bottle that week, intending to send it as a gift, but hadn't figured out a good excuse. This felt like a prime opportunity.

"Rampur!" Sujit's eyes widened with a delight I hadn't quite expected.

"Oh, you like it too?" I teased with a crooked grin.

"You know I do. This can't be a coincidence."

My grin only widened. "I was told this is a limited edition. I hope it's to your liking."

The beaming look on his face said he was more than impressed with it. My heart swelled, and my body warmed at the thought that I had not only managed to impress him but also made him happy. I knew it was wrong in every sense of the word, but I couldn't help falling in love with his happiness.

"You are sly," he said, bringing me from the ether back into my body. "Who did you bribe to get that information?"

"*Bribe*?" I grimaced. "You forget how connected I am. All I did was send an email from my personal account."

"You are very different from what I expected," he said as I poured the liquid gold into a glass and handed it to him.

"You said that once already today." I took my glass of water and settled on a plush chair facing his seat on the couch.

"You're not the hard-ass you portray to be. There's a naughty, playful side you never let sneak out."

I returned a rueful smile as I pulled my knees up in the comfortable chair. "You talked about linguistic code-switching at dinner. Slipping into English and Telugu as needed?"

"Yes."

"Take your shoes off. Put your feet up."

He slipped off his shoes and pulled the tufted hassock closer to him.

"Code-switching is also cultural and behavioral," I said. "Do you know how old I was when I joined Dad's business? Twenty-two. Fresh out of college and before I went for my MBA. I was a nice person. My mom ensured that. But I was also naïve and inexperienced. Neither my privileged upbringing nor college had prepared me for the real world. I assumed everyone was inherently nice and truthful. And if someone lied, it was on account of necessity, not malice or intrigue. In my first year of working for Dad, a staff member asked me for two days off to go see her sick mother in Kansas. Sympathetic to her situation, I gave her the entire week off. I allowed her to take as much time as she needed to care for her mother and passed along her work to her colleagues. Two nights later, I was at a club downtown, and I saw her on the dance floor, drunk and dancing without a care in the world.

"So there I was, sitting with a drink in my hand, in a glittery dress that barely covered my thighs, and I learned the first and most important lesson of my career: people lie. Humans are liars and cheats. That's our true nature. That's our real instinct. Those who don't lie have either overcome their first nature or are efficient in covering up their lies. I let her take the week off because I'm a woman of my word. When she returned the next week, I called her into my office, told her what I saw, and when she denied having been to the club, I fired her on the spot. If she'd accepted that she lied, I would've let it pass. Because guess how old she was?"

"Twenty-two?" he said.

"That's right. And just like me, she'd made an error in judgment. So I was ready to give her the benefit of the doubt, but instead of owning up to her mistake, she lied further to cover her first lie. I fired her and made sure she didn't get another penny from us. When the loss of her job came down on her, she confessed that she had used her mother's sickness as a ruse because her boyfriend was in town, and she wanted to spend time with him. The ironic part was that she did have a sick mother in Kansas who needed care, and she'd used up her allotted leave during the days her mother needed her. She was also the one paying her mother's medical bills. I was terribly upset when I learned, so I made inquiries and sent money anonymously to the hospital where her mother got her monthly dialysis. I did that until she passed. But I didn't hire the girl back. I could've made sure no one in the business hired her, but I didn't do that either because, you see, I'm not cruel. I only hate liars. I may not be a bad person, but I won't be a pushover."

He held his glass close to his chest and looked at me with soft eyes.

"Thus, the Aarti for the people closest to her is different from the Aarti who runs SB Real Estate."

"Completely different."

"We all code-switch though, don't we?"

"Yes. Some of it is benign, like when you adapt to a situation or show respect to the elders in a family or community. But when one is forced to code-switch, it becomes a burden. If you have to do it because you're afraid what others might think of you, if you make it your way of life, if it *becomes* you, it is fundamentally deleterious. Projecting a false image of oneself can seem powerful at first, but the effort required to maintain the façade is...emotionally draining."

Why was I spelling all this out to Sujit? What had prompted it, I wondered. Was it the resounding care in his voice, in his words? Or was I at such a fragile place in my life that I was holding on to the tiny twig in my grasp to prevent myself from drowning?

Sujit pulled the veil off my conundrum. "What are you afraid of, Aarti?" His voice, soft and vulnerable, shot through to my heart. My face heated up, and my eyes felt moist.

I readjusted myself in the chair to recalibrate my breath. "I'm afraid that if I am myself, I will never be taken seriously." His eyes had steadied on me as I continued, "Every now and again, I want to be playful at work, laugh at a joke. But I can't because a friendly woman, especially a young, friendly woman, isn't seen as a strong woman. She's seen as frivolous. Often mistaken for a pushover. My dad and brother can joke and laugh and be taken seriously because they are men in a men's world. If I want to be in a position of power, I need to keep myself aloof from everyone...sometimes even from my own self."

"So, who are you, Aarti? Who are you at your core?" he asked.

It was then I realized that I'd known him for two weeks, and I had shared more with him than I had shared with Sameer in our

years-long relationship. Had Sameer even known the real me?
Had he even tried to know the real me?

SUJIT

"That's the question, isn't it?" Aarti said with a pensive curve of her lip. "Who am I? Is it who I am, or who I've become? And is our self-perception influenced by how others see us?"

I contemplated her questions while nursing the glass in my hand.

"You know how I feel?" she asked, sitting up in the chair. "Like no one has ever loved me for me. No one knows who I am. What I am."

Uncertain if she wanted my verbal input, I reserved my words and kept my eyes on her.

"You know what I love? I love reading, and I love someone reading to me. I used to lay with my head in Mom's lap, and she'd read to me every night until I was almost ten. I love that feeling of sharing stories with someone. I want to share a gasp when something intriguing happens in a book. I love to read aloud sentences that are strung together by the sheer beauty of the language. And you know how many people know this about me?"

I shook my head.

"One. My mom. I was all set to marry him, but even Sameer didn't know this. He never had time. Now I know he never had time for me."

Her eyes glazed, dimming the happy gleam in them from a moment ago.

"What else do you love?" I asked, and she looked at me with surprise.

"You really want to know?" she asked with a lilt in her voice.

"I do." I sat back and crossed my ankles on the hassock.

"I love doing my own makeup. I love pampering myself because only I know what I like. I love a well-made tiramisu."

I smiled. "And here I thought you were a chocolate cake gal."

She laughed in response. "But no one knows any of this about me because no one asked. People always assume things about me because of how I look or who my father is. Right from the first boyfriend I had in high school to Sameer and every other man who wanted to marry me, I've been an heiress who was incredibly hot. I was only ever defined by two things: my looks and my father's wealth."

I let a beat of silence pass before saying, "That's unfortunate."

"You're defined by your wealth, too," she observed. "And it is unfair. Your worth is measured in terms of your assets—the car you drive, the expanse of the home you live in, the brand of clothes you wear, your lifestyle. In today's shallow world, the allure and the enigma of a billionaire surpasses the evils that wealth inequality has created in our society."

Fuck! These were my words in her voice. If I thought I was impressed with her before, she just turned this into a full-blown admiration.

"But," she said, and I reined in my walloping heart. "The burden of the body that women are made to carry is so unfair, so cumbersome."

I wasn't going to argue with that.

"My closest friend in college, Isha, was a fat activist," she said. "She identified as fat, politically. She didn't mince words. No fat *acceptance*, she used to say. Acceptance assumes toleration. Why should fat people expect to be tolerated? We have a right to exist as we are."

I nodded.

"As a fat person, society expected her to hate her body, but she didn't. And she wanted to be with someone who understood that. She didn't want to be in a relationship, even casually, who didn't see her body as a part of her, and vice versa."

Aarti was in the zone now, her eyes fixed on a spot behind me.

"At that time, I didn't give it much thought, because I possessed the ideal body type as defined by society. I thought my situation was different. Then I heard what men had been saying behind my back, and I realized that Isha and I were not that different after all. We both were defined through our bodies. Following in her footsteps, I decided I didn't want to be with anyone who didn't respect my body the same way I did. The only purpose of my body is not to be fuckable, to be there for others' pleasure. She wasn't seen as more than her body, and neither was I."

"I'm sorry, Aarti."

She let out a hysterical laugh. "Are you going to apologize to all women? Because most of us have been through this."

I grew thoughtful. "I think as a society we can keep apologizing to women, and it will never be enough for all the crap we've put you through."

"You got that right," she said with a snort, then her eyes turned soft. "In fact, even though I later found out that Sameer didn't love me, he was the only one who'd made me feel good about myself in a long time. Yes, he used me to reinstate his family name, but he saw me as a person. He respected me. He wasn't faking that. He's a good man, and I hate saying this, but Tara is lucky to have him."

He was lucky to have Tara, but I didn't mention it.

"Do you run into them often?" I asked. "I just realized I don't have to see them or accidentally run into them, but you live in the same city."

She nodded. "Yup, same city, common friends. Even if I don't want to, certain social events mandate our presence. Friends' weddings, business socials, award functions in the desi community."

The soft lines of sadness on her face gave a faint impression of a flower that was preparing to wilt.

"You will find love again, Aarti," something inside me prompted me to say.

"Maybe, but I am not worried about it. I have enough on my plate and more. My family and friends keep setting me up on dates, though I've not found anyone remotely interesting." She rolled her eyes and smiled when I chuckled at her words. A part of me celebrated the fact that her dates had been dull.

"I like this," she said, making herself comfortable in the over-sized chair. "I like that I can talk to you about anything that crosses my mind without fear of being judged or ridiculed."

I leaned back against the couch, almost slouching, and adjusted my face to see her.

"Me too. I'm always closely guarded about what comes out of my mouth, especially after the breakup. With you, I can just be me. I don't have to worry about what you'll think of me, or if I share something, it will somehow appear in the desi rumor mill."

"Here too?"

"Here and New Jersey."

"After Sameer dumped me, they maligned his name, poor thing. Dad's too influential and well-connected for them to come after me, but Sameer lost many big business accounts after that. But hushed gossips didn't spare me either."

"How did you cope?" I inquired softly.

"Not well. I isolated myself, avoided gatherings while I healed. Then I realized that the rumors might actually do me good because people would stop approaching my parents with marriage proposals. And it worked. For months, there was sweet, golden silence on that front. Then, last month, we bought out four big real estate companies, increasing our worth and our influence on the East Coast. And the worms came crawling out of the wood-work. So many pathetic men who don't want to work but instead survive on my father's wealth. They call me damaged goods and hope that I'll settle for a less-than-ideal match to save face."

The cruelty in those words hurt a deep place in my heart.

"They want me to play the dainty socialite who'll stay in my little box after the wedding," she continued. "Fuck that! I'm single-handedly running my father's company. I love what I do, and I'm very good at it. My brother is younger, pampered, married, and a new father. He's still learning the ropes. But I've doubled the company's size and worth since I started. I turned thirty-one this year, and people say to my parents, *how long will you keep her unmarried*? Thankfully, like me, my mom is mouthy. She retorts, *as long as it takes for her to find a deserving partner*."

I poured myself another finger of the smooth liquor.

"So, what's your sob story?" she asked, sipping the water in her glass.

I sighed. "My sob story is that Tara was the first woman I truly loved."

"You're kidding. How old were you?"

I laughed. "Old enough to have sorted out first love and crushes a long time ago."

"I refuse to believe that you never liked another woman until you met Tara."

"Well…"

"I knew it. Tell me everything. Leave nothing out." She grinned and sat up to savor the juicy tale. Except, there was no meat in this story. Literally and figuratively.

I chuckled inwardly before I said, "I never told her I liked her."

"Who was she?"

"Technically, a friend. We were in the same group of friends in college, and I liked her immensely. But before I could gather my wits to tell her, she was going out with my friend, a close friend at the time. That door literally slammed shut on my face. They married after college and divorced a few years later."

Her eyes studied me with curiosity. She knew there was more. I nodded, slightly unsettled by this recognition from her, this connection we shared as if she knew exactly what thought was crossing my mind at that moment. I resisted against it, tried to quash it, but I knew I was weak before it. Before her.

"She contacted me after her divorce and asked me to meet over coffee. I saw no reason to refuse, especially since we operated in the same industry. She confessed that she knew I was interested in her, but chose my friend because she thought he had better prospects. I had to appreciate her honesty. But it was too late. I didn't feel anything for her anymore." I offered a light shrug.

"And you never liked anyone else?"

"I stayed away was more like it. Maybe I'm a true romantic who believes love will find its way to me. Or perhaps I am too scared to acknowledge my desires."

And now, after Tara, even more so. I wondered if Aarti had heard those unsaid words. I evaded her gaze and heard her take a deep breath in.

"I sometimes wonder if who we are is also influenced by who our parents are. And what they aren't," I mused aloud, trying to track the course of my life.

She leaned back in the chair and tilted her head against the headrest. "I'd assume so."

"My parents come from a small village in India. Both grew up in large, struggling families. Dad was a smart kid. He worked his ass off and was fortunate to find a couple of good mentors. Went to college in Bangalore, then came here for a doctorate. He fell in love with a white woman who was doing her Ph.D. with him, but fearing his parents' reprisal, he quietly agreed to an arranged marriage. His only condition was that the bride had to be from a similarly poor family. Only then would she understand his position and the reasons behind his decisions. That young woman was my mother."

Aarti's head was now upright, her eyes glued to my face with curiosity. "Does your mother know about the woman he loved?"

"Yes, my parents' relationship is solid. My mother told us this once. Apparently, he had said, *I won't lie to you. I loved her, and I see her occasionally at conferences. But I will never be untrue to you.*"

"Wow! That was some generation!"

"My mom took some time getting over her insecurities. A small-village girl, dark-skinned, which is seen as a curse in India, could hardly speak English at the time. How could she compete with a beautiful, erudite white woman? Dad had said there was no competition. *I married you, not her. You are my life, she's a friend.*"

"What does your father do?"

"He retired as a professor of mathematics."

"Why does that make complete sense?"

We both tittered.

"Yeah, he's cool that way. That woman he'd loved married one of his friends, and they moved to the same university. They are still friends and my godparents. So much for untangling messy relationships. They made everything look so simple. And here we are, complicating our lives for no good reason."

"Tell me about it!"

"On account of their humble beginnings, my parents emphasized education and a kind, polite upbringing. Do you know when I first used the word 'fuck?' I was twenty-four, and a code had misbehaved. My brother and I were the very definition of straight and narrow. My brother, who's older, once used an expletive, and my dad sat him down and gave an hour-long lecture about why such words should not be used and what kind of social harm they can cause. I never used them partially to avoid hours of lectures. But long story short, not disappointing our parents in any way became more important than any other achievement."

"You said were. As in, you're no longer on the straight and narrow?"

"Well, once I entered the real world, I had to...get real."

"Good for you. You are a good man, Sujit. I hope you know that."

"So I've been told on occasion." I drained the last of my drink. "I need to leave. If Devi finds out I was out this late, drinking, she'll withhold everything that needs my attention tomorrow."

"Are you scared of Devi?"

"Oh, very! She might be my executive assistant on paper, but in some past life, she was probably my older sister, who doesn't let me waver from the straight and narrow. She definitely treats me like a younger sibling."

"And what happens if you find yourself a wild, wanton woman who drags you away from the straight and narrow?"

"Ah, I can only dream of such a day. Anyone who can stand up to Devi and let me take a day off, I'll owe her big time."

"Hmm..."

"No, Aarti, that isn't a dare. You leave that poor woman alone."

She laughed her beautifully musical laugh and turned into the delicate, kind flower that she was.

I stood up, kissed her forehead, and patted her head. "You're a remarkable woman."

"Huh!"

"What?"

"That's what Sameer said when he told me he loved Tara. He said I'm phenomenal, and I deserve someone who'll love me for who I am." She shrugged again. "I guess that's never happening."

"Why do you say that?"

"Did you hear a word I said this evening?"

"Every single one." I smiled. "You are thirty-one. You have a lifetime ahead of you."

"On that note, how old are you, Sujit?"

"Old."

"Oh, come on, I don't see any grays at the temples, so it's safe to say you are under fifty." She shot me a teasing grin.

"Funny. You're funny."

"Are you ashamed of your age? I didn't think men worried about their age. I thought that's the burden women are made to carry."

"I'm not ashamed. I'm thirty-six, will turn thirty-seven soon."

"Oh! No wonder you feel old," she teased. "You *are* old!"

I smiled. Her tall body was sprawled out on the chair in comfort and delight, yet she looked the epitome of beauty and grace.

"Alright, I'm off now. I hope you get to bed too," I said, offering her my hand. "Don't stay up too late."

She put her supple hand with the magnificently slender fingers in mine and pulled herself off the chair.

"Save the rest of this bottle for me," I said as I gathered my coat.

"Of course. Who else am I going to offer a drink in my room?"

"Well, I've heard you've started dating again, so..." I teased with a grin.

She rolled her eyes as I stepped out the door.

"Good night, sweet girl," I said.

"Good night," she whispered and stayed at the door until I turned the corner toward the elevator bank.

SUJIT

"What are you smiling at?" Devi asked as she rushed into my office.

She could always tell from the look on my face when she could come in and when it wasn't wise to bother me.

I hadn't realized I was smiling. My mind had momentarily wandered off toward Aarti and the expression on her face when she thought I was about to spill the secrets of my love life. I cleared my throat.

Devi narrowed her eyes and tapped her pen on the planner in her hand. "You have been uncharacteristically upbeat the last few days."

"And that's bad because?" I asked, looking over the rim of my glasses.

"It's not," she emphasized. "But *why* are you happy?" She cast me a suspicious look again.

I removed my glasses and placed them on the desk. "For months now, you all have hounded me to emerge out of my *gloom and despair*, your words. And now that you think I've found some illusory happiness, you're skeptical about the reason?"

"Hmmm..." The tapping of her pen grew rapid and intense. "The question still remains. What *is* the reason behind this happiness? And now that you broached the subject, I wonder if it's someone new in your life."

I frowned. I had given it away too easily. "Why, so you can go tell Cathy and Amma about it?"

"That's always an option," she said, teasing me with a pensive look, although I completely trusted her. She hadn't divulged my relationship with Tara even though she'd visited me at the office long before I broke the news to my family.

"Was there a reason you barged into my office?" I asked with mild annoyance.

Devi held her stare, then gradually resigned. "I wanted to remind you of a couple of things. The new lease is ready and needs your approval."

I worked hard to keep my face impassive. The lease. Aarti. Her expression. The reason for my smile. No, I wasn't about to go down that line of thought. Not right now.

"I'll take a look at it. Have you run it by El?"

"Yes, she has approved the amount."

"Good. Anything else?" I asked in a bid to rush her out of my space.

"Your mother called and insisted that I remind you about Padmaja's exhibition on Thursday."

I put my glasses back on. "I remember," I said, my reply clipped but not curt.

"And she wanted me to remind you to buy something for her puja room."

I let out an exasperated sigh. "Yes, I remember."

"Hey, don't shoot the messenger," Devi complained.

"I'm not. Sorry. I've got things on my mind right now."

"Yes, like trying to hide a smile behind that massive screen of yours. Like trying to rush me out of your office so you can go back to reminiscing about whoever it is you are reminiscing about."

"Good god, Devi. Do you sometimes forget I'm your boss?"

"And do you always forget I'm Cathy's friend and that you couldn't fire me even if you wanted to?"

"Out," I said with a smile as she pulled up her dignified professional persona before walking out of my office.

Cathy or no Cathy, firing Devi would mean doom for my business. She had been with me since we were a small startup, and she adapted quickly when we ballooned into a million-dollar venture. After it was acquired and I embarked on this new journey, she stayed with me instead of moving to the new company despite their several attempts to poach her. She had her finger on the pulse of this business, and without her, I would not only be left rudderless but possibly be thrown into full-blown chaos. Obviously, I would never tell her that. But the smart woman that she was, she knew it already. She was family, and her loyalty to me ran deeper than our professional association.

I turned my revolving chair to face the skyline before me. My vision blurred over the horizon in the distance, where the skyscrapers reached up to kiss the low clouds. It had been more than a week since our dinner at the Korean restaurant, and I hadn't heard anything from Aarti except a couple of innocuous messages early last week.

In response to my text thanking her for dinner, she had sent a brief one saying that she'd had a wonderful time. I was tempted to ask when we could meet again, but I had typed and deleted that message three times. She did have a busy work life, and she had mentioned she was going out on dates. Maybe spending time with me wasn't at the top of her priority list.

If we had been in touch, though, I would've invited her to Padma's exhibition. It was a black-tie event at some fancy gallery in SoHo. I didn't know the details. I was sure Devi had already passed the information on to Imran.

I sighed as I turned around to face my screen and tackle the steep work week ahead.

IMRAN DROPPED me off outside the gallery on Thursday, and I was glad to step away from the evening chill into the warm hall. The gathering was larger than I had expected. Multiple artists and sculptors were featured at the exhibition as the brochure in my hand informed me. Padma was talented, Tara had gushed over and over during our time together. Maybe this would be her big break. My heart beamed with pride as I looked around for my cousin, but I wasn't ready for what met my eyes.

About fifty feet away stood Aarti, with her back to me. The ease with which I recognized her form unsettled me slightly. She wore a simple black dress that fell just below her knees. The cut of the dress and the fall of the fabric definitely screamed *designer*. Darn, I had too many fashion savvy women in my life that I could spot these things so instinctively.

I'd always seen her in professional mid-heels or sneakers. At the exhibit, she towered over half the crowd with stilettos on her tall legs. I tried to check the admiration on my face. It was a good thing she hadn't seen me yet because I couldn't stop staring at her. She was gorgeous in the truest sense of the word, and it wasn't unnatural to be attracted to her. But maybe she deserved someone better, someone who didn't intermittently think about his ex-girlfriend.

I felt a tap on my shoulder. "Hey, Annayya!"

I turned around to face my younger cousin with the perpetual baby face. "Hello, Bella!"

"Will you give it a rest?" She hit my arm.

"Sorry, I keep forgetting you're all grown up, Ms. Padmaja."

"You are impossible. You know that?"

"Only with the people I love. Now, show me what you've made, and I'll tell you if you're any good," I said.

With a scoff, she threw me an *as if* expression and began escorting me toward her sculptures. "Any other names you've butchered since mine?"

"One. Devi's daughter, Katyayani. That's too long and inefficient. I call her Kitty. She loves it."

"Let me guess, Devi hates it and hates you for it."

"Bingo."

"I forget why you chose that silly name for me."

"We didn't, Bella, you did. Ask Srijan," I said about my brother. "You bugged us for a whole summer to call you Bella."

"Of course I did. I was nine!"

"We still love you the same, baby sister." I gave her a side hug as she pointed at a geometric sculpture of some kind.

I walked around and attempted to study it, but I didn't have an eye for these things. "I have no idea what it is, but I'm buying it," I declared.

Padma smiled. "No, you don't buy something that doesn't speak to you," she argued, instantly reminding me of Tara.

Tara used to say the same thing. And there I was again, thinking about her.

"This is beautiful!" A rich, smooth voice behind me caused a pleasant warmth to unfold in my chest. I swiftly turned around with a smile.

"Aarti."

"Nice to see you again, Sujit."

I stood stupefied and tongue-tied against her beauty. The black dress was complemented by a pair of solitaire earrings and a statement ring on her middle finger. The red on her lips was both classic and powerful. I'd never seen her in a perfect red lipstick before. My trance broke when our eyes met, and she blinked.

I cleared my throat, trying to redirect my own thoughts. "Aarti, may I introduce my very talented cousin, Padmaja R?"

Aarti turned to her with an extended hand. "Padmaja, it is wonderful to meet you. You are a phenomenal artist!"

Padmaja shook her hand and gushed, her baby cheeks flushing with color. "Thank you, you are very kind."

"Padmaja," I said. "This is Aarti Bhatia. She's a...business associate."

Aarti's eyes spied me with mischief, but her composure remained consummate.

We talked for a bit before Padmaja was called away.

"This is soul-stirring," Aarti said when we were alone.

"This geometric structure?" I asked, looking at Padma's creation before me.

She nodded. "See this sort of cage formation here? This is how we are entrenched in different ways. Things we do to ourselves, and things society does to cage us."

"Hmm..." I walked around it and tried to look at it through Aarti's eyes. It did make sense what she saw. I would've never found meaning in it if she hadn't shown it to me.

"I especially love how she's slipped the curves inside the harsh geometric lines."

"What does that mean?"

Aarti looked at me. "I don't know how she intended, but to me it suggests there's fluidity, beauty, and movement inside what seems bulky, unwieldy, and stoic. An allegory for life, don't you think?"

I closed my gaping mouth. I was definitely buying it.

"How have you been?" I asked and walked around the sculpture to stand beside her.

She looked at me with her soft, warm eyes. "Good. Busy. You?"

"Same." I wanted to tell her that I'd missed talking to her.

She slipped a sly smile as if she'd read my thoughts. "I had hoped to hear from you."

"I waited to hear from you, too."

"You could have texted," she accused.

"I didn't want to bother you," I said, then rather audaciously suggested, "But let's grab a drink after this."

Her smile held me for a moment before she whispered, "I need to dump my date first." With her eyes, she directed me to a striking man talking to someone in the distance. My heart dipped.

"He looks nice. Bring him along," I joked.

"Are you kidding? He's clingy. Plus, I want your wit and sass and dimples all to myself."

"Tsk, selfish woman."

She slipped me what had become our secret naughty smile.

"Where should we meet? Any good places around here?"

"Lots. But I was thinking, my home? It's humble but quiet and cozy. And out of the purview of prying eyes."

"Hmm, I'll need to think about it," she said with a gentle frown. "What will my suitors say? Spending the night at a man's place."

"Spending the night? I never offered that. A nightcap, and you're off. Thrown out on your butt if required."

"What a gentleman!"

"Always." I pushed my left hand into my trouser pocket with a grin.

"Okay, text me your address. I will dump the loser and come over."

I saw her date approaching, and the spark left her eye as she prepared to transform into her sophisticated, aloof self.

"Well, it was good seeing you again, Ms. Bhatia. Enjoy your

evening," I said and stepped away to look at an artwork on the wall.

"Are you ready to leave, sweetheart?" her companion said.

Sweetheart! I turned my head to see the cringe in Aarti's measured, held smile, but it didn't seem to have registered with him.

"I was thinking we could get a bite somewhere, maybe a drink," I heard him say.

"I'm sorry, I have another meeting."

"This late? I thought...I was hoping..."

Standing two feet away, gazing at a painting I appreciated nothing about, I pitied the poor fool who thought he was getting in her bed that night.

While Aarti got busy mingling and possibly trying to ditch her date, I found Padma and reserved the sculpture.

"Are you sure?" she tried to ascertain with a wary smile.

I parroted Aarti's description of it and she stood speechless for several moments with her eyes wide in disbelief. When her lips finally parted, she said, "Wow...I...you saw all that?"

I neither confirmed nor denied it.

"It's yours, bro! If this is how you see it, it belongs with you!" She gave me a quick hug, overwhelmed that I'd finally understood the artist in her.

"Now, show me something for Amma's gudi," I said. "I'm sure she called you about it too."

Padma laughed. "She did, and I have just the thing for her, a beautiful painting by a dear friend. Come, let me introduce you to her. She captures the feminine essence so brilliantly. I'm sure Peddamma will love it."

Twenty minutes later, I saw Aarti leave the gallery. I left soon after. On the way back, I stopped to buy two chilled bottles of the sparkling white that she'd loved at Marco's. When I got home, I waited with an eagerness that was aberrant and inexplicable.

She was dating other men, and I was still hurting from Tara. It was safe to assume we couldn't share more than camaraderie at this time. Then why did her presence, her smart words, and her wisdom seem to ease my soul?

She arrived looking relaxed, with a definite lightness in her demeanor. I could vouch for it because she had traded her stilettos for a pair of low-heel pumps. Though she was still in that stylish, simple black dress, she'd ditched her clutch for the tote she usually had on her.

"Nice place!" she said and walked around the spacious apartment, surveying the layout. "Really nice. I thought I heard you assure me it was humble."

"It is. Very humble. Like me." I grinned.

She rolled her eyes and flopped on the couch.

"Did your date drop you here?" I asked for no apparent reason.

"No, I had him drop me at the hotel. I had the car service waiting for me."

"Is the car waiting for you here?" I asked, and she nodded.

"Send it back. I'll drop you."

She narrowed her eyes, then smiled and placed the call.

"Whisky, bourbon, or something else?" I asked when she dropped her phone back into the tote.

"What's the *something else* on that menu?"

"Sparkling white, perhaps?" I asked with a crooked smile.

She laughed. "Yes, please. You know me now, don't you?"

"Only because you ordered it at Marco's. Unlike you, I'm not sneaky. I still don't know how you found out about Rampur."

She smiled as I poured her the wine.

"You're not going to share it with me, are you?"

Accepting the glass I offered, she said, "Maybe someday."

She took a sip of the wine and let out a sigh. "The date wore me out. I don't even know why I decided to go out with him again."

"Again?"

"This was our second date," she said and shook her head in disbelief. "He seemed alright on our first one. We went for dinner, and he wasn't boring."

"You gave him another chance because he wasn't boring?" I asked, intrigued.

"Well, not entirely. My cousin had set us up, so I wanted to give him a fair chance before I rejected him."

"He's a good-looking guy."

"I'll say, and too full of himself. He never asked one question about me. Like *me* me," she said and gave me a look as if I must know precisely what she meant. And I did. She meant the conversation we had the other day.

"He's an investment banker, and all he talked about was money and business. I'm not averse to it, but it's my day job, and I'd really love to talk about other things outside work hours."

She took her shoes off and pulled the hassock under her feet. My eyes darted to her shapely toes, painted deep red, before I brought them back to her face. "Plus, he insisted on being called Ash."

"Ash?" I produced a curious frown.

"Ashutosh. Ash. With Swinstz. That was his introduction," she said and laughed.

I smirked. The CEO of Swinstz was a close business contact. I committed the information to memory. It was one of those things I was good at. I created vaults inside my brain to tag and separate information so I could recall it when required.

"Nice. Was he sweet, *sweetheart*?" I asked with a crooked grin.

"Don't you tease me about it! It was our second date, and he was already too handsy for my taste. And no one calls me sweetheart until I'm in a committed relationship."

"He certainly had other ideas."

She turned her face to me. "Like what?"

"Well, it was clear he thought it was going to turn into a night together."

She shuffled in her place and rested her back against the couch. "That's his problem, not mine. But I bet he'll call for another date."

"Does he stand a chance?"

"Not even if he was the last man on earth," she said, and it set me laughing. "Oh, you know I've been thinking of you all week," she added innocuously.

"Really? Yet, you didn't text or call?"

"Yes, because it couldn't be done over the phone. I wanted to show you this in person." She thumbed her phone open and scrolled. "Mom sent me pictures and résumés she's received over the past few weeks. Let's see what you think of them."

I reached across the coffee table to get the phone from her, but she shook her head and nodded at the couch. "No, come sit here."

I walked over and settled down beside her. Her seductive evening fragrance turned into a soft whisper, holding me in a gentle embrace.

"This one's kind of douchey," I said, looking at the man who sent her a modeling picture.

"Kind of?" She scoffed. "You're nice."

I laughed when she showed me the next picture. "And this dudebro? I didn't know we had desi dudebros!"

"Huh, I wonder which rock it is that you've been living under," she said and flipped to yet another.

"No way! He sent a picture with his biceps showing? Reject! I mean, those are some biceps, but still..."

"I've had a glimpse of your biceps, Sujit. You can't tell me you're not sympathetic to him?" she teased while trying to stifle a laugh.

A smile appeared on my face of its own accord. She'd noticed my biceps, my body? The thought sent a curious feeling zipping through me.

"But I don't live at the gym. Looks like he does. Next!"

We flipped through at least fifteen pictures.

"What, you're going to reject them all?" she joked. "Not one acceptable guy in this horde?"

"Not for you," I declared and sipped the wine.

It was too sweet and too crisp for my taste, but I loved the look on her face as she enjoyed it.

"I smell intrigue," she said.

I grinned. "Must be my cologne."

"Must be you."

She threw her head back on the couch.

I leaned forward and pulled the hassock under both our feet.

"More wine?" I asked.

She lifted her glass, and I leaned to grab the bottle from the table to refill it.

"Want to watch a movie?"

"Sure."

I turned on the TV and handed her the remote.

"You think that's a wise idea? This is literally the remote control you're handing me."

I smiled. "I trust you."

She gave an ominous smirk. "That is a really bad decision, Sujit Rao. You don't know me yet."

I relaxed against the couch and said, "I know you enough to trust you completely."

Her smile was one of surprise and relief as she flipped through the apps to figure out what to watch. We settled on a thriller, but an hour into the movie, her head slipped against my shoulder. She had fallen asleep with an empty wine glass resting upright on her thigh. I gave her a few more minutes to slide into deep sleep before turning off the television. I picked up the glass that had dropped to her side and laid her on the couch. She stirred when I got her a pillow and a blanket, but it didn't break her sleep. What reassured me was the knowledge that the couch was comfortable. I had spent countless nights on it when I fell asleep working or watching TV.

THE NEXT MORNING, she was still asleep when I went into the kitchen to make coffee.

She sat up with a start and looked around. "Shit!"

"Good morning."

"Morning."

"You're a crafty woman, aren't you? You did end up spending the night here."

She smiled. "Where's the bathroom?"

"You can use the master. I've laid out a fresh toothbrush and face wash for you. Don't judge me, though. I haven't made my bed."

"You slept in your comfortable bed while I was scrunched up on the couch? You are a true gentleman."

"Would you have preferred my bed instead?" I asked cheekily.

The last two meetings had changed our equation. We seemed to be getting along like old friends, teasing and joking. It was refreshing.

"In your dreams," she responded with a light scoff.

"I don't dream about you," I said as I turned on the coffee machine.

"Yeah? What do you dream about?"

"I dream of spending a relaxing day somewhere, catching up

on sleep in a hammock on a beach. The other night, I dreamt I had front-row seats to Trevor Noah, with a VIP backstage pass."

"Really? Trevor Noah?"

"He makes my generation look smart and well-read."

"Your generation?" She produced a snort.

"Yes, you young people wouldn't know about that."

"You don't say...but why don't you?"

"What?"

"Go see Trevor Noah. It's not like you can't afford the tickets or the backstage pass."

"It's not always the money." I smiled at her. "I never have the time. Rather, I never make an effort to make the time. Plus, I want someone to enjoy it with. I thought that was something Tara and I would do together, then she vanished from my life...Coffee's ready. Go wash up. I've put fresh towels in the bathroom."

She stood gazing at me for a few seconds, then turned around and stepped toward the bedroom.

After coffee, she prepared to leave. "I've got lots to do today."

"Imran is here. He'll drive you to the hotel."

"That's ok. My car service will be here in no time," she said, unlocking her phone. "I'm sure you have a busy day too."

"I've pushed back my morning meetings. Don't worry, he'll drop you and come get me."

"Pushed back the meetings!" She made a gasping sound. "How did sweet Devi agree to that?"

"Sweet Devi isn't all that sweet. I'll get an earful when I reach work. I'll fill you up on it this evening."

"Evening?" She pivoted with speed to face me. "Are we meeting again tonight?"

I shrugged. "We don't have to if you're busy. I just don't want you spending Friday evening alone."

"Who says I'll be alone?" she said with a cocked eyebrow.

"You won't be," I announced as I walked to the door and held it open for her. "You'll spend it with me."

"Throwing me out, are you?"

"As promised." I leaned in to kiss her cheek. "See you this evening, sweet girl."

She smiled and waved at me from the elevators.

AARTI

Sweet girl, he said, and I loved it. From his mouth, in his voice, in that tone, it sounded neither infantilizing nor patronizing. Ringing with affection, it felt validating. It made me feel special.

I turned and looked at him standing at his door. When I waved, he waved back with a quick flash of his dimples.

He was an exceedingly striking man who made the word handsome sound pedestrian, but he was at ease with his looks. His outward appearance was not what made him. It was incidental to his overall life goals and achievements. But he didn't miss the admiration he got as he strode through the world with confidence and nonchalance.

I had first seen him when he was in Dallas for Tara's exhibition at the art museum. Apparently, he had surprised her by claiming that he had a big meeting he couldn't miss, but secretly made plans with her mother to fly in on the day. Sameer and I were there as patrons of the museum.

The look of love and happiness on Sujit's face as he gazed at Tara had left me slightly envious. My eyes had drifted to Sameer in search of similar validation, but his eyes were on Tara as well. In retrospect, I was jealous that Tara had the undivided love of two beautiful, decent men.

Sujit was surrounded by beauty and glamor that evening, but his eyes never wavered from Tara. The pride on his face when she addressed the audience, his loyalty to her, might as well have been etched in stone, scribbled across the skies. It was unmistakable.

So even as I found myself drawn to this brilliant, kind man, I knew I'd only be second best. I could never have his heart like Tara did. It wasn't that I was seriously considering the possibility, but whenever my mind tried to flirt with the idea, my brain shot it right down.

With a sigh, I stepped off the elevator.

Imran waited for me at the entrance, holding the door open for me with eyes averted in deference. I thanked him and made small talk as he drove me to the hotel. I considered myself savvy, but I couldn't get him to spill anything about Sujit and Tara's relationship. Not that I was obviously prying. I had more finesse than that, but he was smart and loyal to a fault. He made himself out to be "just his driver," but I had seen the smiles and the grins that passed between him and Sujit. Imran was not just a driver. He was a confidant. And Sujit had earned his trust in some way.

I'd just stepped into my room when the phone buzzed in my hand. It was a video call from Mom.

"Hi Beta, kaisi ho?"

"I'm good. How are you?" Just a look at her radiant face and my heart flooded with warmth and calm.

"You look tired. Didn't you sleep well?" she asked with a gentle frown.

I smiled. "I did, Ma."

"Are you eating well? I hope you're not eating too much junk. Try to eat healthy."

"Yes, Ma, I'm eating healthy...ish." I grinned.

"I knew there was an -ish at the end of that sentence." She laughed. "How was your event last night?" she asked delicately.

"You mean, how was my date? Not good. He's not my type."

A look flashed across her face as if she wanted to say something, but she merely nodded.

"Say it, Ma. You know you can still tease me. I'm not so damaged that I can't take a joke."

"No, my darling. You're not damaged. Just hurting. And it will pass. Let it pass. Don't try to hold on to the hurt."

I nodded.

"Okay, here's what I was going to say. Is there any man who can live up to your standards?"

Well, there was one.

I quickly deflected. "How are things in Dallas?"

"Same old. The weather has been good. Looks like the winter won't be as severe this year."

"Ma, don't use the word severe for Texas winter," I chided lovingly.

She smiled. "Is it cold there?"

"Yes, but not severe yet. And *that* is the correct context of the word severe."

She laughed heartily, giving me a full display of her teeth and open mouth. I loved watching her laugh like that. Dad peeked in.

"Hello, Puttar! Sab theek?"

"Yes, Papa, everything is fine. How are you? Hope you are not messing things up without me there."

He waved his hand. "I miss you at the office. Your useless brother has a lot to learn," he said with exasperation.

Mom hit his arm. "Don't use such words for your child!" she chided him with a gasp.

"It's the truth," he tried to argue. "Have I ever used it for Aarti? No. Because she's not."

"Yes, yes, we all know she's your pride, etc.," Mom said. "Now leave. Let me talk to my daughter."

He smiled at me and waved goodbye.

Dad and I talked almost every day, but it was always a work call. He called from his office and never once asked how I was. We got straight to business and hung up as soon as we took care of it. It worked for me just as well. I was cast in my dad's image in many ways. I had my personal time and space and my professional time and space, and I didn't like for them to overlap. Only now, I had transgressed the sanctity of that boundary by forming an emotional bond with a man who technically was a business relation.

But was he only a business relation? The unexpected thought rattled my composure.

"Did you get my email with the pictures, Beta?" Mom asked, and I was grateful for the distraction.

A distraction that wasn't one because it led me right back to Sujit's home, sitting beside him, soaking in his gentle scent.

"Yes, Ma. I..."

"Don't worry. I disliked every one of them. But I didn't want to make that decision for you. You take the time you need. I want you to find love, not an alliance, not an exchange. I want you to thrive in love, my darling. We were wrong to push you towards Sameer and we learned our lesson the hard way."

Mom was the only one before whom I could cry without inhibition. So, I did. I cried for the love I had lost and for the attraction that would never materialize into anything tangible. Mom cried with me.

"All right, that's enough, my baby," she said, finally wiping her tears. You are too strong to let yourself wallow in pain. When you come back, we'll cry together. I can't console you from afar. I need to hold you when you're upset. I need to wipe your tears. Don't cry now when I am far away and helpless."

I smiled through my tears. "Okay, Ma. I love you."

"Now, let me tell you something juicy. That will take your mind off things."

She spent the next twenty-two minutes sharing gossip about the people we knew while I tidied up my stuff. We were very much a part of the desi rumor mill that Sujit and I had talked about. Deeply entrenched in it, although Mom's gossip was innocuous. She wasn't spiteful and firmly refused to participate in spreading malicious falsehoods, but she did enjoy gossiping. She also updated me on the health and well-being of our extended family, venting about how women her age were always bitching about their daughters-in-law and how, like professional life, family responsibilities should come with a retirement age. They needed to take a chill pill—yes, she used that term—and let the youngsters take charge of their own lives and families.

Her chatter did help take my mind off my woes as I got ready and headed out. I stopped by the condo. It looked in good shape to move into on the weekend. Later, I drove to three sites around the city to assess the condition of the properties and got estimates for the cost of repair and repainting. One old building needed its electrical system redone. I called Dad to discuss this, and he agreed with my assessment. That would be a substantial cost that we had not accounted for in this quarter. We would need to adjust some numbers, but we would proceed with the rewiring of the building before we leased it out for commercial use.

By early evening, I was happy, tired, and in need of good food. I texted Sujit to ask if we were still on for that evening. He called me back.

My spirits lifted as I envisioned the sweet smile on his stunning face. "Hey, how's it going?"

"Good, how was your day?" he asked.

"Very satisfying, but I'm bone tired! Are we on for today? If not, I'm going to grab a quick something and crash in bed," I said.

"Here's a counterproposal. I'll pick you up, we can have a nice, relaxed dinner, then you can crash in my guest room, and I can drop you back tomorrow."

"What if I want to stay longer?" My stupid mouth ran itself before I could rein it in. I wondered if he'd regard my jest as presumptuous.

But his reply was instant and unhesitating. "Then bring a bag," he said. "Fair warning, though, Saturday is game night, and it's my turn to host. We're playing Catan."

"Oh, then I'll make my escape before that."

"Why? Don't you enjoy board games?"

"I do, but I wouldn't want to intrude on your nerding-out time, and I haven't played Catan."

"Really? Then you should join us. We are lovable nerds. Plus, you're so beautiful, we might be too distracted and you can outplay us with ease."

I fell silent. My beauty had been commented on for most of my adult life. I had heard variations of the word that could fill an entire thesaurus. Hearing him say it—simple and straightforward —hit differently. My pounding heart expanded with pride.

He had fallen quiet, too, perhaps thinking of ways to backtrack his words.

"Oh, so you've noticed I'm beautiful?" I asked to ease the tension.

"I'm sorry. I didn't mean it the way it sounded."

"How did it sound?" I asked.

"Crass and replete with lechery. In absolute bad taste."

I smiled at his honesty. Most men didn't have the guts to acknowledge their errors in this way. Most men didn't have egos magnanimous enough to offer an apology of this kind. Sujit wasn't like most men, and he'd proved this over and over again.

The warmth in my heart effervesced as mischief. "Then what way did you mean?" I asked, wondering if he'd take my bait.

The brief pause I had anticipated drew out into an overbearing one.

"Sujit?" I prodded with innocence.

"Yes, sweet girl. I'm here. I'm just wondering how to answer that question without putting my foot in my mouth again."

I caught myself blushing. "I think you just did," I said softly into the phone.

"All I can hope for is that it doesn't put a damper on our plans for this evening. Because I was planning on taking you to a different sort of place."

"Different how? Like crass and replete with lechery?"

His sweet laughter boomed in my ears. "Not really, but it's a place cheekily named La Traviata."

"Like the opera?"

He chuckled. "No, like the subject of the said opera."

"That sounds intriguing!" I said, as curious as I was excited.

"Wait till you see the menu."

"Can't wait."

"I'll pick you up around seven. Is that alright?"

"Yes."

"And hey, I was serious about coming back to mine. Pack a bag."

It was unsettling how he had made a way into my life and into my heart. As the oldest child of the family, the eldest daughter, I wasn't known to take instructions from others. I was the one who laid down the rules and dispensed directives. Yet, his bossiness, the appealing assertiveness, didn't seem to bother me. Was this what trust looked like?

For the first time since we'd met, I stood before my closet, wondering what to wear. I wanted to wear something flirty, but I couldn't muster up the courage. Sujit was so straightforward, it'd be like flaunting candy in a kid's face, then eating it yourself. Or like flaunting candy at a kid who thinks sugar is bad for their teeth. Either way, it was a terrible idea.

I chose a knee-length dress with warm leggings and ankle boots. I tried ten different necklaces but finally decided against it and hooked on a pair of mid-length earrings. That was the flirtiest I could imagine getting with Sujit right now.

He was at my door at seven, and I found a glint in his eyes as he looked at my dangly earrings. But he didn't comment. He had toed that line that afternoon, and awkwardness had ensued.

"Scandal under the skirt?" I raised my brows as I read the menu at La Traviata.

"It's a chicken pot pie with their super secret recipe."

"A Bite of Threesome!" I read. "Greek pastitsio with lamb sauce and béchamel.

"That one is really good," he said, looking at me over the rim of his glasses. Those dark, brilliant eyes successfully managed to jumble my thoughts.

I shifted my gaze to the menu. "I love these names. Do you think they'll fly in Dallas? First, Lick the Salt off. Truffle Fries!"

He smiled. "I'm glad you are having fun."

"This is exactly what I needed today. I had a really hectic week. I'm really looking forward to relaxing this weekend. All I need is a comfortable bed and an unlimited supply of coffee."

"I think that can be arranged." He closed his menu and looked at me with a somber face. "Aarti, if you'd rather spend a quiet weekend, I can cancel my game night."

"Of course not," I protested, more embarrassed than defensive. "I'm not about to disrupt your life. I'd never ask or expect that of you."

"You're not asking. I'm offering."

"No," I said with a firm shake of my head. "Being with you feels...comfortable because I can be myself. But I am not about to insert myself in your life and upset it," I argued.

He pushed his glasses up his nose and gave me a glimpse of those dimples that I'd come to cherish. That smile!

"You'll never upset my life, Aarti. If anything, I'm actually rethinking my own priorities."

"Oh?" I asked, raising my brows with hope.

"Yes, talking to you has been both insightful and instructive."

"You shouldn't say such things. They go straight to my head," I said with a grin.

"It's the truth. I like that you don't mince words. And you see me for who I am. Who I *really* am."

"And what's that?"

He grinned. "A hopeless romantic who is now determined to prioritize his own happiness."

I didn't know why it felt good to hear those words from his mouth. He hadn't remotely alluded to *us*, to a possibility of *us*, yet somewhere in his hope, I found a ray of sunshine I could ride all the way to my own happiness.

"What's next?" he asked, nodding to the menu.

I returned my eyes to the last thing I'd read before this conversation. "Wet, Tender, and Delicious. Guess what that is?"

"I don't have to guess. I eat here once a month. Mushroom and pea risotto."

"This is hilarious!" I said.

We chose an unconventional route that evening and ordered martinis.

"You know what the best part about coming here is?" he said when the drinks arrived. "Watching stuffed shirts with a lot of money and old school morality come in and be appalled at the names of the dishes. This is a three Michelin-star place. Being here is a thing to show off at parties and gatherings. But they can't make themselves say it, so they end up using the description. 'I'll have the mushroom risotto.' The servers respond with a straight face, 'Will that be the Wet, Tender, and Delicious, sir?' It's priceless. It's like a harmless revenge of the have-nots against the have-too-much-of-everything, taking a little joy in their discomfort. It's highly entertaining."

"And in all likelihood, they are taking more than their fair share of wet, tender, and delicious behind closed doors," I said with a gentle shake of my head.

"That too," he agreed.

"Point to note, we also fall under the have-too-much-of-everything category," I commented. "We wouldn't be sitting here spending an indecent amount on food and drink if we weren't."

"Yes, but hopefully, we know our place and responsibility in society. Else, it's a waste."

"How do we ensure that?" I asked with curiosity.

He sipped his martini and considered me for a beat.

"A small, good deed at a time..." He took another smooth sip. "But kindness alone cannot remedy social inequalities. So, don't cheat on your taxes."

He was definitely living up to my standards—and more.

"Since our first meeting, I've been trying to figure you out. I think I finally have. You are ethically balanced," I said.

He returned an inquisitive frown. "I've been called a lot of things, but it's the first time I've heard that one."

I pulled my hands down under the table to my lap and fidgeted with the ring on my left index finger. This proximity to him, physical and emotional, was starting to get daunting.

"You know why I'm rich?" he continued. "Because currently, society values my skills more than it does others', like my father. Teachers used to be the most valued in society. Do you know what grade school teachers or even university adjuncts make these days?"

I shook my head.

"Society determines who gets valued, what kind of labor is worth more based on how much money it brings to the most powerful. When I was little, I used to see construction workers and servers at restaurants and wonder why they were poorer than my father, who sat all day and read books. Surely, manual labor must beget more money than reading?"

Hearing him speak about wealth so unhesitatingly knocked down the walls I always put up around me. Since I was little, I had learned to behave as if I was born into money. Talking about our struggles meant that we were new money and thus needed to justify our place among the crème de la crème. Not talking about it signified that our wealth was incidental, a behavior I had learned from Mary Beth.

The truly rich didn't need to showcase their wealth through brands and brags. That was the difference between old and new money. New money felt the need to justify its place in society. Old money took its place for granted. New money needed fancy cars and loud bags. It craved to be seen. Old money preferred its quiet existence because much of it was derived through exacerbating the social inequalities in our societies. Historically, obscene wealth accumulation was made possible only through exploitation, whether it was feudalism, enslavement, colonization, or neoimperialism. This wealth also gave old money the power to define and determine the rules of existence and etiquette.

When the Industrial Revolution led to the creation of a new class of rich in the West, the aristocracy needed to distinguish itself from the nouveau riche. The terms classy, classic, and classical all alluded to this distinction. Where new money was ostentatious and gaudy, old money was "classy." Where new money loved to show off its wealth with loud clothing and jewelry, a "classic" wardrobe became the hallmark of old money. Even today, we use these words as if they don't actually establish the legitimacy of a certain class of people over others.

Etiquette was another way to maintain the divide between the classes. People with wealth created arbitrary rules of behavior—

how to walk, talk, laugh, eat—and called it etiquette. Those without it were uncouth. Not worthy.

As immigrants to a new country, all you ever wanted was to prove that you were worthy. You deserved to be at that table of the richest people with class. Hence, you didn't talk about your wealth. You internalized the rules of etiquette and hoped that you found a seat at the table on an equal footing. But histories of colonization and enslavement meant that people of color had to keep clawing our way out through a sea of racism and privilege. And when we did, some of us turned around and used that privilege to further the exploitation of others.

Not Sujit, though. The resounding conviction comforted me further into this easy camaraderie.

I could let it all out in his presence. "When I was little, Dad didn't have this sprawling business. He was a small-time realtor. Until I was about five, we lived in a small two-bedroom apartment. But both my parents are hardworking. Mom helped by staging open houses and selling Indian clothing and jewelry as a side hustle. This model is pretty commonplace now, but at the time, only a few people did it as a home business. Dad learned the property business quickly, took out massive loans, made smart investment decisions, and the business grew. From fifth grade onward, I only attended elite schools. We moved several times, each time into a bigger house in a richer neighborhood. It was one way to establish status, especially for an immigrant family, but I didn't know that. My brother has only ever seen the riches because he doesn't remember the life before we became wealthy."

I exhaled and let the silence between us get subsumed by the gentle sounds of the restaurant.

"My brother is wealthy because he helps others make money," Sujit said with a laugh. "But if you meet my parents, they behave as if they are still those struggling immigrants. They still think twice before buying anything that isn't groceries."

I'd love to meet them someday, I wanted to say, but that statement came with inferences, implications, and a bitter history of heartache. Wasn't it the same day Tara broke his heart that he'd introduced her to them? I kept my mouth shut.

"Go on, read one more dish on the menu. I know you want to," he nudged.

"Okay, one more. It will be the last one, I promise."

He sat back with his drink.

"For the Love of the Unctuous."

"What? That's a new addition. What is it?" He pulled his menu open and looked for it. "Oh, it's sausage and peppers," he laughed gently.

He ordered For the Love of the Unctuous, and I got Scandal Under the Skirt.

"Potpie is my favorite, but I can hardly find a place that makes a good one. The best places don't have them because it's seen as rustic and homey, not gourmet food. But the best things in life are simple, aren't they?" I said, cracking the delicate puff pastry with the spoon.

He nodded as he sliced into his sausage.

So are the best relationships, I thought as I watched him enjoy his food just as much as I did.

SUJIT

When we drove back to my place that evening, I pulled out Catan while she changed into lounging clothes. I spread the board out on the custom-built gaming table that sat discreetly in a corner masquerading as a console.

Her eyes grew wide and her eyebrows lifted when I drew back the top to uncover it, complete with pull-out player stations to hold cards, game pieces, and drinks. I had dreamed about getting one when I was in college but couldn't justify the outrageous cost of the custom-build. When I moved into this penthouse, it was the first thing I bought, even before I had furniture to sit on.

Aarti settled in a chair I had pulled from the dining table. Getting things custom-built had its advantages. I'd specifically asked for dining table chairs that could be repurposed for gaming.

My friends and I had maintained a strict no friends, no partners policy for our game nights, but I was confident I could get them to bend the rules for my attractive houseguest.

"So settlements go between the tiles and roads along the

tiles?" she asked. I nodded. "But *along* the tiles is also *between* two tiles, isn't it?"

"Yes, but only the settlements will determine what resource cards you get."

"Ugh, this is too difficult. I'm buzzed, and you're taking away all the fun of my martinis."

I smiled, and she steadied her gaze on my face.

"What are you looking at?" I asked, fiddling with the cards in my hands.

"Do you know how gorgeous you are with those dimples?" she let slip, then averted her eyes with a shy smile.

I shuffled in my seat, stumped by her compliment. "Yes, I've been told."

"By Tara?" she asked, looking at me with a diffident gaze.

"Among others. Mostly by the women in my family who dote on me. I heard that even more after the breakup. My family has been walking on eggshells around me. I mean, I'm a grown man, I can handle a little rejection, a little heartache. But everyone from my mom and my aunts to my cousins, my sister-in-law, and even Devi have been treating me as if I'm fragile. For years, they hounded me with pictures and résumés of young women, and suddenly, everything stopped. I think it's my sister-in-law's doing. I think she's convinced everyone I need time to heal."

"I don't get why you're grumbling. It's a blessing to have people in your life who care about you."

Caught by her words, I threw a glance in her direction. "I'm sure there are people who care about you just as much."

She flipped her cards to the table and picked up the glass of water I'd offered her earlier. "You know what Sameer used to say about me? Perfect. That's the word he always used. *You're perfect.* Tara also used that word. And I know they meant it as a compliment, but something pinched inside me. I didn't want to be perfect. I just wanted to be loved like they loved one another."

I made a quick mental note. Perfect was also what I'd used for her since the first time I saw her. That word was never entering my thoughts or escaping my lips again.

"When I first started at the elite prep school, I had no friends because I had a lazy eye and glasses with one thick lens. The kids teased me for it and for the way I styled my long, thick hair in a braid."

"That must have been rough."

She nodded. "The kids in my school came from money. I'd seen it only recently. So I didn't know the expensive brands and the correct etiquette. My father had enough money to pay for our education and sponsor various events at school, but that didn't mean I had *class*. That's what the kids said. *I didn't have class.* When I asked Mom what it meant, she explained politely that it's something that the rich have always used as an accusation to exclude people from their social circle, to make others feel small. She asked me to ignore it and to never use it for anyone else. But Dad overheard our conversation and hired someone to teach us, me and my brother. The teacher claimed with pride that she would make me a proper lady. I hated it. I mean, can you really see me going about like a debutant?" She turned her face to me and rolled her eyes.

I smiled at the thought of her in a flowing gown and crisp white gloves.

"But the next time we were at a school event that required the use of forks of different kinds in accordance with the school status, I stunned them all. Inadvertently so. I was only using the knowledge I'd gained from those expensive classes, but Mary Beth, who was the richest and the most popular girl in my class and the school, turned to me with a whisper of a smile and said, 'Not bad, Battie.' That was what they called me, Battie. They couldn't say Bhatia and didn't want to call me Aarti for reasons that completely evaded me. But everyone at that table saw Mary

Beth's approving smile, and in that moment, I realized, she'd never teased me nor looked down on me. She was above these shenanigans. That's probably the moment the seed of our friendship was sown."

"So you're still friends, then?"

"Yep. She's the one who insisted I come to New York while the celebrations were unfolding in Dallas."

"She's the friend you mentioned the first time we met?"

"Yes, she's married to Ezzie Strauss."

"Ezekiel Strauss? His family *is* New York!"

"Yup, and Mary Beth's *is* Dallas. They met in college, and her family flipped out when she wanted to marry him. But Mary Beth is a force to reckon with. She is smart, witty, and very determined. Poor Ezzie had no choice." She chuckled.

"Have you met him?"

She nodded. "This time, though, I've been avoiding the invitation to their place. Everyone in our circle is privy to how Sameer dumped me, and I don't think I'm in a place to handle it well. Not yet."

"I felt the same way for months until my family and friends cornered me and forced me out of that gloom."

She turned her soft, brown eyes to me. "That's what I mean, be thankful for these people in your life."

"I'm sure your family and friends want the same for you."

As she sighed, I tried hard not to gaze at the chest that rose and fell with the weight of her breath. She was perfect, but now I could never tell her that.

"Mary Beth and Isha are the only friends that I trust with my life and my heart. I was always introverted. I never had a big circle of friends like my brother did. Initially, I thought it was my appearance, so I changed my hair and my clothes, used contacts, and got braces on my teeth. I couldn't wait to be an adult so I could get the surgery done to fix my eye. I was also determined to change my nose and my breasts, but Mary Beth looked at me and sagely said, 'Changing yourself will not make these nincompoops like you any better. You're a brown-skinned rich kid in a rich white school. Don't change who you are. I like you the way you are.'"

I turned to her, and she read my smile. We both burst into laughter as I managed, "She didn't really say nincompoops, did she?"

"She did," Aarti replied, trying very hard to rein in her tipsy laughter. "Maybe that's the reason we're so close. I also thought they were all nincompoops."

"I'll get you more water," I said when I saw her bring an empty glass to her lips.

I returned from the kitchen, handed her a fresh glass, then settled beside her.

"Mary Beth and I have been close since that day. She's dignified, so you won't find her screaming and hugging me, but she'll protect me with the quiet demeanor of a fierce goddess. Ezzie knows it. That's why he loves her so much."

"I like you the way you are, too," I said quietly and slipped away to fetch myself some water from the kitchen.

When I returned, she was busy reading the instructions for the game. As I retook my seat next to her, I asked, "Is that why you came to New York? To avoid the wedding?"

She pulled herself upright with a weary smile. "You're the only one who understands, so I'm not going to lie to you. But if you mention it outside this room—"

"You'll kill me?"

"Don't be silly." She grinned. "I won't get my hands dirty. I'll have someone do it for me."

I laughed aloud. "Maybe we should celebrate the day in our own way," I suggested.

"Celebrate isn't a word I'd use." She turned her face to me, and when I found myself helpless against her soft gaze, she sat up, picked my cards from the table, and placed them in my hand. "Come on, teach me, or I'm going to lose miserably tomorrow. And I really hate to lose."

THE NEXT MORNING, when the car service arrived, we headed over to my favorite breakfast diner. It wasn't a place that took reservations, but I'd called ahead and asked Ms. Dina to save us a table. I was a regular and her favorite, as she'd claimed on several occasions. Ms. Dina's scrambled eggs and waffles were always a treat. No culinary expert could recreate them as I'd repeatedly told her. It was one of the reasons I was her favorite. We also got the petulla dusted lightly with powdered sugar. It was served with honey, strawberry jam, and marmalade.

"What do you think?" I asked Aarti when she'd taken a bite. "And don't say it aloud if you didn't like it," I whispered. "Ms. Dina will ban me if she learns I brought along a date who didn't like her food."

"The waffles are excellent. I concur with you. These are the best I've had."

I raised a brow. "I hear a *but* coming."

She graced me with a smile. "*But* I didn't know this was a date," she said, slipping me her naughty smile that made my body warm up on the cold winter morning.

"A breakfast date. Innocuous. Chaste as they come."

She threw her head back in a gentle laugh before savoring another bite of the waffles. "And the petulla are excellent. I'm going to go find an Albanian breakfast place in Dallas. What do you think is the secret to her waffles? Is it a special ingredient or a specific step in the making process?"

I shrugged. "I'm more sensible than to ask her. She guards her recipes with the same intensity she protects this place. A few years ago, they decided to throw her out and lease it to a hipster joint for a higher rent. The patrons created a ruckus and helped her retain the diner."

Aarti put her fork down and stared at me for a moment. "If I recall correctly, Walter's WM Realty bought out this place about three years ago. So unless I'm mistaken, I take it you had something to do with safeguarding it?"

My jaw dropped, along with the fork in my hand, and remained so until she leaned over and put her finger under my chin to lift it close. "You aren't the only resourceful person around, Sujit Rao."

"Hey, you outdo me in every respect, without a doubt."

Her eyes rose from her plate to meet mine, and her smile widened. I was beginning to love the look of that particular smile on her face, the one that reached her eyes and drew two tiny lines around both corners.

"Like I said last night, you are terribly good for my ego, Sujit," she said and delicately cut into her eggs.

I found myself staring at her as the fork approached her mouth and the eggs slid in. I took in the gentle curve of her lips leading up to the cupid's bow framing her splendid mouth. This morning, she wore a beautiful shade of muted pink. Dusty rose, I think Tara used to call it. And for the first time, Tara's name and memory didn't engender bitterness and sorrow. I felt a strange calm wash over me like a wave receding gently after splashing my feet with perfectly tepid water. Was this how it felt to make peace with one's past? To move on from someone and start something fresh, new, and exciting?

I was still gazing at her when she picked up the striped napkin and gracefully wiped the corners of her mouth. "Just because you're good for my ego doesn't mean you get to stare at me while I'm eating."

My gaze darted from her lips to her eyes and quickly down to my plate. "Apologies. I didn't mean to stare. I was...lost in thought."

She smiled her wicked smile, which she promptly hid behind her glass of water. After a moment of playing eye footsie with me, she placed her glass down and began pouring the pure maple syrup on her waffle in a slow, seductive stream.

"Eat your food, or Ms. Dina's going to give you flak for letting the eggs turn cold," she said, trying to distract me from the steady flow of the syrup.

"Yes, thank you," I said and returned my attention to my plate.

Tara had been bold and exciting in many ways, but I'd never felt like this with her. It was as if Aarti knew exactly how to kindle that special place in my heart and my loins. I'd never felt this needy, this desperate, this helpless with anyone else before. Yet the specter of our connection hovered over us at every moment. We were mementos of a sad, humiliating past for the other. Would we ever be able to get past the ex factor?

With a silent sigh, I finished my food like the good boy that Ms. Dina claimed I was. I hadn't been able to determine her exact age, but she'd lost both her sons in Kosovo long years ago. She'd once told me about them while patting my hand. Only now, this good boy was brimming with unseemly intentions for the beautiful woman who sat across him, enjoying her coffee and another hot waffle.

After I placed the cash on the check that the server had brought us, I began to help Aarti with her coat. I saw Ms. Dina rushing toward us, weaving through the happy, content crowd that flocked her establishment every weekend for her heart-warming food and some much-needed love. Ms. Dina always stopped from table to table, making sure the food was up to the patrons' liking and that they left the place with a smile.

"Ms. Dina," I said, holding her hand in mine, "thank you for getting us the table. I hope it wasn't too much trouble."

"Never for you, dear," she said in her gentle accent and eyed Aarti with curiosity.

"This is Aarti. Aarti, the irreplaceable Ms. Dina."

Flashing a warm smile, Aarti took her hand. "It's wonderful to meet you, and the food deserves every compliment Sujit gives it."

"I'm very happy to hear that," Ms. Dina said, patting Aarti's hand like a grandmother. "He's a very special boy, and that woman hurt him. Please take very good care of him."

"She's just a friend, Ms. Dina," I quickly interjected to avoid Aarti the embarrassment.

Ms. Dina smiled and looked between us before beckoning me down to her low frame. As I bent to give her a hug, she squeezed my arm and whispered in my ear, "I like her, take good care of her."

As if pleased by Ms. Dina's blessing, the sun was peeking out when we stepped outside. Walking away from the breakfast and brunch crowd on that unusually pleasant winter morning, we walked around the corner and waited for my driver to bring the car around.

"What did she say to you?" Aarti asked.

Tempted as I was to brush it off with a joke, the earnest look on her face dissuaded me. "She said she likes you," I said, and I saw the car pull up. I opened the door for Aarti before going around to the other side and slipping in beside her.

"She doesn't know you helped with her problems, does she?" Aarti asked as we started toward the Baccarat, where she wanted to pick up a few things.

"No, I told Walt it wasn't necessary to share that piece of information with her."

Aarti turned her face to scrutinize mine. "And she still loves you the way she does?"

"Well, the love is mutual. She's always caring and kind."

"But it's selfless. No one has loved me selflessly except my mother."

"There's a lot of seemingly selfless love in the world around us. But no love is really selfless because when you give love, you also get it. When you give love, you feel good about it, which makes you happy. If you look at it that way, selfless love is also very selfish. It yearns for happiness, contentment, self-love."

"And that's wrong?"

"On the contrary, it is precious. It makes the world a better place."

"That's too much philosophy to handle this early in the morning without mimosas," she said with a straight face, and I laughed.

For the rest of the way to the hotel, she filled the silence between us with a relaxed, happy look on her face.

SUJIT

*a*dil was the first to arrive that evening. He was surprised to see Aarti when we had a strict no-outsiders rule. Chris and Manoj came soon after. The fifth member of our nerd team was Jaspinder, Jas, but she'd just delivered her second child.

"Aarti will play with us today," I declared with the authority my host status granted me. "And we're playing Cards Against Humanity."

The cards were already out on the gaming table, along with the snacking chips and nuts Aarti and I had picked up on the way. Usually, we ordered pizza, but at Aarti's suggestion, we got some gourmet sandwiches.

I knew my buddies would give me much misery, but that was a headache for another day. I'd also be sneered for shifting from Catan to Cards Against Humanity, and in that context, Jas' absence was a silver lining. She was the most ruthless of them all. I also knew these three renegades would call her the moment they stepped out of my house, and I'd soon have Jas mocking me for giving my dick too much say and such. She would ridicule my head and heart like she had done after Tara crushed my soul. Then again, that was grief best left for another day.

Good thing, too, because that evening I got to see a side of Aarti I hadn't expected. Sitting beside me, she hung up her wine-sipping, urbane self and turned into a beer-swilling, name-calling brat. I was acquainted with her never-defeated, competitive side, but the game night took her competitiveness to another level.

"Now, that's hardly fair," Manoj said when she left him with zero cards won after four rounds.

"What's the matter, Manoj? Are you scared of a little competition from a woman?" she shot back with a smirk.

Unable to resist her charm, Manoj smiled back and shook his head.

"That's right, you men always underestimate *the pretty ladies*, don't ya?"

"Humility isn't one of your virtues, I take?" Manoj teased as he tossed a fresh card to everyone.

"And losing with grace isn't one of yours," Aarti teased him back, and my heart dipped.

Was I jealous of their innocent banter? If it was jealousy, I'd better tamp it down with haste. She wasn't my girlfriend, nor anything else that I should feel so possessively about her.

"Damn, woman!" Adil cried when she continued to wipe us clean, round after round. "I'm glad we're not playing Catan. I don't think my ego could take being beaten so badly in a game I love so much."

Aarti allowed herself a quick, girly giggle, then turned to meet my smiling eyes. That was the reason I'd chosen Cards Against Humanity. I knew Aarti's greatest strength was her ability to read people, and that evening, during the small talk before the game, she'd quickly learned everyone's personality traits and tells. Even I didn't know Chris' tell was that he rolled his tongue around in his mouth— as Aarti divulged later that night—and I'd known him for years.

When Adil declared he'd had enough humiliation for one night, I retreated to the kitchen to grab the sandwiches. We'd have eaten them out of the box they were packed in, but Aarti had matter-of-factly pulled out a serving platter and plates as if any of us rubes cared.

I laid out the platter on the dining table and went to the kitchen to grab the plates and napkins. When I returned, I saw Aarti and Manoj out on the covered balcony with the glass door closed behind them. Installed with heat and lighting, it was perfectly comfortable during the colder months.

Aarti knew Manoj was divorced, and he knew she was single. I hadn't realized their innocuous banter was the start of something devastating for me. Seeing them talking so closely tripped me down a dark hole in my past.

It was the second time Manoj had made moves on a woman I liked.

AARTI

*I*t had been a long time since I had enjoyed myself this brashly. I think the last time I was this uninhibited was in college with my friend Isha. Even when I was with Sameer and my other friends in Dallas, the performative elements in keeping with my social status always haunted me.

I was always Aarti Bhatia, daughter of Satish Bhatia, heir to the Bhatia empire, a socialite—a term I really hated for myself. I could never be just Aarti, the introvert who could be playful under the right circumstances. I had to project my social class and perfection in everything I did. I could never be caught underdressed or overexcited. I could never laugh loudly outside the house. I could never flop around while walking. Such was the burden of being in the public gaze at all times.

And yet, as I barked a rowdy laugh in the safety of Sujit's presence and the security of his apartment, I felt completely at ease. His friends were wonderful. Perhaps because they didn't know who I was, I didn't feel the pressure of being under a microscopic gaze as I always did. But even the feeling of liberation didn't dim my hyper-perceptive senses that I had honed over the years. I noted the intensity with which Manoj was studying me. Little did he know, I was also studying him, only I was smarter than to let it on.

Manoj seemed an anomaly for this nerdy group. Sujit, Adil, and Chris seemed like they could be friends. They were slightly nerdy but very gullible and straightforward. Manoj, on the other hand, was a player and wanted to be seen as one. He was good-looking and a charmer. But there was something about him that bothered me, something I couldn't quite put my finger on. It wasn't anything he said or did. He wanted to appear funny and charming and a consummate gentleman, and he had certainly succeeded in that. But the tiny hairs on my neck, standing on edge, said there was something off about him. And now, he became a challenge I just couldn't resist. I had to figure out what it was.

Playing on my wily charms, the sly smiles, and those *oh-that-was-totally-an-accident* touches as he sat next to me during the game were all ways to disarm him. And sure enough, when Sujit excused himself to get the refreshments, Manoj asked if he could speak to me privately on the balcony. That was the moment I was waiting for.

"You are a sneaky little player," he said as I pulled the door to the balcony closed behind me.

"Hmm, did you underestimate me because of my looks or on account of my gender?" I asked with a crooked smile. "Or did you overestimate yourself, as I suspect you often do?"

He laughed and put his hands up in surrender. "I did, but never again. Not with you, anyway."

I slipped him another sly grin. "Good. A lesson learned, then?"

"Indeed," he said and pulled out a vape pen. "Would you like a pull?"

I raised my palm to refuse the offer. "Thanks."

"This is my only vice," he explained, and I highly doubted that statement.

"What did you want to talk about?" I asked, eager to know what was transpiring in his head.

"No chit-chat, huh?" He tried to endear himself with another smile.

In response, I crossed my arms in impatience. He gathered I wasn't interested in playing his games.

"Since you are in realty, I thought you would be the right person to advise me about this," he said as he pulled in a drag from his device and blew out a cloud of vapor.

I merely nodded in response.

"I have been tinkering with a new idea, and no one knows about it yet." He repeated his motions with the stick in his hand.

I waited in silence.

"That's why I asked you out here," he said and cast a quick glance at his friends, who were gathering around the food at the dining table.

I followed his gaze and found Sujit laying out the spread on the platter as I had suggested. My heart warmed at the sight. I longed to be inside with him, beside him. My unconscious mind had already memorized his scent. I pulled in a deep breath and felt another surge of warmth course through me.

I returned my eyes to Manoj. "Sure, what are you looking for?"

"I can trust your discretion, right?"

"My discretion is conditional," I warned. "I need to trust you first to assure you of it."

He gave a nervous laugh. When I didn't react, he continued, "I'm looking for something similar to what Sujit is hunting for his new venture."

Despite my best efforts, my eyes darted to Sujit again, but this time, I didn't see him around the table.

I drew my brows in. "Sujit is looking for a new space?"

This took Manoj by surprise as his brows drew upward. "He hasn't told you?"

I didn't lie as a principle, but omission wasn't akin to lying, I had determined over the years.

"What has he told you?" I asked instead.

Manoj's face changed as he shuffled and took two steps away from me. He returned to the device in his hand and blew out another cloud of vapor. A bigger one this time.

"He hasn't said anything to me either, but I know," he said then instantly regretted it. "At least, that's the rumor. He's been most secretive about it."

"Then why would you assume he would've shared it with me?" I asked, taking a single, measured step toward him.

Surprised by my advance, he studied me, then unleashed a menacing smile, at once charming and threatening. If only I were someone who would be impressed or intimidated easily.

"Well, I thought..." he said and trailed off, letting the pause linger between us.

I frowned. "Thought what?"

"You both are... aren't you?"

I glanced indoors and frowned again. I was thoroughly enjoying this game. "We are what?"

"For goodness sake, you're fucking him, aren't you? And I'm going to be very disappointed if you say you aren't because he's clearly smitten with you."

Finally, he'd said it, and I had him.

This time, I was the one unleashing a menacing smile. "I didn't realize we were supposed to gratify you and your assumptions. I hope you are magnanimous in embracing your disappointment because we aren't, and he isn't," I said and turned to leave.

"Wait!" The urgency in his words made me gloat. I stopped

and turned back to face him. "Would you like to get coffee sometime?"

"As in getting to know me better coffee or a talk about work over a coffee?"

His lip curved at a corner and he raked a hand through his hair. That might have enamored many a heart, but I was immune to his charm.

"Well, a get to know you better coffee date. Or dinner, if you prefer."

"I'm sorry, I can't."

His gaping mouth said he was taken aback. Men like Manoj weren't used to rejection from women. But then, he had never met me before.

"Can't or won't?" he asked, trying to be witty.

"You want me to find you a space for your new project, don't you?"

"What does that have to do with a coffee date?"

We heard a faint whistle and looked in through the glass door to see Adil beckoning us in. We both smiled back.

"You're a business contact, and I don't date my business contacts. It's not in keeping with my professional ethics," I said and turned to walk out without waiting for his response.

"All right," he said as I slid the door open.

I cast him a quick look over my shoulder.

"A talk about work coffee, then," he said hurriedly before I stepped over the threshold to reenter the living room.

I turned to him and nodded. "Sure. Text me what day works for you."

As I turned back to leave, he said, "I don't have your number."

I looked at him and smirked. "I'm sure a well-connected man like you can find a way to reach me when you need it."

With that, I went back in. The guys had already had their

hands on the sandwiches, complimenting me for the great choice of grub. I got my ham and provolone and settled down by Sujit. I needed to feel his warmth after Manoj's dastardly attempts at wooing me. Sujit was all smiles, but there was something different about his demeanor. I hoped he didn't take my flirting with Manoj to mean anything other than getting under the man's skin. I positioned myself as close to Sujit as was appropriate for the setting, breathing in his masculine scent and relaxing in it. It was all I needed after a perfect night of fun and games.

All kinds of games, I thought as I threw a quick glance at Manoj.

SUJIT

t had been the end of our third semester in grad
school.

With bloodshot eyes from lack of sleep, we raced against time
to finish up our final projects. It'd been on one of those nights
that, in an adrenaline-induced sleepless daze, I'd foolishly told
Manoj, who was my roommate and a close friend then, that I had
a crush on Tejal. She'd been the smartest student in our class but
bold and forthcoming, whereas I'd been a shy, nerdy guy with
glasses.

Manoj's hands flying over his keyboard had halted promptly,
and I'd torn my attention away from my screen to look at him.
His shifty gaze had darted away, and he'd resumed his work.

"What did I say?" I'd asked.

"Nothing," he'd said, shaking his head, then stopped typing
again.

When I'd turned to him, he'd said, "Tejal and I have sort of
been hanging out. Nothing serious, just fooling around. But I'll
end it if you are really interested in her."

In that instant, I'd felt like a chump, uninitiated, ashamed, embarrassed.

"Of course not," I'd blurted. "It's a crush, that's all...you didn't tell me you were seeing her. I've never even seen the two of you together."

"It isn't serious," he'd said with a shrug, eyes back on this computer screen, fingers flying again over the keyboard.

I'd done what my parents had raised me to do. I'd backed off and never spoken about it again. Not even after they got married. It was only after the divorce, when Tejal had asked me for a coffee date that she revealed she'd always known about my feelings and hoped we could reconnect. By that time, I'd moved on. And Tejal's beauty looked less appealing after she'd confessed that she'd chosen Manoj over me because she'd seen more potential, more likelihood of success in him. I had thanked her for her candor, but in the light of it, I wasn't sure if she wanted me back because I'd succeeded in life by her definition. Did she really care for me, or had she only seen the wealth I'd created?

When I'd repaid her candor with mine, she'd pulled back in her seat. "I don't need your money, Sujit," she'd said, a tear forming in her eye. "I'm well-placed. I was just made VP of software operations at my company. I was only hoping for love and loyalty, neither of which your friend has given me."

"Did he cheat on you?" I'd cried, appalled. Although I hadn't had the front-row view of their divorce as Adil did, I'd known enough, but this was the first time I'd heard about it.

"It doesn't matter," she'd said, sniffing back her humiliation. "I'm ambitious, and he took advantage of my unavailability, as he claimed at our divorce hearing. I wonder if he would have seen it as such if he was the busy one and I'd made good use of his unavailability."

I'd taken her hand in mind. "I'm sorry, Tejal. I truly am. I really liked you, but we never got a chance to turn it into something more."

She'd nodded. "You know what's funny? You're rejecting me, yet I trust you more than I ever trusted him. I have no fear of shame or embarrassment with you because I know, despite today, I'll never lose your respect."

And she hadn't, but Manoj had. Tejal had been the sixth member of our game night club, and after their divorce, she'd been dignified enough to let Manoj have his circle of friends. Manoj, on the other hand, continued his braggart and remorseless ways. That was when we instituted the no-outsiders policy. No friends, no partners, no spouses.

I'd gradually distanced myself from Manoj after that evening in grad school, but he had hung on to his friendship with Adil and the others. What changed my opinion of Manoj completely was Adil's revelation that Manoj and Tejal had never been together before that evening. He'd asked her out only after I told him about my crush.

"It doesn't matter if he was trying to hurt me," I'd said to Adil, sitting at his cousin's exclusive club sipping scotch while Adil sipped cola. "There had to be something there. They got married."

"And divorced," Adil had said, turning his soft eyes on me. "Just...be careful around him."

"Why are you still friends if you don't trust him?" I asked.

He shrugged. "I'm not the one he has tried to sabotage. I'm not the one he's jealous of. It's always been you."

When I'd looked at him with a frown, Adil had responded with a frown of his own and said, "How have you survived for so long? He's always trying to be better, more successful than you."

"Why? There's nothing remotely special about me!"

"That's what you think, bro. I think he's overcompensating for his father's fondness for you."

"His father is my dad's friend. That's how we became room-mates that year."

"Yup, and apparently, he couldn't stop talking about how brilliant you are."

"Are you supposed to tell me all this?"

Adil had shrugged with one shoulder, as was his style. "I believe in good deeds, brother, and the good lord knows this is one." He patted my shoulder. "Watch your back."

"Tejal said the same thing," I'd told him.

"Believe her," he'd advised.

Keep your enemies close, they say. That's what I had done. Keeping him close had worked to disarm him. Over the years, his obsession with me had seemed to wane, especially as he struggled with keeping his own company afloat. But I knew that he wouldn't give up any opportunity to sabotage me.

I saw him out on the balcony with Aarti as I placed the plates and napkins on the table. I glanced over my shoulder at Adil, who was already throwing me concerned looks. I nodded in reassurance and wished, yet again, that everyone would stop worrying about me. It made me feel helpless and small, like a kid. And it wasn't like Aarti and I were dating.

"Shall we call the lovebirds back in?" Chris said as he grabbed a sandwich off the platter.

"Sure," I said and settled down before I was tasked with the job.

Adil put his fingers in his mouth and blew a sharp whistle that pierced through my ear drum, and the two heard it on the balcony. When he waved them in, they came back in and settled around the table with the rest of us.

"These look good," Manoj said with a warm smile directed at Aarti. "I take it back. Having a pretty woman on game nights does have its perks."

I tamped down the jealousy rising inside me when I heard

Aarti respond, "As I understand Jas is a part of your game nights. Do you mean to imply that she's not attractive?"

Manoj's jaw dropped.

Aarti put up a finger and added, "I suggest you think very carefully before answering that question."

She picked up her ham, provolone, and arugula as Chris burst into inconsolable laughter. Manoj shut his mouth quickly.

"I'm so glad Manoj's getting what he deserves. He's been having a very easy time since Jas ditched us to care for her baby," Chris said with a grin.

"Yes, that was utterly selfish of her," Adil deadpanned as he bit into his chicken sandwich and nodded with approval. "Good choice, man!" he said to me. "Maybe we should switch our regular menu to sandwiches from this place."

"You'll need permission from Jas," Aarti said with a smile.

Maybe this could save me from Jas' mockery. If I told her how Aarti had had her back all night, maybe she'd consider being a little less harsh on me.

After my friends left and we cleaned up the remnants of the game night, Aarti suggested popping open a bottle of her favorite white.

She revealed how she'd managed to beat us that evening. "It is a game of knowing your opponent."

"You mean friends?" I corrected.

"It's literally called Cards Against Humanity. I'm sure the creators didn't intend it as friendly."

I laughed.

"Adil was the easiest. He's a decent guy, so he'd always choose the least problematic card. That's what I did, too. Chris was just being his charming self and giving me all kinds of hints with his body language. The most challenging was Manoj. He tried to throw me off a couple of times by switching gears, but I needed to win."

"What about me?" I asked, masking my desperation with a cool voice.

Delicately resting the flute on her thigh, she smiled her naughty smile. "You were the easiest, Sujit. I know you quite well now."

I relaxed against the couch with satisfaction. "That isn't good for me."

"I disagree," she said and passed me another sly smile.

AARTI

I didn't want to wake up the next morning. After spending two wonderful days with Sujit, I dreaded the loneliness that would greet me at the new condo. Even so, I had no option but to get off the warm bed and struggle into my robe.

"Morning," I said to Sujit as I came out of the guest room. He was pouring coffee in two huge mugs.

"Morning. Hope you slept well," he said and handed me a mug of the fragrant coffee with the precise amount of cream I preferred and no sugar, as he'd learned in the past two days.

"I wish we could go to Ms. Dina's again this morning," I said with a sigh. "I'm really craving those petulla."

"We can," he offered.

"I can't. I'm moving into my new place today," I explained.

His body, which had leaned against the counter, propelled upright. "Moving in? Is it ready?"

"Yes, there are a few minor things left, but I can get them done later. All the renovations are done. My contractors have fixed all appliances, and I received the furniture sooner as a special favor."

"You don't sound excited," he observed.

"I'm relieved that I can move out of the hotel. It's an excellent hotel, but I need a home now."

"Can I help you move?"

I smiled. "There isn't much to move. I have just the two bags."

He cocked his head. "Can I help you make it a home, then?"

My insides trembled as I gazed into the dark eyes behind those glasses. Would it be completely imprudent to flirt with the idea of making a home with him? I wondered what it would feel like to come home to his warm body, his witty self, and generous spirit every evening. How would his whispers feel near my ear? How would his touch feel on my naked skin?

My eyes darted to his hands around the mug as I imagined his slender fingers gliding along my body. I had a feeling he'd start at my feet, teasing me, trailing his fingers up my shin and along the insides of my thigh. A gasp would escape my lips at the whisper of his touch on my hip, on my pelvis, but he wouldn't pause there, not yet.

Traversing my waist, he'd torture me, avoiding my breasts and strumming his fingers along my arms, neck, and clavicle. Then, when I'd writhe, begging for his touch on my breasts, he'd bring his mouth on them, and I'd lose all purpose. I'd want him to keep his glasses on, peer at me over the rim as he gazed into my eyes with my breast in his mouth, my nipple clutched tight between his teeth, releasing his warm breath on my starving skin.

A plush warmth gathered below my belly and traveled swiftly to my chest. My eyes darted from his fingers to his mouth, just to catch his lips firm around the rim of the cup, his eyes peering at me over his glasses. My rock-hard nipples strained painfully at the sight, my pelvic muscles clenched, and I quickly moved my eyes to the cup in my hand, silently thanking the thick robe for concealing my embarrassment.

"So, what's the verdict?" he asked, and I brought my eyes back to his face. Greeted with a sly smile, I prayed he didn't see the flush under my dusky skin. "Do I get the honor of accompanying you to your new home?"

I gulped the last of my coffee and walked over to the sink to deposit my cup. "You really are persistent, aren't you? If you're so keen on wasting your Sunday, sure, I'd love the company. I do not, however, promise any housewarming treats. The kitchen is barren and cold."

"That's because it isn't a home yet." He smiled and put the cup in the sink beside mine. "But it will be by this evening, I promise."

"Give me a half hour to get ready."

"That's enough time for me," he said and moved toward his bedroom without another word.

When I emerged from the guest room carrying my weekender, he was ready in jeans and a relaxed short cotton shirt, reading on his tablet, which he promptly set on the side table when he saw me. Giving no credence to my protests, he carried my bag down to the parking garage, where the car service awaited us.

Back at the hotel, he helped me pack my bags and got them bussed to the car. Before leaving, he went around the suite, making sure I'd not left anything behind.

"It's the little things," my mother had once said. "Grand gestures will take your breath away for a moment, but the little things will show you how loved you are."

"Like what, Ma?" a young, inexperienced Aarti had asked.

"Like making sure your slippers are right by your bed every night because your feet will hurt all day if you step on the floor first thing in the morning. Like checking that you have water at your bedside every night."

"Papa does that for you?" I had cried with wide eyes.

She'd nodded with a smile. "You know how often he says I love you?"

I'd snorted. "Never?" I loved my dad, but I knew him well. He held that showing emotion was a sign of weakness.

Mom had laughed. "No, silly girl. He used to whisper it to me when we got married, but as life got busier, as he got busier, he didn't remember to say it as often. But every night, there's water at my bedside and my slippers are on the rug by my bed. Even when we've had a fight, my slippers are there. Even after we had a housekeeper, he's the one who makes sure my slippers are by my bed every morning. That's how I know I'm loved."

"So, you're saying don't fall for chocolates and flowers?"

She'd laughed her beautiful laugh. "You can if it makes you happy. Gift them too, if it brings you happiness. But those won't be the instances that will stay with you."

"What's the most touching instance you remember?"

Mom hadn't even blinked. "When you were kids, we went to the Smoky Mountains. Do you remember?"

I nodded. We'd gone with three other families and had the best Thanksgiving break I remembered from my childhood.

"We had rented this lavish home. A grand cabin in the mountains. It came equipped with everything, the kitchen stocked with the staples. But guess what was missing? Sugar."

"Huh?"

"Satish woke up early that morning to make tea and realized there was no sugar. You know he doesn't mind having his tea without sugar, so he could've called the property managers later, and they would have dropped it off, but it would've taken a while. Instead, before I woke up, he drove the long miles down the mountain into the city because he knew I'd never drink my chai without sugar."

"That's not a small thing. It's a grand gesture," I'd objected.

"Yes, but there was no grandstanding about it. He was back

before I woke up, and he'd made the tea for me. I didn't even know about it until that evening when we gathered around the bonfire, and one of our friends complimented me on being such a lucky woman."

The little things.

When I first joined Dad in his business, I studied him. From him, I learned the art of emotional stoicism. I learned how to keep myself guarded against hurt, pain, and manipulation. Decisions with your head, not your heart, he'd ingrained in me. It had taken me months to open up to Sameer, but we had never shared the joys of small things. We exchanged expensive gifts and shared extravagant holidays. We hobnobbed at exclusive parties, but when we were cuddled up in front of the television in his condo, the warmth from his arm around me never managed to reach my soul. It was as if the distance between his heart and mine could never be bridged with the intermingling of our bodies. In the end, he'd taken my heart and crushed it under the weight of his happiness with Tara.

My eyes traveled to Sujit as he scanned around the living area of the suite and asked, "You have the keys to the new place?"

"It has an electronic keypad."

He nodded and said, "Anything we need to pick up on the way?"

"No." I shook my head and followed him out.

The little things, it made perfect sense now.

When we arrived at the condo, he requested the driver to help carry some things from the trunk. I noticed an unfamiliar holdall in the luggage we carried up the elevators. He offered to hold my satchel while I unlocked the door.

"This is it!" I said with a trembling breath. "My first home, exclusively in my name."

As I began to enter, his hand came swiftly around my wrist. "Wait," came his hurried plea.

"What's wrong?"

"It's silly, but my mother always makes me put the right foot across the threshold first."

I smiled. I'd seen and heard this several times before, but I never thought I'd be the one to believe in the good luck that this innocuous step would garner. I pulled my right foot up dramatically, but before I crossed that threshold defined by the door, I pulled it back.

Looking into his face, I took his hand and interlaced my fingers with his. "Will you do me the honor of entering my house with me?"

A look of surprise flashed across his face, and he blinked. A sweet smile quickly appeared, putting two perfect dents in his clean-shaven face. "It would be an honor."

We matched our timing and stepped inside the apartment together. After the ritualistic inaugural entry, we went back out and rolled in my suitcases.

"What's in this one?" I asked, nodding at the extra holdall.

"Something that will help make this a home, I hope," he said with a smile. "Where do you want your bags?"

"In the bedroom, please," I said, rolling a bag toward it as he followed me with the second roller, and it was already starting to feel like home.

When I returned to the living room, having put away my bags, I spotted a large item placed on one of the consoles by the wall. It was surreptitiously covered with a large velvet cloth.

"Do I dare ask?" I said with wide eyes.

"Of course you can. It's a surprise."

My heart grappled with an unrecognizable emotion. Joy? Yes, but it seemed laced with a sorrow of some kind. The kind I couldn't figure out.

"Let me show you the place first," I offered, and he followed me.

After a quick tour of the apartment, during the entirety of which he complimented me on the choice of floor, paint, and furniture, we returned to the living room.

He took a seat on the couch and pulled the holdall onto his lap.

"Now," he said before opening it, "this is something I've seen in my family, and you can absolutely say no. We put rice and milk over the stove and let it overflow. It's said to bring happiness and prosperity," he said and unzipped the holdall. Out came a small container of raw rice, a tetra pack of milk, and a small saucepan.

An entire gamut of feelings ran through me. My wise mother was right. This was exactly the kind of innocuous thing that would stay with me through my life, lending hope in times of sadness.

"I would love that. Would you do it for me?" I asked.

"Sure," he said.

I followed him into the kitchen, where he poured the milk into the pan, added a handful of rice, and turned on the stove. In a few minutes, the milk boiled and ran over the rim of the saucepan. He let it boil over for a few seconds, then turned off the stove.

"Don't worry, I'll clean the stove for you later," he teased as I kept staring at the milk on the stove.

I wasn't worried about the condition of my kitchen counter. What worried me at that moment was the condition of my heart. How was I ever going to get over this man? Why did he have to be unattainable? What would it be like to break all rules and throw myself into his arms?

"You can pray if you want," he said. "My mother does other things, but I don't know any of them. This is the only thing I remember."

Over the years I'd witnessed all kinds of rituals and traditions. Preferences for south-facing homes, not south-facing homes, east-facing windows, no huge trees in certain parts of the yard. From Vaastushastra and Feng Shui to carrying salt or water into the house, I knew most customs, but I never thought I'd be partaking in one with a man I was beginning to really like.

"Now," he said and moved toward the living room again. "I have something for you. A little housewarming gift to make this house a home."

He directed me to the large item on the console, and I pulled the velvet off, squinting with one eye as if it were a bomb that would go off.

He laughed wholeheartedly, throwing his head back, eyes closed, dimples digging deep into his cheeks. Peering over the rim of his glasses, which made my heart thud and clamber, he watched me as I stood speechless by his gift.

It was his cousin Padmaja's sculpture, the one I'd admired at the gallery.

"Oh, Sujit, this is beautiful!" I quickly discarded the velvet in my hand and grazed my fingers along the artwork, admiring it for the prized jewel that it was.

"I'm glad you like it, or I would've felt like a fool buying it for you."

"You bought it for me?" I turned to him.

"Yes, you said such beautiful words about it. It belongs with you, as Padmaja would've declared."

Overwhelmed, I stepped closer to him and asked, "Is it alright if I give you a hug?"

AARTI

gentle scent of spice and sandalwood rose from the warm skin at his neck as he pulled his arms around me. I sniffed a quick breath and basked in his embrace. I felt his hand move up my back, and my nipples hardened against his firm chest. When his cheek brushed against mine, I yearned for the touch of his lips on my skin. I lifted my head to look at him and thought I spied raw desire in his eyes before he cleared his throat and smiled.

"I'm glad you like it," he repeated, a cue for me to regain self-respect and move out of his arms.

Like a saving grace, my phone trilled in my satchel. Flustered from being caught between desire and guilt, I scrambled to pull the phone out. It was a video call from Mom.

"Hi, Beta, have you moved in?" she asked, pride and excitement illuminating her voice.

"Yes, Ma, just did. Do you want to see the place?"

When I mouthed a quick *sorry* to Sujit, he signaled *no problem* with a wave and pulled out his phone to settle on the couch.

It wasn't just Mom on the call. My whole family was gathered around, eager to see my new place.

"Where's Nitara?" I asked about my infant niece.

"She's napping," my weary sister-in-law informed me.

"And how are you doing, Jia?" I asked, taking note of the dark circles around her eyes. "Are you getting enough sleep?"

Her smile turned wider and brighter. "Yes, I'm doing alright."

"I hope Aakash is taking good care of you," I said and gave my brother a stern eye.

Jia rolled her eyes. "He is, a bit, but Ma has been amazing. She's so kind and patient with me, even when I'm not," she said, and tears started to gather in her eyes.

"Arey Beta," Mom handed her phone off to Dad, and I heard her in the background. "I'm not doing anything special, and I have help. That's what you do for your loved ones. You are my family. You and Aarti are both my daughters."

Jia came from an emotionally toxic home with parents too absorbed in their own egos to pay attention to her. She often ended up a target of her mother's ire, who blamed Jia for her marital discord and unhappiness. Her brother, the firstborn, the male heir, got every benefit of the doubt and lorded over Jia like she was a servant girl.

When the brash Aakash and a quiet Jia started an unlikely relationship in college, no one imagined it would last, let alone that they would end up married. During the initial years, Jia refused to be in the same space with my mother without either me or Aakash present. She kept looking for Mom's ulterior motive in her every utterance, every move. Aakash and I had a huge fight about it. I rebuked him for being in a relationship with a woman who mistrusted Mom, disrespected and dishonored her, and it was then that Aakash told me about her past.

Pity and guilt filled me as I imagined Jia unable to trust the two people who should've had her back and made her feel safe. I didn't know what that would feel like. I had asked Aakash if I could talk to her, but protective that he was, he wouldn't let anything bring her discomfort, even if it meant straining relations with his family for a while.

My respect for the brother I considered spoilt and immature, shot up that day. Not only was he convinced of his love for Jia, but he was dedicated enough to give her time to work through her issues. One evening, Aakash and I both sat down with Jia and requested her to give Mom a chance. We assured her that if she thought my mother was as controlling as hers, we'd never insist again.

The transformation in their relationship didn't occur overnight, but it did. "Every child needs to know love," my sage mother had said, "because unless we raise kids with love, they will end up creating a world full of hatred and greed."

Jia turned into a child again when she trusted Mom, and Mom gave her the love and respect she'd never found growing up.

Life is strange oftentimes. We never know where we'll end up finding love.

My eyes shot up to Sujit at the thought. He was typing on his phone with both hands.

"Sorry," I heard Jia, and I looked back at my screen. Her eyes were bloodshot, but there was a smile beneath them. "I think it's the hormones," she said.

"You don't need to explain, Jia. Raising an infant is reason enough to bring tears to your eyes," I tried to diffuse the emotional moment.

She laughed and sniffed back a few last tears. "I've never seen *you* cry," she argued.

"That's because I'm not raising an infant," I said, but I had cried.

I had wept in Sujit's arms, and it had felt good. I wanted it again, to feel free, to cry without being judged, without being labeled as weak. I glanced over my shoulder as I walked into the bedroom with my back camera active. Sujit was on his phone, and if he'd heard any part of the conversation, he didn't let on.

After giving them a thorough tour of the condo, I came back to the living room, ready to end the call. It was the first time Dad didn't have any words of "constructive criticism," as he always put it, and I suspected Mom was the reason. It was my first home, a cause of pride, a source of identity, and Dad had been restrained about what I could have done better. Having been reminded of Jia's past, I was glad there were mothers like my Ma in this world. She wasn't perfect, but she was kind.

"Alright, then, I'll let you all get back to your day. I'll call you tomorrow. Give my love to Nitara."

"Wait, I need to talk to you," Aakash said and grabbed the phone from Mom.

I waited while he made a swift trek across the family room, through the long corridors along the bedrooms, and into the study. I heard the big glass door close shut.

"What's so urgent?" I asked, assuming he had some business-related issue to discuss. "Can it wait until tomorrow?"

"Why, do you have somewhere to be?"

I let out a silent sigh and began walking away from Sujit. "No."

"How are you doing?" he asked as he lowered himself to the couch in the study, but I knew my brother well. His tense tone wasn't meant for that question.

"I'm well. How's everything there?"

"It's been weird," he said. "Everywhere we go, people keep whispering around us because we're the only ones in our circle who wouldn't be at Sameer's wedding. I'm really glad you're not here."

"So am I." I smiled, shooting a quick glance at Sujit, who was still engrossed in his phone.

"There's something else."

"Yes?"

"Are you seeing anyone there?" he asked.

"What?" I felt the blood pump directly into my ears. The unexpected thud was too loud to handle. "Why would you ask me that? And why would it matter if I was?"

"Listen, an acquaintance saw you with Sujit Rao and asked me about it. Do you know him?"

I glanced at Sujit again, and this time, I was sure he'd heard us, for he was looking at me with his eyebrows raised.

"Is he there with you now?" Aakash's eyes bugged out at my shifty glances.

"No," I blurted and fumbled before I could think about it more rationally. "Why would he be here?"

With as much nonchalance as I could manage, I walked into the bedroom and closed the door behind me.

"What about Sujit?" I asked, lowering myself to the armchair in my bedroom.

"Do you know him?"

"Yes, his office is in the building we bought from WM. We met to discuss his lease. What about it?"

"You know who he is?"

"He's the founder of AccessEd. It's a startup aiming to provide accessible education."

Aakash blew out an annoyed breath. "You know what I'm asking, Aarti. You're not naïve."

I met his eye with conviction. "I know he's Tara's ex."

"Are you involved with him?"

"I ran into him at an art exhibition, where I was on a date with someone else, if you want to know."

"That's not the only place you were spotted together. Someone saw you at some restaurant, sharing an intimate dinner."

The lid I was trying to keep on my temper blew off. I jumped off my chair with indignation. "If you already know everything, why the fuck are you asking me?"

His eyes widened. "So, it is true!" The upward lilt in Aakash's voice indicated both shock and disappointment. The next words out of his mouth confirmed it. "This is so messed up, Aarti. I hope you didn't fuck him just to get back at Tara and Sameer."

"You know what, I don't want to have this conversation with you. Ever."

"Wait," he pleaded before I could hang up. "Look, bachchi, I'm only looking out for you."

Aakash and I were two years apart and often toggled the role of the older sibling. Most often, I was the older one, but sometimes, he called me a child and loved me like one.

"You know none of us will second guess you, not me, not Ma, and certainly not Papa," he continued. "You're the smart one, but sometimes, when the heart is hurt, the mind doesn't think straight. I just want to make sure you're not doing anything you'll later regret, that's all. And it's not just you. If this becomes public knowledge, you know what it will do to our family's reputation. To the business. *Again*," he reminded pointedly. "Dad's entire legacy is at stake here, Sis."

"I don't see how any of that will be affected."

"Really? You don't think such a relationship will make us a laughingstock? Of all the thousands of eligible men in the country, you chose your ex's girlfriend's ex? At best, it will come across as vengeance—you slept with Tara's ex because she slept with Sameer. At its worst, it will look pathetic that you fell in love with him. We're in the public eye, Aarti. More so after that spectacular debacle of a proposal. The business is expanding. We need to avoid any scandal."

A boulder from my past landed on my chest and crushed my breath. "I didn't create the scandal," I cried with anger. "Sameer did. He stomped on my heart, and he gets to walk with his head held high. He gets to parade around town with his new girlfriend. Meanwhile, I'm freezing my ass off in New York in the winter."

Aakash's face softened, as did his voice. "It isn't fair, but he wasn't spared either. You know how much he lost financially after that. He says he doesn't care, but we can't afford it, not for a fling, do you hear me, Sis?"

"So, it will always be about the two of them, never about us? Sujit and I will continue to live in the shadow of their happiness?"

"All your life, if you pursue this. That's what I'm trying to say."

I ran my hand over my head and let out a deep sigh. "I'm not involved with Sujit, and I'm most certainly not fucking him. Are you all happy now?"

"It's not just about us, Aarti. It can't be healthy for you either. You'll never get over Sameer if you're reminded of Tara every time you turn around."

My heart twisted in pain. Was this the undetectable sorrow that was lacing my joy, casting a shadow on my happiness? I looked at Aakash's sympathetic face. He felt sorry for me, as did everyone around me. He was sorry he had found his happiness while I was fending off the stigma and embarrassment of a broken engagement.

Then, something hit me. "Aakash, who did you say saw me with Sujit?"

He averted his gaze the slightest before responding, "Just a business contact of mine."

"It wasn't a business contact. You said they *also* saw me at the restaurant, which means they saw me at the exhibition as well. Do you have someone following me?"

"Of course not, Sis!" The indignation in his voice sounded a bit too loud to be convincing.

"Tell me what's going on," I demanded with a stern face.

He didn't immediately divulge it, but I held my silence and

the *I mean business* expression on my face until he came clean. "Papa was talking to someone about your marriage."

The news assaulted me like a knife through my heart. My father, who never made a big decision about his business without consulting me, thought he could make decisions about my life without my knowledge? A tear threatened to gather in my eye, but I blinked it away. Now was not the time.

"Tell me everything, Aakash," I ordered in a smooth, even tone.

"I don't know the details. It's not like Papa is confiding in me about it," he cried with mild outrage. "All I know is the family had heard the rumors about you after the breakup and wanted to judge for themselves. They hired a private eye to tail you and report to them. Fortunately for you, the day this entitled jerk walked into our office, inquiring if you were involved with Sujit, Papa was out. I assured him that it had to be a coincidence and told him that if he didn't trust you now, he should drop the idea of marrying you. You don't want to know what he said after that, but I told him off."

My blood was on fire. "Let me guess. He said I was damaged goods, and that he was doing me a favor by marrying me. That he was a good person to *accept* me despite the breakup and the rumors."

Aakash raked his hand over his head and released a deep sigh. "Something to the effect, and in less charitable words."

"I'm going to talk to Papa. Now," I declared.

Aakash shook his head. "Don't. It will only worsen the situation. He's already angry at how it all unfolded. If he learns I told you about it, he's going to hurt. I don't want to embarrass him, Aarti."

"Did you tell him about the private eye following me and what that jerk said about me?"

"I did. I told him to stop trying to scrape the bottom of the barrel unless he thought that's what you deserve."

"What did he say?"

Another sigh from my brother. "You know he won't accept he made a mistake. But I saw it in his eyes. He was embarrassed for himself and insulted for you. I don't think he's going to try it again, this whole seeking-out-grooms-for-you thing. He seemed defeated and devastated."

The conflict within me felt incapacitating. I was angry at my father, but I was also grateful for his love and protection. He shouldn't have sent marriage proposals without asking me, but when he learned what they thought of me, he was angry on my behalf. He had made a mistake. How could I not forgive him?

Where did that put me and Sujit? Would there ever be a chance for us?

"He blames himself for pushing you toward Sameer and now he wants to somehow remedy it," Aakash clarified softly.

"I don't blame him for Sameer," I said with a frown.

"But he does. He blames himself, and that's why this is so unsettling, Aarti. It doesn't matter how we came about the information, the fact remains that you were spotted with Sujit. You know Papa will never like that. And did you ever consider the possibility that maybe Sujit is using you to get his revenge on Tara?"

"Sujit is not that person," I objected. "He is a kind, considerate man. A good friend. And I am not involved with him."

I wasn't *with* Sujit. I wasn't dating him. I wasn't sleeping with him. Yet all of me—my body, heart, and soul—yearned for him. What did one call such a relationship? A crush? An attraction? An infatuation? An obsession? Or was it something more? Something deeper and meaningful?

"Our business has concluded. We arrived at an acceptable

number, and he has signed the lease for another five years," I added absently.

"Good. That's the last thing we need. Another scandal," Aakash said. "Neither you nor the business can afford it right now. And I care about you, Sis."

"But you care more about the business and its reputation," I spewed out the accusation.

That irked him, and the gentleness of our conversation blew up into acrimony.

"Yes, I care about the business and the family's reputation. We've barely reeled in from that fucked up surprise public proposal to Sameer, and you're going out with Tara's ex, and you don't see how messed up it is?"

"For the last time, I'm not going out with Sujit. He was a business contact. Now he's a friend. He understands what I went through because he did too. He understands it much better than any of you. I'm not going to stop talking to him or hanging out with him because someone somewhere spotted us and thought we were fucking. That's their problem."

"That's *your* problem, Aarti, and ours!" Aakash cried in the same loud tone I'd used.

"Goodbye, Aakash, and don't ever call me about this again."

"Stop this BS, and I won't have to."

I'd never hung up on Aakash. That had never been the spirit of our relationship, but that day I did.

Hurt, angry, and humiliated, I couldn't decide if I should open the door and walk into Sujit's arms or stay here until my anger dissipated. I knew Sujit was outside, worrying, pacing, unsure if he should approach me.

I was right. When I walked out through that door into the living room, he stopped pacing and looked at me with concern in his eyes.

"Are you alright?" he asked from where he'd stopped in his tracks.

"Did you hear it all?" I inquired with a sigh.

"Not everything, but I heard my name mentioned several times. I also heard the F-bomb dropped several times."

I rolled my eyes and walked around him to sit on the couch. "The *F-bomb*, really?"

He sat beside me. "Are you alright?"

"My brother asked me if I was sleeping with you and said it was unhealthy. He also said it would be a terrible blow to our business and social reputation if I had a relationship with Tara's ex."

"What did you say?" The intelligent eyes behind those glasses glimmered with a sentiment I couldn't pin down.

"The truth—that we're friends and that I'm not going to stop hanging out with you because he thinks it's unhealthy."

Sujit nodded and shifted to put distance between us. "Do you want me to leave?" he asked.

I gave him a side-eye. "If I'd wanted you to leave, I would've thrown you out myself. I don't need my brother telling me what I want or what I should do."

"Good, because if you'd chosen to throw me out, you would've had to put away the groceries yourself."

I frowned. "What groceries?"

"Well, I thought you might need some staples, so I ordered delivery while you were on the phone. I hope it's all right."

The little things.

I turned to face him and, looking straight into his eyes, declared, "I'm going to hug you now and possibly cry, and you'll promise not to make a big deal out of it."

He nodded. "Tears of relief or sorrow?" he asked.

"I don't know yet. I'll decide when I'm done crying."

"Alright," he said and opened his arms for me.

I stayed in his arms until the doorman buzzed the intercom for the delivery. Sujit answered the door, collected the bags, and stocked my fridge and pantry while I went to the bathroom to wash away my tears.

"Milk, coffee, butter, eggs. Some bottled water. Took a chance and ordered bread, but I'll get you a fresh loaf from my favorite bakery later. Some fresh pasta in the fridge, in case you feel like cooking, and dried pasta and sauce in the pantry. That should hold you until you can put in a proper order. And we'll pick up some pots and pans in a bit if you want. I also ordered my favorite coffee maker. It's not fancy, but it's the best. It should be here in a bit. And I've already talked to my personal chef. He'll be happy to come make meals for you a couple of times a week if you want."

He stepped over to the counter and picked up a bunch of bananas. "Oh, I ordered some bananas. I saw you eat one first thing in the morning at my place, so I thought that's something you do? Also got some apples. They're in the crisper in the fridge."

I hugged him again and shed a few more tears.

"Frustration," I said, wiping my eyes. "Those were tears of frustration. Not sorrow, not relief."

"We can remedy that too," he said. "Dinner at Marco's this evening?"

"How about La Traviata? I want the potpie."

"Done," he said and pushed the glasses up his nose to look at me. "I'm not a fan of your tears."

"Sorry, but you're the only one who gets to see them, so you'll have to learn to deal with them."

"That's alright, too. I'm not worried," he said with a single pat on my shoulder.

But I was. I was terrified that if I lost whatever it was that we had, I'd never have anyone who'd understand or appreciate my tears.

AARTI

*I*t was a terrible way to go through the week. Between my emergent feelings for Sujit and Akash's words of caution, all I felt inside me was anguish. A sense of helplessness that was debilitating.

Sujit had not only helped me move into my new place, but made the house a home in a short few minutes. I had never felt so loved and cared for. I had never yearned for this kind of connection before. Maybe it was the first-daughter syndrome, but I had always been adamant about being able to care for myself. Then, along came a man whose kindness melted the tough armor I had built around my heart. He had managed to pierce straight through it and he didn't even know it. And I would never be able to tell him because Akash's words held up flashing signs before me. The most poignant of them? Dad's entire legacy was at stake if I continued to indulge in this foolhardy attraction.

His warning reminded me of Mary Beth.

The optics, it's always about the optics, Mary Beth used to say. "Your life could be a glorious mess, but all that the world should get to see are rosy faces in fancy clothes. And don't forget the wide smiles."

Since my move to the city, Mary Beth had invited me several times to visit her. But I hadn't, and she knew why. There was a reason she was my best friend. Her ability to give my introverted self the space I needed to thrive had been one of the most endearing features of our relationship. I didn't want to talk about the breakup or the impending wedding, and she respected that.

That week, though, I missed her presence and her wisdom. I needed to make a headway through my misery.

I texted her.

> Miss you. How's everything?

She texted back instantly

MARY BETH

> Glad to know you're alive. You missed last week's party.

> I didn't miss it and you know it.

I heard her laughter in my head as another text dinged.

> Alright, I missed you then. Come over for a visit. I promise Ezzie won't bite.

> Does he know you say these things about him?

> What do you think?

Of course, he did. He hadn't married her for her money or good looks. It was for her charm and sass.

I will, soon. I promise.

Not soon enough. Is the wedding over?

It's a few weekends away.

Do you want to come over?

No, I have plans.

What plans? Is there someone I don't know about?

Yes, a very handsome building we just acquired that needs my attention.

You know you're not funny. I'm the funny one.

You're funny, smart, and gorgeous. What does that leave me with?

You're the genuine one, the one with all the love and warmth.

Less interesting than being smart and funny.

I might be smart, but you're brilliant

I could visualize her warm smile.

Come over. I'll send a car.

They had an apartment in the city, but they both spent most of their time upstate, at their estate along the water.

She was one of only three people with whom I could be myself in all my glorious weirdness. Mom was my first confidant,

Mary Beth my second. And now, Sujit had made himself my third humraaz. At that moment, I made a quick decision.

> Can I bring a friend? I texted.

MARY BETH
> What friend? Boyfriend?

> A friend.

> Aarti Marie Bhatia, what are you hiding from me?

My middle name wasn't Marie. I didn't have a middle name, so Mary Beth had assigned me one to use in admonishment.

> I'll text you.

My heart bubbled with anticipation and excitement as I considered the idea of taking Sujit with me to see her. If Mary Beth approved of him, I would gain a level of confidence to assess the situation accordingly. The more I thought about it, the more excited I got.

For the next hour, I tried in vain to focus on the mountain of paperwork before me. It was a metaphor, of course, because we no longer used paper. Everything was digital, with backups of backups on server farms far, far away.

Before I could change my mind again, I pulled out my phone and typed, *Wanna come with me to see Mary Beth this weekend?*

Nah, too casual. I deleted it.

I'm thinking of visiting Mary Beth this weekend. Would you like to join me?

I stared at it for several seconds before deleting it. Too formal.

I was in the process of drafting another text when Sujit's call pulled down on the banner.

"Just say it," he said without preface.

"Say what?"

"I've been watching those three dots dancing for several minutes now."

"And may I ask what you were doing that you saw those three dots?" I asked with utmost curiosity.

"Waiting for your text," he said without missing a beat. Haazirjawab, he was. "Just tell me. You know you can tell me anything." It wasn't a question. It was a declaration.

"Alright," I said, "I'm going to visit my friend Mary Beth this weekend, and for some reason, I asked if I could bring a friend...."

I waited for a reaction, but he was smarter. I knew he was flashing his irresistible smile, and it irked me.

"So, would you like to join me?" I asked.

"With pleasure," he said. "I thought you'd never ask."

I rolled my eyes, and I heard him say, "You just rolled your eyes. Tell me I'm right."

"You're so wrong, you could never be wronger," I teased, and I heard his heartfelt laughter. "Are you done?"

"Yes," he said in a soft voice that rustled against my skin and made my insides tremble.

"I'll have the car service drive us," I said and penned down a reminder for myself in my planner.

"Don't," he replied in the same soft voice. "I'll drive us."

The element of romance in that statement, the thought of us driving along highways in the cold weather, the car, warm and toasty, probably soft rock playing in the background...

"Sorry, I have a meeting now, but send me the details—day, time—and I'll pick you up," he said when the silence drew out way too long.

"Better bring your best car," I jested.

"Always the best for you," he replied, and his soft voice was back in action.

"You don't mind accompanying me, do you? Truthfully?" I asked.

"Are you kidding?" he said, "How often does one get a chance to chat with Ezzie Strauss, one-on-one?"

I narrowed my eyes. "Does this mean your willingness to accompany me has nothing to do with me? It's all about meeting Ezzie?"

"Of course, it has absolutely nothing to do with you."

I could hear the smile in his words.

"Have you met him before?" I asked.

"We've been formally introduced on an occasion or two, but I doubt he remembers me."

"If he's met you, he remembers you, trust me," I said softly. Like I remembered him from our two-minute interaction in Dallas.

"Is that right?" he said in a deep, sexy voice that made me want to awaken the rebel in me, abandon all caution, and hurl myself at him.

"Off you go now," I said, "Take your meeting."

"Bye, sweet girl. See you soon."

SATURDAY EVENING, I sat across from Mary Beth, sipping wine. She had chosen a fine Bordeaux from their own vineyards in France while I savored the Château Cheval Blanc. The ride over had been exciting but less eventful than I had imagined. Sujit had remained concerned about the weather and the snowfall that was predicted in the evening.

Right now, he sat cozily with Ezzie across the spacious lounge as if they were old friends catching up. As I had prophesied, Ezzie did remember Sujit and was interested in learning about some new technology that was on the horizon and slated to make waves.

Mary Beth caught me stealing glances at him. I tried to ignore it, but I knew she had her gaze steady on me. When an inadvertent sigh escaped my lips, Mary Beth placed her glass down.

"Alright, out with it," she commanded in a private voice. There was little chance the men would hear us, but she was careful, and I appreciated it. "Do you like him?"

"I do, but I haven't decided if it's a good idea," I said, making peace with the fact that I couldn't hide much from Mary Beth.

I started my tale with the dramatic fact that he was Tara's ex. Her gasp was immediate and involuntary. I told her about our encounter and how it had blossomed over the past few weeks. When I finished telling her about my phone call with Aakash, she blew out a breath. If anyone knew about the gravity of family name and status, it would be the renegade daughter of one of the oldest and richest families in Dallas.

"I see Aakash's point," she said solemnly.

I sat upright. "You agree with him, then? Is it bad?"

She took a slow, thinking mouthful of the wine. "The optics? Most definitely," she said, glancing at the marvelously handsome man. "But it can't be healthy either, as Aakash rightly pointed out. If I were your therapist, I'd use a lot of jargon to explain that this is a textbook case of transference."

I shook my head resolutely. "It isn't. I refuse to believe that my feelings have anything to do with Sameer or Tara, and I don't need an expert to help me decode it."

She nodded in thought and glanced at Sujit again. "Let me ask you, is the attraction only physical? He's a gorgeous man."

"He *is* a gorgeous man," I affirmed.

"If it's physical attraction, that can be remedied easily. A few times with him and it will be out of your system," she advised with the worldly wisdom that was her forte.

"If only it were that easy," I said, letting out a gentle breath.

"Over the past few weeks, he's become a part of my life, a part of me, I'm afraid."

"That's dangerous."

"Don't I know it!" I looked into her stunning green eyes, gazing back at me with concern.

"Tell me how you feel," she insisted.

"I feel happy when I'm with him. It is the ease with which I can talk to him. I can be myself around him. Even when I need to cry, he lends me a shoulder without judgment."

Mary Beth nodded, looking into her glass of the ruby-red liquid.

"Then there's the situation with Dad, as Aakash so firmly warned me," I added.

"He'll be upset?"

I pulled in a deep breath. "I don't know if he'll be upset, or angry, or hurt."

"Parents usually are one of these," Mary Beth said with a chuckle. She had faced an uphill trek, if not a battle, to convince her parents about Ezzie. "But I think you're losing sight of the bigger picture."

"What's that?"

"Your happiness," she said matter-of-factly. "That takes precedence over everything else. You're also misreading another thing."

I raised my brows.

"That maybe your father's interference in your life comes from a place of love and concern, not authority and power. I've known him long enough to know how much he cares about you. I've also seen many a toxic parent in my lifetime, and I can assure you, your father isn't one."

"No, he isn't," I confirmed with conviction. "What does that mean?"

"It means whatever fears your brother communicated to you are *his* fears, not your father's. He said your father's legacy is at stake, but does your father feel that way? Will he be willing to put your happiness on the sacrificial altar to save his name and face?"

Dad had not cared about asking me before approaching some random family with a marriage proposal. Was it in a bid to find me happiness, or was he trying to dispose of me like a risky investment?

I shook off the thought. I knew my father. He had his faults, but the one thing I was always confident about was his irrefutable love for his family—for Ma, Aakash, and me. He called me his pride, and I had never taken it lightly. Neither had he.

"What are you thinking?" Mary Beth interrupted my deliberations.

I shook my head. "All this is futile, anyway. I don't think I can scour up the courage to tell Sujit how I feel."

"Why not?" she asked with a gentle frown.

"What if he doesn't feel the same way? We began on a note of friendship. Something to help us wade through the sea of heartache that was threatening to consume us both. What if he still sees me as a friend or, worse, a charity case? He's a good man, I won't be surprised if he's spending time with me because he thinks I need it, that I'm benefiting from it emotionally."

She extended her hand and covered mine. "Alright, take a breath and calm down. If you ask me, you are overthinking it. You've known him for just over a month, and you're considering life decisions? *Life-altering* decisions," she reminded gently.

I pulled myself out of the quagmire with a deep breath and a sip of the wine. "You're right. I don't even know if we'd be good together. I also don't want to make a decision that could end up hurting my father. Or worse, disappointing him. I am not going to make the same mistake I did with Sameer and jump into a relationship based on an attraction."

"Well..." she said and let her words trail.

"What?"

"I see how you look at him, and believe me when I say this. You never had the same look in your eye when you were with Sameer."

A gasp escaped my lips. "You mean to tell me this time I'm in trouble."

"Deep trouble, Battie. You've found yourself in deep, deep trouble, which makes this even more complicated. He is and will always be Tara's ex, sweetie."

We had polished off a bottle each and a staff member had miraculously appeared with another two and a set of fresh goblets.

"Thank you," I said as Mary Beth handed me a glass.

She picked up her glass and said, "It might be a terrible idea to pursue this, but I think you should still sleep with him. You need it, and I bet he's a fantastic lover."

"Mary Beth Arlington!" I reprimanded her teasingly. "Your very handsome husband is sitting right there, and you're ogling at other men, tsk tsk."

"I'm doing it as a favor for you," she argued with a wicked smile. "And it's Mary Beth Arlington-Strauss now."

"Precisely. Let us not forget that and check out other men," I teased, and we both burst into chuckles just as the two devilishly good-looking rogues approached us.

"I think we should leave," Sujit said. "It's starting to snow."

AARTI

The snowfall was mild, but I spotted a look of worry on Sujit's face.

"Is it the weather, or is it something else?"

He threw me a glance.

"I'm trying to figure out the reason for that frown," I explained.

"Ah!" he responded with a grin. "It's the weather. I'm trying to figure out if we might be able to make it to the city safely."

"What's the other option? I asked.

He hesitated and gave me another glance.

"What?"

"I'm trying to compute if a detour to my family's home might spare us the inconvenience of being stuck in a storm somewhere."

It was the first time I had heard about his family home.

"Do your parents live there?" I asked, wondering how comfortable he'd be taking me home to his family.

"No, it's empty. It's a vacation home that we use during the holidays and when we have out-of-town guests. Mostly, Cathy loves to plan and throw elaborate parties there."

Interesting, I mused.

"Tune in to the road advisory," he suggested and gave me the frequency for an AM channel.

Sujit's suspicion was spot on, probably based on his experience.

The advisory said a blizzard was set to cause whiteout conditions along the highway we were on. The projected snowfall was about two to three inches, it said.

"At least that's a silver lining," Sujit commented.

"What's a whiteout?" I asked.

"It's when the visibility is severely compromised," he explained and added, "Apologies, Aarti, but this calls for an executive decision, and I'm making one. I think it'd be best if we drove to my family home rather than risk being stranded somewhere."

I wouldn't mind being stranded anywhere with this man, but being adrift on a tropical island sounded better than risking a frozen death on the roads.

"I trust you, Sujit," I said like I had several times before.

"And I hope never to disappoint you," he added with a grim look as he took an exit and got on the off-ramp.

Driving effortlessly without any prompts from the navigation system, he pulled up in front of a giant house. It had snowed in the area a lot more than it had in the city, or so it looked. The driveway and the entrance were cleared out, but mounds of snow heaped all around the house.

"At least the property managers are taking care of the shoveling. I hope they have stocked the pantry after my last visit," he said as we drove around the house to the garage in the rear.

He accessed the garage with a pre-programmed button in his car, and the door lifted up.

"How often do you come here?" I asked.

"Whenever I need to get away from people," he said with a quick grin. "Sometimes being here helps me think."

He led me in through a side door attached to the temperature-controlled, four-car garage. We entered through a mud room to a large living area. It was dimly lit and a bit chillier than I expected. Maybe because I had shed my layers before sitting in the car, but Sujit commented as much.

"Darn, the temperature is set to vacation mode. I should have changed it on our way here."

When I returned a questioning look, he explained, "The heating and cooling is connected to an app on my phone."

"Of course it is," I said. "You techies have a compulsion to automate everything, don't you?"

"It's just convenient. Don't you love it when you can turn off the lights with a voice command?" he said, and stepped over to the windows. "It's not bad yet, but the visibility is decreasing. This was a good decision."

I stepped closer to him and peeked outside. The heap of snow beckoned me. Growing up in a region where it doesn't snow seemed to bestow it with a magical feel. Even when severe weather conditions brought snow to Dallas, it never stuck around. It melted away in a day or two. That winter wonderland feel of a soft snowfall had always evaded me, even when I had travelled to snow-capped regions.

"Can we step outside for a bit?" I asked, and he looked at me with a frown.

"It's biting cold."

"I just want to feel the snow on my face. We've got our coats, gloves, and hats in the car," I pleaded like a child. "Please?"

When he assented with a smile and a nod, I rushed to the garage and heaved back our winter clothing.

I had already pulled the front door open and was out while Sujit was still putting on his gloves and hat. The light snow drifting around in the mild breeze made for a great winter greeting card image.

"Damn, it is cold!" he said with his teeth chattering as he stepped out beside me.

It was, but I was enjoying it. Sujit stuck his hands in his coat pocket, waiting patiently while I soaked in the beauty around me. My body trembled slightly as I closed my eyes and put my hands out, allowing my senses to take in the soft snow drifting over me.

"Have you played in the snow before?" he asked.

"Once," I said with my eyes still closed.

Suddenly, something soft hit my arm. Taken by surprise, I looked at Sujit, who stood without his glasses, tossing a snowball in his hand.

"Did you just pelt me with a snowball?" I asked, my voice screeching with incredulity.

Sujit smirked. "I did." He tossed the ball in his hand again. "What are you going to do about it?" he asked in a challenge.

I gasped at the dare, then frowned at his audacity before digging both my hands into the mound to grab snow for a big ball.

"You just made a big mistake, mister," I said. "You forgot how much I hate to lose."

The gloves I had on weren't meant for snow play, and I could feel the cold seeping in. But I didn't care. I flung a hurriedly packed ball at him. With a weak thump, it hit his chest and disintegrated into powder against it.

"Is that the best you can do?" he teased, and I frowned more. He was pushing all the right buttons, and he knew it. "Let me show you how it's done," he said. "Catch!"

I did. The tightly packed, solid ball did not break in my hand.

"And that's how you make a snowball, sweet girl."

I hurled the ball back at him, but he ducked, and it landed in the snow, making a nice, deep crater.

"Well, well, Ms. Bhatia, looks like you are terrible at this," he said, adding fuel to the fire.

When I turned around to gather snow, a soft ball landed on my back while a firmer one smacked my butt with some force. I jumped with a squeal.

"Oh, you're in trouble, Sujit Rao. You want war? You got war," I announced with misplaced confidence.

"Let me see it," he said and tossed the ball in his hand.

The reason behind his arrogant smirk was the three snowballs that lay at his feet, ready to be launched into an assault as needed. In the time it had taken for me to gather enough snow to make one, he had made four, including the one in his hand currently. With quick calculations, I realized that this was his game, and I couldn't beat him at it. But nowhere in the snow-pelting war manual did it say that I couldn't change the rules.

Or the game itself.

Shunting off the lousy ball in my hand, I sprinted toward him. Before he could react, he was on his back in the snow with me on top of him.

Hmm, maybe I hadn't thought it through enough.

I lay on him, pelvis-to-pelvis, stomach-to-stomach. Our chests were separated by the sheer strength of my core muscles because there was nothing I could use to lift myself up. The snow gathered around us, sinking us deeper into it.

"You think that's going to deter me?" he said softly. This kind of proximity to him was disorienting.

Lost in the depth of those warm eyes without the glasses, I failed to notice that his arms at my side were moving. Before I knew it, I felt a cold trickle on my neck. The villain had put snow on the exposed part of the neck. I shrieked, squirmed, and shifted, but he was quicker. Locking me between his thighs, he pulled his arms around me and flipped us over. I lay under him, with my back buried against the snow.

Fuck! If he could do that in the snow, I didn't even want to imagine what he could do if we found ourselves in bed together.

He pulled himself up on his knees, his legs holding me tight. His fingers swiftly came around my wrists to pin me down completely.

"You were saying..." He smirked, but I had forgotten how to breathe.

The world froze into stillness. I lay under his spell, mesmerized by his beauty, captivated by the dent in his cheeks as he teased me. My body was turning numb from the cold, but I felt his warmth against the heat rising below my belly.

The wind had picked up, casting the loose snow flying all around us. The world seemed to fade away, and it was just me and him. No judgmental eyes, no heartache, no exes. Just Sujit and me wrapped in a warm blanket of mutual admiration and love.

Love! The thought reverberated through my body. Was I falling in love with him?

"Let me up," I pleaded softly as his eyes pierced into mine.

Quick as a flash, he jumped from his position and offered me his hand. I grabbed it eagerly, and he pulled me up.

"Let's go inside. You are shivering," he said.

I was trembling, but it was no longer the effect of the snow and the cold. My shivers stemmed from the thought that I had lost myself—heart and soul—to this man.

We shed our outer covers in the foyer, and I realized that my clothes were damp.

"Sujit, I don't have anything to change into."

"I keep extra clothes here. You can use my warm sweats."

Quivering in my skin, I followed him as he led me to the second floor and into the first room along a long corridor.

"This is me," he said. "I suggest taking a warm shower."

I nodded.

"Don't put your hands in hot water first," he warned. "Let them warm up in tap water before turning up the heat."

"Okay."

It felt surreal to take orders, however well-intentioned, from him. I had always been the one to give orders, and I had wielded that right with responsibility and pride. It was unsettling that not only did he care about me this way and knew how to show it, but also that I had little reservations about following his instructions. I had repeatedly said I trusted him, but when had I entrusted myself to him completely in this way?

It was a freedom akin to peeling away the layers of uncomfortable clothing from one's body, like I was doing right now. I turned the shower knob to cold and let the water run on my extremities while diligently protecting the rest from the chilly blast. When I could feel my fingers and toes again, I gradually turned up the temperature and stayed under the shower until the bathroom fogged up.

Wrapping myself in a generous towel, I found a hair dryer, a fresh toothbrush, and body lotion, and got to work.

Back in the room, I looked through a neatly kept closet and found several sets of sweatpants and warm sweatshirts. I also found some formal clothes and a bottle of cologne. I sneaked a quick sniff of the scent and got a heady rush from the memories of his smell. Then my prefrontal cortex took over, and Aakash's words rang in my ears.

My phone dinged with a text at the exact moment. Slipping the cologne back in the closet, I stepped over to the bed where I had dropped it to find Mary Beth asking if we had made it home safely.

I texted her back.

> We took a detour to his family home and will be here until the visibility improves.

MARY BETH

He took you to his family? Isn't that something you both have been trying to avoid?

Not family. Family home. No one lives here.

So you both are alone together on a stormy night?

Yes, but before you suggest it, nothing is going to happen.

You're so boring. Make it happen.

No

I pressed send, locked the phone, and started toward the stairs. What I saw when I reached the landing made me stop in my tracks.

Sujit was at the fireplace, without a shirt, trying to kindle a fire. The light from the hearth reflected off his strong torso. His toned biceps curved as he poked the wood. He wasn't as sculpted as I had imagined when I felt his arm around me. His lines were gentle rather than harsh, their shape more inviting than intimidating. The low-rise pants sat at the hips, and when he stood upright, I caught a glimpse of his tight abs and smooth muscles defining the V.

My nipples wrinkled promptly and turned to stone, the heat in my core sending a jolt up my body. I stood motionless, my mouth dry, my hands cold, with goosebumps covering every element of mine. If I was attracted to him before, right now I stood devastated.

An easy remedy would be to sleep with him and get him out of my system, like Mary Beth had suggested. But Sujit Rao wasn't someone you wanted out of your system. He was someone you wanted buzzing in your nerves, rushing through your veins. He was someone you wanted to lose yourself in.

I wished for us to meld until the boundaries between our bodies disappeared. I wanted to languish in his admiration. I yearned to cherish him, dote on him, spoil him, relish him.

I wanted to be consumed by Sujit, and it was the opposite of getting him out of my system.

SUJIT

I was trying to get the fire going when Aarti came down wearing my sweats. She was only a few inches shorter than me, but her thin frame made the sweats look baggy and over-sized in a way that tugged at my heart. She was wearing my clothes. *My* clothes.

The poker in my hand stilled as I checked her out with greed in my eyes.

It was only when she said, "Hey, looks like you took a shower too," that I realized I stood shirtless before this goddess of a woman.

Clearing my throat, I placed the poker back in its spot and grabbed a T-shirt from the arm of the large leather recliner beside me.

"Are you hungry?" I asked to distract myself from the fiery attraction I was trying to fend off. "I can make some pasta if you want."

"Nah, that's too much trouble. What else do you have in the pantry?"

"Let's check," I said, and she followed me to the kitchen.

I had already watched her studying the artwork on the walls and the accent sculptures on the strategically placed pedestals. I wondered it she remembered it was Tara who had meticulously chosen each piece adorning this home.

When I had suggested driving here, it hadn't occurred to me that the last time I was here with someone else was when I had thrown Tara a surprise birthday party. We broke up that night. Yet, being here with Aarti didn't seem to garner any of the bitter memories I had carried for months. *Au contraire*, I felt happy. Blissful. Completely content.

I browsed the walk-in pantry as she peeked at the world outside through the windows.

"We have canned beans, grains, lentils, nut butters, and jellies of different kinds, a variety of crackers..." I listed, scanning the shelves. "Then, of course, there are my favorite ramen noodle cups."

"Ramen sounds good. Let me make them," she offered.

I gave her a smile as I grabbed two cups from the top shelf. "That's alright, sweet girl. I've got this."

"I don't want to be a burden," she argued.

"Yes, Aarti, you're a terrible burden. I have to use the faucet to pour water into a kettle, then press the switch to the on-position, wait for it to come to a boil, pour it in a cup, *then* hand it over to you. I wonder how you're going to live with yourself after putting me through this kind of toil," I teased.

"Alright, alright, smartass," she said and climbed onto the bar stool at the island.

When the ramen cups were ready, we carried them to the living room to sit by the fire. The home was still heating up, but it was massive and was bound to take a while. I started on my noodles while Aarti pushed her fork around the cup, poking the desiccated vegetables into the soup.

"This was my go-to meal during college, big surprise," I said.

"I always ate at the cafeteria. Never got into the habit of eating instant noodles."

I nodded. "It shows."

"How's that?" She raised her brows in question.

"If you wait too long, the noodles are going to get all soggy and unpleasant."

"But the vegetables are not plump yet.

"They won't get plump, but they are rehydrated by now, trust me."

She rolled the noodles on her fork and put it in her mouth like she was eating a gourmet dish at a Michelin-star restaurant.

"Slurp them. They are supposed to be soup noodles," I said, demonstrating how to do it.

She tried, and the soup flew all over her face. I burst out laughing, and grabbing a tissue from a box nearby, brought it to her lips.

It started out innocuous. I only meant to wipe the liquid splattered on her face. But the heat it turned up became palpable in a single beat. My eyes stilled over her lips, the tissue halting at the corner of her mouth. I heard her breath suspend as I studied the shape of her lips, the small beauty mark on her cheek that I had surprisingly never noticed before. I grazed it with the gentlest touch and felt a shiver run over her body.

"This is so beautiful," I whispered. "How come I've never seen it before?"

She didn't respond but her breath turned erratic. I wanted to lean in and kiss those lips that seemed to have been carved by Michelangelo. After my unfortunate attempt at snow play that ended up with me straddling her, my loins burned with desire. But her words echoed in my ears, *I trust you, Sujit*. I wasn't going to shatter that trust to pieces. My eyes met hers, and I quickly dabbed her face and crumpled the tissue. Sliding away from her, I resumed working on my noodles in silence.

"I hide it with concealer and foundation," I heard her say and looked up. She pointed to her beauty mark. "Someone once commented on it, and I've been hiding it ever since."

"You shouldn't hide it. I think it's beautiful," I said with my eyes on my noodle cup.

When we were done, we chatted about work. I asked her if she had settled in, if she liked living amid the bustle of the city, how she was coping with the cold and the snow, and if she had changed her mind about having my personal chef cook for her. When an expected yawn escaped her tired body, I suggested heading to bed.

"But the fire is too enticing," she groaned. "What if we camp out here instead? I'm too cozy to move anywhere else right now."

I wasn't about to deny her that. "Alright," I said and got up to put away our cups.

"Let me do that," she offered. "Why don't you grab us some comforters?"

While she was in the kitchen, I spread a plush king-size duvet on the rug by the fire, placed two pillows on top, then set up two individual comforters to use as covers.

She returned with two glasses of water and offered me one. I drank like the thirsty man that I was. Drinking half from her glass, she placed it on the side table.

When she slipped under the comforter closer to the fire, I turned off the lights. Laying down next to her, I pulled the warm cover over me.

"This is a beautiful home," she remarked.

"Thank you. I love it here. It's like a little haven of quiet when I need a moment to myself."

"And the choice of artwork is excellent!"

"Yes, Tara did a great job," I said matter-of-factly.

"I'm sorry, Sujit. I didn't mean to...I mean, I didn't remember..."

"Sorry about what?" I turned to her with a gentle frown. "I don't regret it at all."

"None of it?" she asked in a tentative voice.

"None of it," I confirmed with a heart that was at peace. "I love these paintings."

There was a long pause before she asked, as I knew she would, "Don't they remind you of her?"

I was ready with the response. "Not in the way the world thinks. After Tara, my family has been asking me to get rid of them and redo the place."

"How do you think the world sees it?" she asked with curiosity.

"Like they bring me heartache and sorrow."

She was on her side now, facing me, with an arm under her head. "And they don't?"

"Not in the least. To tie Tara to these paintings is to do a big disservice to the talented artists who put their heart and soul into them. I might not understand art, but I do know that looking at these makes me happy. Isn't that the purpose of bringing art into your life?"

"You are..." her voice trailed.

"A hopeless romantic?" I grinned. "I think someone has called me that before."

"Allow me to amend that sentence. You are a hopeful romantic, and don't you ever change."

When Tara broke up with me, I had asked her to tell me something she hated about me. One thing that irked her. She had no answer because she only saw my virtues, not my limitations. If Aarti were to stay in my life, I wanted her to see me in my entirety, complete with my drawbacks.

"When Tara's mother was here," I began, "we kind of formed

a friendship of our own. Tara was in Dallas, and I promised to look in on her mother, even though Tara hadn't expected or demanded it. When we broke up, Tara's mother called me and told me how sorry she was, that it was perhaps her fault that Tara went back to Sameer."

Aarti's eyes shone with curiosity. This was a side of the story she had never heard. No one else knew this.

"How so?" Aarti asked.

"Aai told me how free and happy Tara looked when she was with Sameer. With me, she seemed restrained, like she respected me, but something was amiss. When Tara came clean to her, Aai urged her to consider giving Sameer another chance."

"She told you all this?"

"At least that's what I gathered. Aai spoke in broken English, and I understand none of the three languages she speaks. She said she respected me too much to see me hurt and couldn't leave the country without asking for my forgiveness."

Aarti listened with rapt attention.

"I told Aai she never needed to apologize because she was my friend. And I still call her Aai. That's mother in Marathi," I said in a soft voice, trying to gauge Aarti's reaction.

The problem was she gave me none. I don't know what I had expected when I shared this with her, but she merely blinked as she listened.

"We check up on each other on WhatsApp, and she told me she's taking English lessons back home, so the next time she's here, we can have a proper conversation."

"Why are you telling me this?" Aarti finally asked.

I pulled in a soft breath. "You said you trusted me, and I want you to know everything about me. This is who I am. This is how I think and feel."

She lay completely motionless for several moments before she asked, "Can I give you a hug?"

"Do you feel sorry for me?" I asked with some offense.

"No," she responded with a smile. "I feel incredibly proud to know you."

That wasn't the reaction I was expecting. "And you are not upset?"

"Why would that upset me?"

"I feel like we've become close confidants, and I don't want you to feel like I've been betraying your trust by hiding my friendship with Tara's mother and her friend."

She let out a giggle, the one that I cherished. "You are silly, you know? There aren't many men I know who have such a healthy view of relationships. I am grateful to know you, to have your trust, and to know that I can trust you."

A sense of peace enveloped me. "In that case, come here." I opened my arms, and she slipped into them. When I placed a kiss on her forehead, she snuggled in closer.

"Why does this feel so comfortable, Sujit?" She now lay with her head on my arm. She had slipped out of her comforter and under mine. I readjusted to accommodate her in it.

"Maybe because we can just be ourselves with each other. We don't need masks or excuses." I sighed. "Relationships are peculiar. Look how close we have come in this short time. But I can't explain it to my family, just as I can't explain my friendship with Tara's mother or her friend, Sona, who is still a good friend. Like your brother, I'm sure my family will throw all kinds of advice and words of caution at me."

And this was the moment I wanted her to dispel all fears and tell me that she didn't care about the world or what my family thought of our relationship. Perhaps even admit that she liked me enough to fight against the world.

She didn't, but it didn't crush me. Being with her, having her in my arms, however briefly, felt like a privilege. An undeserving mortal like me shouldn't expect a goddess to stay in my arms forever, but I was elated that at least I had her in my life for now.

I placed another kiss on her forehead and released a satisfied sigh. "You know, I've not felt this relaxed in a long time. I might not have my day at the beach anytime soon, but a snowy day in feels just as good," I said with a chuckle against her ear.

AARTI

*I*t was the little things, as my mother had observed several times. Love and care were epitomized in the most mundane actions of routine life.

But I didn't do *little*. I couldn't. It wasn't in my nature.

Lying in his arms by the fire, I decided I would give him his day at the beach. I was determined to fight against destiny, against him, to give him the happiness that no one else would. I wanted the smiles that were exclusively for me. I resolved to make him happy the way he brought me joy.

It was easier said than done, though, because I couldn't access my wealth. Not without my family finding out about it. I couldn't request a charter plane through my office, nor put any big expense without raising suspicions. By snitching on me to my brother, the world had effectively stemmed my resources. Thankfully, I was friends with one of the country's most powerful couples.

I texted Mary Beth. They had properties all over the Caribbean.

Without any questions, she texted back.

MARY BETH

I'd recommend St. Martin. I'll arrange for the smaller jet, and you can use the château. The staff resides on the property. They'll have everything ready for you.

I had an unabashed demand.

I was thinking something cozier.

There's a beach house closer to the sea, which Ezzie and I use when we travel alone.

I can't thank you enough.

Since when do you need to thank me?

♥

I still think you should sleep with him. This obsession with him is clearly getting out of hand.

That week, I had another important matter to settle. After my visit to Ms. Dina's, I had contacted Walter and we had finally fleshed out the details. Using a subsidiary of our company, I bought the diner from Walter. Ms. Dina would never again feel threatened about losing her cherished place, and Sujit would never lose his sanctuary. I requested Walter to keep this information from both Ms. Dina and Sujit because they really didn't need to know.

Sujit had talked about selfless love that day, and he was right. Doing something good for someone wasn't selfless, for it brought immense joy, satisfaction, pride, or whatever else we were hoping for. I had decided that once I had enough money of my own, I would buy the diner and transfer it to Ms. Dina's name. It was not possible for me at the moment, with Dad holding all of the executive power, and he wouldn't be amenable to helping if he knew Sujit was somehow a part of my calculations. For now, I did have the power to protect her lease.

On Friday morning, I sent Sujit a text.

> How much do you trust me?

SUJIT
Enough

> Enough to let me take over your weekend?

Definitely that much.

> Do you have anything planned for the weekend that can't be rescheduled?

There's nothing that can't be rescheduled for you.

And yet, our connection needed to be kept hidden, an embarrassment we couldn't share with the world. A dash of anger coursed through me as I typed.

> Pack a bag and be ready at 5.

Any hints on what to pack? Tux or Tees?

I smiled. Even when I was feeling the worst, he could always make me smile.

Tees and shorts. Don't forget the swimming trunks. A rash guard if you're averse to showing off your body.

Think turquoise waters.

Mauritius, Maldives, Maui, or the Mediterranean?

It's a weekend getaway, so none of the above. Keep guessing.

Sorry I have to go now. Roy is waiting on the line for me.

Am I supposed to know this Roy?

You should. He's a senator.

Are you allowed to address a senator by his first name?

You are when he's your buddy from college.

All right, big shot. Carry on. I guess if a senator is calling, it has to be more important than chatting with a girl you just met.

I hit send and immediately regretted it. I considered trying to unsend the message—thank you, technology—but I knew he'd already seen it. I saw the three dots and waited for his response with a thumping heart.

Right now, nothing is more important than you, sweet girl. But it is impolite to keep a senator waiting. He's calling about a new legislation on accessible education.

> That does seem more important. I'll let you
> go, then. Go do some good, this shitty world
> needs it.

I typed, pressed the send arrow, and sighed. If anyone deserved happiness, it was Sujit. I was glad I was trying to give him a bit of it, at least.

~

I WAS at his door exactly at five, wearing linen pants and a flowy blouse. "Are you ready?"

He lifted his holdall. "As ordered."

"Good boy," I said and winked.

"You aren't kidnapping me, are you?" he teased while punching in the numeric code to lock the door.

"Maybe. How much do you think your fam will pay for you?" I replied, leading the way to the elevator bank.

"Depends on who you send the ransom note to. If you send it to my parents, they will probably head straight to the police station. If it's my brother, he'll try to negotiate the numbers with you. Your best bet would be Cathy. She'll bankrupt herself to get me back."

"She loves you that much, eh?" I asked with a crooked smile while the elevator doors opened for us.

"Yes, but you don't want to mess with her. There's a distinct possibility she'll find you and ruin you after she gets me back."

That made me laugh aloud. It reminded me of Dad, who'd probably do the exact same thing. No wonder those two were so hurt and offended for us.

"You know, when I saw you at the bar that first night, I would've never guessed how funny you are," I said. "There aren't many people who can genuinely make me laugh. And you do it with such a straight face, one wouldn't know you're joking."

"I wasn't," he said as the elevator doors opened again and we walked out to the car waiting for us. "Cathy has the potential to do everything I just said, and more."

When we arrived at the hangar, the private jet was ready for us. An attendant took our luggage off the driver's hands and carried it on board.

"Wow, Devi wasn't kidding when she said you're an empire!" Sujit said as we climbed on. "Is this your company's jet?"

"No, Dad's very practical that way. He just rents when he needs one," I said as I buckled my seat belt. "Plus, I couldn't tell my family about this, not after that showdown with my brother."

He raised his brows in question.

"This is all Mary Beth. I am officially taking advantage of my friendship with her," I explained with a sly chuckle.

"Wow, I am on board Ezzie Strauss's private jet."

"Probably," I said, looking around at the exquisite furnishing of the aircraft. "Well, actually, definitely his personal one. Mary Beth would make sure I whisked you away in the best way possible," I blurted without thinking. It had been a long day.

He gifted me a wide smile.

"I hope you are impressed. Let the records show that I'm whisking you away in style."

"Well, you've definitely done that. Impress me, that is," he said, and I looked away to hide the flush in my cheeks.

Sujit was asleep a few minutes after take-off but I wasn't that fortunate. Pulling out my laptop, I looked at the documents the office had sent me. It included proposals for several new properties in Brooklyn and upscale Queens. The office had sent me the numbers and their recommendations, and Dad was counting on me to make the final decision. I remained buried deep in the numbers until the captain announced that we were ready for descent.

It had taken us just under four hours to get to St. Martin. It promised radiant waters and pristine beaches, but we'd have to wait until morning to experience the beauty. A car awaited us and soon we were on the way. I powered down the window slightly to enjoy the gentle roar of the waves as we drove along.

The staff was at the beach house, awaiting our arrival. It was huge, with three large bedrooms and a spacious open lounging area. I directed the man escorting us to put my bags in one of the bedrooms facing the ocean and Sujit's in the adjoining one. After making sure we had everything we needed, they drove off in golf carts toward the château to bring us dinner.

When I strolled into the lounge, I caught Sujit looking out at the dark sea with a gentle ripple of a smile across his lips.

"That smile is the exact reason I've brought you here," I said, flopping on a sturdy cane couch with plush cushions. "It's perfect, isn't it?"

"It is paradise," he said.

He came around the couch and sat on a chaise facing me, then slipped out of his shoes and socks and into the slippers that were kept ready for us.

My gaze inadvertently darted toward his bare feet. I didn't remember seeing him barefoot before. He always wore socks with his house shoes, and even at his family home, he wore socks with his clogs. The sight of those runner's feet, the long, shapely toes trimmed and cared for professionally, awakened a primal instinct inside me. I found myself dreaming about those feet against my bare skin. Those toes slipping up my naked calf, my exposed thigh, up my waist....

"Maybe I'll freshen up before dinner," I said and vanished into the bedroom.

He simply nodded and got back up to walk to the window and continue gazing out at the sea.

I heard the faint clink of silverware outside. The staff was already setting the table. I quickly changed into a linen dress and refreshed my perfume.

To keep my mind off my proximity to Sujit, I focused on the delicious food prepared meticulously by the staff. But I could keep neither my mind nor my eye off his magnificent face as he savored the glazed salmon with rice and roasted vegetables. When he suddenly looked up at me from over the rim of his glasses, I looked away.

"Everything is perfect, Aarti. Thank you for giving me my day at the beach. I hope there is a hammock."

"There is. Right on the soft sand by the water." I felt a sense of pride and joy coursing through me.

When the staff cleared up and left, we settled by the windows with a gentle breeze drifting in. I had offered him a scotch from Mary Beth's excellent selection, but he stepped over to her wine collection instead. Curious, I walked over and stood beside him. The walk-in cellar had a fridge in one corner, and I found Sujit standing before it. If the beach house had this kind of collection, I wondered how big of a wine cellar the château had and how many wines it housed.

Sujit picked up two bottles, one in each hand, studying them as if he were trying to solve a major mathematical conundrum. For me, the solution was simple. One was red, one white. There was no decision to be made. I watched him with fascination, wondering why he was considering the options. I peeked over his shoulder to see the labels. One was a Tawny Port, the other a Moscato d'Asti. Both were too sweet for my taste. I preferred a light Reisling or an elegant Gewürztraminer, but I reserved my opinion.

Sujit eyed me, trying to read my expressions. I only returned a smile. He put the Port back in its spot and pulled out another white from the refrigerator. A Passito this time.

"Now?" he asked, and a hearty chuckle emanated from my throat, accompanied by a fear that caused my heart to thud.

He could read my feelings just from the smile on my face. Why couldn't I have met this man sooner? Before the whole debacle that seemed to have defined my current existence. Before we became tagged with the memories of our exes. It would have been so simple.

I pointed to the effervescent Moscato d'Asti. He nodded and put the amber Passito back.

I let out a silent sigh just as a knock sounded at the door.

"Ah, it's here," Sujit said and started toward the door.

AARTI

*W*hen I reached the lounge, a staff member stood outside with a covered platter.

Sujit spoke to him in French. He stepped inside, placed the platter on the small round table by the windows, and stepped over to the glassware cabinet. He returned with two white wine glasses and two small plates. As he placed dessert spoons next to the plates on the table, I stood beside Sujit, wondering when he had the chance to arrange for it all.

The man uncorked the bottle and asked Sujit if we wanted him to pour us the wine. At least, that's what I inferred. I didn't understand French.

Finally, after Sujit had offered an elegant *merci*—in a way that made me wet to my core—the staff member retreated and closed the door behind him.

We were now alone with a chilled bottle of wine and a mysterious platter covered with an opaque dome.

"The suspense is killing me," I said as Sujit eyed me with a triumphant grin.

Pulling out a chair for me, he waited until I was settled, then lifted the cover with a dramatic flair.

On the platter stood two perfect, hearty squares of tiramisu. My heart stopped beating, and my breath jumbled. I blinked at the dessert but could muster no words to emerge out of my mouth.

In my moments of vulnerability, I had shared much with Sujit, but I hadn't expected him to remember anything. Only, he remembered it all. *A well-made tiramisu*, I had said. This certainly looked and smelled like one.

Using the pie server that lay next to the platter, he placed one square on the plate before me. The choice of the sweet wine made sense now. I watched him pour the wine to the perfect quantity in my glass.

"You said you like a well-made tiramisu," he said, creating ripples in my being again. "Tell me if this is up to your standards," he added, nudging me to taste it.

Everything you do is up to my standards, I was tempted to blurt. Promptly, I picked up the spoon and stuffed a generous portion in my mouth to prevent myself from saying anything other than to comment on the dessert.

It was perfect. "This is a well-made tiramisu," I announced with a happy grin.

He exhaled. "Good," he said, then settled in the chair across the table. He served himself the other portion and poured the wine.

"The wine is excellent, as well," I commented.

He took a sip and nodded approvingly. "I can't take the credit, though," he confessed. "I asked my sommelier for recommendations."

"You have a sommelier?" I cried, and he gave me a sheepish look like he was embarrassed.

It was so easy to forget that this man was a literal billionaire with the world at his beck and call.

"Doesn't everyone?" he joked.

"I need their number," I teased back.

"You have me. Everything I have is at your disposal, including my sommelier," he said with his eyes on the tiramisu.

There it was again, that thud in my head, in my heart, pumping through my blood and creating the same cognitive dissonance in my being. I knew I could not have this man, but he was the only one I wanted.

"This is the best surprise I've ever gotten," I said as I watched him enjoy the tiramisu.

His mouth lifted at one corner. "Are you sure?"

I frowned. "What else have you got planned, you sneaky man?"

"Hey, you got Rampur for me. That was sneaky. This is merely a result of good memory."

"You know, if you want to remain in my good graces," I said, polishing off the last of the cream on my plate, "you better let me have the last word now and again."

That made him burst into laughter. "I think you'll be inclined to forgive me after you see the gift I got you."

"Gift?" My eyes widened, then I narrowed them at him. "What kind of gift?"

It was so liberating to be able to joke with him this way. I couldn't imagine doing it with anyone else. I never expected or demanded gifts from Sameer. Even when he did bring me gifts, I hadn't felt the same surge of excitement that was coursing through me currently.

"The kind of gift that I hope makes you happy," he said. "Just like you made me happy by gifting me this weekend."

I turned my gaze away to avoid looking into his eyes. I needed to focus on something else. I saw that he hadn't touched the wine much.

"Let me pour you a scotch," I offered.

He read my thoughts and said, "I'm alright, sweet girl. This combination is perfect."

When we were done, he disappeared into his room and returned with my gift.

Covered in wrapping that resembled an old newspaper, the three items in his hand looked like books.

"What's this?" My eyes were as wide as my smile when he held them out to me.

"Open them."

I tore the paper from the first one and read the title. "*Pinjar* by Amrita Pritam."

"The original is in Punjabi, so I got you the translated version."

I gawked at him, speechless.

"Not what you'd expected?" he asked.

"Not even close!" I said in a soft voice. "Better than I could've ever expected."

"Again, I'm not going to claim any credit. I asked Jas. She's an avid reader of Indian literature. Are you familiar with the book?"

"Of course! You don't grow up in a Punjabi household and not know about Amrita Pritam."

"What does it mean?"

"Pinjar? It means skeleton. A shell. A remnant of one's self. It represents the country at the time of partition, bloodied by communal riots, and women whose honor was linked to the nation. Women became symbols of the nation, and just like the land at the time, murdered and bloodied on both sides."

He wore a look of shock as he sat stupefied. "Perhaps this wasn't the best gift," he confessed tentatively.

"Are you kidding! This is the best gift anyone could have ever given."

Only someone who knew me would think of giving me this. The thought brought a fresh wave of anguish running through me.

"Why don't you open the next one?" he nudged.

My excitement was now approaching its peak. Picking up the slightly thinner of the two, I tore away at the wrapping paper as I chirped, "I wonder what gem is inside this one."

The sight of the book made me jump off my spot on the couch and on to his body. With my arms draped around his neck, I placed a firm kiss on his cheek. I leapt at him so eagerly, his hands came around my waist to prevent him from getting knocked over. Embarrassed, I retook my spot on the couch.

"A collection of Maya Angelou's Poems! How did you know?" I asked.

He smiled in response. "I had a feeling you liked poetry."

"Oh, Sujit!" I said and gave him another quick hug. My eyes were now on the last book.

"What about this one?" I was like a kid at Christmas.

Although, in my family, the kids got gifts on Diwali, not Christmas. Christmas was when we gifted others and when Mary Beth and I exchanged gifts. My heart bubbled with joy.

"Open it," he urged.

My heart was in my mouth as I ripped the cover with wild enthusiasm, and a familiar book greeted me.

"*A Thousand Splendid Suns*! This is one of my favorites. I will cherish this all my life," I squealed like a child, hugging the book to my chest.

"That you will. Turn to the title page."

"What!" I cried preemptively. "No way!"

"Indeed. It's signed by Hosseini."

I quickly opened it and saw the inscription. "Not just signed, it's personalized! It says, *For Aarti*! When did you get this? Do you know him? How do you know him?"

"A gentleman never reveals his secrets," he said with a smirk, and I allowed him the preening.

My eyes were on the verge of moistening, but I turned those emotions into a wide smile and looked away.

"Oh, Sujit! How could I ever thank you for this? Nothing I do or say will ever be adequate."

"You don't need to thank me, sweet girl. And this is only half your gift."

My body perked up. "Where's the other half?"

In response, he shifted to one end of the couch and propped a cushion in his lap.

"Here," he said, patting the cushion. "I'm going to read to you."

A gasp escaped my mouth, and I covered it with my hands. Not only had he appreciated what I had shared with him when I had been an emotional wreck, but he had worked hard to fulfill these small desires of mine. I sat speechless and motionless.

"You don't want it?" he teased. "Alright..." he sighed dramatically and began removing the pillow from his lap.

"Don't you dare move," I said and placed the book of Maya Angelou's poems in his hand.

"I had a feeling you'd choose that one," he bragged and flipped the pages to a poem I had committed to memory during my college days.

"Pretty women wonder where my secret lies..." he began a slow and emotional rendering of *Phenomenal Woman* as if he had practiced reciting it. I reclined, enjoying the beautiful words out of his graceful mouth while he stroked my hair like Mom used to, and all I could do was struggle to hold back my tears.

"'Cause I'm a woman...Phenomenally. Phenomenal woman...

That's me," he ended softly. "Phenomenal Woman, that's you," he whispered to me.

I kept gazing at his handsome face. I knew I could no longer hold back my feelings.

Where we stood looked like crossroads, and we had been forever looking for the right path forward.

I turned over in his lap to face away from him. "Read me one more," I said.

I heard him flip the pages. "*Still Rise*," he read. "You may write me down in history..." He continued to stroke my hair as he read. "...I rise I rise I rise."

Tears were already flowing down the side of my face into the cushion, and he asked, "One more?"

I had no way of responding without making him privy to my tears. Sujit made me feel like I needed nothing else in life anymore. He made me feel cherished and worthy of love again. And he continued to remain out of reach.

The books that lay near me were no ordinary gifts. They were chosen to give me the kind of happiness I desired. Not the kind people thought I wanted. No one except Mom had given me that.

But I wasn't my mother's daughter alone. I was also my father's daughter. Aakash's words resounded in my ears. It was one thing to find solace and companionship in him, but losing myself to Sujit like this was unwise. Especially when I didn't have a way to know if he felt the same. And even if he did, hadn't he said that he couldn't explain our relationship to his family?

Aakash was right. Our relationship would remain mired in shame and embarrassment. The sooner I made peace with the fact that love wasn't written in my destiny, the easier my life would be.

My phone whirred on the table and I wiped my tears to check the banner. Manoj's name flashed on the screen, and I promptly sent it to voicemail. The look on Sujit's face said he'd also seen the caller's name.

"This is the third time he's called me this week," I said, getting off his lap and fixing my hair.

He slammed the book shut as a look passed over his face, one that I couldn't decipher.

"We met over coffee to discuss business. He said he's looking for a place for his new office. I don't usually take such meetings, but I was curious because he mentioned you."

"Me?"

"Yes, at first he pretended to ask me out—" I began.

"He wasn't pretending."

I gaped at Sujit. Clearly, he knew Manoj better than I thought he did.

"I told him I don't date people I do business with, and that's when he changed his tune. He said he was looking for a space, and I quote, *similar to what Sujit wants for his new project.*"

Sujit sat quietly in thought for a moment, and when he finally broke his silence, his voice was tentative. "And did you confirm it?"

I scoffed. "What do you think? I wasn't born yesterday, Sujit. I've been in the business world for almost a decade. I know what is what when I see it. How well do you know him?"

"Well enough," he said with a determined face.

"Is he dangerous?"

"Stalker and killer-type dangerous? No," Sujit said and confirmed the rest for me. Manoj was dangerous in other ways. Nefarious ways.

"I can't imagine how you and he could be friends."

"We aren't anymore, but it's a long story. Some other time, sweet girl." This time, the epithet didn't carry its usual warmth. This time, it sounded like a command. "Tell me what else he has been asking you."

This avatar of Sujit was one I hadn't seen before. That of a fierce, protective warrior. A determined, powerful man who knew what destruction he could rain down.

"He hasn't been talking about business, for sure. He seemed more interested in my personal life. Asked me a lot of intrusive questions in his beguiling, charming way. It creeped me out enough to make the hair on my neck stand up. After I'd deflected every one of his questions, he asked me out again. It's like he is obsessed with me," I said, and Sujit opened his mouth to say something, then changed his mind.

"Don't worry about him," he said cryptically.

SUJIT

aking up early the next morning, I watched the rising sun cast a gentle glow on the darkened waters. As I stood drinking in the beauty of the dawn, I wondered why I had been so secretive about my association with Aarti. Was it for her benefit alone? To save her the embarrassment of being associated with Tara's ex? Or was there a part of me that was worried about it too?

Aarti had become a big part of my life these past weeks, yet I had diligently concealed our association. On the several occasions that she had been in my office, I had always addressed her as Ms. Bhatia, especially when Devi was around. Was I worried that she would tell Cathy if she knew?

This was the reason I didn't take vacations. When my mind wasn't focused on work, it tended to meander in unwarranted directions. Instead of focusing on the what-ifs and the maybes, I should be working to hold on to the one thing that I was absolutely certain of. I liked Aarti. She made me happy. Who else would care enough and have the courage to steal me away from the world to give me a day at the beach? No one but Aarti.

I pushed the large glass French windows open, and a gentle breeze drifted in. St. Martin was windy on its best day, but right now, an easy gust flirted with the calm sea. Inside, the sheer white linen curtains blew in gentle notes.

"Looks like a lovely mornin'." Aarti emerged from her room, glided toward the breakfast table, and began pouring herself some coffee.

"This has been one of the most happy and carefree days I've had in a very long time."

I walked over to the table where she had settled herself in a chair.

"Coffee?" she asked.

When I nodded, she poured me a cup and handed it to me across the table.

I took the cup with my left and held out my right hand for her.

She gave me a look of surprise before placing her soft, warm hand in mine.

"I know I can't ever thank you enough for this weekend, but this can be a good start," I said and placed a gentle kiss on her hand.

She whipped out a smile as warm as the Caribbean sun.

After breakfast, we headed out to the beach. In a brash decision, I relinquished my rash guard, putting my gym-toned torso on display as we took a long, leisurely stroll on the soft sand along the beach. Aarti walked near the water, the rhythmic waves lapping at her feet. She was a sight to behold. She wore a blue one-piece swimsuit with a floral front open coverup that flapped against the breeze. Kimono coverups, I think they're called. An oversized hat shielded her face from the gentle sun.

I could've walked more, if only to hear her talk. She told me about her favorite time at Sanibel Island in Florida picking shells that she later painted and used to decorate her room. It was before they moved to the large house, she told me. When they moved, the interior designers dictated how best to set up her room. After that, they seldom took domestic vacations. It was either Europe or some expensive island in a remote part of the world. It sounded to me like she'd spent a long time doing what was expected of her rather than what made her happy. The longing to make her happy resurged with force within me. If only I got a chance.

"Let's walk back. I'm tired," she said, and we returned to the chaise loungers that had been set up for us. I lay in the heat of the sun, soaking up her warmth, when she said, "You better enjoy the hammock before I grab it."

Begrudgingly, I willed myself off the recliner.

"Do you want the umbrella on you?" I asked. When she nodded, I readjusted the large canopy to shade her body, then silently headed toward the water, where a hammock rocked on its stand.

As I lay with my hands underneath my head, I fought against the breeze that was trying to gently rock me to sleep.

"Are you going to hog the hammock all weekend?"

Aarti's voice near me brought out an unintended smile. I opened my eyes under the sunglasses to gaze at her beautiful face. She stood looking at me with her hands on her slender hips.

"You brought me here for that, did you not?" I asked.

"Yes, but I didn't know you wouldn't share."

"I don't mind sharing. Climb in." I grinned.

"Okay, scoot," she teased.

"Sure." I wiggled my body.

She let out a beautiful laugh before climbing in to rest her head on my arm.

"This is so relaxing," she said and placed a hand on my chest.

"Yes, now don't disturb me while I nap."

I felt the curve of her lip, the movement of her cheek against my chest as she smiled at my words. I felt the entirety of her body against me. Her silky legs, grazing against mine. The soft of her stomach against my hipbone. I could feel the warmth of her body through the two layers of clothing between us.

Then I felt something else. Her breath got deeper and labored. Her body stiffened. The palm resting on my chest moved a few inches inward, then stopped abruptly. I tried to ignore the sensation, but the mind has a mind of its own. And my mind was bossing over me hard. Quite literally.

Then, without a word, she pushed herself up with the hand on my chest.

"What happened?" I asked as if I didn't know the answer to that silly question.

"Nothing, this isn't working. It's uncomfortable. I am all scrunched up. I'll go lay down on the chair."

I nodded and watched her lower herself into the lounge recliner.

I closed my eyes and went back to pretending to nap. Her delicate floral fragrance still hovered around me, nudging me softly. I heard her shuffle.

"I'll be back in a bit," she said.

"Alright," I said with my shaded eyes still closed.

The sea was calm before the evening tide. The sun was making a slow trek toward the horizon with the intention of setting but taking its time, teasing, provoking, wondering how long it would take for mortals to surrender to the beauty of the evening sky. A gentle breeze sang to the sun, asking it to stay a bit longer. I basked in the lull of the breeze and the now predictable rhythm of the waves lapping at the shores. My closed lids began to relax over my eyes, and I was just about to slip into slumber when I felt a pair of soft lips on mine.

My eyes flew open, and my arms lifted up in a defensive posture.

"It's me," Aarti said.

"Aarti, what are you doing?" I removed my sunglasses, dropping them over the rim of the hammock, and they landed in the pristine sand with a soft thud.

She had changed into a skimpy two-piece bikini and stood over me, bathed in sunlight, looking like an ethereal being.

"I thought you wanted this," she said and undid the knot on her top, then pushed it off her shoulders.

I sat up as high as I could in the wobbly hammock.

"What are you doing?" I asked, flabbergasted.

"Do you want me?"

I'd stopped breathing. She touched my cheek gently. "Do you want me, Sujit? Me?"

I sat stupefied. My eyes went to her breasts. They were beautiful. The setting sun had stopped in its track to illuminate her nipples like two pieces of precious, dark rubies set on two perfect mounds of gold.

She moved closer and brought her breast to my mouth. Her hands raked the back of my head as she guided me gently. I held her waist. She let out a loud sigh as my mouth covered her taut nipple. I rolled my tongue over it, and her head fell back, her slender waist arching like an artist's masterpiece.

"Yes, I want you, Aarti. I want the real you, all of you," I said and kissed her chest and stomach.

She held my hand and helped me off the hammock.

I waited while she removed her bottom and reclined on the low chaise.

"You know what I want." She smiled with the mischievous glint in her eyes that I'd come to love and desire more than anything else.

"Teach me," I said.

She took my hand to her perfect brown opening and moaned. "I want your tongue."

"Tell me how." I bent her legs at the knees and coaxed open

her thighs. "You are so beautiful!" I said, and she gave me a shy smile.

Spreading her legs wide open, she showed me how she liked it. I listened, learned, and followed. I gave her exactly what she asked for.

She tasted like sunshine and the sea. She glistened like the lights dancing on the water.

I made her moan so loudly, her back slipped down the recliner.

"You liked that?"

"Oh, Sujit," she said and pulled me into a kiss. My body crushed hers gently, and she moved her tongue deeper and deeper inside my mouth.

Then she got off the chair, pulled down my shorts, and ordered me down on the chaise. She wrapped both her hands around my dick and stroked. I watched her swirl her tongue around the head, her eyes locked with mine. Her coral lipstick turned red, as if my dark skin was bleeding color to her lips, as if our bodies were melting into each other. Her fragrance dissolved into me, my fingers slipped into her hair, I disappeared into her mouth, and her breasts melded to my thighs. Her fingers on my hips leached away the pain I'd held for months. She wanted me to tell her what I wanted, but she'd already given me everything I needed.

Overcome with passion and consumed by fire, she rode me like a tigress. I let her take what she wanted, giving her everything I had in me. We rolled down onto the soft sand. She straddled me again, and I held her perfect bottom in my hands. Her breasts gleamed golden in the glow of the setting sun. I felt her insides clench against me.

"Yes, baby," I whispered, but the crashing waves drowned me out. They got wilder, louder, thudding against my ear, sharing in our pleasure, cheering us on.

Somewhere in the distance, a thunderstorm roared. The sun glinted crimson in admonishment. But emboldened by the gust, the brazen storm continued to forge stronger, heading straight toward us.

Aarti was nearing climax, her moans rising above the roaring waves. She grazed against me, and I felt her insides tighten.

"Oh, Sujit! Sujit...I can't..."

I held her bottom and thrust upward. A few insolent rain drops had the audacity to fall on her breasts and bounce with glee.

"Sujit," she cried again, and I felt the rain on my face. "We need to get inside."

I felt her clamping down on me again, and I kept going. I wanted to give her the happiness that no other man had.

"Keep going, darling, don't stop now. I don't want you to stop," I said.

Unchecked by the sun and roused up by the wind, the storm had gained courage. It poured down with conceited bravado, taking over the skies, the earth, the seas.

"Sujit..."

"Keep going, baby..."

"Sujit...Sujit...hey..."

A soft hand on my wet cheek woke me up.

"Hey, sorry to wake you," Aarti leaned over me in her blue one-piece and Kimono coverup. "It's starting to rain. Let's go inside."

"What?" I scrambled to sit up in the hammock.

"Easy, easy," she said. "Here, take my hand."

Gripping her wrist, I climbed out of the hammock. She led me inside, and I followed her in a daze and with an embarrassingly large bulge in my shorts.

AARTI

*H*e was still holding my hand as we stepped inside the beach house. I let him settle while I fetched a towel.

"Are you cold?" I asked with genuine concern.

"No," he responded as he took the towel from me and wiped his face and legs.

"It looked like you were shivering. And then there is this other condition," I said with as straight a face as I could manage.

He quickly wrapped the towel around his waist. "It's nothing, probably a dream."

"*A dream*? What kind of dream? Were you having a sex dream?" Oh, I was definitely curious.

"No." He responded calmly, but averted his gaze.

"You know, sooner or later, you'll have to tell me who you were dreaming about," I said.

"Not anyone you'd know."

"Oh, so now you're *not* denying it was a sex dream."

"Aarti, didn't you bring me here to relax and unwind? Stop bothering me. I'm going to change out of these wet clothes."

I opened my mouth, but he held up a finger. "No pun intended," he said before I could get in a word. "And FYI, if I was cold, my...thing would be doing the opposite of what it's doing now."

I burst out laughing while he escorted his wet body to the bathroom.

My renewed optimism this morning could be credited to a decision I made last night. I might not get to hold on to Sujit for life, but I was determined to enjoy his company for as long as I could. He was good for my soul. He had helped me heal in a way I hadn't expected. Even after we were forced to part ways, I knew I could hold on to the love, the hope, the kindness in my heart. It sounded like a cliché, but he had made me a better version of myself. I didn't feel broken anymore. I was stronger, more confident with him in my life. He was the definition of the elusive happiness that I'd been searching for.

I walked to the coffee station, brewed two cups, and carried them to the small table by the glass wall. Several delicious-looking pastries and small cakes were neatly arranged on a covered cake stand.

Sujit reemerged from his room, dressed in shorts and a T-shirt. I frowned. He had flaunted his bare torso all day, and now, after that ridiculous dream or whatever, he had chosen to cover up his body.

That didn't mean I was going to let him be. All through coffee, I kept nagging him to tell me who was responsible for his condition in the hammock.

"Okay, at least tell me if that person is real or not."

He frowned. "As in fictional?"

"Or, you know, like a celebrity or something."

"I hope this is not like breaking the truth about Santa, but you know celebrities are real people, don't you?"

I hit his arm.

"I'm not saying," he replied and stuffed a mini cupcake into his mouth.

Turning serious for a moment, I asked, "Was it Tara?"

With a vehement shake of his head, he gulped down the cake with haste. "I've never dreamed of Tara, sexually or otherwise."

When I opened my mouth again, he quickly added, "If you keep bugging me, I'll have to rethink the gifts I got you."

"As in, take them back? Tsk, that's so unbecoming."

"As in, never reading to you again until you stop bothering me."

My pulse fluttered as I imagined us spending a lifetime together, my head in his lap as he read to me every night until my eyelids dropped close.

"All right, you win."

I yielded. Even if it existed in the imaginary plane, it was a vision that would carry me through the toughest days of my life.

"What do you want to do next?" I asked. "It's our last night here. Wanna go dancing?"

He stopped midway to selecting another delectable pastry from the spread and frowned. "Dancing?"

"Yeah, the island has a lot of great clubs."

"I had something different in mind."

"Like?"

"I was thinking of taking another long walk along the sea. Are you game?"

I slumped. "No! You wore me out this morning. I walked..." I checked the data on my smartwatch, "10, 578 steps."

He threw his head back in a laugh. "Alright, then, you suggest."

"Let's—"

"No dancing," he interrupted me.

I blinked my eyes in thought. "Then I'm out of ideas."

"I have one."

"Does it involve walking or running on the beach?"

"No, but it does involve being on the beach."

"Oh?"

"How do you feel about spending the night on the beach?"

"As in sleeping in the sand? No, thank you."

"Not *in* the sand. On the sand. I inquired with the staff during lunch. They have cots with mattresses, and they can set it all up under a canopy in case it rains. But it's not going to rain."

I narrowed my eyes at him. "How do you know that? Do you have an in with the rain god now?"

"No, sweet girl. I have a very reliable weather app." He leaned in to grab my nose between two fingers, and I giggled.

I had assumed it would be a low-key setup with a couple of recliners underneath a canopy. But this was Mary Beth's domain. Her kingdom.

When we walked to the beach after dinner, multiple sets of string lights illuminated two low cots laid with full bedding sets under a regal tent. Dad was rich, but our wealth was acquired, not inherited. This screamed ancestral wealth, which had kept increasing through the generations. We were not nearly in the same league as the Arlingtons or the Strausses. Even if we had the money, expecting or demanding something like this would be inconceivable. I breathed in the sea-soaked happiness around me as I lowered myself to the left cot.

"Now what?" I asked as Sujit removed his footwear and settled himself on the other bed. "We just sleep?"

"No. We listen to the sea, look at the stars in the distance."

"You'll have to turn off these lights for that. Do you know how?" I looked around for a switch of some kind. The person helping us that evening had already retreated to the château.

"Yup. These are battery-operated, and I have a remote right here," he said, showing me a tiny one in his hand.

"Goodness, you have thought of everything, haven't you?"

"Not me. It's the staff. I think they are used to such curious requests from their employers." He chuckled as I removed my silk robe, folded it, and placed it by my pillow.

He pulled the covers on him and lay down with a contented look on his face.

"Are you comfortable?" he asked when I slipped under a plush duvet.

"Yes," I whispered. "You?"

"Very."

We lay there gazing at the dark horizon, where the sea and the sky blended in the same color. Indigo. The color of calm. Of contentment and a higher connection. Just like I had with the man beside me. What was it that I felt about him? What was the spirit of our connection? I listened to the waves and stared at the indigo, searching for clarity and answers.

"Can we turn the lights off?" I asked softly.

"Exactly what I was thinking," he replied as a noiseless click ushered us into darkness.

The château behind us was bathed in dim golden lights, but it looked so far way. The world felt so far away. This space was ours. So was the silence. I tried listening to the rhythm of the sea again. This time, I wasn't looking for answers. Only solace, and I found it in the sound of the waves surfing up to the sand and back. Sujit was right. This was the best way we could have spent the last night here.

"Sujit, are you asleep?" I asked with my sight still set on the horizon.

"Yes, I'm in deep sleep right now."

An unintended laughter rocked my entire body. "This is straight from that Aamir Khan movie!"

As I turned my face to him, he opened his eyes and looked at me.

"Darn, I thought this was as original as it came," he deadpanned.

I laughed harder until I realized I couldn't figure out if he was joking.

"You really didn't know?" I cried with incredulity, then realized not every second-gen Indian kid had grown up on Bollywood. He had said he didn't understand much Hindi. It was possible he grew up on a completely different set of Indian movies.

"Have you watched any Hindi movies?" I asked.

"Some. My parents are big Bollywood buffs. But I needed subtitles, and not many prints had those."

True, they didn't.

"Did you watch Telugu movies growing up, then?"

"Only the ones my parents watched. Mom also watched Tamil movies. And all my superstar idols growing up were from South Indian cinema."

"You are a treasure, Sujit."

"Is that sarcasm?"

I turned to face him. "No, it's genuine appreciation."

My eyes, now accustomed to the darkness, spotted his bright smile. "So are you, Aarti. A genuine treasure. Your work ethic alone surpasses anyone I know."

"Mom sometimes complains that I'm a workaholic like Dad, but I'm not one, and neither is Dad. Dad worked hard to provide for us. Once the business took off, he had to keep up with the pace of its growth. We both love what we do, but we have never prioritized work over people or family."

"I rest my case," he said.

"What case was that?" I teased.

"That you are a genuine treasure." The broad smile on his dark face in the dark night brightened my soul.

"I thought that was my case," I queried with a frown, and the curve on his lips grew wider in response. "What about your work?"

"What about it?"

"I don't know much about startups, but shouldn't someone who sold his for billions be doing something else? Like acquiring other startups or some such? How come you are still tinkering with new ideas yourself?"

"That is a very curious question, indeed. A perceptive one, and one that I have no straightforward answer to."

"Try me. We have all night to chat."

"I've never talked about this openly, but when I began working on the first idea, it was with a goal to make *some* money. It is the ultimate 21st-century dream, after all. All new millionaires were tech nerds. It was a great idea at the time, streamlining healthcare records and accounting systems, demystifying insurance claims and adjustments for doctors' offices, and online payments of balance. All these were needs of the hour. I just hit the right note at the right time. That's what brought in the wealth. I had never imagined it getting this big. I had hoped to help smaller clinics and private practices which already grapple with low-staffing. But everyone from state hospitals to private healthcare giants came knocking, and it turned into a beast I couldn't control alone. That's when I had to bring in bigger teams and imposing C-suite guys. In all honesty, I had hoped for that kind of success, as every startup does, but I had never imagined it would become a reality."

"You still haven't answered my question," I reminded softly when his pause turned into silence.

He turned his body to face me. "All right, sweet girl. Here is the answer to your question. Like I said, most startups identify a problem or a lack they perceive in our system and try to find a solution to it. However, because of the long years and labor involved, the expectation is to make money, a lot of money."

"And that's wrong?"

"Absolutely not. That's what I did too. But once I quote-unquote *made it,* I asked myself what I wanted. And I wanted to work more. I have enough juice in me to keep going another three decades, but this time, the end game is not money. It is to provide accessible education to kids, especially those who need it. Kids with special requirements, kids who struggle to fit into the regimented schedule of our schooling systems. Kids who have all the potential but not enough money or opportunity. What I am trying right now might or might not bring me money, and it's definitely not going to change the world overnight, but I hope it will offer tangible options for some real structural changes in education for everyone."

"And you've put your own money toward it?"

"For now, although I've had investors wanting in on it. Most people see the way I've been working on this venture and assume I'm ambitious and doing it for more money and more glory. But not this particular project. This, I'm doing for myself. Exclusively for myself."

I sighed. "Since I first met you, I've been wondering what makes you different from the other rich guys I know. I think I just found my answer. You care."

He gave me a nervous laugh. "Well, as I see it, there are only three ways to go when one acquires that kind of wealth. The first route is the safe path. You keep amassing more, increasing your power and influence that benefits you and your descendants. This comes from a place of insecurity, but also greed, I suspect. It wasn't something I'm interested in."

"So you choose to spend your wealth creating opportunities?"

"That's the second option. I'm not keen on amassing wealth, but I realized that being thrust into the billionaire's club gave me access to unprecedented power and influence. The kind of influence that can bring about real change and opportunities for happiness in society. Creating something good involves listening to the communities that you are a part of, heeding to the voice of the most disadvantaged. It involves understanding your responsibilities that your status accords you. Given who my parents are, the way my father has raised us, there was no other way for me to be. Of what use are my billions if my neighbor goes hungry?"

My heart warmed at his genuine words, and a proud smile appeared on my lips. But I was curious. "You said there are three ways. What's the third route?"

"The third route is to use your power and influence to actively undermine our shared communities. It is the incarnation of evil on earth. Imagine having the money to single-handedly solve world hunger, but instead of doing good, you choose to spend it on creating fractures in our society. You thump your chest with joy when the rights and privileges of the most disadvantaged are stripped, all in the service of getting you more money and power. That is pure evil."

I paused for thought.

"What about the other project? The one with the creators' studios?"

"Aarti!" he cried.

There was a long pause before he sat up, the duvet pooling around his hips, his thin T-shirt clinging to his toned torso against a determined breeze.

"I know it's a secret, but there's no one else here except us!"

"Not that, sweet girl! I have been looking for a good name for the project, and you just gave me one!"

"Creators' Studios?" Now I sat upright, and the spaghetti strap of my silk cami slipped right off my smooth shoulder, baring my skin all the way to the swell of my breast. But he didn't notice.

"Creators' Studio," he said. "How do you like it?"

"I love it. Congratulations," I complimented.

"Well, it was all you. You can officially claim a share of the profits if this makes big."

"Consider it a gift, sweet man."

"That's a copyrighted term, sweet girl."

"Is it now? I didn't see any copyright notice anywhere."

He shook his head and fell back onto the pillowy mattress.

"Thank you for this weekend, Aarti," he said. "And I know I need to thank you for one other thing."

I threw him an inquiring look. Like me, his eyes had accustomed to the darkness enveloping us.

"Walt told me about Ms. Dina's diner," he said.

I pulled in a silent breath. "I asked him not to."

"He didn't break your trust. I contacted him with an offer to buy out the place in her name. He had no choice but to confess the truth. The shop was hers now for all intents and purposes, he said, and no one could drive her out again."

When I didn't say anything, he prodded, "Aarti?"

"I'm listening," I said softly. I shifted to my back again and returned my gaze to the skies.

"I don't know how to thank you for this. The diner has helped her survive, emotionally and financially. She has been training two women from her country to take over when she's ready to retire, which I hope isn't too soon. You have no idea what you've done for her. You talked about selfless love after the first time we ate at her diner. This is it. *This* is selfless love."

I couldn't hold the lie any longer. "It wasn't selfless, Sujit. Far from it."

"You helped a woman secure the place that has become integral to her identity. It is her entire life. How can it not be selfless?"

"Because I didn't do it for her alone," I confessed. "I did it for you."

The sea turned unexpectedly calm, the thrashing waves barely whispering their presence on the sand as an uncomfortable silence filled the space between us.

"I did it so you didn't lose the space you value so much," I explained.

"I don't know what to say," his gentle voice finally drifted over to me.

"You don't have to say anything," I cried with exasperation. "That was the whole point in keeping it a secret."

I turned to my side to face him and pushed an arm under my head. "You have no idea what you've done for me, Sujit. You brought me out of the despair I had buried myself in and with such effortless ease. You lent me your ear and your shoulder when I was feeling lonely and wretched. You allowed me your company, your unconditional friendship, your unassuming care. This is the least I could do to thank you for it."

"You gave me a new lease on life, too, Aarti. Our friendship was never one-sided. You helped me regain a fresh perspective and a new vision of what happiness entails. Being with you makes me happy."

Oh, thank you, indigo! My heart bubbled with joy at his words. Was this the clarity I was looking for?

"And I am sure we both will carry this happiness with us as we find love again."

All right, WTF, indigo? What are you doing?

"On that note, I also wanted to talk to you about something else," he said when I was nearly done fuming at the universe.

"What's that?" I responded with some annoyance.

"Remember I said we should do something to celebrate on the day of the wedding?"

"Yes, I also remember saying that I wouldn't use the word celebrate," I cried with impatience.

"May I take the liberty of pointing something out?"

"I may regret it, but yes."

"The only way to get from under the shadow of their happiness is to find ours."

Their happiness no longer cast a shadow on mine, but I didn't tell him that. My happiness was overshadowed by a completely different monster cast in the mold of the twisted sense of humor that the universe had unfurled.

"Aarti?" he nudged. "Are you still up?"

"No, I'm in deep sleep right now," I responded, and he laughed.

I breathed in the salty air. "I think it'd be best if I was alone that night."

"Are you still hurting?" he asked.

"Are you?" I countered with some anger.

"No. Are you?"

The honest answer was I *was* hurting but not from Sameer. I was hurting because I couldn't tell Sujit that I was in love with him.

SUJIT

I couldn't bring myself to forget the dream I had about Aarti. It was so vivid, so visceral that its aftereffects shook my world well into the following week. I knew it wasn't just my overactive subconscious at work. It was me, with all the free will involved.

I had spotted desire in her eyes more than once, but the timing of this connection couldn't have been more inopportune. If I had met Aarti outside of our current situation, it would've been a straightforward and rosy path to our happiness together. Our intertwined, murky histories made this a complicated situation.

On several occasions over the past two weeks, I considered disclosing my feelings to her, only to be reminded of her conversation with her brother. She had vehemently dismissed the possibility of us, either from embarrassment or from the fear of losing her family's trust in her. In either scenario, the loss would be mine. If her happiness was closely linked to her family's name and business, I could never be a part of it. On the other hand, if she was put in a position to choose between the two, my fear was she'd choose me, and I'd hate myself for it.

My predicament notwithstanding, I wasn't about to desert her on the night of the wedding. The wedding, or the marriage itself, had stopped being the all-consuming entity it had been a couple of months ago. Now, it was merely a date that, for a reason, was etched in our minds but was destined to have little impact on our lives. I liked it that way. The gift I'd arranged to send Tara on her wedding day was a testament to this.

I studied the invitation to the charity event that I held in my hand. I attended such events only when my presence was deemed mandatory. Usually, my checks were more appreciated than me, I had long surmised. This holiday party, though, seemed like the perfect way to celebrate the night.

I texted Aarti.

> Free for a call?

She called me back instantly.

"How's it going?" I asked.

"Just stopped by the new place to take a look at the renovations. The electrical system needs an overhaul at this property too." The weariness in her voice was surpassed by a sense of pride for her work.

"Well, here's something that might cheer you up."

"Let me guess, you discovered another hidden gem with amazing food?"

I laughed. "Better. How would you like to go dancing?"

"Ha ha, you got me," she said, then quickly added, "Hey, give me a minute."

I heard her give instructions to the crew amid sounds of scraping metal.

"Don't you have people who can do this for you?" I asked when she returned on the call.

"I do, but I trust myself better," she said. "So, you said dancing?"

"Yes, why would you think I was joking?"

"I thought you were teasing me for that night in St. Martin. You are serious."

"I am, and I'm surprised at your surprise."

She hesitated. "It's only because I thought you couldn't dance —wouldn't—didn't, I mean."

"Which is it? Couldn't, wouldn't, or didn't?"

"I mean, you don't seem like the person who'd go dancing in a club."

"Who said anything about a club?"

"Where then?"

"It's a charity event, a ball of sorts."

She burst out laughing. I heard her heels as she stepped away from her crew, and then I heard the sounds of the streets.

"Did you laugh at the image of me dancing at a ball?" I asked.

"No, I just flashed back to the debutant events Dad insisted on me attending."

"Then you can dance, can't you?"

"Oh, I can dance!" I heard the twinkle in her voice. "I just didn't know you could."

"Could or did?"

"Does it matter?"

"It does. If I couldn't, I wouldn't be able to at all. If I could but didn't, I certainly would with you."

"Sujit, this wordplay is getting tedious, and I have a lot on my plate today."

"All right, I'll pick you up at seven on Saturday, and it's a black tie."

"Saturday?" she said and went silent.

"Why? Are you busy?"

"Saturday is Christmas Eve."

"Yes, it is a holiday party," I argued.

"It is the wedding day," she said with some ire. "Sujit, I told you it's best if I am alone."

"And I told you, you won't be alone. Can you trust me on this one?"

"Haven't I repeatedly told you that I trust you? I've trusted you since the first time I saw you at the hotel bar." The annoyance in her voice was loud and clear.

"And that is the troubling part, isn't it?" I softly completed her statement.

"It is," she said with a gentle sigh.

I let the silence hold between us before I spoke again. "Can I ask you something? Seriously, this time."

She hummed in response.

"Are you uncomfortable about being seen with me at a public event with the press involved? Especially on Saturday?"

She sighed. "How much did you hear of what my brother said that day?"

"Enough to get the gist of it."

"They feel it's an embarrassment for them and should be shameful for us."

I didn't react. I was eager to know how she felt about it, about us.

"Sujit?" she prodded.

"I'm here."

"You didn't respond."

"I can't tell you how to feel, Aarti. But I will honor your decision, always. You know that."

I heard a deep exhale.

"I'm not uncomfortable about being seen with you," she replied. "Neither am I ashamed of our friendship."

"And if people arrive at certain conclusions?" I attempted to test the waters.

"They always do, my good man, but that's their problem, isn't it? I just hope to dance my ass off."

Devi knocked on the door to remind me of my next appointment. I waved her to give me a minute. "Well, I promise to be a consummate gentleman and have you back from the ball before your carriage turns into a pumpkin."

"You are a gentleman even if you don't try, Sujit. But I'm certainly not cut out to be a gentlelady. What if I end up wanting to spend the night at your place?"

"That would be absolutely out of the question. You have your own home now. I will make sure that you are tucked in safe and sound, like the sweet girl that you are."

She offered me another short laugh, then whispered, "Thank you, Sujit."

∼

SATURDAY EVENING, I was en route to her apartment, perusing the file that Devi had entrusted Imran to place in the car for me.

"How is Razia?" I inquired about his sister with my eyes on the file in my lap.

"Good. She's happy," he said. I could feel his eyes on me in the mirror.

"How are her courses going? Any trouble catching up?"

"She didn't say, but I will ask her."

I looked at the mirror. "I know she's working at the convenience store."

He sat up straight, then slumped with a sigh. "I told her not to worry about money, to focus on her studies, but she feels like she's a burden on me. I keep telling her you pay me well, but she feels obligated."

"She's a self-respecting person, like her brother, and I appreciate that. But if she doesn't get the necessary skills, I won't hire her, tell her that. She needs to be at the top of her game if she wants to come work for me."

He smiled with relief. That was one threat he could use to get his sister to take her courses seriously. "I will tell her. She says she is already feeling bad that I am paying for her college."

"In the grand scheme of things, it's a very small amount. When she gets the job, she'll be able to repay you in two months."

"That's what I told her, but she doesn't listen. She's stubborn." He shook his head.

"Like her brother," I said with a smile.

"Me, stubborn? Come on, Boss, you won't find a more agreeable person."

"Sure. Absolutely."

He grinned wide.

"How's Afra?" I asked.

He flashed a shy smile at the mention of his girlfriend. "She's good too."

"Did she get the job?"

"Yes, she started this week."

"Good, and the pay bump she was hoping for?"

"Yes, she is very happy. She will be trained by the head nurse, who has already taken a liking to her. I said, that's surprising."

"And how did she take that?"

"Not well," he said with a laugh. "Hit me on the arm and said, you better be careful what you say. I'm a nurse, and I know all ways to make murder look like natural death."

I had to laugh at that. "Good for her."

"She's so smart, Boss. I wonder what she's doing with me."

"You are not bad yourself, Imran."

"But I'm not educated. Can I keep her happy?"

"Those two have no correlation. And you had to quit

studying and migrate to a foreign country to support your family. It's because of you that Razia is an engineer today. Your little brother is on his way to getting his degree. And your mother could have her knee surgery."

He nodded.

"And if you ever want to go back to college, you know you don't have to think twice."

"I know, Boss. But it's too late for me. Now I want to settle down, marry, have kids."

"So when's that happening?"

"Afra and I think after Razia gets back on her feet. We don't want her to feel like she's dependent on us after our marriage."

"That won't be long. Tell Razia I was upset and asked her to focus on her courses."

He nodded.

"Have you talked to Afra's parents yet?"

He blew out a breath.

"What's the holdup?"

"I'm a driver. That's the holdup," he said in a sorrowful tone. "They want her to marry someone educated, someone rich."

"Have you told them how much you make?"

"No, bragging is un-Islamic." He smiled heartedly.

"Then let me brag on your behalf. You'll always have a job with me, you know that."

"Thank you, Boss. But that won't be necessary. Afra is strong. She's got my back."

"Good. I'm glad you have a strong, smart woman in your life."

He eyed me in the mirror with a sly grin.

"Yes?" I asked.

"And you?"

I closed the file and placed it on the seat beside me. "Hopefully someday."

"That day is today, Boss," the sly rascal said as he parked the car under Aarti's building and then came around to hold the door open for me.

I rode up the elevator and waited for Aarti to answer the door. *Lord have mercy!* That was the first thought that hit me when I saw her in the sultry, smooth red gown. I looked at her from top to bottom with complete reverence for her beauty.

"Don't forget to breathe," she teased as she turned inside.

I caught a quick breath and followed her, gazing at her glossy, deep brown hair cascading over a delectably open back. Her perfect curves swayed gracefully with her every step.

"Just need to put my earrings on," she said, grabbing one from the coffee table.

Unable to take my eyes off her, I watched her put the stud in her ear. She laughed with her beautiful red lips as a light from the chandelier caught the stunning solitaire. She grabbed the other stud from the table. The gold setting of the earrings matched the muted gold in her neckline, her proud breasts pouring out generously.

She blinked at me with her long lashes underneath a delicate eye makeup. I noticed she had not used false lashes today, and it did nothing to diminish the beauty of those eyes.

A side slit rode up to her right thigh, drawing attention to her silky, toned long legs. I let my gaze linger and wasn't ashamed of it, for no one else I knew could walk that elegantly in those tall heels like she did. She glided. Her perfume was some sort of magical mix of everything the heavens had to offer. I was certain if goddesses had a scent, they would smell exactly like this.

A goddess, that's who she was. Gorgeous, powerful, brilliant.

Amid my admiration and reverence, I forgot that I had brought along a gift for her.

"Is that for me?" she asked, her eyes darting to the box in my hand.

Shaken out of my trance, I said, "Ah, yes."

When I handed her the box, she opened it and saw the diamond necklace I'd had custom-designed. I couldn't describe what cut it was or how many carats the diamonds were. All I could say for certain was that it was beautiful, and it was created especially for her.

The look in her eyes confirmed it for me. "This is beautiful, Sujit! But you shouldn't have...I mean, there was no need..."

"This isn't from me. This is on behalf of Ms. Dina," I said as I lifted the necklace out of the box and offered to help her put it on.

She pulled her hair to one shoulder as I tried to lock it at her nape. Her scent enveloped me, and I was transposed to an imaginary world where I could take her in my arms and kiss her till our lips were sore.

"Ms. Dina, huh?" she said as I came back around to face her. "So, what did *you* get me?"

I grinned and pulled out a single red rose out of my jacket and held it out for her. "This is from me."

She threw her head back in a heartfelt laugh, showing me all of her teeth, and her nose scrunched up in delight. It was then that I noticed she had not covered up her beauty mark. It wasn't a noticeably prominent size, but there it was, visible under her makeup.

I stepped closer and touched it. "I love it," I whispered against her cheek and placed a gentle kiss on it.

"Don't," she said softly. "This will make it all the more difficult when I have to leave."

This time, I didn't hesitate. "Then don't leave."

SUJIT

From the moment she stepped out of the car, Aarti commanded the attention of every camera around us. People whispered, trying to figure out if she was an actress. Cameras flashed all around us, and the crowds behind the ropes screamed at celebrities to get their attention. Aarti remained unperturbed by any of it. She was used to this. She didn't smile or pose for the cameras. Holding her cool composure, she walked indoors, making sure to maintain a few inches of distance between us.

A host escorted us to our assigned table. When we had settled, I excused myself to get drinks. I waited while the bartender poured a drink for a guest standing nearby. The guy grabbed a bourbon on the rocks and turned to me.

"So you're her latest toy?" he said.

With a quick glance around to ensure he was addressing me, I said, "Excuse me?"

"Aarti Bhatia," he said, taking what he assumed was a cool sip of his drink. "Are you her *date* tonight?"

I knew men like him. That power move of taking a sip

between sentences was so clichéd, it came across as rehearsed. I turned to the bartender. "Two sparkling whites."

"Dude, I'm not the enemy here," the bourbon guy said, and I suddenly remembered where I knew him from.

The opening at the art gallery. The vault where I had stored his information unfolded before my mind's eye.

"Is that right?" I said, now curious about his angle.

"She's a bitc—"

"Watch it," I warned with a stern look.

"Chill, dude. I'm in your corner. I don't know if you're aware, but she was dumped publicly and unceremoniously. Yet has the nerve to fuck around with men. That's a metaphor, of course, she doesn't really fuck. Just toys with them."

I was about to respond when the bartender offered me the wine. With a nod, I signaled him to deposit the flutes on the counter and turned a menacing sneer at the bourbon sipper.

"And that's what bothers you, isn't it? You go on two dates with a woman, and you think she owes you her body."

He smirked. "Hey, man, don't get cocky. You might think you're special, but she's going to toss you away—"

"Like she did you that night after the gallery opening?"

His expression turned quizzical as he tried to place me. I returned a menacing glare. "Ashutosh, Ash, is it? Still at Swinstz?" I said, pushing my left hand into the trousers pocket. "I'd be *very* careful talking smack about her."

Color left his face as he realized the threat in my words. He stumbled backward, fortunately finding the barstool behind him that helped him regain his balance. He gripped it with one hand, the fingers on his other clutching the bourbon tumbler so tight, his knuckles turned white.

"The name's Sujit. Sujit Rao, and no one calls me dude," I said and his eyes darted behind me. I turned around and saw Aarti standing a few feet away. She looked shaken, as if she'd heard it all.

Flashing her my best smile, I offered her my arm. "Shall we?"

Sharp that she was, she recovered swiftly and hooked her arm in mine with an elegant smile, completely ignoring the fool who stood dumbfounded, still gripping the bar stool.

Aarti squeezed my arm, and I squeezed her hand back. I heard her pull in a deep breath. "Did you just do the Bond thing?" she asked with a straight face.

"I did, and we're never going to talk about it," I answered in the same formal tone.

I escorted her to the expansive balcony overlooking the city. It was cold, but the strategically placed heaters made it bearable, enjoyable even. We walked over to the railing at the edge, where couples had lined up with drinks in their hands and lust in their eyes.

Aarti gripped the railing, watching the city lights, and I put my hand on hers. She reassured me with a nod, and I removed my hand. As I did, she spotted someone behind me.

"Is that who I think it is?" she exclaimed with a sparkle in her eye.

I gently crossed over to stand behind her with my hands reaching the railing so I could see the person. It was a famous movie star.

"Certainly looks like him," I leaned in and whispered in her ear. "Unless he's a body double, it's definitely him."

"He's even more gorgeous in person," she turned her neck to whisper in my ear.

I stole a quick glance at him. "Taller, for sure."

She let out a soft giggle as the celebrity turned to her and flashed his trademark irresistible smile. Of course he did. She looked spectacular.

His gaze lingered on her, but she gave an elegant nod and stepped closer, her back flush against me. It was her way to indicate her unavailability, and my chest swelled with pride that she had chosen me to convey it. The warmth between our bodies traveled to my heart.

The movie star now noticed me and flashed a formal smile. I returned a short nod and leaned in toward Aarti's ear. "Well, now here's a really good-looking hunk for you. I hear he recently broke up with his girlfriend."

"But as you also heard, I'll just fuck with him and cast him aside," she whispered bitterly.

"It would be a shame if you let him go before that anyway. He's quite the stud, they say."

That amused her, but she tempered her laugh.

"I'm sorry you had to hear that," I added.

She returned a small shrug. "I've heard worse, unfortunately." Then, moving closer to my cheek, said, "Did you threaten him with just your name?"

"And his. There are some benefits to being known in the industry. And to being friends with influential people."

At that moment, a buzz from my jacket pocket surprised us both. I retrieved the phone she had handed me before we stepped out of the car.

"It's my family," she said, taking a look at the screen. "Probably worried that I'm sad and distraught, eating ice cream in my bed. I'll call them later." She pressed decline and handed the phone back to me.

I slipped it into the inside pocket of my tux. "You didn't tell them about tonight."

But before she could respond, someone opened the door, and we heard music drifting to us.

"Are you ready to dance?" I asked, stepping away from her.

She smoothed her gown and held out her hand for me. "I am."

The tempo was slow, and the crowd was still warming up to

the music. There were only a handful of couples on the floor, and more joining in with the gradual swelling of the music.

"You lead," I whispered to Aarti as she gracefully began the Waltz.

I had claimed I could dance, but I wasn't nearly as blithe or elegant as her. She had received formal training, and it showed. Tapping into my memory, I tried to recollect the correct sequence. But Aarti led us beautifully. With every turn, her gown flew out, revealing her seductive legs, and I didn't miss the looks she got.

"You're a sight, Aarti. Everyone's looking at you," I said as we drifted to my right.

"There's only one person I care about impressing tonight," she said.

I grinned. "Oh yeah, that handsome hunk's got his eyes glued to you as well," I teased her, and she narrowed her eyes at me.

With a light laugh, I swung her, and she dipped with the elegance of a true dancer. The spotlight had caught us and now followed us as we swirled around the dance floor. I'd been in the limelight several times before, but it had never felt this good. When the song ended, Aarti was treated to a heartfelt round of applause, and she took a gentle bow.

We returned to our table with the promised drinks. Two songs later, the Tango music began gently fading in. She got a happy glint in her eye. "Tango?"

"I'm not terribly good at it," I said, returning my scotch to the table.

"You'll be fine," she said and grabbed my hand.

We began, rather clumsily, on my account, but she leaned in closer and whispered, "The eight-step."

I recollected the classes I had taken and attempted again. This time, I didn't fail completely. I grabbed her in my sturdy arms and danced.

"Goodness, you are a sight to behold tonight, Sujit," she cried breathlessly during one of the pauses.

"Just tonight?" I smirked, and she laughed against my cheek.

As the music swelled, she took charge, and I was ready to melt into her arms. Her smile, her laughter, the giggles and tears that no one else got to see, I wanted it all. Her divine fragrance seeped into every pore of my body and I could lie to myself no longer.

I was in love with Aarti.

The music gave way to a resounding round of claps and polite cheers, but I refused to come down from the high of being in her arms.

As I dropped her back and escorted her to her apartment, she said, "Oh, I completely forgot to tell you. I think I have found the perfect space for Creators' Studio. I will call you this week with an appointment to see the building."

"Sounds good. Thank you, Aarti."

She blinked with her soft eyes that were drunk on happiness from the dancing. "Thank you for tonight. You were right. This was good. Just what I needed. I will call my family now. They must be worried and waiting for me to call back."

"Good night, Aarti."

"Sorry you didn't get to tuck me in," she said with a mischievous glint.

"That's alright. I think you can manage that, my sweet girl."

I didn't regret using the possessive, especially when she returned an unfazed smile and said, "Good night, Sujit. You're the best thing that could have happened to me."

AARTI

*Y*es, I said it, and I didn't regret it. Sujit was the best thing that the universe could have thrown in my path after having devastated me with the Sameer situation. Life has a strange sense of humor, I had thought upon seeing him that first night. *Of all the gin joints in all of the towns...*

But apparently, life also has a semblance of kindness, for of all the people that could have walked into my life at that precarious time, he did. Ethically balanced, I had called him. The way he stood up for me, respected and protected me, I had never expected nor needed. And then, there was the thing unsaid between us. Just a touch, a nod, and he could reassure me. I could communicate an entire gamut of my feelings with just a squeeze of his arm, and he understood it all. I knew I had fallen hard for him, but how could I get rid of the baggage that came with this particular desire? How could either of us?

Quickly changing into my night cami and shorts, I wiped all trace of makeup and placed a call to Mom.

"Hello, Beta," she answered on a single ring.

"Sorry, Ma, were you waiting for long?"

"Not long," she replied, but her sleepy eyes said otherwise. "Just wanted to see how you were doing...tonight, I mean."

"I'm alright. I had scheduled a meeting to get my mind off... it," I lied to my mother with a straight face. Love makes us do stupid things, but shame makes us do worse. Which one was it that was compelling me to lie, I wondered.

"Good. Everything will be okay soon, and you can return. I miss you, you know. More than I thought I would," she said.

"I miss you too, Ma. I am glad you have Jia, at least. Do you get to share things with her now?"

"Yes, it's better, but she's a new mom, and she's going through her own stuff. I do get lonely."

"Sorry I've been busy. Do you get to see your friends, though? It must be very awkward."

"My friends have been surprisingly supportive. The Mathurs didn't want to go to the wedding on our account, even though they were invited. I persuaded them to go. Their relationship with the Rehanis is their own."

Mathur Aunty was Mom's oldest and best friend. Her daughter Anju was my friend, although we weren't as close as our mothers.

"I'm glad, Ma. It's overblown, anyway. Mine wasn't the first public breakup, and it won't be the last."

Mom smiled. "I'm glad to see you're taking it so positively, Beta. I have been worried about you."

"Don't be. You know I am the happiest when I'm working."

"Yes, but you used to get some downtime here. I'm worried you're probably overworking yourself there."

"I'm not, and I'm eating well, and I go out too. Don't worry."

"Beta, about that," she said and looked around her, probably to make sure she was alone.

"Yes, Ma?"

She dropped her voice. "Aakash told me he talked to you."

I nodded.

"About Sujit Rao," she whispered as if it was taboo to even utter that name.

I sighed audibly.

"Satish doesn't know, and he should never find out. For his sake and yours."

"Why is it wrong, Ma? Why is it so bad to be friends with someone who went through exactly the same thing I did? Who knows exactly how I feel."

Bright that my mother was, she cut through the BS. "Is it only friendship?"

"It was a business association, if you need to know. I wasn't interested in telling Aakash this, but I've been helping Sujit look for a place for a new project he has in the works."

"In one of *our* buildings?" Mom's eyes bugged out. "Beta, that is a *bad* decision. A *very* bad decision. You know you won't be able to hide it from Satish forever."

"I'm not trying to hide anything," I lied again, this time struggling against both guilt and shame. I was trying to hide every single emotion I felt for Sujit from my family.

The gratitude I felt toward the universe for its kindness seemed to be dissipating fast.

"And when your father learns?"

"I learned to deal with this whole situation, didn't I? Maybe others can too," I cried, bitter from fighting the constant battle. "And did he tell you he was talking about my marriage without consulting me? Did you talk to him about that?"

Mom sighed in consolation. "I did, Beta. I didn't know, and when he told me, I asked him to stop. But you should cut him some slack, my darling. You know Satish took it the hardest. He stood up on that stage and declared to the world that he trusted Sameer. It was more than hurt for him. He believes Sameer besmirched his name, his trust. He lost face because now it was for the world to see his error in judgement."

"I know, Ma. I understand."

"And you have been his pride and joy. He is deeply angry for you. He knows how much you are hurting, and he's not inclined to forgive that family in this lifetime at least."

"But what does Sujit have to do with any of this? Isn't he also the injured party like me?"

"Yes, Beta, but he was Tara's boyfriend. He's already tainted by association in his eyes."

"Ma, he consoled me when I was at my weakest. I sat across from him and promised that I'd help him find a space for his new project, and I am not going back on my word."

Mom sighed in defeated resignation and ran a hand over her forehead. "You are khuddar like your father."

"But this is more than self-respect and honor, Ma. This is about giving him his due respect too. I was in very bad shape when I came here, you know that. I am in a better place now because of him. I am just repaying his kindness like he deserves."

"Oh, Beta!" Mom sighed.

"Am I wrong, Ma?"

"No, my darling, but make sure it's only kindness and nothing else."

"What else could it be?" My lies had gotten significantly bolder over the course of this short conversation.

My perceptive mother dropped the subject and consoled me instead. "You will find comfort and love again, Aarti. You don't have to go looking for it immediately. Take your time to heal. Become your old self again, and you will see I am right."

I nodded. I wasn't going to argue with her, especially when every word out of her mouth was the truth. I was also very tired. I had just spent the most wonderful evening with an incredible man and now I was working hard to lay it on thick how much he didn't mean to me.

Perhaps it was the cumulative effect of it all—the excessive workload, the emotional turmoil, and the blatant lies I had been feeding my family—that I took to bed that week.

I had set aside Thursday afternoon to show Sujit the space I had earmarked for him. But I woke up with a high fever. I took acetaminophen and slept through most of the morning, but when I woke up around noon, the fever persisted. The sheets were damp from my sweat and I was now shivering between them. I texted Sujit to cancel our appointment.

He called back promptly.

"You're not well? What happened?"

"Nothing serious. It's just a mild fever. I should be better by tomorrow," I said, but my teeth chattered so hard, he heard it. He also noted my broken voice.

"I'll be right over," he said and hung up before I could protest.

I didn't know how long he took to arrive because the fever had knocked me out again. When I heard the bell chiming, I unlocked the door using my phone.

He rushed in and put a hand on my forehead.

"Damn! You're hot!" he said with a concerned frown.

I grinned at his words and replied, "Thank you. I was expecting you to say that last Saturday."

"This is no time for jokes, sweet girl. You're burning up."

"Ugh, it's not that bad."

He unbuttoned his cuffs and rolled up his sleeves. My fevered mind wandered to the dance with me swinging in his strong arms. I hummed a tune from that night.

"I want to dance with you again," I said.

"Later," he said as if I was a child making unreasonable demands. "Do you have a thermometer?"

"No," I replied matter-of-factly. "I didn't predict I was going to be sick."

He pulled out his phone from his pocket, placed a call, and put it on speaker while it trilled.

"Where's your linen closet? I need to change your sheets. They are damp."

I pointed to the closet door just outside my bedroom.

The phone continued ringing while he stepped outside and pulled out fresh sheets.

"Yes, Bhai," a sweet female voice answered the call.

Sujit came rushing back in. "Afra, I'm sorry to bother you at work, but I need your help."

"No problem, I'm on my break."

Sujit pulled me up and helped me into the armchair in the room while he continued talking to the woman on the phone.

"My friend is sick. High fever. My concierge doctor is out, and I don't trust anyone else right now. Do you think you can help? Tell me if I need to get her to a hospital."

I rolled my eyes at his question while he put a comforter on my shuddering body. He pulled the sheets off my bed and tossed them to a corner of the room without missing a beat in the conversation.

"Does she have any other symptoms? Headache, nausea, runny nose, rashes, diarrhea? Anything?" Afra inquired.

Sujit raised his brows at me. I shook my head.

"No, nothing else. Just very high fever and intense shivers."

"How high?"

"Not sure. She doesn't have a thermometer."

"Is Imran with you?"

"Yes, he's downstairs with the car."

"All right, let me call him and give him a list of things. I don't think we need to rush to the hospital. Give her plenty of fluids, and if she's not throwing up, have her eat a little. I'll ask Imran to get the rest from the pharmacy."

"Thank you, Afra. I owe you."

She laughed. "Arey Bhai, you can't keep owing me for such small things. You are family. Let me call Imran right away before my break ends."

She disengaged the call, and Sujit finished tucking in the final edge of the fitted sheet.

"Change of clothes?" he asked, and I pointed to a drawer in my wardrobe. He walked into the large closet and returned with a pair of sweatpants and a T-shirt.

"Do you need help to get changed?"

I shook my head.

"I'll wait outside."

Without waiting for my response, he stepped out of the room and closed the door behind him.

"Done!" I called out in a few moments, my shivers having quelled a bit after changing out of the damp clothes.

He entered promptly. "Come on, get back into bed," he directed me.

"Who was that on the phone?"

"Afra, Imran's girlfriend. She's a nurse. A very good one."

"She said you are family. Do you know how lucky you are to have so many people love you this way?"

"Yes, I count my blessings every day," he said with every bit of sincerity as he pulled the covers on me and tucked me in.

"Do you have any food in the house? Anything I can give you before I medicate you?"

I shook my head. "Sorry, my illness came unannounced and uninvited."

He picked up his phone and began typing furiously.

"I've ordered soup from a nearby deli. It should be here shortly. I need to get you some rasam to warm up your insides."

"I love rasam," I said. "I like it with rice."

"This one is more medicinal. I'll ask Amma how to make it."

Before he could run the whole scenario in his head—before I could stop him—he'd placed a call to his mom.

"I need the recipe for your pepper rasam," he said to her.

I held my breath, waiting to see how that conversation would unfold.

Who do you need it for?

A friend.

What friend? And why are you cooking for him?

She's unwell.

It's a she? Who's this friend you are cooking rasam for? And have you ever made rasam before that you think you can crack it now?

I chuckled at the look on Sujit's face. If the conversation hadn't exactly gone the way it had in my head, it was very close.

"No, I don't want you to send it here."

Silence as he listened to her.

"No, Amma, just give me the recipe."

He blew out an exaggerated breath and said, "All right, never mind. Forget I called. I will figure out something else to give her."

Silence again.

"Yes, Amma, it's a her."

Silence.

"I don't want to talk about it right now. Please, Amma."

He ended the call and sank onto the armchair.

"Are you in trouble?" I asked, buried under cozy layers.

He looked up at me with a smile. "More than you know."

"I'm sorry, Sujit. I really didn't want to inconvenience you. You didn't need to come at all."

"Who else do you have here to care for you if you're sick?"

"Just you," I said with a sigh. "But I'm not comfortable accepting help, and I hate to be a burden."

"You are not a burden," he said gruffly.

Gathering my clothes and the damp bedcovers from the floor, he walked out of the bedroom. In the silence of the apartment, I heard cabinet doors open and close in the kitchen, drawers sliding on their smooth bearings and the light clink of glassware.

He returned with a bowl in his hand and placed it on the side stand to help me up. He propped some pillows behind me and handed me a bowl of soup.

"This will have to do until I figure out what else I can feed you. I might have to call Afra again."

I accepted the bowl from his hand but said, "Aren't you being a little too dramatic about a slight fever? And don't you have to be at work?"

"Work can wait. Health cannot."

By the time I was done with the soup, Imran had dropped off a thermometer, a personal humidifier, some over-the-counter medicines, and electrolytes. Suddenly, I was glad I had Sujit in my life, who had so many people who cared for him. But I instantly wondered how much they'd care for me if they knew who I was.

Tainted by association, Mom had said about Sujit. Wasn't it true for me as well? Sujit's family didn't yet know who I was, but when they did, it would unravel so quickly. I wasn't sure I would be able to bear the brunt. It could have been my fever that made me question myself and the validity of my feelings for him, but it was all right there before me, clear as day in my foggy head.

Sujit miraculously managed to get some dal and rice for me. I didn't ask him how. He was a resourceful man with connections. I'd leave it at that. Plus, my brain was tired and hazy from thinking unnecessary thoughts, and I didn't want to tax it further. I let him feed me the warm food, gulped down a tablet, and went back into a fevered sleep.

When I woke up that evening, the sun had already set. Sujit wasn't in the room with me. I pulled the phone from the nightstand to check the time. It was just past seven. Sujit had been with me since early afternoon, and I was grateful. Feeling a bit healthier after the food and the rest, I tried to sit up.

SUJIT

The day had started out wrong and it continued to get worse with every passing minute.

That morning I arrived at the office to Devi's troubled face. I had barely settled in my chair when she rushed in with the news that I had made my way into a tabloid, a news that had gotten the office space animated. Devi had managed to secure a copy for me. On the front page was a picture of me escorting Aarti to the charity event. The angle of the picture shielded her face but mine was visible, elated and enamored. Exactly how I felt around her.

I had hardly parsed through the filth written about us, when my cell lit up with a call from Amma. It was an invitation to come over for lunch on Sunday. Doubts niggled at my heart, but I dispelled them promptly. It wasn't an anomaly for my mother to invite me over, especially when it had been a while. Yet, the timing seemed suspicious. It didn't take long for rumors to spread like wildfire and my extended family spanned all over the region, with everyone's noses in everyone else's business.

Before I could call Aarti to alert her about the development, I got a text from her. My heart thudded at the thought that she had seen the gossip piece and I wasn't near her to console her. Not that I imagined she'd be distraught. She was stronger than that. Nonetheless, it would've been ideal if I'd been the one to break the news to her rather than her finding out about it through others.

When I found out that she'd merely texted to cancel our appointment because she was unwell, it gave me a ray of hope. I was both concerned for her and relieved that perhaps she hadn't seen the untoward gossip.

I heaved a deep sigh as I settled on the couch, just as the intercom rang with the doorman asking if he could send up a visitor.

It was Padma and I was at the door when she came up.

"Are you out of your mind?" she said the moment she had her foot in the door.

I heard Aarti cough from the room and said, "Shh, keep your voice down. She's asleep."

"What in the world are you thinking, Annayya? Or maybe you're not thinking at all!" Padma cried.

"Thank you for the rasam," I said, attempting to rush her back out.

"Unh, unh, you're not getting rid of me this easily," she said and stepped over to the couch in the living area.

"Did Amma call you?" I asked.

"Yes, she called me and your aunt and coordinated this whole thing. Asked me to pick up the rasam from her and get it delivered to you."

"It's convenient that our extended family is spread in every corner of this state," I deadpanned. "How did you know where I was?"

"I called Imran," she said. "Is she the same woman from the magazine?" her voice inflected up an entire octave.

"Amma asked you to pry out a confirmation from me, didn't

she?"

"What do you think?"

"Who else has seen it?" I asked, then quickly added, "I don't care. It's a gossip rag anyway."

"*Tech Billionaire, the New Playboy?* That headline gets a lot of attention when it's a brown man and an unknown, gorgeous brown woman on the cover. Especially when Peddamma is trying to sell you as the most eligible bachelor to our community."

"Well, at least they put a question mark," I said wryly. "Who has seen it?"

"Who hasn't?" Padma said, then after a pause, added, "That family lunch on Sunday isn't a coincidence, bro. You're getting an earful, and I'm forewarning you because I like you."

I nodded. What else was I going to say? I had predicted it the moment Devi showed me the tabloid that morning. I was wondering how to break it to Aarti, and now Padma and I were having this conversation right here in her living room.

"Is she the one on the cover with you, or are you truly juggling women like the tabloid suggested?"

"Seriously, Padma, do you think I've got that kind of game? Or time, for that matter."

There was a soft chuckle from Padmaja.

"I don't know about time, but you've definitely got game, big brother. Glad you don't use it, but you've got it, trust me."

"Did you just roll your eyes at that?"

"Yes, because all my friends keep swooning over you, and I have to work hard to keep them at bay."

"Thank you, I guess," I said with a grin.

She took my hand in hers. "I love you, Annayya. I love who you are. But this?"

"I really hadn't foreseen it," I said with all the guilt that wore me down.

"You might be powerful, but you certainly aren't almighty. You can't foresee everything."

I raked my hand through my hair. "I should have planned better."

Padma looked around. I nodded at the bedroom. "Aarti is resting."

"Does she know?"

"I don't know. Considering it came out this morning and that she's been sick all day, it's safe to assume she hasn't."

"Good thing Aarti's face isn't in any of the pictures, and they don't know who she is yet, but it's only a matter of time. The rats will dig out that information soon enough," Padma observed.

"But it is curious that they got multiple pictures of us over the entirety of the evening, yet none of them show her face."

"What does that mean?"

"I'm not sure yet," I said. "But I'll make sure her identity doesn't get out, for her sake. She's already in hot water with her family about this."

"I don't think you can do much in this situation, bro," Padma advised sagely.

"What do you want me to do? Stop seeing her completely?"

"Are you really seeing her?" she screeched. "Like *seeing* seeing?"

"No," I replied promptly and unhesitatingly. "I'm not *seeing* seeing her, but I like her, and I do go out with her. That charity ball was one such social occasion."

"Stop it immediately, or she's going to end up hurt," Padma said pointedly. "And so are you."

"Who told you about Aarti?" I asked. "About...who she is."

"Word gets around, Annayya. It didn't take me long to figure out you liked her that day at the exhibition, and I wasn't even paying attention. Imagine what someone who's interested will dig out."

"Do you also think it's wrong for me to...be interested in Sameer's ex?"

"I'm not the person to answer that," Padma said with a sigh. "I am living a happy, unattached, childfree life. But if you care, then it matters."

"I don't care," I said softly. "But I care about her, deeply. I don't want to put her in a situation where she ends up being hurt again."

"Then stop whatever it is you think you're doing and get on with your life. Because this is bound to end badly and you both will suffer. Social stigma for sure, but more, I suspect."

"Thank you for the rasam, Padma. Imran will drop you wherever you need to go," I said with gratitude.

"Yeah, I've already spoken to him."

She got ready to leave. "Are you going to spend the night here?" she asked at the door.

"If she's unwell and needs me, then, yes, I am going to spend the night on the couch in her apartment," I replied with indignation.

"Ugh, bro, don't be so theatrical. I'm sure an apartment this size has a guest room with a very comfortable bed."

I tapped her head at the sass and gave her a hug. "Thank you, again, for the rasam. I owe you and you know how to collect," I teased with a smile.

"That I do," she said and turned to the door. "And be very sure about what you're doing, Annayya. Chronic heartache is not a healthy condition to live with."

My weary body was ready to collapse on the couch. I lay my head back and closed my eyes. It gave me no respite. I leaned forward, elbows on my thighs, two fingers gently resting on my forehead, my eyes closed. I needed to find a way out of this. And soon.

A soft hand landed on my shoulder. "Sujit," Aarti said.

I jumped up instantly. "Hey! How are you feeling?" I checked her forehead with the back of my fingers. "Good, no fever."

"I'm better," she said and quickly added, "I heard some voices. Was someone here?"

"Yes, Padmaja was here to drop off some rasam."

"Ah, looks like you got your rasam after all. Next stop, family reprimand?" she said with a grin.

"Something like that," I said and asked her to take a seat beside me. "There's something I need to tell you."

I told her about the pictures in the tabloid and the trashy news item that accompanied it. "They haven't figured out who you are, but we need to be prepared…"

"In case we break the internet?" she cried with a frown.

I sighed. "I have no idea how it happened, but I assure you I won't let it get any bigger."

"Can I see it?"

"You don't want to. It's a tawdry tabloid."

"All the same, we must be prepared, like you said."

I pulled up a digital copy on my phone.

"*Tech Billionaire, the New Playboy,*" she read.

"*The New Playboy?*" I corrected with a smile. "There's a question mark there."

She continued reading.

After a disastrous and humiliating breakup earlier this year, the South Asian golden boy of tech, Sujit Rao, is attempting to make waves.

She looked up at me. "That's very bad writing."

I shrugged. "Told you it was a cheap gossip magazine."

"But they could employ some decent writers to get more copies sold."

I returned a tight smile and walked to the kitchen to get us water, while she continued reading aloud,

He was spotted over the weekend at a charity gala with an unknown woman, possibly a model.

"A model?" She grimaced, then returned her eyes to the phone.

The couple seemed very intimate as they shared giggles and whispers, which convinces us that there is something spicy brewing here...

She shook her head. "This is just terrible writing."

The mystery woman created quite the storm on the dance floor, fetching adoring looks and roaring applause. Could this be the start of something big for Rao, or is it just a passing fancy? Will it end in love or is there more heartache in his future?

Ugh, I've read enough," she said, offering the phone back to me.
"Read the final lines," I suggested.
She scrolled down the drivel.

The identity of his glamorous companion is unknown at the moment, but it is only a matter of time until we discover who she is and uncover her connection to Sujit Rao.

Her eyes bulged. "Uncover her connection? They used the word *connection*. This is a threat, Sujit!" she cried with anger.
"Yup. And a thinly veiled one, at that."

"Whoever wrote this is privy to our history. This is a fucking threat!" Aarti bubbled with rage and jumped from her seat.

"What's the endgame here, though? I haven't been able to figure that out."

I handed her a bottle of water and we both cracked the seals in tandem and sipped in silence.

"The curious thing is that if they had wanted, they could have gotten a clear picture of your face and outed you right here, but they didn't. Someone who wanted to target me but not you..." my voice trailed off as I realized whose handiwork this was.

Aarti sat upright. "You know who it is, don't you?" she said.

I glanced at her. She had enough to worry about. I wasn't about to add to her troubles.

"It's probably a prank. It will blow over soon enough." I got up swiftly and grabbed a container from the coffee table. "Come on, let me give you this rasam. This is what will get you back to health."

SUJIT

*I*t wasn't a weekend I was looking forward to. Aarti was
better, but I still didn't want to leave her side. Or
rather, I didn't want to leave *her*.

But everyone in my family had called to confirm I was coming
to lunch on Sunday. I had expected calls from Amma and Cathy,
but when Nanna and Srijan called, I knew it was a siren for deep
trouble. Then my nieces called, courtesy of Cathy, to remind me
how much they were looking forward to seeing me that weekend.

This time, Imran refused to let the car service drive me. I was
already feeling coddled and claustrophobic, but Imran insisted
that it would be best if he drove me on Sunday. Lacking the
energy to fight back on another front, I assented. He insisted that
he was thinking of visiting his cousin anyway, and this would be a
perfect opportunity.

"You've had a tough week, Boss," he said as we approached
my parents' home in the quaint town of Princeton.

My father had retired from the university, but they hadn't felt
the need to move away from the town. That both their sons lived

within reasonable driving distance was one of the reasons, and they were surrounded by family up and down the state.

"Kanna!" Amma squealed per her usual happy demeanor, although I didn't miss the tense look she exchanged with Cathy as I crossed the threshold into the house.

My nieces came hurtling toward me. "My little rabbits!" I said, grabbing one in each arm and giving them a warm embrace.

"Your rabbits are now turning into clever foxes," Srijan said, giving me a hug.

Nanna gave me a pat on my back. "It's been too long this time, Sujit," he said.

Cathy was the last one to smile at me.

"Hi, Suj," she said.

"Come on, Cath," I teased. "You can do better than that." I took her in my embrace and hugged her like we usually did.

Srijan smirked. "You're in big trouble," he whispered near my ear as we all headed inside the home.

"I know, Padma warned me," I whispered back, and he chuckled.

Lunch was no different than usual. Laughter, chatter, and silly jokes from the girls. Now that the older one was in the fifth grade, everything was dramatic. A lot of things were "sus," and most of the boys in her class had become "so annoying."

Not to be left behind, the younger one shared tales of playground politics and allegations of favoritism by teachers.

"Eat your food," Cathy kept reminding them intermittently, and they harrumphed each time before deferring to her instruction.

It was late afternoon when the girls finally disappeared into Dad's library. It was their favorite place in the home. Dad and Amma had curated a special section for them over the years, with their own personalized reading nooks, complete with comfortable oversized recliners for both. The girls were their first grandchildren, and their only ones, they suspected.

I chuckled at their conviction as Srijan handed me a whisky he'd poured for us. Cathy had refused. Dad and Amma didn't drink, but instead of retiring to their room, this time they joined us in the family room.

Amma said something to Cathy in Tamil. I didn't understand the language. Amma spoke both with equal ease, so it was very convenient when Srijan fell in love with Cathy, whose family was from Tamil Nadu. Now the mother-in-law and daughter-in-law had their own secret language, which worked excellently to exclude the men of the family. Dad didn't speak Tamil, but I suspected he'd learned a few terms over the years. He chuckled at Amma's words, and she threw him a quick reprimanding look.

"All right, let's get on with it, then," I said to Cathy.

Cathy frowned with annoyance that she had lost the upper hand in the conversation already.

"If you know why you are here, then you also know what I'm about to say," she began.

I nodded and took a slow drink.

"It's not healthy, Sujit. You are smarter than this."

"Please elaborate," I said, mainly to vex her, but I also wanted to get an insight into what exactly it was that I was doing wrong.

Cathy looked at Amma and said something. Amma nodded and said to Dad in Telugu, "It's best if we let the kids talk alone."

Dad sighed as he lifted himself out of the chair and gave me a reassuring nod. I nodded back.

"Srijan," Cathy ordered and my brother took off just as swiftly.

"Well?" I said when I was alone with Cathy.

"Look, Sujit, you know I've loved you like a little brother."

"Yes, I know."

"So let me tell you that what I'm about to say comes from a place of love and concern, not judgement."

I nodded and placed my whisky tumbler atop a coaster on the glass table before me.

"Aarti is not Tara," she said.

"She definitely isn't," I reassured.

"She's not a substitute for Tara either. She walked into your life when you were reeling from hurt, pain, and humiliation. You met her when you had received the invitation to Tara's wedding."

Her words gave me pause. "How did you know about the invitation?" I asked softly, fending off shame and embarrassment.

She sighed. "Devi mentioned it inadvertently. She didn't know we weren't supposed to know. Everything goes to her desk first, remember? She thought I knew. Otherwise, I wouldn't doubt her discretion one bit."

I'd never doubted her discretion either.

"Why did Tara send you the invitation, Suj?" Cathy asked with concern.

I shifted back in the chair and reclined against the back. "Because when we parted, I said we would be friends. This is her way of showing she still cares about me and wants me to be a part of her life. She wants me to be happy for her."

"Are you happy for her?"

"Absolutely. I wouldn't wish her anything but happiness."

"Are you still in love with Tara?"

I laughed. "At this point, it seems all of you are more obsessed with Tara than I could ever be."

"Don't deflect. Answer the question."

I put my ankle over my knee and leaned back in the chair. "If you'd framed that question differently, the answer was yes."

"Differently how?"

"I love Tara as a person. I care about her. I respect the choice she made for herself. But I am no longer in love with her, if that makes sense."

"That's psychobabble."

"That's the reality of human emotions. Tara brought joy to my life. She taught me how to love, how to have fun. She made me laugh—"

"She also made you cry, dear brother," Cathy argued.

"She did, but not with malice. She was distraught too. I cannot *not* give her the benefit of the doubt just because she put her happiness before mine. That's everyone's right, isn't it? How can I hold a grudge against her for that?"

"So where does that leave you?"

"With the ability to love others."

"Do you love Aarti?"

I smiled wide. "Well played, Cathy. There's a reason I liked you since the first time Sri introduced us."

That made her grin.

"And your answer is?" she prodded.

"You already know, but the answer is yes, I admire Aarti deeply. She is strong, assertive, and savvy. She knows how to run her business."

"That's called transference. Classic transference. Tara was also strong and assertive. She was independent and savvy. You can't have Tara, but you see Aarti, who reminds you of what you had with Tara, and you project your feelings onto her. So, you take your friendship with Aarti and turn it into the feelings you've repressed for all these months."

I roared with laughter and picked up my whisky. The ice was melting, and so was my patience with this conversation.

"If that isn't classic psychobabble!"

"That's psychological insight," she cried with exasperation, "not psychobabble."

"Then let me put your mind at ease. Number one, I have no

repressed feelings. I have allowed myself the time and space to grieve and heal. Number two, I know exactly how I feel about Tara and about Aarti. I am not seeking solace in Aarti's arms just because our exes sought solace in theirs. And number three, to keep comparing Tara and Aarti is to do a disservice to two unique, phenomenal women, whose existence is neither defined nor circumscribed by the men they choose to associate with."

She shook her head as if to clear her thoughts. "But you do have deeper feelings for Aarti. You can't deny that."

"Now, that is a completely different conversation, and I'm afraid our time is up."

She grinned at the joke but instantly said, "Hold on, this was exactly the line of conversation I was trying to have."

"I disagree. You were trying to gauge if I saw Aarti as a substitute for Tara, and we have just established that I don't. You were trying to figure out if I was thinking straight, if all this was unhealthy for me. We also determined it isn't. I think that concludes our conversation, does it not?"

"Sujit," she reproached sternly, but I merely sipped my whisky in response. "This whole idea is too close to your hurt for you to be comfortable with it. I refuse to believe you don't think of Tara when you're with Aarti."

"I don't." I met her eye with conviction. "I've never thought about Tara when I'm with Aarti. Not in the way you imagine, anyway."

I looked at her and saw the concern on her face. Cathy was thrilled to meet Tara that evening at the surprise party. She had loved Tara and was glad she was getting a sister-in-law who was as strong-headed and ambitious as her and who could eventually become her friend and confidant. So when it crumbled at the end of that day, she took the utmost umbrage. She was hurt for me and for herself.

She was hurt for my parents, who she thought were left

humiliated and deserved better. Mostly, I suspected, she was angry at me for being so gullible that I didn't know a heartache was imminent in my future. Whatever her reasons, she was profoundly upset. She had wanted to call Tara and express her displeasure, but of course, I wouldn't allow it.

This wasn't like a traditional arrangement of marriages where one's family is humiliated when the girl refuses a match. The problem had been between Tara and me, a fact Cathy refused to accept easily, *Not after you introduced her to your family!* As if women can't change their minds after having met their partner's family.

"All right, then, let's talk about the optics. This is scandalous for someone in your position. You aren't just an ordinary man, not anymore. Not since you shot into the echelons of the rich and the famous."

"You know I detest that word." *Optics*, I always hated the way it was used these days. For the engineer in me, optics was a field of study, a very interesting one. I was resentful of what it had been transformed into in the American jargon.

"I know," she consoled. "But it is the truth. Unsavory, but the truth. The reality of being in the public eye."

"That's what Aarti's brother said to her," I whispered as I returned my glass to the same spot on the coaster, adjusting to set it parallel to the edges of the table.

"What?" Cathy, now intrigued, sat up with rapt attention.

"That it was embarrassing, it wasn't right."

"That's what I am saying! It isn't right, at least not for families so vividly in the public eye. And despite your arguments and convictions to the contrary, I think it is also very unhealthy."

I paused for thought.

"When the newness fades away, when the excitement wears off, you'll be face-to-face with this reality, Suj. She will always be Sameer's ex to you, and you'll always be Tara's to her. The Tara that broke your heart and the Sameer that stomped on hers. The public humiliation that you both dealt with will resurface when you're done with this initial attraction. And if your relationship becomes public, when this is over, you both will face the same humiliation all over again. You'll never rid yourselves of their shadow. *Never*."

This was also why it irked me that Cathy was smart. She had the knack of showing you the mirror exactly how it was, no matter how dusty or bloody.

"Suj," Cathy said with a hand on my arm as I got off the chair.

I nodded. "You're right. Say bye to the girls for me," I said and left without a word to anyone else.

Imran started the engine when he saw me walk out and was about to rush over to open the car door for me. I waved him to stay put and came around. Slamming the door with some rage, I signaled him to go.

"Are you okay, Boss?"

I didn't have to look in the rearview mirror to see the concern in his eyes.

"Yes, Imran. Everything is good," I said rather curtly, then added, "Thank you for driving me today. I appreciate it."

He nodded as I placed a call to Devi. It was Sunday, but we never cared about weekends since our startup days.

"Yes, Boss," she answered in a chirpy voice. Sunday was when she spent quality time with Kitty, and I felt slightly guilty about encroaching on it.

"Just a quick thing, set up a call with Vinay first thing tomorrow."

"Vinay Rathod?"

"Yes. First thing tomorrow," I repeated and disconnected without pleasantries.

My parents had raised me to be kind, but I was never meek. Even when I was deferential, I was never meek. My friends knew this, as did my competitors. Now, it was time to unleash this side of me for everyone else to see.

As I felt the world closing in on me, I was certain of two things. One, I really, really liked Aarti. She had made her way into my heart and deservedly so. I wasn't going to give up on the possibility of us without a fight. The question was, did she like me enough to stand up against her family, her father, for me? Only she could answer that.

And two, whatever my equation with Aarti, whatever our future held or did not, I wasn't going to let Manoj have his way. Not this time.

I was on a warpath, and this was just the beginning.

AARTI

*T*he calendar had turned that week, kindling a renewed conviction in me.

After our pictures appeared in the tabloid, we'd avoided going out openly. We never spoke about it but we had started meeting at our homes instead of stepping out for meals. The heartwarming dinners had halted, although the conversations had stayed the same.

Sujit had an invitation to a New Year's party that he couldn't refuse. He had made an appearance and left the soirée early to be by my side at midnight. We celebrated with a tiramisu that he had ordered and a chilled bottle of wine. At midnight, he'd kissed my cheek, and later, I'd fallen asleep on his shoulder while we watched a movie.

That week, I decided to regain control over the reins of my destiny, my happiness. It all hinged on one important factor: my father's approval.

"I really don't feel like attending a party, Ma," I said over the phone when I called my mother to inform her of my visit to Dallas.

It had been a while since I had seen my family. I was homesick, but this visit to Dallas was an impetuous decision that I hoped wouldn't backfire. I reserved the real reason for my visit, but Mom took it as a sign to finally throw the party she'd been planning. She wanted to introduce Nitara to the world with a splash and was waiting for me to return. There would be no celebration without me, they all had repeatedly asserted.

I was in no mood to celebrate, not yet anyway. The wedding was still fresh in the memory of our clique. And I had more pressing issues to deal with. Except, Mom had made up her mind and she was a force of nature.

"It's not about you, Beta. This is about Jia and Nitara," she tried to persuade. "It's about making them feel special and loved."

"I understand, and I want all the happiness for them, but I'm still not keen on making public appearances."

Mom let out a quiet sigh. "That's alright, Beta." And there it was. I knew I was going to lose the argument the moment those three words came out of her mouth. "We'll do it later. I'd hate to put you in an uncomfortable position. But it's time to stop hiding. Sameer got married in one of the biggest weddings this year, and you shouldn't be the one shouldering the burden of that breakup. Come with your head held high. You have nothing to feel embarrassed about."

Wise as my mother was, I hated that she was usually—well, always—right. I delivered a deep exhale into the phone, which Mom accepted as my reluctant acquiescence.

"Good," she said, and I could hear the smile in her voice. "Good decision. I'm glad."

I called Sujit to give him the news. The idea of being away from him, of not seeing him for a prolonged period of time, caused an unprecedented frenzy inside me.

"I was just about to call you," he said.

"Yeah? About what?"

"Do I need a reason to call you?" I heard a happy ring in his voice.

I sighed with relief. "No, you don't. You never need a reason to call, but I called to share some news. I'm going to Dallas for a bit."

There was a brief pause that followed an unmistakable shift in his breath. "Is it a casual visit, or did something happen?"

As much as I wanted to share the real reason for my visit, I couldn't. Not yet anyway. If the conversation with my father didn't work out the way I hoped, it would save us both the unavoidable heartache. The very thought threatened to crush my breath and my soul.

"Relax. I just want to see my family. I miss them. And Mom has planned a party for Nitara and she really wishes for me to attend," I offered instead.

"Nitara?"

"My niece."

"Ah."

"I'm sorry to abandon you like this. I know you'll be lost without me."

He laughed his throaty laugh. "That I will be, for sure, but I'm glad you are going back. It's your life, your city, your people. Reclaim it all."

"Whoa!" I uttered. It was weird to hear the fire in his words. Like he was angry and ready to take on the world. "Is everything alright?" I asked tenuously.

"Everything is good. It's about to get even better," he answered cryptically. "You enjoy your time there. Have a safe trip, and let's catch up when you're back."

"Thank you." I stayed on the line since neither of us was ready to hang up. "You know what's reassuring?" I said softly. "Mom said she heard Sameer and Tara are on their honeymoon, so there'll be little chance of running into them."

Quietly, I mused about the word honeymoon, the act of unabashed and blatant fucking cloaked in the sweet mask of a linguistic masterstroke.

"That's good," he said. "And let's talk when you are back."

"Talk? That's a rather specific word. Is it important?"

Another quick pause that I didn't know how to decipher. "Yes, but it can wait until you're back."

"Are you sure? I can make time if you want to meet up before I leave."

"Yes, sweet girl. It can wait. I'm not going anywhere."

"Where were you supposed to go?" I teased, and he broke into a laugh.

"Go on now. Don't you need to pack for your trip?"

"Not much. Mom will probably insist on getting me new clothes for the party anyway. I'll send you a picture," I blurted.

"I'd love that," his soft voice reassured me.

"See you, Sujit. Be a good boy."

"Not this time, sweet girl."

I frowned in confusion. "What do you mean?"

"I'll tell you when you're back. You go enjoy yourself. You deserve it."

"Bye, Sujit."

"See you soon."

~

Two days later, I arrived in Dallas and learned that I was spot on about the new clothes. Mom had set up everything for Jia and me to go shopping for the party.

Jia was relieved to be with someone who wasn't Aakash, Mom, or the household help. She drank decaf coffee and talked my ear off while I smiled and nodded, sitting at a local café.

At the boutique, she complained about her bulging, shapeless belly, and I promptly delivered a lecture about the need for women to break the shackles of social pressure to return to their pre-pregnancy bodies in six to nine weeks after delivery.

"You're barely human in six to nine weeks," I said to her. "That's why I really admired Aishwarya Rai when she had her child. I was young and totally buying into celeb bodies being back to flat and fit within weeks of their deliveries. Then along comes Aishwarya, the former Miss World, and says, f-you all. I will take the time I need, and I won't let you shame me for it. And she didn't hide inside her house either. She flaunted herself at the Cannes the same way she had carried her slender self on that red carpet before the baby. So take your time, Jia. Be happy. Don't force yourself to do anything you don't want to. Rest up and become stronger."

Jia smiled at me as she held up a gown one size larger than she wanted. "I'm so glad Nitara will have you as a role model growing up. I want her to be like you, strong and fierce."

"And like you, strong and loving." I smiled at her in the mirror, and her fair face flushed with humility.

I held her shoulders and leaned in to whisper, "You're not going to cry, are you? I might be good at many things, but I really can't handle tears. I'm not Ma."

Jia gave a quick laugh and turned to me. "Alright, I won't. How's this one?" she asked, holding the gown up again.

"I'm not loving the sequin work. How's this?" I showed her a black gown with muted shimmer.

"Black! Are you trying to get me ostracized? People will talk about it for ages if I wear black to my baby's first event."

"People will always talk, Jia, and no one knows it better than me. What do *you* want?"

She peered straight into my eyes. "I want you to be as happy as I am right now."

I frowned. "You're miserable right now. Nitara's been keeping you up all night and my useless brother has been pushing off all responsibility on Ma."

She laughed. "That's true. Breastfeeding alone is wearing me out. But I still want you to be happy."

I took her hand. "I'm very happy, Jia. Nitara makes me happy. You all make me happy."

Her eyes caught a pastel grey dress in the selection the stylist had brought out for us. "I like this one." She held it up for me. It had a beautiful sheer lace shoulder and long sheer sleeves.

"I love it too. That cascading embroidery is really elegant. Try it, and if it looks good, we'll get that."

I got myself a flowy skirt with a crop top and a jacket, and Jia got the grey dress of her choice.

Jia looked stunning the next evening. With Aakash in a smart tuxedo and baby Nitara in pastel pink, they looked the picture-perfect happy new family.

"So good to see you here, Aarti," Anju said, giving me a hug.

"Thank you, it's been rough," I said as I grabbed a glass of white wine from the server.

"Tell me about it," she said.

Recently divorced, Anju had moved back from Atlanta and had been subjected to similar gossip and speculations about the real reason for the breakup of her marriage.

"How's New York?" she asked, and a quick smile appeared on my lips in response.

The thought of Sujit filled me with warmth. That gorgeous face, the quippy mouth, those bright eyes, the generous heart. And the dimples, those darn dimples that made my knees wobble.

"It's good. Keeps me away from unnecessary thoughts."

"I'm glad you weren't here for the wedding," she said in a hushed voice. "It was all anyone would talk about for days before and after."

"Yes, Aakash told me."

"Ran into Mihir there. He was with someone new, big surprise. Some FOB this time."

I shook my head at her use of the slur, but she didn't notice. "It's really bizarre," she continued, staring at the wine in her glass. "She's unlike any of his previous girlfriends."

Mihir didn't have girlfriends. He didn't believe in relationships, but I didn't remind her of that. Anju had been obsessed with Mihir since I'd known her. Hopelessly so, because for one, Mihir wasn't the kind to settle down like she wanted, and two, they were poles apart. Their personalities were just too incongruent. I had tried telling her that years ago as teenagers, but she claimed I was making a move on Mihir myself and wanted her out of the way. I'd zipped my lips after that. I'd known Mihir for just as long, but he wasn't my type. Sujit, on the other hand, was someone I could dream about with my eyes wide open on those lonely nights when I lay awake in bed trying to quell the fire between my thighs.

"Come tomorrow," she said, breaking my reverie. I trained my eyes back on her. "Mom mentioned your parents are coming alone. But I want you to come. You shouldn't be hiding and shying away."

Anju's brother was getting engaged, but I'd told Ma I wouldn't be attending any other parties at this time.

"I'm not hiding," I argued. Well, I wasn't anymore. "But I'd like to avoid Sameer right now."

"He isn't coming. They are...out," she said.

And I remembered. "On their honeymoon."

"Come tomorrow, I insist," she cajoled with another smile.

"Let me see," I offered truthfully.

Later that night, when I told Mom about this conversation, she agreed. "That's not a bad idea. Maybe you'll meet someone there."

"Ma," I cried and rolled my eyes at her. "Why does everyone assume that not being attached means I'm lonely and miserable?"

"I'm only teasing." Mom smiled and pulled my hand in hers. "But Sameer's parents will be there. Will it bother you?

"I can ignore them."

"Yes, and it's bound to happen. We've excused ourselves from events for months now, but these are our friends, too. We can't miss their kids' birthdays and weddings because Sameer's family will be there. Plus, they aren't missing anything."

I squeezed Mom's hand. "You're right. I think I'll come. This embarrassment BS is like a blanket that we've pulled on ourselves. It's time to shed it."

"Well said, Beta. Chalo, you go to bed now."

Before I turned in, I texted Sujit, and he called me back.

"Why are you still up?" I asked as I cozied underneath my warm duvet. "You're an hour ahead. Shouldn't you be tucked into bed like a good boy?"

"Who said I was a good boy?" he said, and I could picture the glint in his eyes, the one that twinkled from behind his glasses.

"You're not. You are very naughty, a very bad boy," I teased and resisted the thought of him doing nasty things to me.

He laughed. "How was the party?"

"It was wonderful. I'm glad I came. Nitara looked so stinking cute, Mom did her nazar tonight."

"What's that?"

"Something to get rid of the evil eye."

"Ah, yes, I think my mother does something similar for my brother's kids."

"Your brother has kids?" I asked and realized we'd never really talked about his family. "How many siblings do you have?"

"Just the one brother and Cathy, who fusses over me like a mother hen. They have two girls, ten and six. Both a handful, much like you."

"Hey," I complained with faux indignation, "I'm a very good girl!"

"Yes, you're a sweet, sweet girl," he said, and my heart dipped. I wished we were on video call so I could see the look on his face. "Well, I'll let you sleep now," he added with haste.

"Wait," I cried and let the pause say everything I wanted to.

He breathed into the silence, and it felt perfectly peaceful. Bliss, they call it.

"Good night, Sujit," I whispered into the phone.

"Good night, sweet girl."

It was with his voice in my head that I woke up the next day. Sweet girl, the words and the voice carried me through the day and into the party that evening.

Jia had decided to stay home and rest while Aakash was catching up on work. Mom, Dad, and I were almost ready to leave when Nitara threw a fit. Not her mother, or grandmother, nor her nanny could calm her down. It was only when I cradled her in my arms that she lulled into drunken-like drowsiness. Not wanting to put her down until she was in deep slumber, I asked Mom and Dad to go ahead. Mom didn't want to miss the ring exchange. I nodded at them and turned my attention to the calm child in my arms.

AARTI

wenty minutes later, I lay my niece in her crib, peaceful as an angel. An angel no one would believe had screamed like a banshee just a few minutes ago. I put Jia in an armchair with her feet up while the housekeeper brought her herbal tea. Dropping a kiss on Jia's forehead, I grabbed the keys to my Audi.

I had missed driving my car since I left. There was no way I was driving in NYC, and the thought brought me sadness, as if I was slowly wrapping up my life here and moving there for good. A sudden, loud thud echoed through my heart. The thought was exciting and nerve-racking at the same time.

As I entered the heavily decorated banquet hall, hoping to run into friendly faces, I ran straight into Tara.

"Aarti!" she exclaimed with a slight gasp as Sameer appeared by her side. She wore a beautiful evening gown that accentuated her gloriously curvy shape—proud breasts and shapely hips.

"Hi, Aarti," Sameer said, and I gave him a side-eye.

"I was told you were on your honeymoon," I explained with

my eyes resolutely planted on Tara's face. "That's the only reason I decided to come."

She exchanged a quick look with Sameer and returned a warm smile. "We had to cut it short. I got invited to an exhibition. And you don't have to miss anything on our account, Aarti. We'll excuse ourselves from events. This is your community. These are your friends. I'm a newcomer. You have more right, more love here."

I returned a tired smile. "You never made it easy for me to dislike you."

Sameer, too worked up to smile, touched Tara's elbow. "People are staring and whispering. We should move along."

Tara scanned the crowd around us with a gentle frown, then pulled out a wicked smile. "Since they are already talking about us, let's give them something to talk about. Would you like to get a drink, Aarti?" she asked, nodding at the bar.

"That might not be a good idea," Sameer tried to interject, but she gave him a stern glare, and he shut up promptly.

I loved that look on him. He'd always been a larger-than-life figure, a striking, powerful man with enough machismo to melt panties. It was gratifying to see him cower before Tara's ferocity.

"I'd love that," I answered Tara, partly to vex Sameer.

"Go on, I'll catch up with you," she said to Sameer and started walking toward the bar without waiting for his response.

"White wine?" she asked when we'd crossed the small distance to the bar with all eyes glancing and glimpsing at us.

"Sameer told you?"

She nodded. "Sparkling white, right?"

"What are you having?"

She shrugged with a naughty curve of her lips. "I've always been a whisky gal."

"Then make it whisky for me as well."

We grabbed two on-the-rocks and stepped over to a table in

the corner. I looked around for my parents but didn't spot them in the crowd around us.

"Here's to you and Sameer," I said, raising my glass.

"And to you." She clinked it. "How's New York?"

"How did you know...ah, the desi rumor mill."

She nodded and sipped her drink.

"It's good. The work keeps me busy, and it's the best place I could be right now."

"The city is bewitching for sure. I lived in Brooklyn for five odd years," she said.

"We bought some property in Brooklyn, but I've not had a full experience of the place."

"If you need someone to show you around, my friend Sona lives there, and she's amazing. Knows a lot more about the region than I do. She's in Dallas right now, but she'll return soon."

A light flickered in my head. "Is she the one Mihir is seeing?"

Tara looked at me with incredulity. "Is there *anything* people don't gossip about?"

I shook my head and sipped my whisky. "Not much."

"It's a really, *really* small world, and I'm very claustrophobic," Tara said with a graceful sigh.

I looked up at her, and suddenly, I was glad she found the man she loved and who loved her so intensely. She deserved it.

"I heard the wedding was beautiful," I said amicably.

She looked down at her glass. "Yes." She held the silence for a moment, then, looking up at me, said, "I'm sorry it has been awkward for you. When I broke up with Sujit, we ended on a positive note. I don't doubt that I hurt him, but we had a chance to talk it through, to put all emotions out in the open. I realize you never got that chance with Sameer, and I'm sorry for that."

"You aren't the one who should be sorry," I said when her words roused up memories of hurt and humiliation, razing through my heart like a tornado.

"I also realize I never apologized to you," she said, and I looked into her eyes, where I saw warmth and concern, not contempt or deceit.

"You didn't cheat on me," I replied.

"But I did betray your trust."

"Maybe, but I was never angry at you, Tara. I did say some horrible things to you, and I'm sorry, too, but it wasn't about you. I thought I was going to have this wonderful, happy life with Sameer and suddenly, it was gone like sand slipping from between my fingers. I opened my fist, and it was empty."

As her eyes traveled down to her glass again, I caught Sameer from the corner of my eye walking toward us. He wore a perfectly tailored suit in a shade of blue that I used to love on him. And yet, he didn't take my breath away. It didn't shake me to my core as I'd experienced with only one man.

"How's it going? Everything alright?" he asked with diligent caution as he approached us.

Tara looked up at him. "I'll join you when we're done."

He looked at me and sucked a quick breath. "Yes, sure. Take your time," he said to her. Then quickly whispered, "People are talking and wondering if it's going to get heated."

"What, like we're going to end up in a catfight?" Tara scoffed. "I thought you knew us both better than that. Are your parents worried?" She glanced around him toward the crowd.

Sameer shook his head. "Mom also knows you both well."

I took the opportunity to spot my parents again. I saw Mom eyeing me with concern, but I gave her a knowing nod and a smile. She nodded in relief and turned around to join her group of friends.

Tara put a hand on Sameer's arm. "Go on," she said with a love-filled smile. "I'll join you in a bit."

Sameer smiled at her first, then at me, and turned to leave.

"And let them talk," Tara said to his back. Sameer turned his face and gifted her a most brilliant smile.

"I never loved him, Tara," I said when Sameer was out of earshot. "I thought I did, but now I know it wasn't that."

She nodded gently.

"I know because I met someone and felt something."

Her eyes bulged wide before softening with a warm smile. "I'm very happy for you."

She ran her finger on the rim of her glass, gazing into it. I understood why Sujit had a high regard for her. Now that I knew the full story, I got it, too. I thought she had stolen Sameer from me, but he was never mine. *I* was the other woman. Even if I had married him, I would've always been the other woman.

"How did you know?" I asked, and she looked up. "How did you know Sameer was the right person for you and not your New York boyfriend?" I purposefully left out Sujit's name.

"My mother saw it first," she said, reiterating what Sujit had already told me. "She said Sameer lit a fire in me and that I won't be happy without it in my life."

"Do you believe that's true?" I asked.

"Well, if that fire meant annoyance, he definitely does that. He annoys me to no end," she joked and laughed. I didn't.

I waited with anticipation. I really wanted to understand why she chose Sameer over Sujit, who was incredibly kind and a hundred times wealthier.

Tara took a small sip and pulled in a deep breath. "As much as I regret hurting Sujit, at the end of the day, the question was, with whom could I see myself growing old and wrinkled? For me, that person was Sameer."

She looked at my earnest face and leaned in to whisper, "Listen, it's very simple. If you think you can fart in the presence of this man without fear of embarrassment, then he's your person. I couldn't imagine it with Sujit." She lifted one shoulder in a matter-of-fact shrug.

Her blunt words shocked me, but I could totally see myself in any situation with Sujit without fear of judgement or embarrassment.

She grinned at my expression. "Looks like you got your answer."

I gave her a shy smile that I promptly hid with my glass. Around us, a few aunties huddled, whispering and stealing badly hidden glances at us.

"They're never going to make it as spies," I remarked.

"Nope. Mata Haris, they are not," she said and let out a marvelously loud laugh.

I discarded all inhibition and joined her. We both laughed raucously as people stared at us with scandalized eyes and disapproving head shakes.

"Fuck, I'm just going to say it. You're awesome," I said. We clinked our glasses and took a big gulp of the sharp whisky. "Thank you for today, thank you for this," I said softly after the taste of the whisky on my tongue had mellowed.

"Thank you for being generous," she said and squeezed my hand.

"Tara...I was wondering if we could talk again before I leave. Somewhere more private?"

Her eyes studied me for a brief second, then creased at the edges. "Absolutely. Do you want to come over to the condo, or would you like to meet somewhere else?"

"Not the condo, for sure. Too many memories."

"I understand. How about that favorite bistro of yours?"

I was about to nod when a strange realization hit me. She wouldn't have known about my favorite bistro unless Sameer had shared it with her, and it assured me of two things. One, Sameer did care about me. Even though he'd broken my heart, I had occupied a place of importance in his life. If I hadn't, if I'd been insignificant, he wouldn't have bothered telling Tara so much about me. And two, their relationship was solid as a boulder. You don't talk to your wife about your ex's favorite bistro and her love for sparkling wines unless you both have complete faith in the relationship.

Aakash said Sujit and I would live in the shadow of their happiness all our lives, but they were also living in the shadow of our memories. It was a strangely comforting thought. Sujit and I were not discounted, dismissed, or made invisible, but rather, held with love and reverence in their relationship. Maybe that's where Sujit and I could begin.

"Yes, let's meet at the bistro." I breathed in a satisfied whiff.

AARTI

The next morning, I sat at my favorite brunch place in Plano, along an artificially created lake, pristine and well-groomed. This was the last place I had shared a meal with Sameer before all the threads had unraveled, but its memory didn't garner bitterness. Not after my chat with Tara last night.

For the short time I'd known her, Tara had always been graceful, gracious, and proud. I'd been hurting because I'd not had closure, as Tara pointed out, but talking to her and laying out my feelings had aided the healing process.

That evening months ago, I had barged in on them having an intimate dinner at his condo. I was about to rush out, angry, humiliated, and injured, when Tara suggested that I should hear them out. Her words were still vivid in my memory. *You have a choice. You can stay and let Sameer explain. Or leave with this rage and carry the grudge for life.* I was ready to jump on the bandwagon of carrying the grudge for life, but then I heard her say, *Neither can change the fact of his betrayal, but you can choose how you want to resolve this.*

There it was. Betrayal. It was out in the open. Spelled out in red. Spoken in bold. She had called out Sameer's actions for what they were. Betrayal.

I stood at the door, tears in my eyes, and made the decision to step back in. I wasn't sure I had made a wise decision, but it felt like the right thing to do at that moment. Their apology was unconditional.

It was Tara's honesty in calling a spade a spade that brought me back into the apartment. As Sameer started confessing how I'd been merely a means to his ultimate goal—getting back the wealth and status they had lost in India—I felt more and more like a fool. A fool who had thought she was in love with an honest and loving man.

I'd returned home in tears and confided in my family. Dad had called Sameer's father and pelted him with angry words and vengeful threats. Dad was a powerful man, but I'd not known him to be vindictive. Mom and I had talked him down. It was better we'd discovered the truth before the wedding. It would've crushed my heart if I'd spent a lifetime trying to win Sameer's love only to realize it would never have materialized.

It wasn't the breakup that hurt me. It was the public declaration of our betrothal that unnerved me. People break up all the time. It's not a big deal. But I'd announced to half the city that I was in love and planning to marry the man of my dreams. That's the part that hurt the most. It was about my ego, not love.

As he had promised, Sameer had come to apologize the next day, and the next, and the day after that, but I'd refused to see him. I'd asked Mom to turn him away. He had spoken to my parents with humility, accepting his guilt in all of it. He'd confessed about his strained relationship with his father, who'd instigated the surprise proposal. But I hadn't seen him, hadn't given him a chance to explain, hadn't told him the extent of my hurt, and that's where I'd faltered. If I had, I probably have had some semblance of closure sooner.

Tara arrived with a smile, dressed in leggings, high boots, and a smart quilted jacket over a black top. A handmade long necklace and a beautiful bold purple on her lips marked her as the artist that she was.

"Hey," she said as she pulled a chair across me. "You look great."

I didn't need to glance down at myself in jeans, a top, a jacket, and ankle boots. "You do too." I smiled.

We placed our order amid a bit of initial awkwardness. After a few minutes of small talk, she went straight to business.

"So, what did you want to talk about?"

"You're not going to let me have my coffee first?" I teased, and she smiled.

I readjusted myself in the chair. "I told you yesterday I met someone and felt something?"

She nodded just as the server approached and placed two artistically finished lattes before us. Tara grabbed the tiny tongs, dropped three sugar cubes from the ceramic holder, and put the lid back. I eyed her as I brought my cup to my lips.

"Go on," she urged, stirring hers.

"It's Sujit."

Her spoon dropped in the cup, slumping against the rim. "*Sujit*? *My* Sujit?" she asked, and I laughed.

"Yes, the one you ditched for Sameer," I teased, and her eyes traveled to the table with a smile.

"Tell me more. Tell me everything," she said, looking back up at me.

When I finished narrating how we had met and how the friendship had evolved over the months, I confessed, "I think I might be falling for him."

The smile on her face had grown systematically wider, and she finally lifted her cup to her lips. "I don't blame you, he's very lovable."

I looked into her eyes. "Did you really love him, Tara?"

She placed her cup back and interlaced her fingers resting on the table. "I did. I still do, in a way. I care for him deeply, but when I saw Sameer again, I remembered what we had. The heat, the need, the hunger, it was deeper, more urgent. I felt it in my heart, in the pit of my stomach. But when I am in his arms, it's peaceful, quiet, and comfortable. I don't know how to explain it."

"I know. It's how I feel with Sujit. This yearning that arises sometimes in the heart, sometimes below the belly, and takes over completely. It's warm and needy. It's the kind of frenzy I can't understand. But it's more. I feel calm, grounded, and protected around him."

She smiled and leaned in to pat my hand. "That sounds awfully like more than feelings, Aarti."

"Don't say it, don't say the word."

"I won't. I know it's scary. Been there, done that. Twice." She nursed the giant cup in her hands.

"I feel like you're the only person I can share all this with. I fear people will judge me for my desires. Ridicule me. With you, I have an upper hand since you stole my boyfriend and all," I teased.

She gave me a wicked smile and said, "Not boyfriend, *fiancé*, remember?"

I shook my head as I drained the last of my coffee. "Don't remind me." And we both burst out laughing. "I don't know what I was thinking."

"I was so envious of you, Aarti. The first time I saw you, I thought I could never compete with her. She's the definition of perfect—beautiful, gorgeous, stylish. It pained me to see how good you both looked together."

"And I was envious of how he looked at you with so much love and admiration. I'm still a little envious of how happy you are together."

She turned more somber despite the slight smile gracing her face. "Have you told Sujit how you feel?"

I shook my head just as the server came back out again and put the omelets before us.

"You're scared," she observed as I picked up my fork.

"I'm terrified."

"Because?"

Tara was a smart woman, and I was glad I was talking to her about this. She had the distance from me that made her objective, and she knew Sujit intimately, which made her the perfect person to advise me.

"Because even though I think he feels the same way about me, I can't be sure. And because the world might ridicule us for falling for each other."

She put her fork down with a frown. "What do you mean?"

I told her about my conversations with Aakash and Mary Beth. "I don't know how my father will take it. He hates everything associated with Sameer. Both my brother and my best friend warned me that Sujit is and will always be your ex. Is it shameful to fall for him? Aakash says it reeks of desperation or vengeance, you know, because you fucked my boyfriend, I fucked yours."

She laughed a nervous laugh. "That thought never occurred to me, but tell me..." She dabbed the corners of her mouth with a napkin. "What does it matter what anyone thinks and says? If he makes you happy and you make him happy, isn't that the only thing that matters?"

"Aakash says it might hurt our reputation, our standing in the business world and in society."

"Does that bother you?" she asked.

I knew Sameer had declared he would put his and Tara's happiness before the business, but it was his name at stake, not his father's, not his family's.

"I can't believe I'm telling you this. I haven't even told Ma, but I'm here to talk to my dad. I'm going to explain everything and beg him to give me and Sujit a chance at happiness."

Tara reached out and grabbed my hand while my eyes remained downcast with everything that was weighing me down —the desire, the guilt, the shame, and the embarrassment about the shame.

"I don't know your father, but Sameer speaks very highly of him. He also told me how much your father loves and respects you. So here's my unsolicited advice. Don't beg. Demand. You shouldn't have to beg for your happiness from the people you love and who love you. You should expect it, and demand it."

My eyes shot up to her, staring at her with incredulity. "Damn, girl! You've got your perspective all sorted out!"

There was strength and conviction in her voice when she said, "When you've grown up without much, your ambition and happiness are the only things you can unflinchingly stake a claim to."

The words stabbed at my heart. Unlike me, she'd had to claw her way to the top. I'd grown up with privilege, and even though I worked hard, some doors were already held open for me. Not for someone like Tara.

"You know, we could have been best friends in another life." I surprised myself with this honest confession.

"I don't believe in other lives," Tara responded, shaking her head and sticking a gentle fork in her breakfast potatoes. "Yes, if things were different, we could have been close friends, but nothing's stopping us from being friends now." She met my eye. "You are always welcome in our life, Aarti. Sameer has nothing but the highest regard for you. When you find it in your heart to forgive us both, we would love to have you as a part of our lives again. If that's something you want too."

I nodded. "I don't make friends easily."

"I know. All the more reason to keep us close, yeah?" Her warm smile enchanted me completely.

At that moment, I understood what Sameer saw in her. She completed him. She grounded him.

Sujit was right. Relationships are peculiar.

"I'd like that," I said. "And I know we both will get along well. For one, I'll be the perfect sounding board when Sameer annoys you. No one better to bash him than me."

"Whoa, that's definitely an unforeseen advantage," she joked.

She reached across the table to pat my hand. "I'm genuinely happy for you and Sujit. Tell him the moment you're back in New York. If I were the type, I'd be squealing and screeching with joy right now."

Retracting her hand, she turned serious. "He's a very good man, Aarti. Sona calls him a unicorn. Hurting him is something I'll have to live with, but if you two make it work, please take very good care of him. Give him the love he deserved from the start. Did he tell you about Tejal?"

My eyes flickered in thought. "He didn't mention her name, but he did share the story."

"He had carried that hurt for a long time, and I turned around and crushed his heart. It doesn't help that he has to keep seeing that bastard Manoj every so often."

I sucked in a breath. "Tejal was married to Manoj?" I cried with a gaping mouth.

She put her fork down. "He didn't tell you that part?"

I shook my head as it all made perfect sense suddenly. Manoj's approaching me for the property, his interests in the same buildings I was showing Sujit, his asking me out. The puzzle was solved, the picture crystal clear before me.

"Thank you for telling me," I said. "I suspected there was something off about that man. I just couldn't figure out what."

"Everything is off about that man," she said and picked up the glass of orange juice before her. "Sujit must have a very good reason not to shove him out of his life. God knows, he should've years ago."

Tara sipped her orange juice. Then she dabbed her mouth delicately and replaced her napkin by her plate.

This newfound camaraderie led us to exchange stories about our jobs and their stresses. The excitement in Tara's voice was unmistakable as she told me about embarking on a career as an artist. Something she'd always wanted and worked for and which was finally within her reach.

"You get the guy and the career of your dreams, eh? Talk about finding your happily ever after," I teased as I finished up my egg and placed my silverware down.

She blushed, then studied me with a doe-like tender gaze. "You shouldn't worry about what others think. I'm talking for real here. You are *the* Aarti Bhatia, and he's Sujit freaking Rao. You'll be the most charismatic, most dynamic power couple since...hell, I don't even know any other power couple who can hold a candle to you. It's a fucked up world, Aarti. Its lust for the misfortune of others will never be satiated. You go get your happily ever after. Claim it, grab it, and never let it go."

I did the only thing I wanted to do at that time—grin wide and be grateful for the woman sitting across the table from me. "I think I'm going to do just that."

"Now, that's the kind of billionaire romance I can really root for," she said with a wink.

SUJIT

I knew it was Manoj the moment Aarti confirmed my suspicions.

Never before, since becoming Sujit Rao, the billionaire, had I captured the paparazzi's fascination. I'd had dinners with politicians, some of whom were my friends from college. I'd attended parties with celebrities and high rollers, but it had never been newsworthy. And certainly not tabloid-worthy. If I had ended up on the cover of a gossip magazine, a tawdry one at that, it had to be for one reason alone. Someone was bothered by my proximity to Aarti.

The choice of the tabloid was no coincidence either. It was a careful attempt at causing insult, injury, and humiliation. The only reason Aarti's face wasn't plastered all over the tabloid was because someone didn't want to get on her bad side. Someone who had hopes that he could somehow charm her.

I didn't have to look or think too far to figure out who that snake was. Well, scratch that. Apologies to all snakes everywhere. He was a human. A malicious human with everything devious that humanity is made up of. A human who dressed well and smelled good to hide the rot that was inside him.

Manoj was smart. A charmer who could sweet-talk his way into or out of anything he wanted. During college, I had held that he was smarter than me. But instead of using his brilliance for good, he had squandered away his energies trying to outdo me. Initially, it had been a response to his father's affection and high regard for me. I'd been merely a pawn in his quest to gain his father's validation and approval. Yet, in the long years he'd been obsessed with me, his envy had intensified. He was consumed by it. His actions were no longer motivated by gaining his father's approval. This was about me.

Ironically, he also owed his success to me. Cyber security was new and hot at the time, and he'd nicked the idea from my notes, I later came to realize. We'd been brainstorming ideas one week, and the next, he said he had found his niche in cyber security. I had made detailed notes only days before. It felt uncanny that he had come up with an almost identical proposition, but I was naïve, and I trusted our friendship. After all, what person would do that to a good friend?

I let him pursue his startup idea as he gathered people and resources around him quickly. He was terrific at that. I was bookish and nerdy. Manoj was worldly-wise and a convincing orator. So while he tinkered with the options for cyber security and flaunted his new relationship with Tejal, I retracted to my safe zone in front of a computer and discovered another idea that I really liked. Software solutions for healthcare management. I had seen my uncle and aunt, both doctors, struggle with insurance filing and patient information paperwork. It was their kind faces that I kept before me as I worked hard to build viable solutions for small clinics.

For years, Manoj had toed the line and then looked for a reaction from me. Much like an errant child doing what it's instructed not to do, then looking challengingly at the parents. I had kept him as a part of the group because neither Chris nor Jas knew about the real Manoj. And because Tejal had warned me to keep my enemies close. That's what I'd done.

I had kept tabs on him for a long time. It wasn't uncommon for companies to recap, but his frivolity and lack of vision kept running his to the ground. He used his charm and his beguiling ways to keep attracting capital to pump into his failing enterprise. The second time he was on the brink of a recap, I had asked Vinay to invest in his company. He did it as a favor to me, knowing full well that the company was headed downhill.

Manoj had made it his mission to become bigger and better than me. I didn't mind that. My ego was neither bloated nor fragile to be intimidated by his ambitions. But this time, he had crossed the line. If he thought he could use Aarti to get to me, he had clearly misjudged me for all these years. There wasn't much he could do to undermine me, but the day he learned that Aarti wasn't interested in him, the next issue of that tabloid would be replete with filthy lies about her. That was a surefire way of hurting me.

I was about to make certain that didn't happen.

Vinay was Dad's former student. His first student who'd made it big in the tech industry and who had become a venture capitalist by the time I graduated. It could have been his regard for Dad that made him unflinchingly invest in my startup when it was still rough around the edges. He had always insisted that he saw the merit of my project. He knew the gaps in the industry, and he had long prophesied its massive success. I had never thought it would be sought after by everyone in the healthcare industry. But after it went big, Vinay had patted my back and sagely said, "I'm not going to say *told you so*, but I did call it when I sent you that first check. Maybe now you can finally accept I'm a savvy investor."

I don't remember the exact moment our business relationship turned into friendship. But over the years, it had slowly and quietly blossomed into a form of trust and loyalty that was rare in the cut-throat competitive market in which we operated.

Devi had given his office a heads-up, so Vinay was ready when I called.

"Hey, Suj," he said in his deep, throaty voice. Authoritative.

A voice quite asynchronous with his gentle visage and mild manner. But then his mild manner also quite effectively masked the astute, ruthless businessman inside him. It was his ruthlessness that I needed right now.

"Vinay, I think it's time," I stated without preamble.

With Vinay's acumen, we had a plan in place. He had already talked to the other investors about his interest in buying them out. He had primed them about the bloated valuation of the company, highlighting the need to change the leadership. While two major investors had agreed to sell their shares to Vinay, one had offered to support his decision to rid the company of Manoj. A change at the helm would get him a better return on his investment, he had argued. Vinay had been careful to keep my name out.

I didn't believe in playing dirty, but Manoj had started it and had transgressed the boundary that he shouldn't have. I was ready to do whatever it took to ruin him.

"Our best option is a leveraged buyout," Vinay informed me. "It will shatter his credibility in the industry."

"That is what I want."

"It will take a few months, but he will be out."

"Leave him with nothing," I demanded.

"He will be left with a little," Vinay countered practically, and I knew I would have to make peace with it. For the moment, at least.

Once Manoj was out, I would eventually buy the company. It

was my idea after all, implemented badly, and I was determined to rescue it and build it to its fullest potential. My anger spiked at the thought of every backstabbing act Manoj had carried out over the years.

"I want him ruined. I want him out."

"He will be when we are done with him," Vinay assured.

"And no one gets laid off. AccessEd will absorb his employees if needed."

"That's your headache, not mine," he reminded me.

"No mercy, Vinay. None. I need him running scared and desperate by the end of the month."

"Be careful," Vinay cautioned like the big brother he had always been to me. "This guy is not going to go down easy."

"I will. I can take care of myself, but I won't let him hurt others. Not anymore."

Vinay's voice shifted from professional to personal. "Can I ask you something?"

I hummed in response.

"Why now? You've been waiting patiently for years to see him drown himself."

"Yes, I knew he'd ruin himself sooner or later. That I'd not have to lift a finger for his downfall."

"What happened this time?"

"This time, he messed with the wrong person."

AARTI

I spent that weekend luxuriating in the warmth of Tara's words. I was ready to grab my happy.

If I had read Sujit correctly, I knew he liked me. But he had enough reasons to tamp down on his feelings. After all, I wasn't the only one in the public eye. That event with our picture in the tabloid had made it clear that Sujit had as much to lose. And if he thought our relationship would mark us for ridicule, I would understand and accept his decision.

But I wanted him to make that call because I was ready to take the plunge.

My nerves kept jangling all weekend, excited to go back into Sujit's arms and terrified of my father's reaction if our relationship actualized. That was the reason I chose not to divulge any of this to Mom. I hadn't told her about my meeting with Tara either.

The society assumes and expects women to catfight over men, like they were prizes to be won. And there we were, Tara and me, sharing brunch and developing a friendship that would've been seen as suspect by anyone who knew our situation. The crux of the matter was, I wasn't jealous of Tara, and she wasn't insecure about me. I didn't want what she had, and she didn't suspect I would become a thorn in their relationship. In fact, I was mildly, albeit pleasantly surprised at her reaction to my interest in Sujit. Unlike my feelings for Sameer, her admiration for Sujit hadn't waned. She wanted him to have the happiness that he had granted her.

Although I had never cared about accolades, it was reassuring to learn that she respected me enough to believe in my happiness. To believe that I could keep Sujit happy for life. It was a grown-up, healthy approach to relationships that I hadn't encountered before.

The mountain I needed to scale right now was my impending talk with Dad. *Demand, don't beg*, Tara had advised. Finding the right words to do just that was the herculean task before me.

"What's bothering you?" Mom asked, looking at my hand. We were at the table having a family dinner.

I stopped fiddling with the ring on my left index finger and shook my head at her. "Nothing."

"If you don't want to go back, you don't have to, my child. It's all done now. The buzz has died down," she reassured.

"Yes," Dad added to my surprise. He usually chose to stay silent on the subject.

I decided to tread that forbidden line. "Have you forgiven them now?" I asked in a gentle tone to suggest I wanted him to. But to my dismay, he shook his stubborn head.

"No. Never. They hurt my little girl, and I will never forgive them for it."

I unleashed a quiet sigh of dejection and threw a glance at Aakash. He returned me a somber *I told you* look. Mercifully, Aakash had chosen to underplay the gravity of our last conversation, opting instead to revel in the misconception that I had given up all association with Sujit. That was his folly, and I chose not to shatter his delusions.

Jia didn't know about any of this and continued to eat her food in blissful ignorance. I was glad about that.

"You should return now," Dad continued. "I miss you here." His voice was soft, but he quickly cleared his throat and gruffly added, "The business needs you."

I glanced at Aakash again, who shook his head and got back to his food. I burst into a quick laugh, and Dad realized his error.

"Err...I didn't mean to imply Aakash isn't doing a good job—"

"It's all right, Papa," Aakash interjected. "We both know she's more qualified than me to handle it."

"Yes, but that doesn't mean you are not holding it on your own," Dad consoled him, then turned to me, "But we are still awaiting your return, Aarti."

"Darn, he must really miss you," Aakash said with a grin. "When's the last time you heard him express his feelings so vocally?"

Mom chuckled in response and said to me, "We all miss you, my darling."

"And we want you to be back here," Jia added. "For good."

I smiled around the table at everyone. "I have some unfinished business in New York. As soon as I see it through—"

"You'll take the next flight back," Dad declared without looking at me. He had his attention on his food, enjoying his favorite aloo ki sabzi with dal and chawal.

It was another thing we shared. We both loved this particular potato recipe that only Mom could make perfectly.

I took the opening to broach the subject. "About that..."

Dad sat upright and glared at me. "What? I knew there was something fishy when you decided to buy that condo there."

"Is that true?" I heard the panic in Mom's voice. "Are you having second thoughts about coming back?"

Now Aakash joined in. "Come on, Sis. This is ridiculous." He huffed. "You can't let Sameer drive you out of your own hometown. This is your birthplace. You can't just up and leave because he broke off an engagement."

And then Jia chimed in. "Aakash is right. I can't imagine Nitara growing up without you around her."

"Will you all just calm down?" I cried with a frown. "No one is driving me out. I'm neither timid nor fragile to be frightened off so easily. But the expanding nature of our business means we need another home base. And New York seems like a logical one, doesn't it, given how much property we've already invested in?" I looked pointedly at Dad, who returned a resigned, sheepish look.

"We can find someone else to conduct business there," Aakash suggested.

"Yes, and you can travel there whenever you need to, but don't even think about moving there!" Jia said with a panic in her voice. I understood her fears and empathized. New York wasn't a place of particular fondness for her. She grew up adjacent to the city where she had experienced the worst years of her life.

I reached over and placed a hand on her arm. I had no real words of comfort to offer, and I didn't want to lie if only to assuage her.

"Nitara will never grow up without me in her life," I said. This was the truth. Even if I were across the world on another continent, I would be in her life and she in mine. "I can't imagine growing old without her in mine either."

"Old?" Jia said and burst out laughing. "Please, you're never getting old. You're like fine wine. You'll age like Angela Basset or Jane Fonda."

Mom smiled lovingly at Jia first, then at me. "Or like Rekha, the Bollywood icon of agelessness."

"Or like our own Ma right here," Jia said with a love so pure, it existed only in the realm of the spiritual. Mom beamed and gifted Jia the most brilliant smile I had seen on her in a while.

"Alright, alright, you both!" I chided lovingly and was instantly reminded of Sujit. If he were here, he would have agreed with them and probably added a few more names to the list. Michelle Yeoh, perhaps.

A wave of gentle warmth brushed my heart at his thought, and suddenly, the idea of being away from my family halfway across the country didn't fill me with dread. Instead, I found myself daydreaming of a fulfilling life with him. I looked at my father, his blissful self enjoying a satisfying meal with his family.

We gathered in the anterior room and chatted until Dad excused himself and retreated to the study. A tired Jia went to her room to spend time with Nitara.

"You both head up too," I said to Ma and Aakash. "I'll talk to Papa for a bit, then turn in, or I'll be tired on my flight tomorrow."

Ma gave me a tight hug. She did miss me but I wasn't worried because she had found a daughter in Jia. I knew she'd be loved and cherished in my absence. I also knew I was only a phone call and a four-hour flight away if she ever needed me.

Outside the study, I spent a few moments admiring my father hard at work before I knocked. He waved me in.

He turned around in his work chair as I took a seat on the couch.

"You're leaving tomorrow," he said.

This was as close to *I love you* as he could get.

"Yes, Papa. I wanted to talk to you about something before I left."

A smile and a nod as he interlaced his fingers, resting them on the slight paunch of his stomach.

I pulled in a deep breath, mustering all my courage. If there was ever a time to be brave, now was it.

"I met someone in New York, Papa. Someone that I've come

to like and respect," I said with as confident a voice as I could manage.

His smile disappeared and was replaced with a thoughtful frown.

"You haven't been in New York that long." Read, how did you meet, connect with, and come to trust someone in such a short period?

"We have been able to spend some time together."

"It is not difficult to impress someone if you are so inclined." Like Sameer, who had efficiently managed to fool us all. My mind completed the unsaid part.

"I've had the chance to witness his true nature and personality. I trust him."

"Have you done a background check? Do you want me to?"

I shook my head firmly. "No. But I need your blessing."

The frown deepened. "Here is what I know, Aarti. If you were confident in your choice, you wouldn't be here talking to me."

I took another deep breath. It was time to drop the bomb. "It is Sujit Rao." I wondered if Papa knew his connection to Tara.

"That name sounds familiar," he said and turned his chair to his desk.

If Sujit were anyone else, he would've made sure that everyone knew who he was, what he was capable of. Thankfully, Sujit was not just another billionaire. He was the kind of billionaire the world needed more of. A benevolent king who'd spend his riches trying to do good for humanity.

The big screen of Dad's home computer lit up as he did a quick search for Sujit. What he read must have pleased him because this time when he turned to face me, his frown was gone.

"Sounds like a decent enough guy."

"There is one thing Google search won't tell you, and that's the reason we are having this conversation, Papa," I said in a gentle voice, preparing him for the next words that were about to come out of my lips.

The frown reappeared, along with the interlaced fingers and the stern look in his eye.

"Sujit was Tara's boyfriend."

That got me the reaction I was waiting for. The bomb had exploded. He jumped from his seat, his anger and disappointment fumbling for words. He stood, gawking at me, as I slowly rose from the couch.

"I know what you are thinking—"

"What were *you* thinking, Aarti!" he cried. I stepped up to him and coaxed him back into his chair.

I kneeled at his side and told him everything. Our chance meeting, the connection over the breakup, how he lent me his shoulder to cry on. I told him about my conversation with Aakash and his fears if our relationship became public. Dad heard me out patiently, never once interrupting.

When I was done, he pulled in a deep breath and said, "And despite all that, we are here, talking about it."

Which meant I liked him enough to put everything at stake.

"Yes, Papa. You remember we had that wall calendar one year when I was younger? It had all those clichéd quotes, and one of them said, *Happiness is like a butterfly. The more you chase it, the more it eludes you. But if you turn your attention to other things, it will come and sit softly on your shoulder.*"

Dad looked at me like I had completely lost my mind. Maybe I had.

"It felt like that. When I was busy chasing love, I didn't find it. But when I buried myself in work, I was landed straight before Sujit."

Dad frowned. All this talk of love and men was making him uncomfortable.

"Looks like you've made up your mind," he said with a slight slump. "What are you asking of me?"

I stood up and retook my seat on the couch. I needed to look into his eyes when I told him this.

"I've made up my mind," I began, "but I still haven't told Sujit how I feel. I think he likes me, but we haven't had the conversation. I said I'm willing to risk it all, but I have yet to find out if he is willing to do the same."

He leaned forward in the chair. "You chose to speak to me before you find that out?"

"Because I need your blessing. You always say I'm your pride. But you are my pride too, Papa. You and Ma. I am proud to call you my parents. Your hard work, your ethics, these are the principles I've founded my life on. It's not only that I don't want to displease you, but I would never want to put you in a position where you can't hold your head high."

He looked away promptly as I spied a slight shimmer in his eyes. With rapid blinks, he tried to regain his composure.

"You've consulted me before making any major business decision in recent years. I'm asking that you trust me to make the right decision about my life."

He rose and walked to me with small steps. I stood, and he gave me a quick hug. Then he put a hand on my shoulder and said, "I am not good with words like your mother, but I have always trusted you, Puttar. You know that. But I'm ashamed...." his voice trailed.

My heart sank. It appeared that my father shared Aakash's fears after all. He was unwilling to let the stigma of my association with Sujit taint his name and business. It was a source of shame for him.

A tear threatened to gather in my eye. I had never cried before Dad. I was his strong Bachcha, molded in his image. I swallowed hard to push down all the emotions rising inside me, including a feeling of betrayal and shame. I wasn't about to put his legacy at risk. I would kill all desire for love and happiness rather than malign the reputation of my hardworking parents. I hoped he knew that.

"I won't do anything to risk our family or our business, Papa. I will remove myself from his life swiftly if you don't approve of our relationship."

Dad shook his head vigorously. "No," he said. "That's not what I meant."

I took his hand in mine. "It is alright, Papa. I understand. I am not a regular woman who can live her life according to her own rules." Like Tara, who could choose her own happiness. "I know I bear the burden of being the heiress to the Bhatia estate. You never have to worry about it, Papa. I will never put myself before our family's repute..." my voice broke.

I stopped talking. I wasn't going to let my father bear witness to the pain of my shattered heart. My broken life.

To my amazement, Dad grinned. *He grinned!* Blinding me with a dazzling look, the one that crinkled the skin around his aging eyes. He put a hand on my head and tapped twice.

"This is the reason you're my pride, Puttar. I can always count on you to do the right thing. But I want you to count on me to do the right thing too. I'm ashamed..." He paused and let out a sad smile. "I'm ashamed that you think I wouldn't risk absolutely everything to get you the happiness you deserve."

This time, I allowed the tear to slip off my eye and down my face. A lone tear of a warrior who had won the battle. Dad patted the hand he held, and I swiped my tear away with the other.

"But I am worried," he said and settled down on the couch. I lowered myself beside him. "A father can't stand by and watch his daughter's heart being shattered. *Again.* What if this Sujit boy is unwilling to commit? You said he has as much to lose."

The conviction that the two men I loved—my father and Sujit

—had awakened in me rang through my strong voice. "Then it will be on me. It was my decision, and I am strong enough to weather the consequences. But if I give up without trying, it will be unfair to me."

Papa nodded multiple times. "Your mother always said, if Aakash can do what he wants, Aarti also should be able to. If we didn't object when Aakash chose his life partner, how can I deny you that right?" he said and let out a deep sigh. "I didn't grow up thinking like that. Our family was very conservative, with strict gender roles and expectations. Women were not allowed to spread their wings and fly. My mother was a smart woman, but she remained buried in housework all her life. She could have been a world-class singer, but women were not allowed to sing in our household. She wanted to be one, but she made peace with her life."

I had heard my grandmother sing, but I'd never given it much thought. Hearing my dad talk about his mother's missed opportunities and her unfulfilled dreams put everything in perspective. Every generation of women benefitted from the struggles of the generations that came before them. I was benefiting from both my grandmother's and my mother's missed opportunities.

As if reading my thoughts, Dad said, "Your mother showed me the error of my ways. She could've been a powerful woman in her own name, but she chose to support me after we moved here. I regret it every single day. I would've loved to see her on stage with the world's most influential women, but she isn't there because of me. I feel more indebted to her than I can ever tell her."

My mouth gaped at my father's confessions. He was always guarded about his most intimate thoughts and feelings. Yet, here he was, spilling it out to me because he wanted to show me his faith in my happiness.

I squeezed his hand. He patted it and smiled. "Your mother made me a better person, and it looks like this Sujit has made you stronger, more firm in your beliefs. That is good." He offered a pensive nod. "It is good," he repeated.

I sat tongue-tied. In all of the scenarios that I had run through my head, none came close to what was unfolding before me right now. Papa and I had a close relationship, but it had been a silent, muted one. We knew how much we were loved and respected. We never had a reason to voice it as such. So whatever was emerging from my father's mouth this evening felt like an aberration or an anomaly in the grand design of the universe. Either that or our relationship had just taken a beautiful turn.

I leaned in and hugged him. "Thank you, Papa. I won't let you down," I said with my head in the nook of his neck.

"I know you won't, Puttar. I won't let you down either. I know I did with Sameer, but I won't make that mistake again."

I looked him in the eye. "Sameer wasn't your mistake, Papa. You didn't push us together. You never forced me into the relationship. If you are carrying the guilt of that breakup, I want you to stop. It was not your mistake." When he didn't respond, I took his hand in mine and reiterated, "Papa, it wasn't your mistake. Not your burden to carry."

He returned a slow, resigned nod.

"What happens now? You plan to move to New York?" he asked with his trademark frown.

"I'm already there," I teased.

He sighed. "It's good in a way. Now I have a trusted employee to take care of my operations in that region," he teased back, and we chuckled.

AARTI

The moment I landed in New York the next day, I texted Sujit. But before I could call him, I found a voicemail on my phone.

"Hey, it's Manoj. I was hoping we could meet up one of these days.... just...give me a call. You have my number."

My temper flared. After what Tara had shared with me, I was determined to cut Manoj down to size. He would never bother Sujit when I was done with him.

I called him the moment I was back at my condo, and he answered on the first ring as if he had been expecting my call.

"Hey, how is it going?" he said in a pleasant tone that irked me.

Shrugging the warm coat off my shoulder, I grabbed my bag and walked toward the bedroom.

"Going well. Did you call for a reason?" I was done playing games with him.

"Right to business, huh?" he teased, and I chose to ignore it.

He cleared his throat. "Well, I was hoping we could meet for dinner sometime?"

"I'm afraid that's going to be difficult. It has been pretty busy lately. But if you email me your requirements, I can have someone working on it promptly."

He laughed a nervous laugh. "I thought...*you* were going to help me find a place."

"It's still my company, so it *will* be me helping you find the place," I replied in a vacant tone.

He laughed again. A vicious one this time. "You are making it difficult, aren't you?"

"Making what difficult? You need a rental space for your business. I assure you, you'll get one."

"I wanted to have a chat with you. Over dinner."

"Sounds like a date."

Having put away my clothes during this short conversation, I stowed my luggage, and was eager to step into the shower. I put a hand on my waist and waited for his response.

"If you want that, sure," he said, attempting nonchalance.

But I was adamant. "I thought I already told you I don't go out on dates with people I have business associations with."

"You did." His voice reflected a smile. "So, not a date then. Consider it a dinner with a friend. Like you do with Sujit."

The tiny hair on my neck stood on edge now. He knew that mentioning Sujit was a sure-shot way to touch my Achilles' heel.

"Sujit *is* a friend," I said, making a point. Manoj wasn't.

"All right then, consider it a business dinner. I have something important to show you. It's about Sujit's pictures in the tabloid."

"What does that have to do with me?" I asked, as my anger rose and my nerves jangled.

"I know it's you on the cover. I have managed to get the rest of the pictures."

The rest of the pictures. Meaning there were more, probably with my face, revealing my identity. I was right all along to be distrustful of this vile man.

"What do you want with me, then?"

"I care about you, Aarti," he said in a gentle tone. "I want to personally meet and give them to you before they fall into the wrong hands."

They were in the wrong hands already, but I didn't bother spelling it out. I was interested in knowing how far he was willing to carry this charade. Just how far would he stoop to hurt Sujit?

"When do you want to meet?" I asked with a quiet sigh.

His voice brightened. He erroneously assumed I had bought his words at their face value. That he had lured me into his honey-laced—well, hornet-laced—trap. "The sooner, the better. Trust me. How about tomorrow?"

"Sure, text me where you want to meet."

That is when he really shook me out of my skin. "How about Marco's? You like their food, don't you?"

Either he had been keeping tabs on us, or he knew it was Sujit's favorite bistro and that he would have taken me there at least once.

"See you at seven," I said and hung up before he could get in another word.

Tired and exhausted, I retreated to the bathroom. I had planned on taking a quick shower and getting into a warm bed ASAP. But after the conversation with that slimy man, I needed more.

Turning on the faucet in my bathtub, I dropped in bath salts. Then I walked over to my rather sparse bar and poured myself a small flute of wine. On my way to the bathroom, I made a quick halt at the bookrack and picked up the poems of Maya Angelou. It had been a long time since I had sought solace in the comfort of poetry. Sujit had gifted me this soothing feeling from my past, and I was never letting it slip again.

Samuel Barber's *Adagio for Strings* played on the Bluetooth speaker connected to my phone. I pulled the bathtub tray and placed the wine and the book on it. I lowered myself into the tub and soaked in the fragrant water, now covered in kaleidoscopic bubbles. The cool wine warmed my insides as I turned page after page, getting increasingly absorbed in the beauty of those lush words.

When the water had gone from warm to tepid, I closed the book and put it away. I took the last sip of the wine and considered calling Sujit. But calling him while I was naked was a decidedly bad idea. I was tired, needy, and furious at Manoj. If I called Sujit, there was a good chance I'd plead with him to come over and devour me.

My left hand slipped beneath the bubbles. My right deposited the wine glass to the side and greedily grabbed at a breast. My nipple was already taut and wrinkled at the thought of Sujit. The hand inside the water then moved along my thigh right to my core as my knees parted and made way for it. I moaned as I imagined Sujit's warm, naked body against mine.

Since I had seen him shirtless at his family home, I'd been dreaming of touching that silky, broad chest. *The abs, firm but not muscular, the biceps, toned and strong.* As my finger found the perfect spot, I grabbed onto it for life and rubbed tighter. *His plush lips on my mouth, then slowly moving down my body while my skin sizzled and my senses lit up like fireworks.* My finger ached sweet and bitter as I pushed past my sensations to focus on his image.

Standing at the edge of the bed, he thrust into me hard, his lustful eyes roving over my desperate, naked body. As he bent over to grab my breasts in both his hands... a loud moan erupted from deep in my stomach, and I scrambled over the threshold.

I sighed, feeling tender and unfinished. Then I did it all over again before washing myself off and heading to bed satisfied, for the moment, but unfulfilled.

AARTI

S ujit's text greeted me the next morning. He had sent the text late into the night after I'd finished fantasizing about him and was snug in my bed.

SUJIT

Welcome back, sweet girl. Sorry I'm just seeing your message. Guess you must be asleep by now. Talk to you tomorrow.

And then, a few minutes later,

Glad you're back.

I was glad to be back, too. Although the idea of meeting Manoj that evening was the first thing on my mind, seeing this text from Sujit had raised my spirits. I wasn't one to be flustered easily, but Manoj had the knack of getting on my nerves in all the wrong ways.

After I learned about him from Tara, I harbored even more animosity toward him. He had messed with the wrong person this time. Sujit might be kind, but I was not. I believed in just deserts, not blanket kindness. By the end of the day, Manoj would be out of our lives for good.

By the end of the day, I'd also know if Sujit would be *in* my life for good.

I called him the first thing after coffee.

"Good morning," he said in his sexy, husky voice, and I melted right away.

"Hi," was all I could manage.

"How was Dallas?" he asked.

"Wonderful!" I said. "I can't wait to tell you all about it."

"I can't wait either, sweet girl. Wish we could have dinner tonight, but I have a standing date."

"A date, huh?" I teased. "Is she pretty?"

"Very pretty. Like an angel."

A silly place in my heart sank. "Is it a *date* date?" I asked, trying very hard not to sound jealous.

"A dinner date," he clarified. "Why? Does it bother you that I'm having dinner with other pretty girls?" he teased more brashly than he had before.

"Not at all," I said sweetly. "In fact, I have a dinner appointment myself. Although I wouldn't call it a date."

"Yeah? What would you call it?"

"I'd call it a raging tempest."

"That explosive, eh?" he teased and I laughed.

"Sujit..."

"Yes, Aarti?"

"I can't wait to see you," I said simply.

"Can I come over after dinner, or do you think you'd be occupied with your raging tempest?"

"The tempest should be razed to the ground by the time dinner is done," I said with fury.

"Is everything alright? If you want to meet sooner, I can."

"Thank you, but it's nothing I can't handle."

"There is nothing you can't handle," he replied.

A warmth coursed through my being, bringing a smile to my face. I was so proud of this man, and I wanted to take him in my arms and tell him just that.

～

I BLAZED THROUGH MY WORKDAY, awaiting the evening when I could finally tell that slimeball Manoj what I thought of him. This time, I decided not to toe but step over the line.

Instead of picking a sensible dress that would indicate my disinterest in him, I picked a low-neck mini sheath. Instead of opting for a sensible bra that wouldn't draw attention to my breasts, I retrieved a push-up from my drawer and jacked my bouncing breasts up to my chin. I covered up my beauty spot completely. He didn't deserve to see it. Instead of choosing a soft, muted color on my lips, I reached for the bold red that was my signature power shade. And instead of slipping on my trademark cool demeanor, I channeled all my anger and wrath. Today was the day Manoj would finally stop messing with Sujit. Forever.

I found him waiting by the valet when I arrived.

"Hi, Aarti," he said with a smile that would enamor many a weak person. I wasn't one. "You look spectacular." The lecher's eyes landed straight on my chest.

Of course I looked amazing. I had planned it that way. I merely nodded.

"Are you not going to say a word?" he said as the maître d' escorted us to our table. A prime spot, or the "display tables," as they called them. Visible to the people walking in but distant enough from the entrance to avoid the draft from the door. Not in proximity to either the kitchen or the back of the restaurant toward the restrooms. I wouldn't expect Manoj to choose anything else. He knew how to show it up. That's what people like him lived for.

He also made sure to take the coat off my shoulders and hand it to the maître d'. Then he pulled out a chair for me. I let him. It was best to allow him the illusion that I was impressed by his chivalry.

"What would you like to drink?" he asked after we had settled, and I had buried myself in the menu without a word.

I looked up at him and returned the menu to the table. "What do you want to talk about?"

He unleashed a Grinch grin that instantly reminded me of that Tim Curry scene in *Home Alone 2*.

"Enough with the games, Manoj," I stated in a cool voice. "I'm running out of patience."

"You know, you could at least be grateful to me," he argued, dropping the menu on the table as the server came for our drinks order.

"Get us your finest red," Manoj delivered the line straight from a movie.

I suppressed a snort. If he knew me at all, if he had paid even the slightest bit of attention, he'd know I preferred white. But that was the thing about such men. They didn't care about others. The only person they saw was themselves. He wasn't Sujit.

An untimely softness surged through me at the thought of that kind, gorgeous man. I couldn't wait to see his handsome face and the reassuring smile that ended in two perfect divots in his cheek.

The door opened again, and my eyes drew to the party walking in. For a moment, I wondered if it was a figment of my imagination. If I had somehow summoned Sujit with my sheer willpower. He was walking in behind the maître d'. With him was Devi and a young girl, who appeared to be Devi's daughter. She chirped something to Sujit, and he gave her the smile that I was just daydreaming about.

Our very visible table meant that he saw me too. Our eyes met, and his smile broadened. But one look at my companion, and he stilled. With a quick nod, he asked if I wanted him to come over. With just my eyes, I conveyed I had this covered. Another nod at my conviction, and he turned his attention to the girl.

This was the fucking connection I'd been waiting for all my life. And like hell I was going to give it up without a fight. Manoj was a non-entity; I'd fight the gods for Sujit.

While the maître d' pulled a chair for Devi, Sujit did so for the girl and handed their coats to a wait staff who had appeared at their table.

Manoj followed my gaze. "Well, well," he said. "Our secret is out now." He cast his Grinch grin again.

"What secret is that?" I marshaled my cool and sipped the water from the goblet on the table.

"You and me at this table," he said as the server returned with the wine, a fine Malbec.

I patiently waited as they went through the tired routine of sampling and okaying the wine. I was tempted to say something about not being fond of red, but I bit my tongue.

"Here's to you, Aarti. The fabulous woman that you are," he said, raising his glass at me.

I sipped mine without a word. It wasn't a bad wine. A bit heavy but very good. A nice mouthful with notes of plum and sweet tobacco. Certainly a wine that someone like Manoj would choose. But then, he didn't choose it, did he? He let the restaurant do it for him. He couldn't even be trusted to pick a good wine for himself.

Sujit, on the other hand, knew exactly what he wanted. Like the scotch he chose at our first meeting. My eyes drew to Sujit and Manoj's were glued to me.

"What is the deal with the two of you?" he finally asked.

"What did you want to talk about, Manoj? I really don't like the idea of being threatened like this."

His eyes widened with a dramatic flair. "Threatened?" Then he shook his head with the same vehement theatrics and added, "No, you've got it all wrong, Aarti. I'm worried about you."

"Worried about what?"

He hesitated for effect, as if he had planned it. Then, placing the wine glass back on the table, said, "I know about you and Sujit. About your connection."

He used the same word that had been stated in the tabloid. I frowned. "What connection?"

He let out an exasperated breath as I continued to deny him the pleasure of what he sought. Flustering me.

"I know you're Tara's husband's ex-fiancée."

"So?" I returned a quizzical frown again.

"I know you both are hiding it from your families and from the world."

"There's nothing to hide," I replied in a calm voice, even as every word from his mouth infuriated me.

"Then you wouldn't mind if these pictures made their way to the news, would you?"

He placed an envelope near him on the table. I didn't reach out to grab it like he wanted me to. That seemed to irk him further.

I sat back in my chair with a conceited smile. "I didn't mind the first time they did."

"Oh, but they *didn't*. See, that's the point I'm trying to make."

"So the first time was about cornering Sujit. And now it's my turn, is it?"

Perturbed at being seen so visibly by a woman he had clearly underestimated, he drew his brows together.

"This is unfair, you know," he cried in a defeatist tone. "I brought these to you. Can't you see that?"

He grabbed the envelope and tossed it across the table toward me. It flopped next to my wine glass. I picked up the glass and took a sip before placing it at a distance from the envelope.

"The question I have at this moment is," I asked with a menacing calm. "How do you have these pictures in the first place?"

His brows flew off his forehead. "What, you think *I* had something to do with this?"

"The thought definitely crossed my mind," I said. "How else would you have *the rest of the pictures*, as you put it?"

He shook his head and blew out a breath. "I care about you, and that's why I went to great lengths to retrieve these pictures. If I hadn't, these would be splashed across the front page of a magazine next week."

Ah, there it was! The threat I was waiting for. I turned up my lip in a sneer.

"And the price of keeping them away from the public eye?"

He smirked as if he had won. "Your gratitude," he said.

"And nothing else?"

"Your friendship," he had the audacity to demand. "Aarti, I'll say it again. I care about you, and I know Sujit. I don't want you to end up hurt like the other women in his past."

I glared at him, but he spotted the curiosity in my eyes and latched on to it.

Whipping out an obsequious grin, he said, "You don't know about it, do you?"

Despite my best efforts, my eyes drifted to Sujit. Just a glance, and I saw him laughing with Devi's daughter. Devi observed the two with a sweet curve on her lips. Manoj saw this and pulled out another sneer.

But instead of responding with anger, I relaxed against the

chair, a cool move I'd learned as a great intimidation tactic. It worked every time.

"I know men like you. I know women like you. You derive your sense of self, your identity, from seeing others fail. You'll never be good enough, so you put roadblocks in Sujit's path, deter him, and attempt to demoralize him. But you don't fool me," I said, leaning in. "Not one bit. I know exactly who you are, Manoj. You are a petty man who doesn't think twice before backstabbing a person you call a friend. Don't assume I'm unaware of your past. I know exactly what you've done."

His face had changed. His fair skin was turning red with humiliation. This was precisely what I wanted.

I tapped the envelope with my red nails. "This is your doing. It has your fingerprints all over it. You aren't even smart enough to mask your juvenile envy for Sujit."

His anger was evident now. His right hand resting on the table clenched into a fist as he tried hard to avoid creating a scene.

"You've fucked with him long enough, Manoj, but no more. Try it one more time, and I'll fuck you up so bad you'll have no recourse but to leave the city. If you don't remove yourself from his life, I'll dedicate the rest of mine to fucking up yours. You want to splash these pictures in a gossip magazine? Go ahead, do it. You don't scare me. But mess with him again and see what I'm capable of."

It wasn't intentional, but my protective mode was on, and my eyes flitted to Sujit again.

Manoj had found the opening he was hoping for. "Fuck! You are in love with him, aren't you? This is so messed up."

"That's none of your business," I retorted.

"Then here's a friendly tip for you. He's fucking her," he said, throwing a quick glance at Devi. "You should know that. She's his side-piece, always has been. He's the reason she's divorced. That right there is a messed up happy family. And like you asked me to remove myself from his life, I strongly suggest you do the same. Not for his sake, for yours. He might look and appear like a nice guy, but he's a fucking manipulative bastard. He fucked my ex-wife before she was my ex. And after. Then tossed her aside when he found Tara. It was karma that Tara dumped him the way she did. He isn't the person you think he is."

I produced a final superior gaze as I gathered my clutch and prepared to leave. "Here's what I do know, Manoj. Sujit can fuck who he wants. But I want *you* to stop fucking with him. Now. Or you'll see what my wrath looks like. You don't want me as an enemy, believe me."

His eye twitched, and I spotted a tremble in his hand. "And I prefer white wine."

I stood and tapped the table twice with my perfectly manicured nails. "Nice talking to you, Manoj. Take care."

With a brilliant smile, I walked off, completely avoiding eye contact with Sujit.

As I exited the restaurant, I saw Imran walking toward me.

"Ms. Aarti, do you wish to go back home?" he asked with his usual courtesy.

"It's all right, Imran," I said with a smile. "I have the car service waiting for me."

"Please let me drive you," he insisted and I was curious.

"Sujit will need you," I argued. "When they are done with their dinner."

"Boss will be here for a while. I will be back in no time."

I shuddered against the cold and acquiesced. "Thank you," I said with a short nod.

"I'll bring the car around. Please wait indoors if you need to. It's a cold day."

In about two miraculously short minutes, Imran drove up and rushed to hold the door open for me. I called my driver and asked him to retire for the night.

"I hope you are alright, Ms. Aarti. I know it is not my place, but I hope things are good between the Boss and you."

I smiled with surprise. "The Boss and me? What do you know, Imran?" I asked with a curious lift of my brow.

He responded with as sheepish grin which I spied in the rearview mirror.

"Only that my boss cares about you very much," he replied. "He is a good man. I'm requesting you to give him a chance to show you."

I sighed deeply. "I wish it were that simple." I was already dreading the impending conversation with Sujit.

He tried to read me in his mirror. "Whatever it is, he will know of a way to resolve it. He always does."

"I know you're his friend, a close confidant. But you don't know who I am."

He didn't miss a beat. "I know you, Ms. Aarti. I've known about you before anyone else did. And I am still here assuring you that he's never been this happy—truly happy—before you."

"He wasn't happy with Tara?" I asked with utmost curiosity.

"He was happy, but not this happy. Not this relaxed, this comfortable. It's different with you. From the first night I drove you both to Marco's. That's why I'm asking you to give him a chance."

"You love him, don't you?" I asked with a smile.

"He was there for me when I had no one to turn to. He's done more for me than any family would. He loves me like a brother, and I respect him like one."

I heard his breath quicken as we neared my building.

"He's a really good man, Ms. Aarti," he repeated, as if he needed to convince me of it. "He is going to come over tonight. I'm sure of it. I'm kindly requesting that you don't close the door on him."

I smiled wide at his metaphor. "You are a smart, sharp man. I am glad you have Sujit's back."

His eyes were averted but he waited as if he were eager to hear those words from my mouth.

"You don't need to worry, Imran, because the truth is I like your boss and I care about him, too."

There was a wide, giddy, happy grin on his face as he came around to hold the door open for me.

"Thank you for everything," I said softly and he returned a quizzical look. "Thank you for keeping our secret and for believing in our happiness," I explained. "Thank you for everything you do for him."

He grinned again. "I'll also be here for you, Lady Boss."

That made me laugh. "And I hope to support you and Afra just as much."

His smile turned shy at the mention of her. "Thank you, Lady Boss." He grinned. "I should get going."

"Good night, Imran."

"Good night, Ms. Aarti."

SUJIT

I knew Aarti wouldn't willingly meet with Manoj. Which meant he had something on her. He had either blackmailed or threatened her. I trusted Aarti to hold her own, and I saw her walk away without a look of worry on her face. That knowledge did little to calm the feeling of restlessness and unease inside me.

I was furious that Manoj had the guts to put Aarti in this position. And I was irked that Aarti had chosen to deal with him without confiding in me. She had clearly voiced her mistrust for him on our last night in St. Martin. She should have trusted me and told me about this.

I was so consumed with Aarti that I forgot why I was at the restaurant with Kitty. I tried to be present at the table, nodding to her chatter and laughing at her jokes. But my mind remained occupied with Aarti, and I knew Devi saw it too. She didn't mention anything, though.

When we dropped them back home, I promptly instructed Imran to drive me to Aarti's. I needed to make sure she'd emerged out of her dinner meeting unscathed. I also had to finally confess how I felt about her. A sudden, unexpected feeling churned my stomach, and Imran saw it as I readjusted myself in the backseat.

"Everything will be okay, Boss," he said with his usual silly grin. "Today's the day."

"Whatever you think is going to happen, Imran, I assure you it isn't," I teased back with a straight face.

"Oh yeah, it's happening." That wide grin again. "Should I wait or leave, Boss?" he teased as we entered the portico of her magnificent building.

"Depends," I said as I opened the door to step out. "I'll let you know."

Ignoring the anxiety and anticipation coursing through me, I rode the elevator to her floor. I couldn't wait any longer without telling her what she meant to me.

I rang the doorbell, and I knew she saw me on the camera. But instead of unlocking the door with her phone like she usually did, she answered it in person this time, in a mini satin cami dress and a short robe.

"Sujit," she said. "I wasn't sure you were coming tonight."

"I said I would," I reminded her. "Can I come in?"

"Yes." She drew the robe close over her thin camisole and stepped aside.

"I had to make sure you were okay."

"Why wouldn't I be?" she said without inflection.

"I saw you with Manoj."

"You don't need to worry about that. Or him." She sighed and continued, "He called me yesterday, saying he had pictures of me from the party."

I opened my mouth to express my displeasure, but she quickly added, "He wanted to meet and blackmail me into being seen with him. Or ending my friendship with you—"

"He—"

"I don't know what he wanted. I never let him finish. But he's finished, believe me. He doesn't have the means to hurt me in any way. Nor the balls."

I smirked. "That means he's worried."

She frowned. "Worried about what?"

"His entire life is unraveling before him. It has begun, and he's running scared. That's the reason he contacted you. You were his last hope. That column in the tabloid was his way of using you to irk me. Now that his hands are tied, he was trying to use you to get me to help him."

"Yeah, little did he know that this house cat is actually a tigress in the wild."

I grinned, then turned somber. "You should've told me, Aarti. I would've taken care of it immediately. You would've never had to see him at all."

"I wanted to see him. I needed to look him in the eye and tell him to fuck off. And to stop fucking with you forever. After today, he won't hurt you. I promise you."

"He won't. Not anymore." I told her everything I had planned with Vinay.

She gaped at me with wide eyes. "I...well...that's...I..."

"You didn't think I had it in me?" I filled in the blanks.

She returned a sheepish look. "Something like that."

"He's always tested my limits. But this time, he crossed the line."

"This time?" she asked with a tentative look.

"He came after you, and I couldn't allow that."

She took a startled step back. "What are you saying, Sujit?"

"I like you, Aarti. A lot," I said with my gaze planted in her eyes. They widened, then softened instantly. "That's what I needed to talk to you about. I like you and need to know how you feel about us."

She fiddled with the delicate diamond ring on her left index finger like she did when she was anxious or musing about something.

"Manoj tried to throw me off," she began. "By saying you have an ongoing affair with Devi. That's the reason she's divorced."

My heart bubbled with rage, but I saw Aarti roll her eyes.

"As if I was going to buy that BS from him. By the way, your date was as pretty as you said. Like an angel," Aarti added with a warm smile.

"It was Kitty's birthday. Ever since her father walked out of their lives, it has been our ritual to celebrate with a dinner at Marco's followed by ice cream at her favorite creamery."

"Her name is Kitty?" she asked with a suspicious cock of her head.

"No, it's Katyayani. It's a mouthful, so I call her Kitty. And Devi's marriage ended because her husband broke her trust and chose to be with another woman."

She smiled. "You don't need to convince me. That trust I keep talking about, I don't say it lightly. I trust you completely, Sujit. I can't believe Manoj thought I'd buy it."

"It was his last hurrah. He would've tried anything to create a rift between us."

"If he were even a slight bit smart, he would've known..."

I held my breath for her next words. "Known?"

"I like you, Sujit. I like you enough that I had a heartfelt conversation with my father and sought his blessings before returning to you," she confessed.

My heart leapt off a cliff as I stepped toward her. "Is that the truth, Aarti?"

"How did you not know?" she cried with incredulity and frustration.

"How did *you* not know?" I asked in return.

"I knew," she said. "But you'd said it would displease your

family, and I wasn't sure if you were ready to take the brunt. To stake it all."

I laughed. "My family will be relieved that I am happy. And despite the pathetic attempt in the tabloid, the truth is that the world isn't really interested in my personal life. It never was."

"It will be once AccessEd becomes the big thing it's destined to be," she said matter-of-factly.

I beamed at her staunch conviction. "Maybe. Until then, I'm free of that burden. But you...whatever your brother said. I am ready to take the chance, Aarti. I am ready to stand by you and face whatever filth the world throws at us."

"I don't care about the world. But I do care about you. And our families. I don't want to hurt anyone close to me in this process."

"Are you scared?"

"No. For once, I'm certain we won't live in the shadow of Sameer and Tara anymore than they're living in ours. And I like you with an intensity I've never felt before, and I don't want to give it up without a fight."

"All right, then." I heaved a deep sigh of relief. "I want the happiness that you give me, Aarti. But I need you to be absolutely certain about this. You have more to lose in every way than I do. I need you to be sure that this is what you want. I don't want you to regret us later."

She scoffed and took two confident steps toward me. Then, without warning, she pressed her mouth firmly against mine. Her fists tightened around the lapels of my jacket and tugged at it as her tongue breached my mouth, rendering me helpless. Before I could remember to breathe again, she retracted.

Taking one step back, she smoothed my lapels and said, "Is that certain enough for you?"

"Good god, Aarti!" I cried and raked a hand over my head. I loosened the tie to release the heat rising up my body.

She cocked her hip and crossed her arms. Her breasts burst upward and out over the silky satin dress.

"I need to make just one call before we do this," I said and hurriedly touched the second number in my favorites.

"Imran, you can leave."

I heard his gentle chuckle as I tossed my phone on the couch without disconnecting it.

SUJIT

Stepping toward her, I pinned her to the wall. Everything I had been waiting for in life was within my reach. She was the fire I needed, and I didn't even know it.

Aarti's lips parted and her eyes glimmered with desire as I gazed at her intensely. I ran a firm thumb over her lower lip and watched her tremble against me.

Placing my hands on the wall, I caged her between them. "Now, I need to know how far you want to take this tonight," I said, bringing my hand to her waist. "Because once I start, I'm not inclined to stop—until you ask me to."

A shuddered gasp met my question, and I ran my hand down from her waist to let it rest on her hip. "Tell me. How far should I go tonight?

She curved her index finger and beckoned me. I drew closer until my nose brushed with hers. "I want you to stop only when you've filled me up completely and I'm dripping down my thighs," she whispered against my lips.

My cock came alive at her words. At the visual. "If you keep saying such things, I'll have to keep doing it over and over again, my sweet girl," I threatened.

"I want you to," came her trembling words. "I want you to fuck me over and over and over again until I can barely walk. I want to be devastated, Sujit. I want to be devastated by you."

I stepped back. My body was burning up. I ran my fingers through my hair. "Damn, Aarti!"

She leaned in. "You're not the only one who's hungry," she whispered in my ear. "I've been starving, and you're the only thing that can satiate me."

"I've been waiting for this moment for an eternity, Aarti Bhatia."

I moved closer and breathed on her lips. They parted, and she panted with need. Her hands clasped into fists at her sides. Gently, I placed my mouth on hers. Her plush, warm petals felt perfect between my lips. She tasted like sunshine and happiness on a cold, dreary winter night. I tugged at her lower lip and allowed it to fill my mouth. A moan escaped her, and her patience broke. When she pushed her tongue in, I held her shoulders and let her kiss me with the ferocity of a wild cat. Then I pushed her deeper against the wall and crushed her gently with my weight.

With her hands on my chest, she bought just enough space for me to flick the robe off her shoulders. As the garment dropped to the floor, I pounced on her again.

"You know, I was always a gentle lover," I said against her cheek.

"Was?" Her lips curved into a smirk.

"Until I met you. You are fire, and I run to you like moth to a candle, knowing full well it means my obliteration. But I can't help it. I want to burst in your flames."

"Ah, poetry! It's prettier in Urdu."

"Yeah? Tell me." I gripped the string of her nightie in my teeth and tugged it down her shoulder.

Her breath caught, and she waited with anticipation. Her bare shoulder was the most beautiful thing I'd ever seen. I placed my lips upon it with reverence.

"Don't get distracted, sweet girl."

With a choppy breath, she said, "Candle is called shamaa... moth is parwaanaa." A gasp as I slid my hand up her thigh, lingering at her hip.

With my eyes on her, I whispered, "That's beautiful, lyrical. Tell me what happens when the parwaanaa flies close to the shamaa."

The warmth of my words sent another shiver rippling across her body. Her skin came alive with goosebumps. My fingers felt the string of her slight underclothes, and I hooked a finger into it. "Go on, tell me what happens when my moth flies into your flame."

I reached down to kiss the swell of her breast, and she threw her head back in a sigh and fisted my hair.

Her breath shuddered. "The flame says, don't come near me, you stupid moth. You're going to burn. You'll die."

I gathered her hair and kissed her neck. "But the moth doesn't heed, does he?"

With another broken breath, she shook her head. "The stubborn Parwaanaa responds, I'll die for my love, become one with the flame."

"Romantic, but stupid."

"Yeah? What would you do?"

"I'd kiss the flame, just enough to let her know what she'd miss if she engulfed me. Tease her, torment her." I placed a tender kiss on her lips, just a graze. Then moved my mouth to her chest and neck and jaw, while my hand moved to her bottom. She shuddered.

"You think that'll work?"

I brought my eyes back to her face. "No, it'll never work. If she stops being a flame, he'll not be attracted to her. He can never dull her brilliance, her power, for that's what makes her who she is, what she is. That fire is what attracts him to her."

She stared into my eyes for a few seconds, then kissed me like it was our first kiss. Hunger, passion, and anticipation in a single touch. When I tried to remove my glasses, she held my hand.

"No!" she cried urgently. "Keep them on."

"Is that what you like?"

With downcast eyes, she returned a shy nod. "Whenever you look at me from over the rim of your glasses, I find myself dripping wet."

My heart rumbled. "How about we test that theory?" I teased.

Peering over my glasses had been an old habit. But no more. From here on, this was for Aarti alone. I looked at her like she wanted me to.

"Is it working?" I said, running my hand along her inner thigh. She sighed aloud. I inched my fingers toward her panties. She readily parted her legs for me.

"Check for yourself," she offered.

I moved the delicate fabric aside and ran my finger between the perfectly swollen lips. I didn't have to venture too far. She was dripping, alright.

"Fuck, Aarti! You wanted me to devastate you, but I'm going to be the one to end up devastated."

A proud smile illuminated her face, and she clamped her legs closed around my hand. With sighs and moans, she gyrated her hips, grinding on my finger.

"I never thought I'd be this needy, Sujit. What have you done to me?"

"My question exactly, sweet girl. What have you done to me? Do you have any idea what effect you have on me?"

She rubbed her hand on the front of my trousers, feeling my

hardened cock against her palm, and giggled. "I think I'm getting an idea."

Yanking my hand out from between her legs with urgent need, she pulled off my jacket and shirt to fling them away. Her fingers began to trace every inch of my torso, setting my skin ablaze. Sighs and hisses escaped my mouth as her lips landed on my neck. I gripped her shoulders to ground myself when her soft kisses caressed my chest and all the way to my abdomen. My muscles tensed as her soft palm cupped the strong bulge. I threw my head back as she gave it repeated gentle squeezes. It was getting harder and unbearable in my skin. My legs struggled to find their strength.

I gripped her hand and brought it back to my chest.

"Have some mercy, my darling," I pleaded, fisting her hair tenderly.

It was impossible to keep my eyes off her face. They roved in worship, admiring her every flawless feature. Her seductive lips, their wide curve crowned with the most perfect bow. Her smooth skin and that beauty mark that I could kiss for life. The strong cut of her jaw and chin. The powerful eyes with the most brilliant deep browns I had ever seen. She could kill you with those eyes. Nothing I had ever imagined or dreamed about could come close to having her in my arms like this.

She was the epitome of power and grace. A goddess. A queen.

"It was you," I whispered against her cheek before placing a light kiss on her beauty mark. "It was you I dreamt of that day at the beach. You were responsible for my condition that evening."

A surprised gasp escaped her lips. She held my face between her hands. "I need to tell you something, Sujit. I...I feel so helpless, and I don't want to be left looking like a fool again."

As her hands dropped to her side, I stepped back to give her the space she needed. I lifted her chin with my finger. "You know you can tell me anything, sweet girl."

"I said I liked you...a lot. But...that's not the whole truth."

My brows furrowed in confusion.

"I think I'm in love with you."

My hand dropped as my frown deepened, and she got a look on her face like she had just made the biggest mistake of her life.

"*Think*?" I prodded. "So you aren't sure?"

She blinked. "I am sure." The words that came out were tentative.

"I thought you didn't believe in love and rosy endings?" I continued my sweet torture.

She saw the jest behind my serious facade and rolled her eyes. "I didn't. Then I met a hopeless romantic who changed my worldview."

"Is that right?" I said and gripped her earlobe between my teeth.

"Sujit," she said, putting her hand on my chest. "You aren't bothered by it, are you? This is no longer a what-if situation. It's a what-now one."

I smiled. "We don't have to worry about what-now because I know exactly what's going to happen next."

"What's that?"

"We are going to say fuck-you to the world and live happily ever after because I'm absolutely, positively, life-threateningly in love with you."

She brought her hands around my nape and pulled me in for the most rapacious kiss I could have ever imagined.

My breaths came in short huffs, my hands incapable of deciding where to rest.

"Bedroom. Now," she ordered, and I pounced on her mouth again. Her breath was alluring and reassuring. Her touch, both fire and its salve.

She held my hand and rushed us to the bedroom. At the edge of the bed, she dropped the nightie down her glorious body and stood before me. The dark red rubies gleamed with pride on those mounds of gold. She brought my mouth over them, one after the other, and sighed as I licked and nipped at her nipples. They were so tight and felt so right in my mouth. As if they were made for me. I wanted more of her. All of her.

"Let me taste you, sweet girl," I said, and her face flushed.

She slipped up the bed and opened her thighs very slightly. Reluctantly.

"Wide," I instructed. "Wider for me, Aarti."

Her back arched at my words, and her toned, shapely thighs parted for me.

I slipped off my shoes and tore off my socks before climbing on the bed to hunch on my knees. As her eyes met mine, peeking over the rim of my glasses, she took her lower lip between her teeth.

"I never thought I'd have a glasses kink," she said with a mischievous glint in her eye. "Or maybe it's a Sujit in glasses kink? Yes, that's it. I have a Sujit-in-glasses-eating-me-raw kink," she declared.

"Good, because that's exactly what I plan to do. Eat you raw, my sweet, sweet Aarti." I bent and placed a tender kiss just below the wisp of fine hair. Her eyes dropped shut, and her back arched. A smile beamed on my face.

"Look at me," I whispered, and she did.

I kept my eyes on her and ran a soft tongue between her slit. A gasp, but her eyes remained on me.

"You'll have to tell me what you like," I said.

She nodded with greed, and I watched her fist the bedsheet in preparation. I pushed my hands under her to lift her buttocks and licked again. I ran my tongue from her bottom hole, sliding all the way up, ending at her clit, and swirled my tongue around it.

For the next few minutes, all I heard were gasps followed by long moments of breathless silence. I pulled my right hand from below her and threaded it around her leg. With two fingers, I coaxed open her plush, swollen lips to reach her clit. Full, erect, and ready to burst. I flicked it with my tongue, and her pelvis rose with a jerk. I pulled back and sucked on her fleshy lips instead. I let my finger roll around the wet clit as I nipped at her outer flesh.

The next time I reached her clit, she slipped her hand into my hair and clutched it in her fists.

"Slightly to the left," she directed, indicating the sweet spot for her.

I shifted my tongue to my left. She whimpered. "The other left. My left," she instructed.

"Sorry."

When I brought my tongue to her desired spot, she shuddered and let out an audible gasp.

"Fuck, Sujit! You are a fucking god!"

My chest flushed with pride, and I felt myself leaking, but it wasn't my turn. Not yet.

Carefully, I added varying amounts of pressure as I devoured her.

"Please!" she cried finally. "Please let me breathe!"

I looked up at her and cocked an eyebrow. "Shouldn't I be the one begging for breath, considering it is my face that is buried?"

An unexpected laughter rocked her body as she closed her legs and beckoned me. "Come here, you sassy man."

I slid up her body and put my mouth on hers, allowing her to taste herself on me. In turn, she kissed me with a voracious greed that inundated every raging cell in my body with pleasure.

"Take it as a huge compliment when I say that you're even better than my toys."

I smirked. "You got any here?"

Her eyes twinkled. "What do you think? I've been living alone, trying to fend off my intense attraction to a man who sets my loins on fire. Of course, I have my toys here."

"Go, get your favorite one. I want to watch you use it."

"In time, my good man. I want to enjoy you first."

The words sent a thrill down my body. She straddled me, grazing herself against my cock, straining through the fabric of my trousers. I felt her warmth through the two layers of fabric.

"Tell me what you want," I rasped in her ear as she bent over to reach my mouth.

"I want you naked, right now," she whispered. "I want you ramming into me, pounding me so hard that I forget myself. Until there's no me and you, just us, melded together. I want to linger at that threshold where pleasure and pain become one, until I cease to exist."

A distinct recollection from my French philosophy class flashed before my mind. "Sounds like jouissance," I said with a gentle frown.

Her eyes widened. "What?"

"Jouissance. It means—"

"I know what it means," she cut in. "I didn't know you did!" The surprise had widened into a grand smile.

"Well, then get your toy," I ordered. "We'll need it for jouissance."

She raised a suspicious eyebrow.

"Hey, I might be good, but no man is jouissance good, no matter what porn tries to sell you. It's either fingers or your toy. You choose."

Her head lolled back in laughter before she said, "How do you manage to make me fall in love with you over and over again?" She grazed against me and softly added, "Only a god confident in his sexuality can acknowledge this truth. Most men think they can rock a woman's world with only their dicks."

She leaned in to give me a quick kiss and jumped off me. Rushing to the bathroom, she returned, waving a wand in her hand.

"Good choice," I said as I got off the bed.

She cocked a hip and placed a hand on it. "Is it weird that we're in the toy zone, and I have yet to see your dick?" she mused with a gentle frown.

I smirked. "We can certainly rectify that," I said and began to unbuckle my belt. "I hope it lives up to your expectations."

As the belt swooshed off the hooks and landed on the floor, she stepped closer and swatted my hands away. "I want to do it," she demanded.

I held her shoulders and kissed her cheek. "Everything I have is yours, my sweet girl. Take what you want."

It was torturously slow, the way she unbuttoned and unzipped my trousers, stripping me down to my boxer briefs. With a smile of approval, she ran her hands on my bare thighs and covered buttocks. Watching her enjoy my body gave me a high like I hadn't known before. Her hand hooked in my waistband at my back. She ran her soft finger around the band, her lower lip disappearing between her teeth. I knew she was tormenting me. The mischievous glint in her eye said she knew I knew.

"Babe, if you wait any longer, I'm going to burst out of these briefs. I'm so hard, it's starting to hurt, darling," I begged.

"Okay," she whispered breathily and pulled down the underclothes.

My cock sprung free, and I huffed a relieved exhale. Her eyes shone, reflecting the recess lights in every shade of gold.

"Sujit!" Her breath came in broken, heavy gusts as she cupped my face. With unusual tenderness, she peppered several appreciative kisses all over it.

"I've always hated the word perfect," she said against my lips.

"I remember," I replied.

"But you're as perfect as perfect can get."

"I don't want to be perfect," I confessed. "I just want to be yours."

"You *are* mine," she declared and led me by my hand to the bed. She lowered me to the edge and slipped between my legs. "You have no idea how badly I've been waiting for this," she said.

The lust in her eyes drove me wild. I clenched my jaw. "Show me," I demanded.

Her lips parted wide, and I watched myself disappear in her mouth. My eyes dropped shut, the warmth driving me out of my mind. It could have been a minute or a lifetime because it felt like a moment and an eternity all at once. I found myself growing harder against the expert acrobatics of her tongue. It swirled and twisted and twirled around my cock. I had no idea what she was doing except inching me toward destruction. Jouissance. I was heading straight toward it.

"Stop," I cried and touched her shoulder. She pulled me out of her mouth, my cock throbbing hard. "I don't want to come. Not yet." I panted as I pulled myself upright. "Not before you."

I positioned her at the edge of the bed and grabbed the wand.

"Lube?" I asked, and she pointed to a drawer by her bed.

I slathered it on the wand and handed it back to her. In her dancing eyes, I spotted mischief and shyness, desire and fire.

"Open those legs for me, sweet girl, and keep them wide open."

AARTI

A shiver swept across my body at his words as I waited for him to enter me.

I had surprised myself all evening, from kissing him like there was no tomorrow to blowing him the way I had always wanted. Right now, he stood above me, ready to thrust his formidable dick inside me, and I still couldn't believe I was about to fuck Sujit Rao. *The* Sujit Rao. *My* Sujit Rao.

My fantasies stood before me, shaped in reality.

"I can't believe this dick is mine. *Mine.*" My back arched as the words escaped my lips.

He bent and brought his mouth to me. "Only yours," he reasserted. "Along with everything else that I have."

His weight felt wonderful as he brought his knees around me on the bed and kissed me. I wasn't a slight woman, but his big palm cradled my face as if I were a delicate doll. His breath was the most comforting thing I'd felt in a long time. Like him, his kiss was calm, assured, tender, but held the passion of a roaring wildfire.

"Fuck me, Sujit. I can't wait any longer."

"Neither can I," he said and kissed me again.

He stood and positioned himself at the edge of the bed. When I opened my needy, wanton legs, a smile rippled across his lips.

"Look at you, my darling. You are so beautiful with your legs open for me. I can gaze at you all day long."

I felt my face flush, and I pushed my breasts closer with my arms.

"How about now?" I teased.

He raked his hand through his hair and shook his head.

"You have no mercy, do you?" he said and grabbed my tits in his big hands, squeezing them. All blood rushed to my nipples, which were plump and erect, ready for his mouth again.

He read the anticipation in my eyes. "Tell me," he whispered. "Tell me what you want to see."

My back arched again. There was a difference between *what you want* and *what you want to see*. He knew exactly what I wanted. I wanted to watch him feasting on me.

"Grab them between your teeth," I said.

My breath was lava as I watched him clamp down on my nipple. His tongue swiped the small area available to him as he held the big nipple tight. A light groan emerged from my chest. He pulled it upward, creating a sweet tension in the breast, then bit down hard. It was only a couple of seconds of brutality, but it unleashed a thrill that had me grinding against his leg like a cat. Begging to be taken. Then he moved to the other breast and did it all over again.

"Mark me, Sujit. Mark my body as yours," I begged like I never thought I would. With him, I could unleash my desperation without fear.

"Where?" he asked, unflinching at my request.

I pointed to the swell of my left breast. "Here."

His mouth closed on the area—all suction. This fucking god knew how to deliver a perfect hickey! I luxuriated in the warm pinch. Gazing down at the beautiful bruise on my chest, I pointed to my shoulder.

The underside of my breast came next, and a final one on my neck.

"The next time we go out, I want you to keep your neck uncovered. I want the world to see my mark on you, Aarti Bhatia," he said.

I couldn't hold it any longer. "Please," I said with an edge in my breathless voice. "Please fuck me. I need to feel you inside me. Deep. All the way to my core." I was not ashamed to beg. I would beg all my life to be fucked by him.

This time when he stood upright, he rubbed his cock all over the opening. When it crashed against my clit, an electric bolt ran through me. I saw him guide it in, tenderly and carefully.

I became the deep moan that emerged from my chest. Wet and ready as I had been, having him inside me set a new bar for what it meant to be dripping. With every thrust, an exhilaration flooded through my walls. In the silence of the room, I heard the slick sound of my body, which aroused me further.

When I flicked the switch on my wand, it whirred in a quiet rhythm. The moment I placed it where I wanted, the sensations became overbearing. The way he filled me up was already giving me a heady rush. Adding my sensitive clit to the equation threatened to tip me over the edge. I modulated the pressure, allowing my body to retain some semblance of lucidity. My legs, bent at the knees, spread wider to give me the maximum contact with Sujit.

He leaned over to reach my breasts, gently at first. Then, as the heat washed over us, he squeezed them tight. He closed his fingers around my nipples, and I felt the effect of the pinch in my stomach. My muscles clenched, and I slammed the wand harder on my erect clit. An unexpected shriek escaped me and the toy slipped from my grip. I was losing it fast.

Chasing the dancing toy with dexterity, he brought it back to the desired spot, his dick firm and steady inside me.

I guided his hand holding the wand to the tender-most spot, and groaned as he pressed it snug. His thrusts resumed—slow, rhythmic, steady. My only option was to surrender to his movements rocking my body. My eyes dropped closed as he turned up the speed, his cock ramming into me like I had demanded. The wand cinched tight.

The tremors hit my belly first and I clutched the sheet beneath me. My breath hitched and remained suspended, awaiting the tidal wave that would wash me into the deepest recesses of the sea. My legs began to close up.

"No, sweet girl. You need to keep them open," Sujit urged, and the tsunami I was waiting for crashed into me. As if his voice held the validation it needed, my orgasm torpedoed through me, and I reached for his hand holding the wand. He swatted it away.

"Jouissance," was his pithy reminder.

My arms flailed about, trying to find something to hold on to. I grabbed the pillow underneath my head and clutched it in my fists.

Sujit withdrew his cock and put his fingers against my G-spot for the final stretch that would sink me to the ocean floor. With the wand firm and steady, he rubbed against the roof. My body turned to a weeping mess as I lost control over every faculty. My muscles gave way, and I screamed the hell out of my lungs.

The pleasure transformed into pain, then evolved back into pleasure. My soul shattered and reconstituted in the same moment. I lost myself to the destruction and found myself in it. My euphoric body vaporized into nothingness, then landed like a heavy mass of boulders, lifeless.

"That's my girl," he said as I continued to spasm through the sensation of loss and gain intertwined as one.

A tear ran down the side of my face. The wand disappeared, as did Sujit's finger. His mouth was now between my legs, tenderly licking my warrior's wounds.

As I emerged from the deluge, another storm ravaged through me. Unexpected, inconsolable tears now flowed down my face. Healing tears. The pain I had carried for all the years that I had not known Sujit became the tide flooding my eyes.

He slid up beside me and enveloped me in a tight embrace. I felt his lips on my forehead. "I'm here, my love," he whispered. "Nothing's going to hurt you anymore."

At his words, all barriers around my heart came crashing down. The gates to the fortress I had built flew wide open, and the torrent turned more savage.

"I've got you, sweetheart. You're safe in my arms. I'll protect you and your heart."

The little girl who had fended off ridicule and contempt, who had strived and failed to find acceptance from her peers. The young woman who had wanted the world to see her in her own right, who didn't want her tears to be taken for weakness. The lover who'd been wronged, who had found no love in return. They all healed in his arms that night.

When my tears waned, I found my breath back. I was stronger with him. I was stronger because of him.

Slipping one leg between his, I sniffed away those unwarranted tears. "And I'll protect you right back," I promised.

"I know you will," he said and hugged me tight until our bodies were one. I lay helpless—and the happiest I'd ever been.

I think I could be excused for having no recall of what happened next. I do remember straddling him, grinding myself against him. I remember gazing into his eyes as I lay below him. I remember the gush flooding me when he came inside me. I remember him saying how much he loved seeing it drip out of me. How we got there, I didn't quite recollect.

Wrapped up in his arms, I took in his spicy masculine scent, heightened by heat and sex. I let my hand rove over his body, feeling the shape of his hip and thigh, the muscles on his chest and abdomen, and the soft, clean cheeks where his dimples appeared when he smiled. I reached up and kissed the tip of his nose and the soft lips below it. I drew my hand to his ear and tugged at the plush lobes. I traced the deeply intricate crevices of his beautifully carved ear with my finger, my face buried in his chest. When he kissed my forehead, I wished we could remain suspended in this moment forever.

But then, I needed to pee. Begrudgingly but with haste, I pushed myself off his chest and pulled the robe that had fallen to the floor.

"Aarti," Sujit called, and I glanced at him over my shoulder. He shook his head with a domineering look in his eye.

"What?" I said, one shoulder into the robe. "You want me to walk to the restroom naked while you watch me?"

His lip turned up in one corner. "No clothing this weekend."

I returned his smile and shrugged the robe off my shoulder. "That works both ways, I hope. I'd love to watch your cute ass as you walk away."

He shook with a gentle laugh and pulled my hand to grab me.

"Don't!" I cried hurriedly. "I'm going to burst."

He placed a quick kiss on my hand and let me go. Rushing to the bathroom, I released all the tension pent up in my bladder. I rinsed and cleaned, gargled and deodorized in preparation for what awaited us next. As I fluffed my hair, I admired Sujit's marks on my body. When I walked out into the bedroom, I heard the sound of a soft snore.

Sujit's peaceful face greeted me and I gleamed at the sight before stepping away, sans clothing, to get a drink of water. As I crossed the living room on my way to the kitchen, I heard a silent buzz of a phone. I scanned around and remembered Sujit had tossed the phone onto the couch. The persistent buzz did help me locate it, but I stopped short of picking it up when I saw that it was Manoj calling.

I wondered if I should wake Sujit, but then why would I disturb his rest for this man? He got what he deserved. Now all he might want was to either abuse Sujit or try to appeal to his decency, yet again. Only this time, Sujit was in no mood to entertain either. The phone stopped buzzing, and I continued my trek to the kitchen.

Grabbing two glasses of water and a coaster to cover his, I tiptoed back to the bedroom. Sujit had rolled onto the other shoulder now, away from me, and I pulled a light cover on his naked body. Then, on a whim, I walked back out, retrieved his phone, and placed it by the nightstand on my side of the bed.

Wondering how to kill time while I waited for Sujit to wake up from his nap—I hoped he would soon—I pulled out my laptop and AirPods. I rarely got time to catch up on any of the series I kept adding to my watchlist. Today looked like a great opportunity to watch at least one episode of a series while I waited for the man of my dreams to wake up from his dream and make love to me again. I chuckled inwardly at my girlish thoughts and turned on a spicy Spanish period romance drama that I had left midway.

Talk about girlish! I was crushing hard on the young hero. The series, set somewhere in Cantabria, was lush with glorious castles and expansive landscapes. I was grinning like a schoolgirl at the banter between the two lead characters when a gentle tap on my shoulder made me jump out of my skin. One AirPod popped out of my ear, and I saw Sujit staring at me, amused.

"Not funny," I reprimanded, pulling the other AirPod out and dropping it all in a drawer beside me.

"What are you watching?" he asked as I clicked the spacebar to pause the movie.

"Nothing that might interest you," I said, promptly pushing

the laptop screen down. "I got you some water, thought you might be thirsty after...you know..."

I placed the glass in his hand, and he downed it in under five seconds.

"Gosh, you were thirsty!" I remarked.

He grazed a finger along my jaw. "I'm hungry too. But let me freshen up first."

As I collected the glass from him, a pleasant thought hit me. I *was* capable of the little things! I had always suspected I was all about larger-than-life gestures, that's what I was good at. But being here with this kind, brilliant, ridiculously gorgeous man, I found versions of me I had never noticed before. My father was right. Sujit made me kinder, better, stronger. He made me feel cherished.

Sujit returned with his face fresh and dewy, hair slightly damp, and full-frontal nudity that created ripples in my stomach. He snuggled against me and pulled the duvet over us.

He gazed at my face with a desire so powerful, I bit my lip and my eyes lowered on instinct. He smelled of mint and herbs. The spicy scent of his body danced around me as he moved closer to my face. But instead of touching my lips, he reached for my cheek and placed a gentle, adoring kiss.

"You are the best thing that could have happened to me," he whispered in my ear. "I've never felt like this before. I feel alive, full of hope. I look forward to waking up each morning because I have you in my life."

He paused, then grinned. "I can't resist thinking, I'm grateful Sameer broke your heart, and I'm glad Tara broke mine."

AARTI

*M*y eyes glazed in thought, and I fiddled with my ring. He read my signals with ease.

"Tell me," he urged.

"Will you be upset if I told you I spoke to Tara when I was in Dallas?"

He kissed my cheek again. "I'll never be upset about anything you do, Aarti. That's one thing you can be assured of in this relationship. If anything bothers me, I'll talk to you about it, but I won't resent you for anything you say or do."

I rolled my eyes right into my head. "God!" I cried with exasperation. "This was a simple question, and you turned it into a mini-lecture on expectations in our relationship."

The thunderous sound of his laughter rumbled against my skin as he hugged me tight. "All right, sassy girl. What did you two talk about?"

"Well, you know her better than I do. She just asked me right there at the party, with all eyes watching us, if I wanted to have a drink with her."

He smiled. "That sounds like her."

"She apologized for having betrayed my trust. I told her she wasn't the one who should be apologizing to me."

I turned in his embrace to face him. "She said you two had a chance at closure that I never did, and she regretted it."

"Did you get to talk to Sameer, then?"

I shook my head. "I realized I didn't need to. He wasn't the one I was seeking closure with. I was seeking it within myself. Talking to Tara helped me with that. And you helped me see it that first night I cried in your arms. When you encouraged me to spell out that my grief was my own doing."

"Did I do that?" he asked with every bit of sincerity as if he had no idea what that first night meant to me.

His support made me into a person I trusted again. He made me fall in love with my life again.

"Then I told Tara about you," I said with downcast eyes.

"About me as in about *us*?" His voice inflected.

"I thought she would be the perfect person to confide in. And I'm glad I did." I blushed with another coy smile, then looked up at him. "I like her, Sujit. I'd love to have her in my life. Will you be good with that?"

He returned a smile. "I like her too. I am actually happy she found what she wanted."

"She said hurting you was something she'll have to live with, but she was happy for me. Asked me to keep you happy."

"You already make me very happy. Just by being you."

"You make me very happy too. You make me laugh like no one else can. But I'm also glad I can cry with you when I need to. Without judgement, without shame."

"But I'd rather you didn't have to cry anymore, sweet girl. Your tears wreak havoc on my heart."

"I can't promise that," I confessed truthfully.

"That's all right too, I'm always here."

When I paused again, he wrapped his arms around me and kissed my forehead.

"Aarti, you know you never have to think twice before saying what's on your mind. Just say it, sweetheart."

He said *sweetheart* and my heart skipped a beat. How could something so simple, so innocuous, create such strong ripples in my being?

"Tara warned me about Manoj." I glanced at the phone on the side table by me. "He's been calling you. I didn't want to disturb your nap, but I brought the phone in."

Just then, as if I had summoned the devil himself, the screen lit up again with his name. The whirr of the phone echoed in the silent bedroom. Sujit reached across and grabbed it. He declined the call, and in a second, it buzzed again in his hand. He declined it again.

"I don't get why you're ignoring his calls. I would've answered the phone and tore him a new one."

"Because I have nothing to say to him. Why would I waste my words this way? He got what he deserved, and actions speak louder than words anyway."

I agreed with him. In theory. "But it would be so satisfying."

The phone buzzed again, and Sujit cocked his head. I wasn't about to persuade him to compromise on his ethics, but I sincerely wished to see him blast Manoj to smithereens with his words. Giving me his sweetest smile, Sujit answered the phone and put it on speaker.

"Yes, Manoj," he said in a very formal, distant tone.

"I know it was your doing, you fucker. I thought you were my friend. Do you have any idea what I've been through the last few days? I know you can stop it. Stop it, *now!*" he screamed like an ill-tempered child.

Sujit's composure remained unruffled. "I gave you a long leash all these years, Manoj. But this time, you messed with the wrong person. You fucking messed with the *wrong person*." He enunciated each word through clenched teeth.

That seemed to have rendered Manoj speechless. There was only silence at the other end. Clearly, he had misjudged Sujit's determination.

"You were never my friend, Manoj. I only kept you close because Tejal asked me to keep an eye on you. You stole her from me, yet she trusts me more than she trusts you. How's that for fate, eh?"

"You bast—"

"I have to thank you for one thing, though," Sujit said and ran a finger along my jaw. "I have to thank you for trying to use Aarti to fuck with me. If you hadn't, I wouldn't have realized the intensity of my feelings for her. And for that, I'll leave you with just enough to save you from bankruptcy. Consider it a gift. But you're done, Manoj. You are done." Sujit ended the call before Manoj could muster up a response.

The words sent pride surging through my heart. This was the kind of passion I yearned for. The kind I'd seen Sameer show for Tara. After years of tolerating him, Sujit destroyed Manoj just because he had targeted me. I took Sujit's hand and kissed his palm.

"Of course, my love. That is how strongly I feel about you."

He raised his index finger. "But wait for it. He'll call back in one minute because he'll need that time to think about what he's going to say next."

In about another minute, the phone buzzed in his hand, and Sujit declined the call. In another few beats, Manoj called again. This time, Sujit powered down his phone and pushed it under the pillows.

"There, that's taken care of." He brushed a finger against my cheek. "Now, where were we? Oh yes, naked and in bed. Wasting time talking about futile things."

"What would you rather do?" I asked provocatively.

"I'd rather spend time kissing my girlfriend."

"*Girlfriend*, huh?"

"Indeed," he said and leaned in with a kiss.

In only a few minutes, we had knocked the pillows off the bed and rumpled up the sheets.

"It's safe to say you've ruined me for other men, Sujit Rao," I said this time.

"It's a good thing then that there will be no other men for you, Ms. Bhatia," he declared and took my mouth in a possessive, fervent kiss.

It was past two in the morning, but we sat wrapped up in each other's arms. On his insistence, I had pulled out my laptop to watch the series together. He sat with his back against the head-rest. I sat between his legs leaning against him. His idle hand caressed my arm and thigh underneath a warm cotton duvet.

"Who's this guy, again?" he asked as the secondary villain appeared on the screen. I explained, and we returned to watching it.

His hand traveled to my chest and strummed my nipple, distracting me from the very interesting exchange occurring on screen.

I swatted his hand away.

"Hey," he said. "You keep watching, I'll keep playing."

"I can't focus on the dialogue," I complained, slapping his hand away again.

"That's too bad because I can't seem to keep my hands off you," he said in my ear and kissed my shoulder. A shiver ran through me instantly. "You have the most beautiful shoulders. I love how perfectly brown they are," he said and ran a finger along the edge while kissing the side of my neck.

I lay my head back against him and moaned as he kissed the other shoulder and traced his finger along it and down my arm.

On the screen, I saw the heroine walk into the frame to confront the hero in his chambers. There had been a huge misunderstanding brought on by the villain, and this was the scene where the two main leads were expected to have a showdown.

In my bedroom, I felt my hero's armor getting thicker underneath me. "See what you do to me," he said. "I can't get enough of you."

"Hush," I fake scolded. "This is an important scene."

Sujit's hands now came around me and cupped my breasts as the heroine continued her tongue-lashing on the screen.

I shuffled in his lap and reached behind to grab him. Thick and long, he felt wonderful in my hand.

"What just happened?" Sujit's grip on my breasts loosened as the couple on the screen was now tangled up in a hot kiss. "They were arguing, now they are kissing?"

"I wouldn't know because you distracted me," I teased and slipped out from between his legs.

As the onscreen couple began undressing each other, I turned on my haunches and lay flat on my stomach to face my hero. I gripped him with both hands as the head glistened in the dim lights of the bedroom, with a perfect drop crowning it. I ran a slow, firm tongue to lap it up, and he released a loud moan just as the onscreen hero pinned the heroine against the frame of an intricate 19th-century bed. Soon enough, he'd have his dick inside her, but we weren't bound by similar time constraints.

I took my time, sucking, licking, running my hungry tongue along his beautiful length. Meanwhile, the heroine was moaning, more sensual than heated, as the juxtapositional frame showed the villain walking a long corridor toward the hero's chambers. Heightened music accompanied the frames.

Sujit's hand slipped into my hair and gripped it gently, guiding me to where he loved it most. I obliged, then ran a firm tongue over his sac, and a hiss escaped his mouth. I did it again, and his grip on my hair tightened. I took him in again, attempting to swallow him entirely. Sounds of wanton moans and rhythmic music flowed from the screen. Sujit's grip on my hair moved from the nape to my scalp. Heat rose up my body, and I sucked harder, feeling the vein underneath get plump and taut.

The temperature in the room shot up several degrees. Neither said a word. Neither invoked any deity. Suddenly, a hard cry from the screen made me stop and gawk. We both burst out laughing just as the villain pushed open the door, attempting to catch the couple red-handed. Only it was a different room, with a different horny couple going at it hard and strong. Too loud, too coarse.

I tittered and shut the laptop screen. Sujit grabbed it from the bed and gently deposited it to the side table.

The relaxed censorship on streaming platforms had allowed for desire to be openly displayed on screen but it remained arrested in the shadow of binaries. There was "good people" sex, and then there was "bad people" sex. One was soft, partially shielded, passionate, tender. The other, exposed, vulgar, kinky, bawdy. Nowhere was this more pronounced than in period dramas.

Which category did Sujit and I fall under, I wondered as I lowered myself down on him. His heat and thickness instantly took over me. My head fell back as I rode him with enthusiasm. He gripped my breasts, tweezing my nipples with the same intensity.

"Oh, Sujit!" I cried, out of breath, and paused to kiss him. I drove my tongue deep into his mouth and was reciprocated with vigor. His hands moved to my bottom and squeezed my cheeks, sending a thrill up my spine.

When I found my breath again, I grazed against him, his clean softness rubbing tight on my clit. He felt my pelvis tighten and brought his mouth to cover my breast.

"Yes...tease me," I urged, hovering at the edge.

He sucked harder and rolled his tongue over my rigid nipple. It was becoming hard for my weakening body to keep up the rhythm. I felt him pulsate inside me. He reached around me and put a moist finger on my bottom.

With his finger teasing my sensitive nerves, he said in my ear, "Come, sweetheart. Come hard for me."

That was the moment the dam burst open, and my legs tightened around his hips. I let out a gasp, my voice thwarting inside me. The sweet spasm contracted all the muscles in my abdomen and pelvis. His thick dick remained steady inside me, fighting against the contractions. I loved how he stretched me all the way to my core and touched my soul. I loved the way my body could swallow him whole and garner that satisfied smile on his face. My muscles were just about to relax when I felt him throb and come inside me, and they tightened all over again. I was falling in love with the feeling.

I collapsed on his chest, surrendering to the cool of his skin against my raging heat. I wiped the beads of sweat on my forehead with the back of my hand and panted into his shoulder.

He brought his arms around me and softly said, "You are so sexy, Aarti."

"And you're so freaking hot!" I moaned.

AARTI

I'm not certain what time we fell asleep, but I saw the dawn approaching through my window just before I slipped into a deep slumber. By the time my eyes opened on their own accord, a soft sun was showering happiness upon a cold winter day. Soon, the frosty clouds would swallow it up, but for now, it was shining grace upon us.

Sujit stirred and turned on his side to face me, the sunlight gleaming on his brilliant visage. I moved in and buried myself against his chest, breathing in the scent of his body. A smile appeared on his lips and he placed a kiss on my forehead.

"I'd say good morning, but I see it's a great one already," he said with his eyes still closed.

"Not yet," I said, reaching for him and getting tingly instantly.

He flinched. "Easy! There's a lot going on there right now."

I laughed as he excused himself to use the bathroom. While he freshened up, I drew a sheer robe over my naked body and walked out of the room. After washing up in one of the spare bathrooms, I turned on the coffee machine. It dispensed two cups of espresso with the perfect coffee-to-crema ratio. It was Sujit's favorite coffee machine for a reason. That man had impeccable taste. And now *that* man was *my* man.

My cheeks turned warm at the thought as I frothed the milk to make a latte for me and turned on a kettle to make an Americano for Sujit. It was wonderful to start a relationship where I already knew how he liked his coffee.

Sujit walked up to me in his boxer briefs just as I finished making the two cups.

"Thank you, sweet girl." He took the cup I offered and placed a kiss on my cheek. "You didn't need to. I could've made it."

"No milk, no sugar, right?" I asked.

"That's right." He reached for my waist and pulled me closer. "Love the sheer clothing, although I would've enjoyed it more if you were completely naked."

I raised a brow. "Says the man who walked up here in his boxers." Balancing my cup in one hand, I reached over with my free hand and grabbed his ass.

He gripped my earlobe between his teeth, and I dug mine softly into his chest. He threw his head back, barely maintaining his grip on his mug.

"Careful, you better not spill coffee on my exquisite wooden floor."

"All right," he resigned, retracting his arm from around me. "Breakfast at Ms. Dina's?"

"Sounds perfect," I replied and sipped my latte. It tasted especially good this morning. "I can finally tell her I intend to keep her golden boy very happy."

He beamed with his trademark deep dimples. "She's going to dote on you for life." Then softly added, "As am I."

I gripped his arm. "Hey, you aren't going to tell her about me buying her diner from Walter, right? I don't want her feeling obligated."

"No, sweetheart. It's not my place to share that information."

"Thank you," I said.

As he leaned in for a kiss, the intercom rang with a call from the building desk. I answered it.

"Yes, please send him up," I said and turned to Sujit. "It's Imran."

I rushed to the bedroom to put on my plush robe and dashed back out. Sujit had answered the door. Imran stood outside wearing a concerned look.

"Hello, Ms. Aarti," he said with apologetic eyes.

I responded with a nod. The expression on his face said something was wrong. And that something was about me and Sujit.

"Sorry, Boss," he said to Sujit. "I've been trying to call, but it's going to voicemail. Everyone's been trying to call."

"What's wrong?" Sujit signaled him in, and he stepped only a foot inside the house. Sujit didn't seem bothered that he was still in his underpants.

"There's another feature on a gossip website. It picked up fast and is now highlighted as a banner on a major newspaper site." He stole a guilty glance at me. "Everyone has been trying to get in touch with you."

"What feature?" Sujit had his back to me, and I couldn't see his face, but his voice was laced with anger, worry, and impatience.

Imran hesitated and threw another quick glance at me.

"It's about you and Ms. Aarti," he said, his voice just above a whisper. "It's...not good."

"It has filth about Aarti?" Sujit asked. Even though his face remained shielded from me, I could visualize the angry frown on his forehead.

Another guilty nod from Imran as he confirmed our suspicions.

Manoj stood at the brink of destruction but his zeal for

vengeance against Sujit, the need to show him up, to demean him, did not quell. That man was incorrigible.

Imran looked at me, then back at Sujit. "Your family has been trying to reach you. When they couldn't get in touch with you, they called me to ask if I knew where you were. I...I didn't tell them, but they assumed."

This time, he avoided making eye contact with me. "They asked me to find you and give you a heads up. There are reporters outside your home."

Well, good thing he was here, although it would only be a matter of time before they found out where I lived.

"I'll be with the car," Imran said. "If you need me."

Sujit nodded and closed the door behind him.

"I'll get my PR team on this immediately," he said in an eerily calm voice, like the one before the storm. I knew exactly what he was capable of.

I grabbed both our mugs and deposited them in the sink. Sujit had stepped into the bedroom and turned on his phone.

His forehead creased in a gentle frown that got deeper as he kept reading.

"Fuck him!" I was surprised to hear a deep growl from Sujit.

"What is it?" I asked, nervous and infuriated.

"This is deeper than us, Aarti. This is a smear campaign. They got a whiff of the legislation we've been working toward."

He handed me the phone. Bracing myself for the wretched words that would greet me, I read the headline. "Heartbroken Billionaire Finds Solace in the Arms of His Ex's Husband's Ex."

There are tragic stories, and then there is the tale of Sujit Rao's unrequited love. A source close to Rao, who has requested anonymity, disclosed that earlier this year, the enigmatic tech billionaire suffered a humiliating breakup, which shattered him completely.

*Tara Kadam, an up-and-coming artist, was Rao's girlfriend for
almost a year, and Rao was all set to marry her. It seems he had a
custom-designed ring ready to propose to her.*

I looked up at Sujit. "Did you have a custom-designed ring
ready for the proposal?"

With his anger intact, he shook his head. "It's a bunch of lies.
I probably would have done that if things had turned out differently, but it was too early in the relationship for a ring."

I smiled at him, and he frowned more furiously. Stepping
closer, I placed a kiss on his lips.

"I don't understand. What's the smile and the kiss for?"

I gave a quick peck on his cheek. "You could have lied to me,
but you didn't."

"Lied about what?"

"Lied that you had never considered creating a custom ring."

"You know everything, Aarti. Why would I lie, and why
would I ever lie to *you*? You're my life now. You're my everything."

I placed a hand on his chest. "It's your decency that has led
you into this mess in the first place," I faux-chided him. "If you
had nipped it in the bud, you'd not be facing this now."

"If I wasn't good, I would never have you. I'm not inclined
to give it up anytime soon. And as far as bullshit is concerned, it
comes with the territory. If it wasn't Manoj, it would be
someone else. At least with Manoj, I know where he's going to
hit."

"Your heart?" I said, my eyes flickering.

"Exactly." He drew me close and placed a kiss on my temple.

I continued reading.

*Unfortunately for Rao, his girlfriend went back to her ex, leaving
him holding the ring and a broken heart. It is still unclear how
Rao got in touch with Kadam's lover's ex-girlfriend, but sources*

speculate that it was with the goal of seeking retribution against the exes who had jilted them.

The woman in question is Aarti Bhatia, heiress to the SB Group, a real estate giant based in Dallas with properties all over the country.

"Oh, Papa is going to be furious!" I cried. "It's a good thing I've already confided in him. He will know exactly how to handle this shit."

A look into Bhatia's past makes the retribution claim quite convincing. It seems that Bhatia had proposed to her then-boyfriend, Sameer Rehani, at a high-profile party in Dallas, where he owns an investment firm. One can only speculate why he would break up with the heiress to marry Kadam. Post-breakup rumors suggest that it was because of Bhatia's lack of commitment toward him. It was suspected that she was in love with her brother's best friend, and Rehani found out about the affair. Bhatia's teaming up with Rao could be a way to ruin Rehani and Kadam's marriage.

It is ironic that their plan of foiling the lives of their exes turned on its head, and Rao fell for Aarti Bhatia. It has yet to be confirmed if Bhatia shares Rao's feelings or if she's playing him to get revenge on her ex. If the rumors about Bhatia are true, Rao might be looking at yet another humiliating heartbreak.

This stain on Rao's personal life might cause some problems for his social standing. It is speculated that Rao has been pushing a legislation for accessibility in education. Considering the dubious decisions in his personal life, one wonders if he can be trusted to weigh in on an issue of such magnitude. As a close family friend noted,

Rao's shacking up with his ex's husband's ex, the one whom Rehani rejected, is a less-than-desirable optic for the influential billionaire.

I paused for thought. "Why did they feel the need to include this?" I mused aloud.

But Sujit didn't need to guess. "It's clear Manoj has gotten in bed with the detractors of the Bill."

"Detractors? Why would anyone want to oppose a Bill for greater accessibility in education?"

"Because free and more accessible education hurts the deep pockets. There's a pipeline from private schools to Ivy Leagues and boardrooms. Greater accessibility means their privilege and power is threatened."

My mouth gaped. "This is the reason I hate people."

He let out a sad chuckle. "Yes, we are the worst species on earth."

Manoj had stepped on Sujit's Achilles heel. Accessible education was the mission of his life, and for this alone, I was determined to destroy him to the point of no return.

I wanted to keep going but Sujit gently retrieved the phone from me. "No reason to read on, sweet girl. I'll call my PR team right away. We can give a joint statement or something. Let me see what they recommend."

I pulled my arms across my body. "That's one way to go about it."

Sujit eyed me intently. "What are you thinking?"

"The thing is, I hate being backed into a corner. I hate being put on the defensive. And I hate being blackmailed. I'd warned Manoj I'd come after him if he didn't leave you alone, and that's what I intend to do."

"Oh?"

I took his hand and stepped over to the bed. Lowering myself to it, I asked him to sit with me.

"Do you trust me, Sujit? This is no longer your fight or mine. It is ours, and we need to be on the same page."

The brilliant smile that adorned his face brought out the dimples that I cherished. "I love you, Aarti, and with that love comes trust."

Then he pulled his brows together. "Or maybe I trusted you before I fell in love with you?" he contemplated. "Either way, I love you and trust you completely."

I pulled in a deep breath. "He wants a spectacle, and we will give him one. Just not the one he expects. He wants us to feel ashamed and embarrassed. I want to give him the opposite. I want to show him, and the world, what you mean to me."

My plan, of course, hinged on the certainty that Sujit was ready to announce our relationship to the world.

With another confident inhale, I asked, "How comfortable are you making our relationship public?"

A small smile tugged one corner of his mouth. A smile that transformed into a wide grin. He knew what I was asking. In that moment, I was reassured that our connection ran deeper than the intermingling of our bodies and hearts. We understood the other's unspoken words. We read each other's thoughts and body language.

"If you're wondering if I have doubts about our relationship or that we'd face more public ridicule if it doesn't work out, I want to assure you right now that I'm confident in my feelings for you. And I'm comfortable sharing this with the world."

"Sujit..." I grappled for the right words.

"The truth is, I've never felt this way before."

A warm blush spread across my body. "Me neither," I whispered. "Since the first night I met you."

"But I hate that we're forced to take our relationship public before we're ready. I hate that we've not been given the time and space to do it on our own terms."

"On the contrary, I think we've been given a golden opportunity to prove that love is not bound by social norms and conventions. We chose to be together despite our past, and I want to show the world that this is what love looks like. I hate that heteronormative monogamy has confined love to a narrow definition. I know you will always love and respect Tara, and I don't resent it. You're a better lover because of her. You are happy for her, and she's elated that you've found your happiness. I want the fucking world to see the beauty of this connection. I want to flip Manoj's script on its head and show him for what he is. A petty, narrow-minded egotist. Are you in?"

His grin reappeared. "Let's do this. Tell me what you are thinking."

In the short time since I'd begun reading the gossip article, my mind had already devised a plan. I took Sujit's hand and interlaced my fingers with his.

"Here's what we're going to do..."

AARTI

wo days later, we arrived at the Ritz-Carlton for the party. Sameer and Tara were right behind us in the car we had arranged for them. The sidewalk was lined with reporters and paparazzi. Tourists and local crowds thronged alongside to get a peek at their favorite celebrities.

Cameras flashed as Sujit exited the car and came around to hold the door for me. I stepped out in a designer gown accessorized with a specially created Bvlgari necklace.

Sujit and I waited, smiling for the cameras, as Sameer and Tara joined us. Tara looked luminous in her gown with a smart updo. I had ordered a special bracelet and earrings set for her, which now adorned her body. Sameer looked dashing as always, but I only had eyes for the man who ruled my heart.

Sujit looked breathtaking, effortlessly so. We posed for pictures, talking, laughing, and taking our sweet time to step indoors. Every act was meticulously choreographed.

When I spoke with Tara two days ago, she was thrilled at the idea. Shattering bigotry and challenging regressive social conventions were among her favorite things. She readily agreed and assured me that Sameer would be happy too. Sameer's peaceful face said he was here willingly. That Tara had not needed to force him to participate in this scheme.

As hosts, we were the first to arrive. Soon a long line of luxury vehicles dropped off high-profile guests, most of whom were here because Sujit had personally invited them. Mary Beth and Ezzie arrived soon after. Food, drinks, and music flowed. People who needed to network found their connections and chatted. Friends found each other and settled around the tables. There was no agenda to this party, except to showcase the four of us together, Sameer and Tara, and Sujit and me.

When we had finished going around the room, saying hellos and welcoming everyone, the four of us sat with a carefully chosen group of reporters at a table. Sujit's PR team had already sent them a statement, which we had looked over and edited.

The questions posed by the reporters were friendly, and we chatted.

"Tell us how you met," one of them asked.

We shared our story, leaving out the personal details of having connected over our heartaches.

"It was a business association that turned into a comfortable friendship," I said, casting a smile toward Sujit.

"Which turned into love," the reporter completed, a sincere smile gracing her muted pink lips.

"Yes," Sujit said and held out his hand for me. "I mean, how could I resist her? She's beautiful and brilliant. I stood no chance."

As a wave of gentle laughter rolled around the table, I found myself blushing at his words.

Both Sameer and Tara had wide grins on their faces.

"And we couldn't be more thrilled for them," Tara added.

"What caused the breakup, if you don't mind my asking," another reporter inquired, directing the question at Tara.

"Not at all. We were college sweethearts who grew apart. We just met at the wrong time, and things blew up from there." Tara briefly shared their story.

Sameer leaned forward. "And I want to add that the rumors spread about Aarti after the breakup were misogynistic and completely unacceptable." I was taken by surprise at his furiously strong words.

Tara nodded. "Yes, it was between two people, and to drag someone through the mud like that was evil. The rumors were just that, lies and fantasies. They didn't have a kernel of truth to them."

A warmth spread across my chest and enveloped me. In addition to Sujit, both Sameer and Tara had my back. Maybe this was what true friendship looked like. My circle of friends was increasing and it didn't fill me up with dread. Quite the contrary, it made me feel loved and cherished.

The reporter who had asked the question agreed. His lips parted in appreciation, scanning the four of us. "It is certainly not commonplace to see the kind of cordial relationship you seem to have with your exes."

"The truth is, it is because we respect our exes that we are able to find solace in their happiness. If you really care about someone, how can you see them unhappy? Why would you want to see them unhappy?" Sujit was a master with words. And here I thought I was the more astute one. I smiled with pride at the man who'd be my partner for life.

Under the table, I squeezed his hand. Without glancing at me, he squeezed it back with love and reassurance.

"Can you talk a bit about this rumored legislation?"

Sujit elaborated on the need to eliminate systemic hurdles to education to create a more equitable playing field. "For too long, people with means have controlled everything from education and opportunities to sexual autonomy and rights of minorities, often to the detriment of societies. I can't change everything, but I will certainly try to change what is within my capacity. That means equal and accessible education for every child, regardless of where they live and who they are."

Their recording devices were on, but all reporters took furious notes on their pads.

"And do you foresee any opposition to this?"

Sujit chuckled. "Well, if it has found its way into a gossip column, someone certainly is worried."

"Are *you* worried?"

"I'm never worried when doing the right thing," Sujit answered with honest conviction. "On the other hand, those who are resorting to spreading filth and lies are certainly worried. As they should be."

My heart thumped. That was a direct threat to Manoj and I knew at that moment that he was done for.

The interview wrapped up after a few more questions, and I heaved in relief. Sujit escorted the reporters toward other influential people who would be quoted about this party.

Tara covered my hand with hers. "How do you feel?"

"Happy," I said and as I looked up at her, my eyes fell on Sameer.

He held me in a gentle gaze, a soft smile trained on me.

Tara's eyes flitted between us, and she said, "I need a drink. I'll be back in a minute."

Sameer gazed at her lovingly and nodded with gratitude. When Tara stepped away, his unfazed smile returned to me.

"Can you forgive me, Aarti?" he asked, his voice filled with guilt.

I moved to the chair Tara had vacated. I smelled his cologne, enigmatic but now unfamiliar and distant. "I must apologize to you, Sameer—"

He didn't let me finish my sentence. "Never," he said with

determination in his voice. "I hurt you. I'll be the one apologizing to you for life."

"I apologize for never giving you a chance to say your piece. You kept coming to my home, and I kept refusing to see you."

"That was your prerogative. I don't hold that against you."

My eyes darted to Tara in the distance. "I see the kind of friendship Sujit and Tara have, and I feel envious. When I confided in Tara, she was happy for Sujit. I want that with you. I want you to be happy for me. I want to be happy for you. I *should've been* happy for you."

"We can start anew," he said. "You'll always have my utmost respect, Aarti. Nothing can take that away. I owe you for being kind and generous when we were together. If we had married, we might not have been this happy, but you would've always had my respect and loyalty."

His honest words tugged at my heart. I was grateful to him for spelling it out without duplicity. I raised my tentative eyes to his. "Are you happy for me, Sameer?"

He took my hand and patted it. "Very," he replied. "If you remember, I'd said that you're a phenomenal woman, and you deserve someone who loves you for who you are. Someone who would appreciate you completely. I'm glad you found him. I'm even more pleased that it's Sujit, because I was ready to give up Tara to him."

"What?" My brows furrowed in confusion.

"When I first met Sujit, I was so impressed with him, I thought Tara deserved better than me. Tara deserved him. I told her so."

"Didn't she smack you for that?" I teased with a smile.

He chuckled. "Well, we did have a fight, but we sorted it out. What I'm trying to say is that if there was anyone I would've wished as a partner for you, it would be someone like Sujit. I'm not just happy, I'm thrilled for the both of you."

A tear threatened to run down my cheek. He swiped a napkin from the table and snuck it to me discreetly. He knew I hated displaying tears. His gesture conveyed he still cared for me and it comforted me.

So this was what closure felt like!

I swiftly dabbed the corners of my eyes, and we saw Sujit and Tara walking over with flutes in their hands.

"Champagne for everyone, sparkling white for Aarti," she said, placing a long-stemmed glass before me.

"To us," I said.

"To true love," Sujit said.

"And great friendships," Sameer added.

We all looked at Tara. Her eyes flitted between the three of us, and she shrugged. "What? You took all the good ones. What do I toast to?"

We laughed.

"Okay, here's one. To our happily ever afters."

"Amen," I said, and we clinked our glasses.

EPILOGUE

SUJIT

The door to my office was locked, and the switchable glass walls were turned opaque. Holding Aarti at the waist, I ran my hand up her thigh and around to her butt. The pencil skirt she wore today was gathered unceremoniously at her hips.

She tugged the jacket off my shoulders and tossed it to a chair behind her.

"We have fifteen minutes before the staff arrives," she warned breathily.

"And only ten before Devi does," I added and leaned her against the table.

Descending to my knees, I moved the lace aside and ran my tongue between her delicate lips. She moaned and pushed her hand into my hair. I put my eager, diligent mouth to work.

A few silent beats passed as she tried to modulate her breath. "Wait! I can't do this!" she cried.

I stopped and looked up at her with a cocked eyebrow.

She pulled me up by the collar of my shirt. "I'm too turned on."

I ran a finger through her dripping-wet slit and said, "I can see that, and I want to lick it all off you right now."

Yanking my hand out, she guided my fingers to my mouth. I licked them like they were covered in honey. When I caught her gazing at me with raw desire, I put the same fingers in her mouth and sighed as the warmth of her tongue enveloped them.

"You look so beautiful right now," I whispered, helpless against her touch. "Let me eat you until I'm satisfied."

"There's not enough time for that," she argued. "Ten minutes isn't going to cut it. I need more of you. I need to feast on your body, swallow you whole."

The words had barely left her mouth when I pounced on it, thrusting my tongue deep. She moaned and sucked it like she sucked my dick. With my hands on her lower back, I pulled her closer to me. Our unseemly slobbering sounds echoed in the quiet office.

Finally, she put her hands on my chest and pushed me away.

"Lunchtime?" she asked breathlessly. "We can make a quick getaway."

I nodded just as we heard shuffling outside my office.

"Good thing," she whispered. "Devi's here already."

Quiet as mice, we pulled on our clothes and smoothed out any evidence of mischief. I grabbed her one last time and kissed her hard.

"Careful! Lipstick!" she warned softly.

With the handy makeup wipes she'd begun carrying, she cleaned our faces. Clearly, I couldn't be trusted to keep my mouth off her. Or my hands. Then, quickly reapplying the color on her lips, she dumped everything in her bag.

We retook our places on the chair and couch, per our usual routine, and I switched the glass back to transparent. Devi had occupied her throne behind her desk and was already at work.

It had been six months since Aarti had relocated to New York

City. We kept base in our own apartments but often spent time together for days on end. She had become comfortable around my family and with my staff. Well, it was her staff now.

We had entered into a formal partnership with Creators' Studio. In a short time, Aarti had managed to not only build it from the ground up but also define its shape and character. She had brought Padma and her friend on as consultants, whose guidance helped build tangible features into the program. Aarti also consulted with Tara, often course-correcting according to her suggestions.

Starting a non-profit to address child hunger had been a long-held dream of Aarti's. Last month, she'd started the procedure to create one. It was slated to begin its operations in the U.S. and gradually spread across the globe to end child poverty and hunger.

As I watched her with intense admiration, she brought her eyes to meet mine.

"Focus," she reprimanded with love. "Did you take a look at the documents I had sent?"

"Yes. I agree with everything you suggest."

"Hey." She gave me a stern look. "*Did* you read everything?"

"I did, yes, ma'am. And I agree with everything you suggest," I repeated with emphasis.

We had bought out Manoj's company from Vinay, who was glad to have it off his hands. Manoj had thrown petty tantrums when he was ousted, but Vinay had managed the takeover spectacularly. He let the world see that Manoj's behavior was no better than an entitled frat boy, while he remained the untouchable, immaculate investor with the private equity who had swooped in to save the day. Manoj's disgraceful reaction also ensured that he would find no support in the industry for many years to come. My conviction had held true. He had managed to ruin his own professional credibility.

After the party at the Ritz-Carlton, the press had continued to tout Aarti and me as a power couple, a force to look out for. We were featured everywhere from fashion magazines to editorials about social change. None of this fazed us, though. We continued to work quietly on projects that were meaningful to us.

The noise, however, effectively drowned out the narratives that expected us to be shameful of our relationship. With a singular, dignified interview conducted by a prominent news outlet, Aarti had spectacularly destroyed Manoj without once uttering his name. She had left just enough breadcrumbs for people to be intrigued and take it upon themselves to figure out who had dared to blackmail her. Once Manoj's name was discovered as having slipped the rumors to the tabloid, his personal reputation had dwindled as swiftly as his professional. She had relegated him to the point of no return.

The previous month, I bought the company with backing from new investors who saw the promise of growth under new leadership. Aarti managed to convince her father to invest in it, although the money now was Aarti's. Her savvy had finally convinced her father to let her pursue her own path with a share of the wealth she'd earned and deserved. He was still bitter about her moving away from Dallas and, ergo, threw me a cold shoulder now and again, but I wasn't worried. Everyone else in her family had accepted me as the reason for her happiness, and I was certain in time, I would win over her father.

"There is only one person I envision as the COO of this venture," Aarti said as we fleshed out the list of possible C-suite candidates for the cyber security company.

My lips turned up as I looked at her from above the rim of my glasses. "Are you thinking what I'm thinking?"

"Tejal," we both said in unison.

"Definitely Tejal," she said making several lines on the paper in her lap. "Oh, how I wish I could see his face when we make that announcement."

She tapped her pen several times on the folder in thought. "I think it's time she reclaimed her rightful place in your game-night group. Now that Manoj's out, why don't you ask her?"

"Or you can, when we call her in for the position."

"It's not my place, Sujit. I'm not a part of the group, and I don't wish to be. That's your space, your nerding-out time. I wouldn't dream of encroaching on it."

"Why don't you just come out and say that you have better things to do?"

She smiled. "That too, but I really want you to have your own time. I promise it's not a ruse."

My eyes stilled on her again, my sight glazing over her face.

Aarti Bhatia was power personified—Shakti herself—a goddess walking the earth, and I felt both proud and humbled that she had chosen me as her consort.

"What are you looking at?" she said as a blush tinted her bronze cheeks.

I closed the file in my lap and placed it on the coffee table between us.

"Aarti, we both have been scarred by surprises," I began. "So I will never surprise you with a marriage proposal. But I want you to know that I'll be ready whenever you are. You just have to say the word."

Her mouth gaped as her eyes widened. "If I didn't know any better, I'd think you are proposing to me right now."

I returned a sheepish smile. There was nothing standing between us anymore. "May be I am."

She frowned. "This looks suspiciously like a surprise."

"It's not." I reassured, holding my palms out. "See? No ring."

She returned a bright smile, then got off the couch and stepped over to me. I stood with her, my heart lurching in my mouth.

"Yes. I will marry you," she declared in the understated manner that had been the essence of our relationship.

Our bodies stunned to stillness for a moment before she gasped and placed a hand on her mouth.

"Shit! Did we just..." she cried.

"I think we did."

Devi's knock on the glass door shook us out of the limbo.

When I waved her in, she entered with a curious expression, studying our stunned faces.

"What's wrong?" she asked urgently.

I exchanged a look with Aarti and we both grinned wide.

"I think we just got engaged," I announced.

Her jaw dropped open, then a wide grin appeared on her face, crinkling her eyes.

"Oh my goodness!" she squealed.

She stepped over to Aarti and me. "I've never done this before but I'm going to do it today," she warned before taking us both in a tight hug. "I am so happy!"

When she released us from her embrace, she declared, "I'm going to reschedule all your meetings for today. You both should go and celebrate, and we need to plan a grand party." The wheels in her head were already spinning.

As Devi rushed out, I turned to Aarti. She averted her shy eyes.

My love, gratitude, and reverence toward her became the swift kiss I placed on her cheek. "I need to pinch myself. I can't possibly be this happy."

She looked at me and delivered a pinch on my forearm.

"Ouch!" I cried.

"Satisfied?"

"Yes. In so many ways, I can't begin to express."

"I need to call my parents," she said and rushed over to retrieve her phone from her cherry red tote.

I pulled out my own and stepped over to the window.

While I waited for Amma to answer her phone, I heard Aarti's voice, "Ma, I need to tell you something...something good."

I stared at her jubilant face and found myself powerless against her brilliance and grace. As I watched her talk to her family, wearing the look of a lovelorn teenager in my eyes, I silently thanked our exes. Without them, we wouldn't be here.

∾

THE END

ACKNOWLEDGMENTS

It takes a village, the saying goes, to raise a child. I feel the same way about my books. Writing might be a solitary affair but it can't go far without the help and support of all the wonderful people who make writing worth it.

First and foremost, I thank one of my best friends since school, Himika for beta reading this book. It is an understatement to say that she knows me. She knows my soul and she knows my characters. That's the reason she gives me the best feedback on my work.

Fazal Gupta is my go-to friend for all things startup. He is astute but also incredibly kind and believes in my work. His insights on the workings and failures of startups has helped me sharpen those aspects of the story.

Since I'm not well-acquainted with Telugu, I want to thank my friend Sirisha who helped me with the terminologies and customs I've used in the book. It goes without saying that I bear full responsibility for any mistakes.

Allie Oleander, in addition to being a phenomenal writer, is a kind and generous friend. She's the one who helped me create the blurb for this book and I can't begin to express how much I love it.

Sherri Shackelford has been my editor since my debut and I can't trust anyone else with my book. She believes in my writing and my voice. Her invaluable guidance has made my books stronger each time. I thank her for being in my corner and for trusting me to tell a good story.

My gratitude, once again, to Zuchal Rosyidin for the phenomenal cover for this book. He takes the time to understand my vision and makes it better each time.

My husband Vaibhav is always present to pick up the slack in our everyday life as I drown myself in my work, forgetting myself for days at end. He's the kind of staunch partner who inspires my stories. He is my real life Sujit. Thank you, my love.

No note would be complete without a mention of my son, Aadi who inspires me to be a better person, a better writer every day. Thank you for making my life more meaningful.

Last and most importantly, I want to thank my readers who took a chance on my books and loved it. I appreciate your messages and emails more than you know. You give credence to my existence as a writer.

ABOUT THE AUTHOR

Varsha Chitnis is an award-winning author of heartfelt, angsty romance.

Born in Mumbai, Varsha grew up in the beautiful city of Baroda. Through her Ph.Ds. in Political Science and Women's, Gender, and Sexuality Studies, and a fulfilling teaching career, she has remained a storyteller at heart. She loves writing about South Asian characters and their multifaceted lives. Her work combines romance with high drama and sizzling heat. Her debut novel won the *Indieverse Award for Best Romance*.

Varsha enjoys baking a little more than she should. She loves jewelry, and is seldom spotted without her big, oversized earrings, and her trademark bright lipstick. She has lived in several places in the U.S. and currently calls California her home.

You can find out more about her writing at
varshachitnis.com.

BOOKS BY VARSHA CHITNIS

The Art of Taking Second Chances

The Rules of Playing with Fire

The Ex Factor

∽

WRITING AS VARSHA C.

Un/Bound

www.ingramcontent.com/pod-product-compliance
Lightning Source LLC
Chambersburg PA
CBHW031031030726
47497CB00004B/1096

* 9 7 9 8 9 8 8 9 1 9 0 2 5 *